The Gibraltar Conspiracy

THE
GIBRALTAR
CONSPIRACY

JACK ULDRICH

Mark,

To a great
Brother-in-law!

Jack

Copyright © 2000 Jack Uldrich

ISBN: 0-9679877-0-9

First Edition, June 1, 2000

Cover design: Scott Zosel

LC: 00-102040

Prepress by North Star Press of St. Cloud, Inc., St. Cloud Minnesota.

Printed in the United States of America by Versa Press, Inc., East Peoria, Illinois.

Published by: Mortyn Press
                  4901 Emerson Avenue South
                  Minneapolis, Minnesota 55409

Dedication

To my wife, Cindy,
and daughter, Meghan,
for their support, encouragement and love.

Acknowledgements

It has been said that the care and feeding of a first-time novelist is a delicate task. In my case, this is particularly true. When I first imagined this book almost two years ago, I had no idea how many people I would come to rely on. I owe much to the following:

My wife, Cindy, for her patience, understanding, and encouragement as I stole precious time from her—and our daughter—to toil on the book in the wee hours of the morning, late into the evening, and on numerous weekends.

To my youngest sister, Catherine Glynn, who acted as my early editor and kept me pointed in the right direction.

To my editor, Marilynn Taylor, for her advice and superb editorial skills.

To my friend and former campaign manager, Eric Snyder, for his many constructive comments and insightful political analysis.

To Chuck McShane, for his painstaking review and attention to detail.

To my older sister, Anne (Nan) Zosel, for her valuable contributions, and my brother-in-law, Scott Zosel, for his work on the cover design.

And to everyone else, including John Fisher, Dick Ficken, Brian McEnaney, Scott Brenner, Jennifer Moriarty, John Allen, Richard Fong, and Frank and Shar Romero. But, especially, to my mother and father for providing me every opportunity I would ever need to pursue my dreams.

As always, all errors and omissions in the book are mine and mine alone.

The Gibraltar Conspiracy

CHAPTER ONE

R obert T. Colfax, the maverick governor, dusted the rich, damp black soil off his right knee and made the sign of the cross. He then whispered a few words to the only mentor he had ever known, Father Otto Wilhoit. The old priest gave him a steady look and placed his weathered right hand on Colfax's chiseled face, pulled him close and said, "You don't have to do this."

"Yes, I do," replied Colfax to the man who practically raised him after his father's tragic death. "Luke 12:48: 'For unto whomsoever much is given, of him is much required.'" Wilhoit knew the quote well. He had taught it to Colfax thirty-five years earlier.

"'And to whom they have entrusted much, of him they ask more,'" said Wilhoit, finishing the verse. "Are you prepared for those demands?"

"I am."

"May God bless you, Robert Thomas."

Colfax embraced the elderly priest and walked over to his wife, Linda, who was seated on a massive red pine trunk that had been torn from its roots in a violent wind storm years earlier. She had been quietly watching the scene between the two old friends. Linda was one of the few people who understood the true depth and meaning of their relationship.

Colfax took his wife's hand and, knowing that their life was about to change forever, strode with her three hundred feet down Schoolcraft Trail, past the brilliant fall foliage of northern Minnesota, to the headwaters of the Mississippi River. Wilhoit walked in the opposite direction and said a silent prayer for his former student.

Reaching their destination, Colfax gently squeezed his wife's hand, looked her in the eye and asked if she was ready for the journey that lay ahead. Receiving an affirmative nod, he softly kissed her cheek, and the pair walked to the podium, which bore the state seal of Minnesota. Directly behind Colfax, the deep blue water of Lake

Itasca shimmered brightly, and a gentle, unseasonably warm breeze pushed small waves to the shoreline. To the right of Colfax stood a one-hundred-year-old white pine. Even closer was a gigantic wood stump into which were carved the words: "Here 1,475 feet above the ocean the Mighty Mississippi begins to flow on its winding way 2,552 miles to the Gulf of Mexico." To his left, a few dozen large stones bridged the headwaters. Minutes earlier his two daughters, Catherine and Colleen, had scampered across the boulders, declaring themselves to "have walked across the Mississippi." Upon the podium itself was an awkward clump of microphones of various sizes and shapes. Beyond those were thirteen television cameras, at assorted heights and angles, from a host of different news organizations. Behind the cameras stood hundreds of supporters and friends, all of whom, save one—an unimposing, middle-aged man with gray hair—Colfax would have recognized if only the bright klieg lights had not limited his vision to a few feet. The gray-haired man noticed the priest take up a position well away from the throng of supporters and made a note.

In an almost relaxed manner, Colfax pulled a folded copy of his prepared remarks from his left breast pocket and placed the text on the stand before him. Having no intention of looking at the text—he had written every word himself—Colfax straightened his lean, athletic body to its full height of six feet, three inches, cast his eyes over the cameras and announced that he was running for the presidency of the United States. The announcement was not unexpected. Colfax's supporters, many of whom had been with him since his first campaign for Congress in 1982, had known it was only a matter of time before he sought the land's highest office.

"I stand here at the headwaters of the Mississippi—a national treasure which Mark Twain once called 'the Body of the Nation'—because this river represents everything that I hope and trust my presidency will accomplish," Colfax began. "The mighty Mississippi joins North and South—and it connects East with West. And it does so without prejudice," said Colfax, falling into his patented speaking cadence. "It nurtures cities—and assists the farmer; it fuels trade and commerce, but does so in a way that reminds us that without a healthy and sustainable environment, commerce is not possible; it has been a source of exploration, and it has aided immigration." Colfax paused and then added, "And my—our—administration will hold these same tenets. Our country's future, like this mighty river's, is big and broad. But it must flow in a manner so all of our citizens can share in its bounty. Under our administration, it will!"

The crowd roared its approval.

Colfax, speaking from his heart, continued, "It is time for principle to triumph over politics, purpose over partisanship, substance over style, character over cynicism and vision over vacillation. It is time for our leaders to stop cowering before public opinion and time they start shaping it. I will be just such a president," Colfax bellowed to a suddenly energized crowd. Then, with a pause, he leaned into the podium to draw the crowd closer in and dropped his bombshell.

"And I will do so as an independent!" Many in the crowd were temporarily stunned at the announcement. Almost everyone had expected him to return to his roots and run as a progressive Republican. "The pundits and the politicos will say it can't be done. But I know that it can, and it will be done—with your help!" Without waiting for applause, Colfax continued, "The major political parties have become beholden to Washington insiders. It is time for us to put the general interest of our citizens ahead of the money and influence of special interests. Together, we will eliminate the national debt. We will fundamentally reform Social Security. We will preserve the environment. And we will eradicate corporate welfare and the corrosive effects of special interest money once and for all!

"Just as the Mighty Mississippi makes its humble beginning here at Lake Itasca, so does my candidacy. And just as the river gathers strength as it winds its way through this diverse and rich country, so too will my campaign. With your help, and the Lord's blessing, we will triumph!"

The cheers of his supporters echoed across the lake into the surrounding forests.

With that, Colfax turned to his wife and, over the sound of clicking cameras and shouts from reporters, asked, "Are you sure you're ready?"

She nodded. She was nervous, but she understood her husband felt this was his calling. Colfax rather self-consciously kissed her and turned back to the microphones. Almost simultaneously, the Great Seal of Minnesota, which was electronically projected on the front of the podium, was replaced with a Colfax campaign logo, which prominently displayed the campaign web site: www.colfax2000.org.

* *

Within minutes, the site had logged over a thousand hits, mostly from political junkies who were watching the news conference live on C-SPAN and were intrigued by Colfax's announcement to run as an independent. The site would receive thousands more hits after the announcement was featured on the major networks and the *Larry King Show*. Hundreds of thousands more hits came the next day as various papers, including *The Washington Post, The Washington Herald* and *The New York Times* picked up Colfax's picture and web address.

One person who did not visit the web site but read a confidential report on Colfax's entry into the presidential campaign was Win Murdock, the seventy-seven-year-old chairman, CEO and president of Holten, Inc., the world's largest privately held company. A massive conglomerate of gas, oil, mineral, chemical and agribusiness interests, the company, which was an ubiquitous sponsor of Sunday morning talk shows where it billed itself as "feeding and fueling a growing world," had in recent years relied exclusively on government subsidies to remain competitive— something only Murdock and a handful of trusted lieutenants knew.

The single-spaced, one-page memorandum, drafted up the night before by the unimposing, middle-aged, gray-haired man, said that Colfax was highly critical of "special interests" in his announcement but spoke only in generalities. The consummate insider, Murdock knew it was only a matter of time before Colfax got specific and made "corporate welfare" a key campaign issue.

A methodical and calculating man who left nothing to chance, Murdock also knew it was in his best interest to terminate Colfax's candidacy sooner rather than later—before the Secret Service got involved. The Secret Service was the only federal agency he had never been able to influence.

Casting aside the report, Murdock took a sip of coffee and shook his head. He was surprised it had come to this. "Bobby," he said quietly to the empty room, using Colfax's nickname, "you could have been president. All you had to do was accept my help—and my money."

* *

Sergeant Lee Manning had not noticeably moved for hours. Even as the captor forced the frightened second graders to systematically reduce the odds of a successful shot by taping paper over window pane after window pane, the sharpshooter stayed perfectly still, hidden from the view of the former school janitor by a high row of hedges. The rifle remained pressed hard against the sniper's solid, compact body, and the former active-duty Marine never lost focus throughout the long and tortuous hostage negotiation phase of the standoff. The concentration of Raleigh's most skilled Special Response Unit member never wavered, even as a contingent of television helicopters hovered overhead.

The call finally came. The target, Marcus Delaney, recently fired from the school, had begun to show signs of dangerous instability. "Okay, Manning," said the lead hostage negotiator and officer in command, Thurman Smith, "if the target presents himself, take him out. You've got one shot. It has to be an instant kill. No collateral damage."

With that final command, an almost imperceptible smile flashed against the sniper's normally stoic face. Manning replied, "Roger that—one shot. Instant death."

As darkness settled beyond the school, now surrounded by an eerie glow from the lights of all the television cameras covering the scene, Delaney moved past the fourth windowpane, which had been crudely covered with construction paper by the student hostages hours earlier. Manning picked up on the movement by the faint shadow that Delaney cast over the paper. Moments later, Delaney lifted the lower left corner of the paper from the left-most window and peered outside. Manning radioed confirmation to Smith. "The target is confirmed." The sniper's steely eyes settled squarely on Delaney's acne-scarred face.

"Fire at your discretion," responded Smith, adding, "Good luck, sergeant."

"Luck has nothing to do with it," said Manning, confidently. The twenty-eight-year-old North Carolinian had been waiting for this moment ever since 1991, when the secretary of the Navy decided not to employ Manning's sniper skills in the Iraqi dessert.

Recalling the lessons of anatomy that all Marine Corps snipers are taught, Manning adjusted the Leupold Mark 4 Ultra scope and focused it on the small indent of Delaney's lip just below his nose. The trajectory would place the bullet directly through Delaney's central nervous system and instantly incapacitate him.

Letting out one last full and evenly paced breath, Manning waited for the moment when the body is precisely between exhaling and inhaling, when the body is utterly still, before ever so gently drawing in the right index finger on the taut two-stage trigger.

Instantly, in less than one one-hundredth of a second, the hammer violently slammed home on the pin. Traveling at three times the speed of sound, the Teflon-coated bullet smoothly exited the barrel and covered its upward trajectory over the parking lot in less than a second. It effortlessly pierced the glass and violently smashed through the target's front teeth, severing Delaney's brain stem and halting any message that his brain might have tried to send to his right hand, which still held a 9 mm Beretta.

The bullet's destruction was not, however, complete. It continued through Delaney's brain and exploded through the lower half of his skull before lodging itself in the temple of Tim Barlow, a second grader who happened to be standing in the wrong place. Manning never saw the little boy.

Instead of touting Manning as a hero, television coverage of the incident fixated on the two body bags being hauled away by the coroner's station wagon.

The child victim happened to be the only son of Jean Barlow, a prominent liberal city council member from the more affluent part of Raleigh who had frequently touted her son's attendance at the inner-city school. She was also a vocal critic of the Raleigh Police Department, which she perceived as racist and prone to unnecessary violence.

Immediately following her son's funeral, Council member Barlow, held a news conference in which she launched a crusade to reform the police department. Barlow's wrath was directed at the city's Special Response Unit and, in particular, at Sergeant R. E. Lee Manning, whom she called, among other things, "a frustrated and confused Marine," "a fascist," and "an accident waiting to happen."

* *

Lee Manning was not happy about being ordered to go see Nancy Reiser. Manning thought the whole thing was bullshit—the babbling-brook-like fountain, the soothing music, the plants and, especially, the intrusive questions. The hour-long session was almost over when Reiser, a police psychologist, scribbled the phrase "abnormally normal" in her notebook.

* *

Secret Service Agent Sean McGowan had been in Lagos, Ghana, for almost a month. As the lead liaison with the Ghanaian Special Forces and the police, the thirty-five-year-old bachelor was charged with coordinating the 15,000 soldiers and police the African nation had made available for the president's visit to its capitol.

While in Lagos, McGowan had daily flown by helicopter along all potential motorcade routes that the Secret Service might use for the president's trip, looking for vulnerabilities. He also led the threat assessment team, which checked and secured every building along all possible routes. The result of McGowan's work was a 220-page security document that every Secret Service agent on his team had read. McGowan's report left nothing to chance. His work was meticulous. Since graduating from Notre Dame in 1986, McGowan was one of the few young agents believed to have a serious shot at becoming director of the Secret Service.

* *

The fall day was hotter and more humid than normal. The temperature was approaching eighty degrees by 8:00 A.M. and would rise to ninety-three degrees before the president's motorcade would reach Independence Square in the heart of Lagos. McGowan had not expected to be in the motorcade—advance team members rarely work the details for which they do the advance work. A fellow agent had grown ill the night before, however, and McGowan was reassigned on protective duty to Ghana's president, Paul Mahama.

All along the twenty-mile motorcade route, thousands of Ghanaian boys and girls—many in crisp blue-and-green school uniforms—feverishly yelled and waved their small plastic Ghanaian and United States flags. Overhead, helicopters flew in front of the motorcade and swept the low-level buildings with sophisticated electronic equipment. Within the motorcade itself, Secret Service agents in every car eyed the crowds and scanned the rooftops for any movement that might portend a threat to the man—and the institution—they were charged with protecting.

Inside the square itself, half a million people lined the outer walls and crammed into its center. Despite standing and waiting for hours in the oppressive tropical heat and humidity, the citizens of Ghana who were lucky enough to be in the square to witness this historic event—the first-ever visit by a sitting American president—were genuinely enthusiastic. One man, who had arrived almost twenty hours earlier than anybody else and was now located at the base of the stage, did not join in on the enthusiasm. Kwabena Sulemana was on a personal mission.

The president's press secretary was ecstatic. Facing domestic troubles and low approval ratings at home, the president's staff was desperate for a public relations victory, however small. The White House staff spun the trip as a vital ingredient of President Donald Butler's overall strategic Africa policy initiative. With little more than a year left in Butler's second term, the discerning observer would have recognized that his administration did not have anything remotely resembling a strategic policy toward Africa and didn't really need one. Despite this, the Ghanaians were still pleased that the United States president had chosen to visit their country.

When the American and Ghanaian leaders took the stage, the roar that greeted them was deafening. As far as McGowan could see from his position on stage, near Mahama, Ghanaians young and old were stomping and clapping their approval. Thousands more waved *akwaaba*, or welcome, posters. For McGowan, the crowd represented half a million different threats.

Joining the two presidents on the stage was a host of tribal chiefs and local politicians, all dressed in the colorful and flowing traditional gowns of Ghana. A large choir, whose sole responsibility was to sing the national anthems of both countries, created a vibrantly colored backdrop. As the last note of the Ghanaian national anthem was struck, 3,500 white doves were released and sent flying over the crowd. Members of the White House public relations team flashed self-congratulatory smiles at one another. The scene made for great TV.

President Mahama welcomed President Butler and spoke for a few minutes about the geopolitical importance of the United States.-Ghana relationship. Butler returned the kind remarks and launched into a carefully drafted speech, peppered with ever-so-slight catch phrases about African-American relations, which only diplomatic officers around the world would bother to decipher for their nuances.

From McGowan's position, just seven feet from Mahama, the day was going well. The principals had arrived safely, and the speeches were almost over, which signaled that the most dangerous part of the day was also coming to a conclusion. In forty-five minutes, the president of the United States would be back on Air Force One, along with McGowan, returning to Washington, D.C.

Then, out of the corner of his eye, McGowan saw Mahama lean over and ask Butler a question. McGowan didn't hear the question but saw that Butler was only too happy to oblige an answer. McGowan sensed the request was not good news for the president's protectors.

The president turned to his lead Secret Service agent, Jerry Trebtowski, and said, "President Mahama has graciously asked if I would personally greet a few of his citizens. Given his great reception, it's only appropriate."

"Mr. President," said Trebtowski, "we're on a tight schedule. I can't recommend—"

Cutting him off, the president snapped, "I'm doing it."

Instantly, Trebtowski was on his radio informing the contingent of Secret Service officers that "Trailblazer," the codename for the president, was on the move. McGowan's initial suspicion was confirmed. Protecting a glad-handing politician in a large crowd was an agent's worst nightmare.

Quickly surveying the situation, Trebtowski guided the two presidents to the base of the stage, the most secure place from which they could engage in the age-old political ritual of shaking hands. Trebtowski knew that every president loved it and that it came with the job of protecting a president, but he—and the Secret Service—still hated it and advised every president against doing it. They also knew that every president would inevitably ignore their advice. Butler was no exception. In fact, more than most, he seemed to thrive on—and even derive energy from—human contact.

As the presidents, with their contingent of protectors, approached the crowd, which was contained by the metal barriers at the base of the stage, people surged forward for their chance to touch history. Those closest to the barrier were immediately thrust against it. The pressure was so intense that three people instantly collapsed, and a dozen more had the wind knocked out of them.

President Butler, seeing that the once friendly faces had now become stunned and frightened, was the first to detect that all was not right. "Back up, back up!" he yelled in vain to the crowd. "For Christ's sake, back up!" the leader of the free world implored, but thousands of Ghanaians continued to surge forward.

With a suddenness that startled everyone, the metal barrier directly to the left of the two presidents crumbled under the pressure of the crowd. A wall of people that, moments earlier, had been unable to breathe was now propelled to the ground.

They had no chance to get up. A second wave of people then fell on them, adding to their misery.

Through it all, Kwabena Sulemana was able to maintain his composure and his focus. Sensing that the opportunity was divinely inspired, Sulemana was pushed to within ten feet of his target.

Within a fraction of a second of the barrier collapsing, Trebtowski was on his radio informing every agent that Trailblazer was being withdrawn. Masses of sweating, frightened people, however, enveloped the two presidents and their protectors and clogged the path back to the stage. Within seconds, the helicopters that had been hovering over the square began to converge on the scene. Behind the stage, the drivers of every car in the president's motorcade awaited word that Trailblazer was secure so they could depart the scene.

While barking commands into his radio, Trebtowski laced his hand through the president's belt loop and placed his body between President Butler and the crowd. McGowan was doing the same with Mahama. Sulemana edged closer.

As the helicopters neared, the crowd became more frantic and pushed even harder. A second barrier—this time to the far right of the president's entourage—crashed to the ground. Hundreds more Ghanaians flowed through the opening like water rushing through a breached dike.

Then suddenly, as he continued to scan the frightened crowd, McGowan caught sight of Sulemana. His face didn't look right. It was calm, almost serene. In spite of the chaos surrounding him, McGowan locked onto Sulemana. His sixth sense told him that this guy was trouble.

Sulemana, unconcerned with the dangerous situation around him, did not notice McGowan. Three feet was now all that stood between him and his eighteen-year-old dream of retribution. Using the only hand that he could, the former Ghanaian Army private unsheathed a razor-sharp wooden knife that he strapped to his stomach just below his right ribs. Instantly, McGowan saw the weapon. "Knife, ten o'clock," he screamed into his radio as he thrust Mahama back to the protection of the Ghanaian agents directly behind him and hurled himself toward the lunging assassin.

Hearing McGowan's warning, Trebtowski ceased pulling on Butler's belt loop and literally lifted the president up and began carrying him out of harm's way. At the same time, the wall of agents squeezed tighter around Trailblazer and began forcefully creating a human tunnel through the crowd to the stage.

As Sulemana thrust the knife in the direction of the Ghanaian president, McGowan, with violent swiftness, cracked the assassin's left wrist with his hand and redirected the knife. Only slightly deterred, Sulemana continued on. McGowan countered with the fleetness of a professional lightweight boxer and hit the attacker's float-ing rib. The blow caused Sulemana to drop the knife. In almost the same motion, McGowan located the attacker's center of gravity and pulled him to the ground.

Lying on top of Sulemana, McGowan quickly and efficiently searched him for additional weapons. Finding none, McGowan pushed himself up by pressing Sulemana's torso to the ground. By this time, two other Secret Service agents and a Ghanaian military officer had surrounded the attacker.

As Mahama and Butler were propelled through the human tunnel, up the stairs and across the stage to the awaiting vehicles, the Ghanaian military began to regain control of the crowds.

Thirty-seven seconds after the words "Knife, ten o'clock" had been uttered, the lead cars—with Presidents Mahama and Butler securely inside—were safely on their way away to the airport via an alternate route that had been developed weeks earli-er by Sean McGowan.

By the time the motorcade arrived at the airport, McGowan and the Secret Service officers who stayed behind were safely on the stage above the carnage and interrogating Kwabena Sulemana. To their surprise, his intended target was Mahama and not Butler. Eighteen years earlier, Sulemana, a lowly Army steward who had been working for then-General Mahama, had been accused of stealing a sterling silver shoehorn from the general. The punishment was the loss of his right hand and the termination of an eleven-year career in the military. It was a crime he hadn't committed.

Four hours later, with Air Force One well over the Atlantic Ocean, the full extent of the tragedy in Lagos began to come clear. Fifty-seven Ghanaian citizens— thirty of whom were teenagers—had been killed in the stampede. Hundreds more were injured.

News of the tragedy was picked up by news agencies around the world, while reports of the foiled assassination were officially denied by the Ghanaian govern-ment. Sulemana was quietly executed at a military base southwest of Lagos later that evening.

Ten days later, Sean McGowan was awarded Ghana's highest military honor. A month later, he accepted the Secret Service's highest honor—the Exceptional Civilian Service Award—with little emotion.

* *

Nancy Reiser had worked for Raphael Baptista for seven years before she returned to Raleigh. Baptista's request a year earlier had surprised her, but she was happy to keep an eye open for someone with the characteristics for which her former employer was looking.

"Are you still looking for someone for your special project?" asked Reiser.

"I am," replied Baptista.

"Then I think I've found your person." Reiser went on to explain Lee Manning's unique credentials and situation. "In our business, we call someone like this 'abnormally normal.' What it means is that the person can do very abnormal things—such as your task—and still conduct themselves in a normal manner."

CHAPTER TWO

P ete Sawyer, Robert Colfax's twenty-nine-year-old, bespectacled campaign manager, surveyed the main ballroom of the Mayflower Hotel. Satisfied that the lights were well-positioned for C-SPAN II's cameras to pick up the campaign's web site address and toll-free number, Sawyer, always cognizant of an opportunity to promote his candidate, spotted Ellen Moriarty, Washington's hottest political reporter and author of the influential Internet newsletter, *The Moriarty Minute.*

"Ms. Moriarty, I'm Pete Sawyer. I'm glad you could make it."

"Wouldn't miss it for the world," said Moriarty, a bit sarcastically as she surveyed the room with a bored look.

"I appreciated your full coverage of our announcement last month. Every other major daily put our story next to the obits."

"The majors," said Moriarty referring to the largest newspapers, "never know a story until it bites 'em in the ass. Plus, I've liked Colfax ever since he resigned as secretary of Navy. He had balls then, and his willingness to run as an independent tells me that he still has them." Moriarty looked at Sawyer for a reaction but got none. "Plus, win or lose, he's going to add some excitement to this race. The thought of Martin Byrne and C. Elliott Prescott duking it out with their vapid ideologies of 'practical centrism' and 'common-sense conservatism' is enough to make me puke. Your boy might actually force them to do some creative thinking—or least force their overpaid political consultants to expend a few brain cells on something other than hard liquor."

"That's the plan. If we can get them engaged in a campaign of big ideas, we can win," said Sawyer. "And, like you, we're going to use the Internet to level the playing field."

"So, what's your boy got in store for tonight?" asked Moriarty. "Anything worthy of my fifteen million netizens?"

"Without giving away the story," said Sawyer, "'my boy,' as you so fondly call him, is going to highlight corporate welfare in tonight's speech. But unlike the other candidates, he's going to name names."

"I think I'll stay for the show," said Moriarty, who with a satisfied smile returned to her laptop computer.

*   *

Colfax looked out over the large audience of the National Small Business Coalition, the country's pre-eminent trade association for small to medium-sized businesses. "Thank you for inviting me to your fifty-third annual Capital Conference. I am pleased to be here, even if I am not your first choice," he said with a smile, referring to the fact that he had been asked only the day before to fill in for C. Elliott Prescott, the governor of Pennsylvania and presumed Republican nominee for president. Prescott's father, a former U.S. senator and secretary of state, had suffered a stroke two days earlier, giving Prescott a convenient excuse for canceling his appearance before a group that he already felt was squarely in his camp. "But like a small businessman who finally gets his chance to pitch his product to a large prospective customer, I intend to make the most of this opportunity."

A few appreciative smiles glittered in the crowd.

After working up the crowd over the unfairness of taxes for a few minutes, Colfax began to hone in on his audience. "I was speaking with a local food distributor back in Minnesota last week. Do you know what she told me?" Colfax paused for crowd to take the bait. "She told me her company was regulated by sixty-three different local, state and federal agencies. Sixty-three! She employs 154 people. That works out to more than one agency for every three employees. As president, I will do something about this," said Colfax. "We don't need sixty different federal agencies issuing 1,800 rules a year. And we sure as hell don't need a Code of Federal Regulations that's 130,000 pages long. Before one new rule is issued under my administration, we will first review every federal regulation and remove those that are unnecessary, redundant, outdated and just plain stupid."

The audience responded with a loud round of applause and a few hoots and hollers.

Colfax then moved in to close the sale. "Before I conclude, I would like to address one last issue. Actually, it's two issues—but they must be addressed simultaneously in order to fundamentally change the way Washington operates. These issues will receive my immediate attention—eliminating corporate welfare and reforming our campaign finance system."

Moriarty stopped typing into her laptop and, for one of the few times in her career, really listened.

"As owners of small and medium-sized businesses," Colfax continued, "I know you don't come to Washington looking for handouts or special breaks. In fact, it's just the opposite. You come to Washington to ask to be left alone—to be able to quietly make a profit so that you can provide for your family and improve your communities. Unfortunately, not all businesses think the same as you. There are some among us that aren't pulling their weight. As president, I will require every business—I repeat, every business—to compete on the merits of its product. No longer can businesses expect their friends in Washington to save them from their own ineptitude. All corporate welfare does is take money away from proven entrepreneurs—like you," said Colfax, gesturing at his audience. "What's worse is that your money is then redistributed by clueless politicians—many of whom have no business experience—in the form of subsidies and tax breaks to the only people who matter to them—the people who contribute to their campaign coffers."

Ed Kielty, a successful software developer, leaped to his feet and cheered. He also wrote down the Colfax2000.org address.

"If I am going to ask educators, seniors, and welfare recipients to tighten their belts, you bet your you-know-what that I am going to ask corporate America to do the same," said Colfax. "If we're going to have time limits for welfare recipients, we sure as hell ought to have time limits on corporate welfare. And, according to my watch, their time has run out." He then listed the names of the some of America's biggest oil, chemical, telecommunications, agribusiness and defense-related companies in the country and the public largesse that they received.

"Holy shit," muttered Moriarty as she returned to her laptop, "he *is* naming names. My readers are going to love it."

Colfax continued, "I feel so strongly about these issues that I want to single out a company that no one has had the courage to call on the carpet. From the multi-million-dollar special tax breaks for gas and natural oil that it receives, to the $700 million subsidy for ethanol, to the special mining rights Congress bestows on it, this company is the epitome of everything that is wrong with Washington. And its president occupies the largest seat at the public trough. The company is Holten, Inc., and the man to whom I refer to is Win Murdock.

"Let me give you just one example: ethanol. I will seek the immediate elimination of this outrageous subsidy. It was intended as a temporary measure—twenty years ago—to help address the then-perceived energy crisis. Two decades and nine billion dollars later, it is still in existence. Why?" bellowed Colfax at the crowd. "I'll tell you why: greed and corruption. Holten, Incorporated, America's largest agricultural concern, has derived a stunning forty-one percent of its profits over the last ten years from ethanol—and last year it would have been in the red without taxpayer subsidies. That's greed. The corruption comes from Win Murdock's dealings with Congress and the White House."

Colfax's passion was being widely embraced by the audience.

"Don't you find it a bit strange that Mr. Murdock gave over $200,000 to both the president and the president's challenger in the 1996 election? Isn't it odd that he would feel compelled to give over 2.5 million dollars to both the Republican and Democratic parties in 1998? If he is such a shrewd businessman, why doesn't he just close his wallet to both parties? The net is exactly the same," said a grinning Colfax to his laughing audience. "I'll tell you why: easy money. Win Murdock has learned that if he keeps lining Democrats' and Republicans' pockets, they'll keep lining his. A nine billion dollar profit is a pretty good return on the investment of a few million dollars in campaign contributions, don't you think?"

Ed Kielty shook his head in disgust. Colfax had hit the nail on the head, he thought to himself. Right then and there, he vowed to get involved in Colfax's campaign.

"The problem is that this nine billion dollars came directly from us. If we weren't underwriting one of the wealthiest men in America to the tune of over a billion dollars a year, we could be fixing our worn-out roads, repairing our crumbling bridges, paying our teachers more, or lowering taxes."

David Pollard, the vice president of government affairs of the National Small Business Coalition, silently nodded his approval at Colfax's impassioned remarks. Looking around the room, he could see that he was not alone.

After the speech, Moriarty grabbed Sawyer and handed him her business card. "Here's my personal e-mail address. Keep me informed of Colfax's plans." Then in an altogether earnest tone she also uttered, "If he can survive Murdock, your boy just might have a chance."

Across town, a former Secret Service agent watched the speech on C-SPAN II and wondered if a man of Colfax's character could actually make it into the White House. Jaded by her experience with the current occupant of the White House, Stephanie Freeberg was not optimistic.

* *

The first winter storm of the year had engulfed the sweeping Nebraska prairie and was hurling a furious combination of snow and sleet at the fifth-story window of Win Murdock's luxurious office complex. From his vast state-of-the-art command center, with its host of high-powered computers and television monitors that simultaneously ran CNN, BBC, and the Asian News Network, Murdock commanded the seventy-seven billion dollar conglomerate that he had almost single-handedly grown from a small commodity brokerage in Iowa over half a century ago. Presently, Holten, Inc., had 113 foreign operations and employed over 88,000 people worldwide.

"Give my regards to the senator, and I wish you the best with your event next Friday," Murdock said to Miriam Harder. "You know, I had a nephew die of leukemia many years ago," he said, lying. "If you need more than $100,000 to make your charity gala a success, just give me another call. I have a few friends who could contribute."

"Thank you, Win. I'll be sure to give Gene your regards," said Mrs. Harder, indicating that Murdock's generosity would make its way back to her husband, Senator Gene Harder, chairman of the Senate Commerce Committee—the real target of the $100,000 contribution. Murdock could not care less about leukemia. Using a wife to get at a politician was one of Murdock's favorite ways of applying additional grease to the wheels of Washington, D.C. Plus, Murdock figured, it was an easy way to avoid all the negative press the do-gooder political organizations heaped on Holten—and Murdock in particular—for their political contributions. The Federal Election Commission would never know about the contributions.

"David," Murdock barked at his ever present executive vice president and trusted protege, David Luther, "cut Ms. Harder a check for one hundred grand and have it FedExed. Also, get Thompson on the phone."

A minute later, Jerome Thompson, senior vice president for international marketing for Holten, Inc., was nervously waiting for his boss to speak into the secure phone. Finally, after what seemed like hours, he heard Murdock's distinctive Midwestern twang come over the line.

"Jerry, give me the good news."

"Mr. Murdock," responded Thompson with more courage in his voice than he actually had, "we've only been able to identify three of the agents. We can't make our pitch until we know them all."

"Goddamnit, Thompson," Murdock exploded, "if you don't pull your head out of your ass and find that fourth agent, we're fucked. Do you hear me? Holten's screwed if word of this investigation is leaked to the media. You find that son of a bitch, now," screamed Murdock. "Once you do, do whatever it takes to turn them to our side. I expect a report at 7:30 tomorrow morning." Murdock slammed down the phone.

"David," said Murdock, "arrange a conference call with Ambassador Wiley for tomorrow morning at eight and instruct him to set up a lunch with his old friend Tom Geary at the earliest possible date."

Luther returned to his small, windowless office adjacent to Murdock's and called the executive secretary for the former ambassador to China, Harold Wiley. While waiting for an answer, his eye caught the image on the small television situated in top right corner of his suite. Luther couldn't hear what was being said, but he saw that Robert Colfax had the attention of his audience.

Luther reached for the remote, but before he could to turn up the volume to hear Colfax, the ambassador's executive secretary was back on the line, confirming that Wiley had canceled a scheduled breakfast for the next morning in order to speak with Murdock. She also informed Luther that she would arrange a lunch with FBI Director Thomas Geary as soon as possible. Luther thanked her and hung up the phone.

He quickly pushed the volume button for the small set. The voice of Robert Colfax filled the room. ". . . I am going ask corporate America to do the same. The days of sugar-coated subsidies for Atlantic Petroleum and TelCommNet and U.S. Rail & Freight will come to a grinding halt when I become president—"

Seconds later Luther heard Colfax start talking about his boss. He sprang to his feet and raced into Murdock's office. "Turn on C-SPAN II," said Luther, grabbing the remote on Murdock's desk and changing the channel from the Asian New Network to C-SPAN II before Murdock even knew what was happening. "Listen," said Luther.

". . . the corruption comes from his dealing with Congress and the White House . . ." Murdock heard Colfax say. In silence, the pair watched as Colfax outlined his case against Holten, Inc., and Win Murdock.

Rubbing his temple with his thick fingers, Murdock quietly moaned, "What a fucking day. Luther, get on the phone and arrange a meeting in Washington tomorrow afternoon. At a minimum, I want members from the World Corn Association, the Alternative Fuels Consortium, and the Sustainable Agriculture Council there. I expect you to chair the group. The outcome of this meeting will be to drop a load of shit on Robert Colfax so goddamn fast that he never brings up the issue of ethanol, my name, or Holten's name again—ever! Do I make myself clear? You may avail yourself of the company plane, David. I want a report by four tomorrow afternoon." Luther turned to go back to his office when Murdock stopped him. "And, David, since you're going to be in Washington, why don't you meet with Ambassador Wiley. Tell him I want him to get Geary to stop the bureau's investigation." Murdock worried that if the last special agent wasn't found, the FBI's investigation of Holten's price-fixing scheme might result in a huge fine and a few of their vice presidents going to jail.

Later that evening, in weather in which no commercial airliner would ever take off, David Luther settled into the leather seat in Gulf Stream IV as it rapidly made its way down the icy runway at Holten's private airstrip.

* *

The courtroom was well lit, air-conditioned and comfortably decorated with contemporary beige and light brown chairs, but it still had a cold, sterile, institutional feel. From Manning's perspective, the room also lacked the awe-inspiring quality of the older, more classic courtrooms. Justice did not seem guaranteed in the room—it was a feeling the police sergeant could not shake.

"Sergeant Manning," intoned Jeff Piccone, a thirtyish, slightly overweight and balding lawyer, as he began questioning his final witness in the wrongful death case of Timothy Stensby Barlow, "you are a seven-year veteran of the Raleigh Police Department?"

"Yes, sir."

"And you have served on the Special Response Team for the last four years?"

"That is correct, sir," said Manning.

"You are also former Marine. Is that correct?" asked Piccone, as he pushed his glasses back up his sharp nose.

"Yes, sir. I still am a Marine. I'm an active member of the Reserves," replied Manning proudly.

"Excuse me," said Piccone, suddenly shifting gears. "In your seven years as a police officer, have you ever fired your gun or rifle in the line of action?"

"No, sir," said Manning.

"As a Marine, did you ever fire at the enemy in live combat?"

"No, sir."

"Although you are trained as a Marine sniper, you never employed your skills in a real-world situation. Is that correct?"

"Yes, sir," said Manning, bitterly recalling that the response should have been no—if only the policy of the United States military had allowed the then sergeant to engage the enemy in 1991 during the Persian Gulf War.

"So this was your first shot with real consequences?" said Piccone. "Life and death consequences?"

"Yes, sir," Manning replied calmly.

For the next half hour, Piccone methodically and relentlessly questioned Manning about the training and habits of snipers, the schools they attended, the courses they took and, in general, the daily stresses and pressures that snipers experienced. Just as Manning was settling into a groove and feeling comfortable with the line of inquiry, Piccone's easy-going drawl picked up an edge, and the attorney focused his eyes exclusively on Manning.

"Did anything touch the barrel of your gun?" he asked.

"No, sir."

"Are you sure?"

"Yes, sir."

"How can you be sure?"

"I'm a professional, sir," replied Manning, in a tone revealing a rising level of anger.

"In the course of the eight-hour event nothing—absolutely nothing—touched your barrel? Tests, if they were conducted on your barrel, would not find any dirt or residue from the surrounding area?" asked Piccone.

Manning again responded "No, sir," although this time with an edge of doubt that Piccone detected.

"What was the wind direction when you fired your fatal shot?" Piccone asked.

Manning paused before answering. "Northwesterly."

"Are you sure? We can consult the weather reports for October 6th."

"Yes, sir, I'm sure."

"What was the speed of the wind?"

"Variable. Between seven to twelve miles an hour."

"At the precise moment of your shot, what was the wind situation?"

"It was calm," said Manning.

"Is it possible that there was a gust of wind?"

"It's possible. But given that the shot was taken at approximately 100 yards, the effect of the wind on the bullet would have been insignificant, sir."

Piccone ignored Manning's response. "Tell me, Sergeant Manning, did you consider how the bullet would go through the glass window? Isn't it true that when a bullet hits a medium like glass, it can be expected to be deflected to a certain degree?"

"Yes, sir," admitted Manning.

"Is it also possible that Delaney pulled away from the window just before you shot?" asked Piccone. Manning hesitated. "Is that possible, Sergeant Manning?"

"I—yes, sir. It was possible. But not very likely."

"Not very likely . . ." replied Piccone, who let the phrase hang in the air. "Did you know how thick the glass was?" he asked after a moment.

"No, sir. I assumed it was a standard quarter of an inch."

"You assumed?" asked the lawyer, wiping some sweat from his receding hairline. "Wouldn't that have affected the angle of the bullet as it passed through the glass?"

"Not necessarily, sir."

"Interesting," said Piccone before asking his next question. "Did you know where all the students in the room were, Sergeant Manning?"

"No, sir."

"Did you consider the possibility of collateral damage?"

"Yes, sir," replied Manning.

"And how exactly did you consider this possibility?"

"Given my position on the ground and the assailant's position in the second-story room, which I calculated to be seventeen feet above my own, and knowing the distance between myself and the target was ninety-three yards, I determined that if the bullet successfully severed the target's medulla oblongata and exited his cranium, it would continue in an upwardly direction above the head of the average second grader. I also figured that because the target was at the very end of the classroom, the likelihood that a student would be behind him was remote."

"Impressive, Sergeant Manning. Did you consider that once the bullet reached Mr. Delaney, that it could strike his teeth and or skull and thus be further deflected?

"No, sir."

"No?" said Piccone, incredulously. "Let me get this straight. You consider yourself an expert sniper?"

"Yes, sir, I do."

"Wouldn't an expert sniper know if the target was directly up against the window? Wouldn't an expert know how thick the glass was? Wouldn't someone of your level of expertise know whether innocent people were in the path of your bullet? And wouldn't an expert know that a front-on face shot might be deflected?" Manning was visibly angry now and wanted to throttle the weasel-faced lawyer, who the sniper reckoned to be some liberal, Ivy League-educated lawyer.

"The target was unstable," said Manning. "I was told to fire at my discretion. I took every precaution against collateral damage. Unfortunately, the boy was in the wrong place at the wrong time. Marcus Delaney should be the one on trial, not me."

Piccone ignored Manning. For the third time, the lawyer switched gears. "Sergeant Manning, tell us about the time in 1985 when Maggie Long was raped."

Manning was dumbfounded by the question. "What? What does that have to do with anything?"

Over the mild objection of Manning's lawyer, the judge allowed the question after Piccone argued that it got to the question of intent.

"Ms. Long," Piccone continued, "was raped and brutally beaten by three men—three black men. You were heard to have said afterward—I have affidavits—and I quote 'the niggers should be shot.'" Manning's attorney did not object to the question. "Are you a racist, Sergeant Manning?"

"What? Ah—no," said Manning. "No, I'm not. I served in the Marine Corps with blacks. I've got nothing against blacks. What happened to Maggie was a crime. I was young. I was angry. I may have said those things, but I am not a racist."

"The fact that Marcus Delaney was black had nothing to do with your willingness—your recklessness—to set aside your concerns about having less-than-complete information just to have the opportunity to kill Delaney?" asked Piccone.

Desperately scanning the courtroom for Thurman Smith, the detective who had ordered the shot, Manning replied no. Thurman had left the room before Manning was called to testify.

"Your willingness to fire into a situation that had not been fully thought out was in no way related to your eagerness to kill Mr. Marcus Delaney, a black man—and in the process, Timothy Barlow?"

"No," said a genuinely confused Manning, staring out at the courtroom filled with the grieving relatives of Tim Barlow and what appeared to be a number of underemployed lawyers, including the same unimposing, middle-aged man with gray hair who was in attendance at Robert Colfax's announcement. He was there to see first-hand what an 'abnormally normal' person looked and sounded like.

"Were you trying to prove yourself to your colleagues? Prove you were as good?"

"No, sir."

"I have no further questions for the witness, your honor."

The judge dismissed the jury for the day, and, as Manning exited the courtroom, Jean Barlow, now a candidate for attorney general, was holding a news conference before a pool of reporters and cameras, expressing her disbelief at the reckless disregard for procedure and the blatant racism that still pervaded the Raleigh Police Department.

As Manning's lawyer fielded some questions about his client, the seven-year police veteran escaped through the side door of the courthouse, thinking that for the second time in a very brief career, the "system" had failed to recognize the skills of an expert sniper.

CHAPTER THREE

Matthew!" screamed Sean McGowan as he bolted upright and stared straight ahead into the darkness. Before he could get his bearings, Stephanie Freeberg rushed into the small bedroom.

"Sean, what's wrong? Are you Okay?" she said as she sat on the edge of the bed and gently placed an arm around him, drawing him into her body. "It was just a dream."

"Huh?" said McGowan, looking around, still not fully awake.

"You just had a bad dream."

"Yeah," said McGowan, softly, "it's always the same. And there's nothing I can do to change the ending."

"Tell me about it," said Freeberg, suddenly very curious about the possibility of gaining a glimpse into the heart of her new lover whom she had aggressively pursued since leaving the Secret Service.

"It's about my brother."

"I didn't know you had a brother."

"He's three years younger than I am and still lives with my parents. He's a quadriplegic."

Freeberg looked McGowan in the eyes and encouraged him to continue.

"Twenty years ago, we were at our cabin in Wisconsin. It was late August. Matt and I were playing football in the yard between the cabin and the lake. He was pretending to be Walter Payton, and I was Jack Lambert," said McGowan, referring to the former Chicago Bears and Pittsburgh Steelers greats. "Football practice was starting the next week, so I decided to teach him a drill I knew the coach would have him and his teammates doing. I figured he could benefit from the experience. Plus, being older, I wanted to toughen him up a little," said McGowan with a crooked half-smile as he recalled his stubborn little brother. "So I had him lay on his back with the Nerf football. I then laid down so that our heads were almost touching but our feet were pointed in opposite directions. On the count of three, we would both get up as quickly as possible. It was Matt's job as the running back to try and elude me. It was my job as the defender to tackle him." McGowan stopped.

Freeberg stroked his arm. "It might help if you talk about the dream, Sean."

McGowan nodded. "After pounding him pretty good for the first few times, he decided to cheat a little. On the count of two, he sprang up like a cat, and before I knew it, he darted left. Still on my knees, I threw out my right hand to stop him, but he leaped over it like he really was Walter Payton. Once past me, he began to mimic Howard Cosell, 'Payton's at the twenty-five, the twenty . . .' 'Offsides!' I yelled, 'offsides, the play is going to come back.' But Matt continued to rush headlong toward the lake yelling, '. . . the fifteen, the ten, the five—Payton's going to score!' as he sprinted down the dock. At the end, he screamed 'Touchdown!' and dove head-first into the lake with the football stretched out ahead of him—just like Walter Payton.

"'Matthew,' I yelled after him, 'you cheated.' Then I waited for him to come out of the lake. When he didn't come up, I rushed to the end of the dock. I saw the football floating in the murky water, and then I saw his body lying at the bottom of the shallow lake. I'll never forget that moment. That's how the dream ends every time—just like it happened that day."

"Sean, I'm so sorry," said Freeberg, wondering how much this experience had fostered McGowan's protective instincts, a trait most Secret Service agents possessed. "Do you see your brother very often?"

"Whenever I go home to Chicago for the holidays. It's still hard. I see him and I blame myself. I see my mom and blame myself that she looks twenty years older than she is. I sometimes think that if only I hadn't tackled him so hard the first two times, he wouldn't have felt the need to jump on the count of two. Or, if only I had been able to grab his right foot as he jumped over my outstretched arms. So many 'what-ifs.' What if we hadn't gone to the preseason game between the Packers and the Bears? Matt would have never seen Walter Payton dive into the endzone. What if it had rained more that summer, then the lake wouldn't have been two feet lower than normal," said McGowan as his voice trailed off. "What if—"

"I know the feeling," said Freeberg. "I have a younger sister who's deaf— it was preventable." It was the first time Freeberg had ever told anyone the story of her sister. "My mother was away taking care of her mother, which left my dad to watch the three of us for a week. Lisa came down with a really bad ear infection, and my dad didn't take her to see a doctor. She's been deaf ever since, and my dad has never forgiven himself."

The pair spoke for almost another two hours before Freeberg fell asleep in McGowan's muscular arms. Her last thought before sleep was that she could really fall in love with someone like him.

*   *

McGowan woke up alone but could hear the TV in the next room. He walked into the sparsely furnished living room. "C-SPAN II," drawled McGowan when he saw what Freeberg was watching. "You're pathetic."

"It gets me hot," joked Freeberg. "Mutter sweet nothings about family values or the politics of inclusion, and I'm all yours."

"Seriously, don't you get enough politics at the Center for Squeaky Clean Politics?" asked McGowan, with a mischievous look.

"It's the Center for Ethical and Responsive Politics, thank you very much, and no, I don't."

"So what exactly do you do in your new position?" asked McGowan. "What's your official title?"

"I'm director of research. I'm responsible for monitoring the fundraising and donation activities of organizations that intend to play a role in the 2000 presidential campaign."

"You follow the soft money?" asked McGowan.

"More than just the soft money. I track the independent expenditures and the issue advocacy dollars."

"Good luck. I hope you have the budget to send a few team members to China," he said with an easy laugh. "So, are you still happy to have left the Secret Service?"

"Absolutely. Going back for my master's degree was the best thing I could do. I love my new job. I feel like I felt when I first started with the Secret Service—like I'm doing something that matters."

"Really? Do you miss the service at all?"

"I miss the camaraderie. But since I mustered up the courage to call you, ask for a date, and eventually seduce you," said Freeberg, "that feeling has subsided. Seriously though, no, I don't miss it at all."

McGowan knew she was telling the truth.

"I suppose I shouldn't say this about the man you are now protecting—you know, the Secret Service code and all—but I couldn't stand him. I didn't go through all that training—put in those eighteen- and twenty-hour days—all those years just to protect a sleazebag like him. The way he treats women is awful. It's demeaning. It finally got to the point where I couldn't handle hearing one more comment about the size of some senator's wife's breasts or his wagering about the oral sex skills of some female staff member. The man is a creep. The only way to salvage my self-respect was to resign. I've never looked back," said Freeberg, closing her bathrobe tightly over her well-defined and shapely thigh, as if trying to shut out any thought of Trailblazer. "How about you? Is working the presidential detail everything you thought it would be?" she asked.

"Yes and no. The professionalism and the pace are certainly what I expected. The petty politics and the personalities are difficult. The worst part is tolerating the young staffers who think they're God's gift to this country. The dumbshits don't understand that we're assigned to protect the president of the United States—that's our sole responsibility. Like you," continued McGowan as he looked at Freeberg and wondered how her attractive facial features and light brown skin had failed to capture his attention during the six months they had worked together at the White House, "my respect for Trailblazer is wearing thin. When I first interviewed with the service out of college, the thought of protecting the president thrilled me. The idea that some day I would be responsible for protecting a Harry Truman, a John F. Kennedy, or a Ronald Reagan gave me a rush. Honor, courage, respect, love of country were—and still are—real concepts to me. It is frustrating to have to protect someone who you wouldn't be proud to introduce to your mother."

"I know the feeling," said Freeberg. She was even more convinced that she could fall in love with the man sitting across from her.

Changing topics, McGowan said, "Did you hear the rumor that Director Andersen is planning on retiring?"

"Are you serious? Jesus, he's the fourth director to leave under Butler. The way he's going through directors, you may yet become the youngest director."

"Morale is pretty low over there," said McGowan, referring to the White House. "Andersen is leaving to take a job at the Social Security Administration. The damn Social Security Administration!"

"Why?" asked Freeberg.

"Same reason as you. He didn't like looking the other way at all of Trailblazer's extracurricular activities. And do you know how the White House is spinning his departure? They're saying Andersen is taking the new job because of heart problems."

"That's what I can't stand about the service," said Freeberg, "Anderson is as decent and moral a man as there is, but in the service you either suppress your own standards when they conflict with your responsibilities to protect the president, or you resign."

"Andersen will be the good soldier and go along with the lie. I am sure he's happy to be leaving, though. I would be," said McGowan.

"Why don't you leave?" asked Freeberg. A long silence followed.

"To tell you the truth, I am. I put in for a field assignment last week. I said I wanted to go somewhere in the Midwest to be closer to my brother and my mom."

At this Freeberg felt a lump rise in her throat, "I would have called you for a date sooner had I known the clock was ticking," she said, getting up from the couch and snuggling into McGowan's lap. "If you get it," she continued, "you could be assigned to cover Robert Colfax."

"He doesn't stand a snowball's chance in hell," said McGowan, "I don't think he'll make it to Christmas." Colfax was still at one percent in the polls.

"I don't know. I think this country is ready for an independent president. I just saw him last night on C-SPAN II. He's courageous. He just roasted Win Murdock —pretty much labeled him the poster boy for corporate welfare. Plus, I don't think that most people know he's independently wealthy. He can stay in the race until the end."

"I thought I read somewhere that he said he isn't going to spend an unlimited amount of his own money," said McGowan.

"He said he will only match the contributions his campaign receives. He doesn't want to be like Cross and spend untold amounts of his own money," said Freeberg, referring to Stanley Cross, the rich cable television mogul who was challenging Elliott Prescott for the Republican endorsement. "Apparently, he doesn't want to appear that he's just buying his way into the campaign like Cross. At the same time, he doesn't want to rely on any special interest money. I think his plan to match people's contributions is an intriguing idea. It's going to require some amazing grassroots support before he's a legitimate contender."

"Good intentions—but I still don't think he'll make it."

"If he does though, he won't be beholden to any special interests—and that'll be really interesting," said Freeberg.

"Do you honestly think people will contribute their own money to a multimillionaire?" asked McGowan.

"If I had some money, I would," said Freeberg. "When I joined the service, he was the kind of guy I thought I'd be protecting."

"Well, who knows? If I am assigned to the Minneapolis field office, you might catch me standing at the side of Robert Colfax," said McGowan. Freeberg pressed a little closer into McGowan's hard body and began softly kissing his weathered face. She didn't want to waste the little time she had left with him.

* *

Manning was contemplating ordering a second beer when the decision was made by someone else. The bartender motioned that the gray-haired man at the end of the bar had purchased the beer. Manning acknowledged the gesture and watched the well-dressed man make his way across the room.

"If you're a reporter, thanks for the beer, but piss off," said Manning. "And if you're hitting on me, you can really fuck off."

The man was not at all startled by the comment.

"I'm not a reporter, and I'm not hitting on you. I'm a lawyer. I have been following your case since the time you shot that son of a bitch. I just wanted to say that I admire your skill and, perhaps even more, your courage through this whole ordeal. The very fact that you are on trial is a travesty."

"Thank you," said Manning, still somewhat unsure of the friendly overtures of the lawyer. "It's all political."

"I know. It's just that it isn't fair when honorable people get sucked into political situations. From everything I've read, you kept your boss appraised of the situation prior to the shot and informed him of the dangers that the shot involved. Yet it's your ass that's on the line." The man scanned Manning's face. "If you don't want to talk about this, I understand."

With a subtle nod, Manning indicated it was all right for the lawyer to continue. "You sure?"

Again, Manning nodded. "What I meant was that while it was you who took the shot, the shot couldn't have been taken without your boss' approval. Right? Whatever happened to the concept of responsibility? I mean when things go well, everyone wants credit. When they go sour, everyone looks for someone else to dump the shit on."

"It was my responsibility," said Manning coolly. "I would have preferred a shot at a point just above the bastard's ear—but it didn't present itself. I was only given the face-on shot, and I was comfortable with that. Given the same circumstances today, I would do the same thing."

"I know you feel bad about the kid," said the lawyer. "I just think that your superiors at the police department could be more supportive of you. How come none of them has testified? And how come Detective Smith isn't being held to as high a standard? I mean, he's the one who ultimately ordered the shot."

Manning said nothing.

"Do you know why I think he's not testifying?"

"No," replied Manning, who was told by superiors that the trial was merely a political show to placate Jean Barlow.

"Smith won't be called by the plaintiff's lawyer because he's black and that doesn't fit their racist scenario. And your lawyer won't call him because they are setting you up to take the fall for Timmy Barlow's death."

"What?"

"I heard from some of my lawyer friends that the plaintiff's lawyers today brought up the rape of a friend by a group of black men."

"She was my best friend and she wasn't just raped, she was brutally gang-raped. I would have wanted to kill whoever did it. Black or white," said Manning. "That doesn't make me a racist."

"In the eyes of the jury it might," said the man trying to gauge Manning's reaction. "Just be careful. They'll probably dig up more from your past. They'll thoroughly review your military record and talk with your friends. They'll want to know about your mother and your father." The man let the last sentence hang in the air.

"What the fuck does my old man have to do with anything?" demanded Manning. "He was a piece of a shit. Why would he be brought into this?"

"The plaintiff will portray you as the product of a racist and bigoted upbringing— even if you weren't." The gray-haired man knew that Manning was. "What's worse, you're being set up. Your attorney should have objected when the other side claimed to have affidavits—but he didn't."

The man did not explain his role in making that happen. He just ordered the sniper another beer and introduced himself. He did not use his real name. Nor did Raphael Baptista tell the sniper he was not really a lawyer.

* *

Elizabeth Vandiver had met Win Murdock on numerous occasions and had been the beneficiary of his bipartisan generosity throughout her distinguished public career as a congresswoman, governor, and now ambassador. Murdock was among the first to congratulate her on her decision to disregard Republican Party elders and resign as governor of Maryland to accept President Butler's offer to become ambassador to the United Nations. He suggested it was a shrewd political decision and that she would be uniquely positioned on the short list of vice-presidential candidates in the year 2000. Vandiver herself was less concerned with the political implications of her decision. She wanted a new challenge—and she had personal reasons for wanting to get out of Annapolis.

When Murdock called in early November and suggested that she use his company jet to fly to Davos, Switzerland, where she was scheduled to give a presentation at the Annual Conference on Global Economics, Vandiver accepted the offer gratefully. The Holten jet was already making the trip, so the ambassador could, for the price of a first-class ticket, save a good deal of time by flying "Holten Express."

The Gulf Jet IV had every convenience. Upon stepping into the multimillion-dollar plane, Vandiver was greeted by an immaculately dressed steward who asked if he could take her jacket and her bag. He then brought her a glass of her favorite wine. The steward offered the same to Vandiver's bodyguard, but he opted for a cup of coffee. In seconds, the steward returned with the wine and a cup of piping hot coffee.

The ambassador relaxed in the wide, plush Corinthian leather seat. Next to the seat was a secure telephone, fax, computer terminal, and video monitor. Further aft was a well-stocked wet bar and small galley. From his station in the galley, the steward could monitor a computer screen for a signal that any of the plane's occupants required service.

Three hours into the flight, somewhere over the north Atlantic, the steward walked toward the cockpit. He had not been beckoned by anyone in ninety minutes. The Holten executive was thoroughly engrossed in a briefing his staff had slaved over the night before, and the ambassador was fast asleep. The bodyguard was preoccupied with the recent edition of *Sports Illustrated* and barely looked up when the steward passed by.

Upon reaching the closet, he quickly sifted through the contents of the ambassador's purse. Having found what he wanted, the steward expertly placed the distinctive key into a mold he had drawn from his pocket. He delicately removed the key with a pair of tweezers and then repeated the process, taking the imprint of the other side of the key. With a solvent from a small vial that he kept in his breast pocket, the steward dabbed a hanky and cleansed the key of any residue.

CHAPTER FOUR

David Luther took his seat at the head of the large mahogany table that occupied half of the eighth floor conference room of Washington's most powerful and influential law firm, Lawrence, Mance & Scott. Directly across from him sat the president and CEO of the Alternative Fuels Consortium. The executive director of Sustainable Agriculture Council and the head of the North American Corn Council sat along the sides. Also seated at the table were three former congressmen, each of whom owed his lucrative lobbying career to Win Murdock's generosity. The Washington insiders were still making small talk when Luther called the meeting to order.

"I want all of you to see something," he said, turning in his swivel chair and hitting the button on the video remote control. Directly behind him, a six-by-six-foot screen descended from the top of the wall. On it was projected a video clip of Robert Colfax's speech to the National Small Business Coalition. The men sat in silence as they listened to Colfax outline his case against the continued federal subsidization of ethanol.

"Obviously, Holten is not pleased with Mr. Colfax's portrayal of ethanol. And we are certainly not happy with his characterization of our chairman, Mr. Murdock." Looking directly at the leaders of the three trade groups, Luther continued, "Therefore, Holten Incorporated would like you to make it known to Mr. Colfax, in no uncertain terms, the error of his ways." Everyone at the table knew that their comfortable lifestyle rested in large measure on their ability to keep Win Murdock pleased, so they listened attentively.

"Specifically," Luther said, eyeing each person at the table, "your organizations are to instruct your members to contact the Colfax campaign through personal letters, phone calls, and e-mail to voice their displeasure. The campaign is not to appear to be organized. It is to look like a genuine outpouring of concern from corn processors and ethanol advocates all cross this country."

As each person at the table was making notes with their Mont Blanc pens, Luther continued to issue orders like a colonel to a room full of eager second lieutenants. "Each person at this table should also work their contacts at the newspapers and talk radio programs in the Midwest. Mr. Murdock wants Colfax refuted quickly and firmly. He wants a special emphasis made in Iowa."

"But," said Joel Wykoff, president of the Alternative Fuels Consortium, "Colfax is running as an independent. He doesn't care about Iowa—he doesn't have to participate in the caucuses."

Luther showed no signs of annoyance but replied curtly, "Perhaps you would like to tell me why Mr. Colfax has a speech in Dubuque tonight and another in Des Moines before Thanksgiving if he has no interest in Iowa."

Wykoff, a former high-level official with the U.S. Department of Agriculture, shifted uncomfortably in his seat. He didn't have an answer.

"Colfax hasn't even registered as a blip on the latest presidential polls," ventured Phillip Cunningham, a twenty-eight-year veteran of Capitol Hill and the most senior of the three former congressmen at the table.

"Precisely," responded Luther, "and we want to keep it that way. The man is making a full frontal attack on our most important product. We are not going to sit by idly while his attacks go unanswered." The tone in Luther's voice conveyed the priority Holten, and Win Murdock, ascribed to this job. "I expect each of you to quantify the numbers of calls, letters and e-mails your members have made by the end of the week." Smiling, Luther added, "We are asking each of you to earn your $50,000 quarterly retainer for a change."

Turning to the former congressmen, Luther said, "I expect each of you to use your connections with your former colleagues in the House and Senate to do what they can to discredit Mr. Colfax. I also expect you to work your contacts on the editorial boards of the largest papers in the Midwest and have them criticize Mr. Colfax's foolish position. Mr. Murdock is willing to pay an additional bonus of $25,000 for every negative story or editorial you can place against Governor Colfax."

Just as each participant was thinking how they might be able to delegate their weighty responsibilities to their more capable underlings, Luther stopped them. "There is one last thing. I expect each of the trade associations at this table to contribute $500,000 to the creation of Washington, D.C.'s, newest issue advocacy group, the Coalition for a Prosperous New Millennium. From those of you on retainer," he said, looking at the ex-congressmen, "I expect $100,000. You can give me your checks as you leave." Luther pushed himself up from his chair to indicate the meeting was over. "Thank you for your time, gentlemen—and, yes, you will be reimbursed by Mr. Murdock for your contributions."

* *

The alarm clock announced the beginning of day with a loud, irritating buzz. Robert Colfax, having gone to bed just four hours earlier, sprang from the stiff mattress and slapped the alarm off. He walked to the bathroom, splashed his face with cold water and began putting on his running gear. After completing a simple routine of stretches, Colfax exited the hotel, took a deep breath of the cool Iowa morning and began easily jogging toward the river.

The night before, Pete Sawyer had given the candidate a map of a five-mile loop through the streets of Dubuque so that he might conduct his daily run with relative efficiency.

A mile into the run, Colfax glided past the Dubuque City Bank. The flashing sign proclaimed the time to be 5:17 A.M. The temperature was twenty-eight degrees. As he drifted toward the river along the deserted streets, Colfax wondered how much longer he could continue his pleasant runs without Secret Service protection. He figured he had about two more months when at least one hour of his day was his own.

Colfax, after extending his run a few miles—something he did whenever he could, returned to his hotel room drenched in sweat. Inside, he found Sawyer, who tossed him a copy of the *Des Moines Daily Tribune*. Sawyer had folded the paper so that the lead editorial was prominent. The headline was simple: "Leave Ethanol Alone." It went on to outline the many benefits of the product and suggested that if anyone should understand this, it was the governor of Minnesota. The editorial also ventured that if Colfax wished to be taken seriously as a candidate for national office, he would reconsider his position on the issue.

"They're wrong," said Colfax, throwing the paper back at Sawyer. The campaign manager didn't bother to tell him about the front-page article that all but dismissed his candidacy.

Colfax started his daily ritual of push-ups, sit-ups and pull-ups. The routine was one Colfax had learned thirty years earlier from some Navy SEALs with whom he served when he was a young officer in the Navy patrolling the MeKong Delta. The routine consisted of four different push-ups, the most difficult being the fingertip variety, and seven abdominal exercises. He concluded his workout with two different types of pull-ups and five minutes of jumping rope. Through it all, Sawyer briefed him on the daily news, the day's upcoming events and tidbits about local politics and personalities that the candidate would need to know to navigate his way through the day.

Only when Colfax was almost finished doing his cool-down stretches did he start to ask questions. "What time do we address the Chamber of Commerce?"

"They're expecting you at 7:45 and would like you to begin speaking precisely at eight. Everything should be wrapped up by 8:45. Apparently, these guys like to be at their jobs and behind their desks by nine o'clock sharp."

"I would expect nothing else from our good neighbors to the south," responded Colfax. "So we have time to do a little retail politicking?"

"Absolutely," said Sawyer, who was always amazed at his candidate's willingness to do the extra things that were small but essential for winning the presidency.

After a quick shower, Colfax dressed and was working the voters in several cafes and diners. Two hundred and thirty handshakes later, Colfax was on his way to his first scheduled meeting of the day.

The Hawkeye Room of the Dubuque Holiday Inn was a typical hotel meeting room. The walls were adorned with photos of University of Iowa athletes who hailed from Dubuque and its surrounding area. The carpet was slightly worn, the lights were a little dimmer than they should be, and the pungent smell of chlorine permeated the entire facility. The main table, at which Colfax and seven local dignitaries sat, was a large, round, wooden table covered with a simple white cloth. The other seventy members of the Chamber of Commerce sat around similar tables.

Colfax and his guests talked about the next week's Minnesota-Iowa football game as well as the upcoming Big Ten basketball season. Colfax impressed his guests with his facile discussion of the relative strengths and weaknesses of every team in the conference.

A little before eight, the president of the chamber began his introduction. He cited many of Colfax's accomplishments as governor of Minnesota and then added a personal wish that he would like to see Colfax become president if for no other reason than Iowa businesses would stop fleeing to the business-friendly climate that Colfax had created in Minnesota.

Colfax graciously thanked the host for his kind words and, relying solely on Sawyer's earlier briefing, proceeded to acknowledge every local dignitary in the room. Colfax quickly moved through his standard introduction about why he was running for the presidency and dived into the real topic of this speech—campaign finance reform.

"As residents of Iowa, you will no doubt be hearing from a lot of presidential candidates in the next two months. They will all call for tax cuts. Some will call for a cut of ten percent, others for thirty percent and still others for a flat tax or a cut for the middle-class. The problem is that none will ever see the light of day," said Colfax. "Tax reform will not become a possibility until campaign finance reform becomes a reality. This is because the only way to lower taxes is to eliminate the thousands of special interest tax breaks and loopholes. And those special breaks and loopholes will not be eliminated as long as the special interest groups that benefit from them continue to line the pockets of the major presidential candidates and members of Congress." Colfax paused and let his remarks hang over the room.

Most heads in the room nodded in agreement.

"Do you really think the vice president, the man they call the 'solicitor-in-chief,' is going to risk alienating his major campaign donors by telling them he is going to work to abolish their precious tax breaks? And do you think the governor of Pennsylvania, C. Elliott Prescott, is really going to eliminate a tax loophole that benefits gas and oil benefactors? It ain't going to happen folks!"

More heads nodded.

"To break their stranglehold, we need major campaign finance reform."

The normally staid Iowa businessmen and women applauded, and for the next few minutes Colfax outlined in detail his campaign finance reform initiative.

"The people should be able to know immediately, via the Internet, who contributed to whom and how much. Also, there is no reason why a candidate for the House, the Senate, or the White House should be able to take money *after* an election. The only reason people give money *after* an election is to curry favor with a candidate that they didn't support before the election. They are buying access, pure and simple. And it is access that the average person can't afford. I want to abolish this practice. It is nothing more than legalized bribery!"

The applause flowed naturally.

"I also want to prohibit our elected officials from raising money during specific periods of time—say, a year before election, so they can actually concentrate on doing the job that we sent them to Washington to do. This way they won't have to spend their evenings and weekends groveling for dollars." Adopting a more somber tone, Colfax continued. "But regardless of whether I win or lose, I would like all of you to engage your elected officials on the issue of campaign finance reform. Ask them where they stand. Their refusal to address this issue is a crime. They use their power to remain in power—and they do it by redistributing our tax dollars to their friends. I say the use of power to remain in power is an abuse of power. And it must end. And as president, you have my commitment that I will end it."

At the conclusion of his speech, Colfax was given a standing ovation and a plaque commemorating his visit to Dubuque. The head of the chamber then asked if there were any questions from the audience.

John Blair, a farmer, businessman and member of North American Corn Council, asked the first question—a question the executive director of the corn council had instructed him to ask. "Governor Colfax, I liked a lot of what I heard today, but your stance on ethanol troubles me. The farmers of Iowa rely heavily on ethanol, and if you end the subsidy, you'll push even more family farmers off the land." A number of heads nodded in approval of the question.

"I appreciate your question. The *Des Moines Daily Tribune* called upon me this morning to reconsider my position. My response is simple—I won't. In the late 1970s, when we faced an energy crisis and it appeared that ethanol could help address that crisis, a reasonable argument could be made that a subsidy was needed. Twenty years—and nine billion dollars later—we know the answer: no. Ethanol is expensive. It takes as much energy to produce a gallon of it as it saves, and it is environmentally unsound. Furthermore, it only benefits the massive agribusinesses, like Holten. I understand the plight of the farmer, but I will not put the interests of one small group over the national interest. Next question," said Colfax, confidently pointing to the next questioner.

Colfax handled the next five questions easily and to the satisfaction of his audience. Most found his candid responses refreshing. The final question came from John Blair, the same man who asked the first. "Governor Colfax, do you think you can win? You're at two percent in the polls, and an independent candidate has never come close to winning the presidency."

"Another excellent question. I ask myself the exact same thing every day," Colfax said, flashing his trademark crooked smile at a chuckling audience. "As I said in my opening remarks, I still believe that ideas matter. I still believe character matters. And I refuse to believe that money should be the deciding factor driving politics today. I will win because I am the one candidate who, above all else, will always put the national interest ahead of special interests—even when that means disagreeing with citizens like you over subjects like ethanol."

The meeting concluded at precisely 8:45, and as Colfax was talking with the chamber president and Pete Sawyer was taking down the large "Colfax for President" banner with the web site address, John Blair walked up. "I just wanted to say I appreciated your answer on ethanol," said Blair, shaking Colfax's hand. "I don't agree with you, but I respect your honesty." Gripping his hand and looking him in the eye, Blair wished Colfax good luck. As he walked away, Blair could imagine himself voting for Colfax, despite what his colleague at the corn council had said about the candidate. Colfax seemed like a decent man. "Hell," thought Blair, he even liked Colfax's firm handshake—a handshake strengthened and callused from three decades of pull-ups and push-ups.

* *

Since being placed on administrative leave, Manning spent the better part of each day at the public library reading hunting and fishing magazines, the occasional military journal and a lot of military biographies. Manning's favorite subject was military snipers. Manning had just finished a book on the legendary Marine Corps sniper Carlos Hathcock when the slender man with gray hair, hard blue eyes, and professional demeanor sat down across the table and began speaking in a quiet, clipped, unaccented voice.

"Good afternoon, Sergeant," said the man, waiting for the sniper to look up. Manning instantly recognized Raphael Baptista as the man from the bar the night before. His passive eyes were neither inquiring nor threatening. "Do not attempt to talk. Just listen. Your career as a law enforcement official is over. As is your career in the Marine Corps." Manning began to speak, but Baptista ended it with a frozen stare. By the look in his eyes, Manning knew what he said was true. With no emotion in his voice, Baptista continued, "You possess a very valuable skill. A skill my employers would like to utilize. If you voluntarily resign from the Raleigh Police Department and the Marine Corps, the information the plaintiff's attorney possesses will not be used against you. I'll see to it. If you do not voluntarily resign, your career as both a police officer and a Marine will be terminated anyway. The choice is yours," said the man as he held up a hand to discourage Manning from asking any questions. "They know about your father and what he did to you."

The sniper just stared at the man across the table.

"The skill we seek is your extraordinary talent as a sniper. You will be compensated at a level significantly higher than your combined salary as a police officer and a Marine reservist. Your talents will be used sparingly and professionally, and you will not be asked to serve in a manner that would be inconsistent with your current duties.

"You have exactly twenty-four hours to respond to this offer. If you consult with anyone, the offer is void. I will visit you again tomorrow at the same time and location. Good bye." With that, Raphael Baptista disappeared as quietly as he had arrived.

* *

Sean McGowan looked around the White House one last time. He had arrived in the fall of 1996 so proud and certain that his career choice was among the most noble of all callings. Three years and three Secret Service directors later, Sean McGowan was no longer so sure. His opinion of the Secret Service itself and the people with whom he served with had only grown in stature, but his opinion of the man he was responsible for protecting had plummeted. At thirty-five years of age, Sean

McGowan was burned out. He knew it was time to let another young hard-charger take his slot on the prestigious presidential detail.

Two weeks earlier, McGowan had asked for a reassignment. The newest director, Max Walters, had sighed heavily when he read the letter and made a half-hearted attempt to talk McGowan out of it. But he understood all too well what McGowan was feeling.

Effective with the receipt of the letter, McGowan was placed on nonprotective duty. The status meant that his days of traveling with and protecting Trailblazer were over. He didn't care. All he was missing was twenty-hour workdays as the president furiously crisscrossed the country in his last year in office, attempting to manufacture a legacy.

Instead, McGowan's last two weeks were filled with eight-hour workdays that consisted of little more than ensuring that no unwanted visitors accessed secured areas, thereby threatening the First Lady, who seemed to relish the distance from the president as much as McGowan did.

In fact, the only real challenge McGowan faced during the final two weeks was warding off the overly aggressive advances of the assistant press secretary to the First Lady who thought it appropriate that McGowan should be given a going-away present in the privacy of the Lincoln bedroom. The young assistant didn't take McGowan's rejection lightly and suggested that if she was good enough for the president's press secretary, then she was damn well good enough for him. McGowan smiled and said nothing. He knew he had made the right decision in leaving. The assistant press secretary's actions were everything that he had come to despise about the current occupants of the White House.

On Friday, November 19, at a few minutes past five o'clock, Sean McGowan signed out at the White House Security Desk and did not look back. He was going to the Secret Service's field office in Minneapolis, where he was looking forward to tracking down counterfeiters and being closer to his brother and mother.

* *

From outward appearances, Josh Parker looked like a typical college student, complete with the baseball cap, faded jeans and a shirt from Abercrombie & Finch. The nineteen-year-old Drake University economics major had recently joined a fraternity but only because he thought it would increase his prospects of meeting women. It didn't.

The son of a successful investment banker in Chicago, Parker had grown up in the well-to-do suburb of New Trier, Illinois. What distinguished Parker from the other students at the Des Moines school was that his father had taught him at an early age the importance of investing and, more important, the power of compound interest. With gentle nudging from his father, a life-long Republican with a libertarian bent, Parker had become a big proponent of privatizing Social Security.

On a whim, Parker had enrolled in a course in presidential politics in which he had been assigned to write a term paper on the political views of any one of the candidates running for president and assess the candidate's prospects for victory. He had made no progress on the assignment by the time he went home for Thanksgiving. The paper was due the following Monday.

During halftime of the Thanksgiving football game, Parker confided to his father the difficulty he was having in selecting a candidate for his paper. He felt the major candidates were, as he put it, "lame." Parker's father smiled in agreement.

"Have you read anything about Robert Colfax?" his father asked.

"No, who's he?"

"Do you read the paper over there in Iowa, Josh?" asked his father incredulously.

"Yeah, sometimes."

"Colfax is the governor of Minnesota, and he recently announced that he is running for president as an independent."

"Oh, yeah—I've heard about him."

"I'd suggest that you find out more about him. Not only would he be an excellent topic for your paper, you might actually find that he is the best candidate and worthy of your vote next November. His position of Social Security reform is very intriguing—you and your classmates would stand to benefit greatly if his plan makes it into law."

"Do you think he's for real?" asked Parker.

"Isn't that the purpose of your term paper?" responded his father.

"What do you know about him?"

"There's an excellent article about him in the last week's *New Republic*. I'd start there."

The next day Parker began his research. Four hours later, he had downloaded from the Internet articles from the *Wall Street Journal*, the *Minneapolis Star Tribune*, the *St. Paul Pioneer Press*, the *Washington Post*, the *Washington Herald*, *Time*, and *Newsweek* and a host of other political magazines and journals. He had also accessed the Colfax2000 web site and downloaded Colfax's position paper on the creation of personal retirement accounts. By the end of the day, Parker had not only finished his assignment, he was convinced that Colfax could become the next president. Rereading the paper, he was very satisfied with the final product. He was also happy because he could now party with his old high school buddies that evening with a clear conscience.

"How's your assignment coming along?" asked his father at dinner that night.

"It's done," said Parker proudly, "and I think Colfax can win."

"Really?" said his father, slightly surprised. "Why?"

"Five reasons," said Parker in rapid succession, "issues, demographics, experience, technology, and money."

"Go on," said his father, who was delighted with the level of thought his only son had given the matter. Maybe, he thought, his son was getting an education that justified the high cost of tuition.

"Well, first, he's the only candidate actually talking about any meaningful issues. I think his approach to problems is refreshing. His willingness to let people invest more of their own money is just what Social Security needs. I think his position will appeal to a lot of people, especially young ones. That's why I said demographics. Did you know that there will be more voters under the age of forty than over in the 2000 election? I think the young voters will also respond to his other positions. He's good on environmental issues, and he isn't hung up on social issues like abortion and gay rights."

"Do you think they'll vote?" asked his father.

"I do. That's why I mentioned technology. You should check out his web site. It's awesome. It's got video clips of him explaining his positions on issues. It has a financial calculator so that people can see how they would fare under his proposal for personal retirement accounts and under the current system. It has also position papers. It even has political cartoons. It's pretty cool."

His father had never seen his son so animated and encouraged him to go on.

"That's why I said technology was one of the five factors in his favor. I think Colfax is going to use the Internet like Kennedy used TV in the 1960 election. Did you know that by this November, seventy-eight million will have access to the Internet? And most people who use the Internet tend to be pretty close to Colfax's political philosophy—fiscally conservative, socially liberal.

"He's so far ahead of the other candidates that he has the potential to blow 'em out of the water. I e-mailed the campaign a question this morning and got a response back this afternoon. I even subscribed to receive his weekly web campaign update."

"You also mentioned a few other factors," said his father.

"Experience and money," responded Parker. "Did you know Colfax was wounded in Vietnam and was awarded the Purple Heart and the Congressional Medal of Honor? He was also a congressman and secretary of the Navy before he became governor. So, although he'll be running as an independent, I think the political establishment will take him seriously. He's nothing like Stanley Cross," said Parker, refer-ring to the wealthy aristocrat, who had never held office, seeking the Republican nomination.

"You mean he's not just another rich guy on some wild ego trip who thinks he'd be make a good president because he inherited some money?" said his father with a hearty laugh.

"Precisely," said Parker. "I think Colfax will win for the first four reasons I men-tioned, but his wealth will certainly help matters. Did you know that he sold his first company, a marine electronics manufacturer, for six million dollars in 1981, when he decided to run for Congress? He placed the entire amount in a blind trust run by Alfred Sanger," said Parker, referring to one of the greatest institutional investors of the century. "It has since grown at an annual compounded rate of twenty-eight per-cent. That six million dollars is now worth over $500 million."

"Ah—the beauty of compound interest. Probably explains his passion for per-sonal retirement accounts."

"And then after he resigned as secretary of the Navy, he returned to Minnesota to head up a fiber optics company. He was compensated almost entirely in stock. It was worth thirty cents a share when he began. When he stepped down to run for governor, it was selling for over sixty dollars."

"So what's his net worth?"

"Forbes estimated it to be over 800 million dollars."

* *

Two days later, as he and three of his fraternity brothers drove across the barren plains of eastern Illinois to Iowa, Parker, with the report about Colfax fresh in his mind, persuaded his buddies to become Robert Colfax supporters. Unwittingly, he also took his first step toward becoming one of the more influential political activists in the 2000 presidential race.

* *

Robert Colfax had put his youngest daughter, Colleen, to bed three hours earli-er and was still upstairs in his study when his wife, Linda, entered. He appeared to be staring straight ahead at a thirty-year-old photo of the platoon he led in Vietnam. In the photo, Colfax was the only man wearing a T-shirt. He also stood apart from the others because he was the only one not holding a beer—or smiling.

"What are you thinking?" asked Linda.

If her presence surprised him, Colfax didn't show it. He turned to face her. "I've just been thinking about the campaign—and Vietnam. You see that photo?" said

Colfax, motioning toward the wall. "Of the twelve men in that photo, only three made it out of Vietnam alive. One of the reasons I'm not smiling in the picture is because I had just learned I had to lead my men up the river the next day."

"Is that the day you saved O'Neill's and Isaacs' lives?"

Colfax nodded. He had been awarded the Congressional Medal of Honor for his actions that day. "You know, I was feeling sorry for myself a little earlier—for being only at two percent in the polls. And then I remember their sacrifices," said Colfax, glancing at the yellowing photo, "and it reminded me of one the reasons I'm doing this. It's not just for Catherine's and Colleen's futures, it's for the people like Gomez and Moss and Hankinson. Every one of those men killed came from poor families. I'm tired of seeing the elite use government solely for their benefit. Today's special-interest beneficiaries are direct descendants of the same weasels who avoided the draft back in Vietnam. Whether avoiding their civic responsibilities in time of war or avoiding taxes in peacetime, they're always trying to figure out how the system can benefit them. They could give a shit about anyone else."

Linda Colfax could feel the stress in her husband's shoulder and neck as she gently massaged them. "You just have to keep going," she said. "Fight the good fight."

"That's what I did in Vietnam and it almost got me killed."

"That's not how O'Neill and Isaacs see it. You made a huge difference—and you'll make a huge difference as president."

Colfax placed his hand on Linda's and drew her around onto his lap.

"Why else would people already be attacking you in Iowa?" she continued, "It's because they know you're serious—you're a threat to their privileged positions."

CHAPTER FIVE

The third meeting between Lee Manning and Raphael Baptista lasted less than two minutes. Baptista presented the police sergeant with two resignation letters—one for the Raleigh Police Department and the other for the Marine Corps. Manning signed both without a thought. The sniper had no choice.

"Now we can get down to business," said Baptista, sliding a large manila envelope across the table to Manning. "Enclosed is a one-way ticket to Colorado Springs and verification that $25,000 has been credited to a bank account in your name. In the next twenty-four hours, you are to pack up all your possessions and personal items. You will have no need for anything for the next few months. Upon arriving in Colorado Springs, you will receive further instructions." Baptista knew Manning's disappearance would go unnoticed—the sniper had no close friends.

The next day, the freelance sniper was in a modest motel room on the west end of Colorado Springs. Inside the room was another manila envelope with more instructions.

Among other things, the instructions informed Manning that an MA40A1 rifle and 4,000 rounds of ammunition were in the closet. Also included in the envelope was a map to an isolated firing range and a note instructing the sniper to practice a minimum of two hours a day. The only qualifications were that the practice rounds should be conducted when the temperature was between fifteen and forty degrees Fahrenheit, and at least half of the shots had be fired in the evening hours and at a distance of between 400 and 600 yards.

Manning reread the instructions. The note provided no clues about the sniper's new employers, but it was clear from the level of detail that they were professionals.

* *

Pete Sawyer was speeding down the highway in the jet-black Ford Explorer. Colfax, on a cell phone in the passenger seat, conducted a live radio interview with an ultraconservative mid-morning talk radio host from a small 350-watt radio station located just outside of Burlington, Iowa. As Colfax expounded on his position on free trade, Sawyer was mentally trying to figure out how he would spin the situation if he and his boss were pulled over for speeding. He came to the conclusion that at this point in the campaign any press, even negative press, was good press.

"What was that last question?" Sawyer asked Colfax, seconds after his boss turned off his cell phone.

"Our Rush Limbaugh disciple," said Colfax, "inquired into the odds of a successful presidential bid. Specifically, he cited the recent poll numbers in a hypothetical race between Prescott, Byrne, and myself. He seemed to imply that Prescott being at fifty-one percent, the vice president being at forty-three percent and me having only two percent—tied with 'undecided'—should give me cause for concern."

"Doesn't it?" asked Sawyer, who struggled with the question every day.

"I have the most strategic and cunning campaign manager in the country—so I don't have to think about it. That's your job," replied Colfax, flashing a quick grin at Sawyer.

"Seriously," said Sawyer, nervously glancing at his watch. He knew that Colfax hated to be late for scheduled events.

"What do I think? I think that two months ago I was at one percent in the polls, and this month I'm at two percent. I've doubled my numbers! If we keep doubling our numbers, I'll be home free by August," said Colfax, still smiling. "And if I'm not—I'm going to can your ass."

Sawyer laughed. Having worked for other politicians, he had come to enjoy Colfax's calm, almost detached, perspective of things.

"Seriously though, the numbers don't concern me—not yet. Everyone knows Prescott is the frontrunner. Hell, he has forty million dollars more than any other candidate—with the exception of Cross."

"And you," interjected Sawyer, "for that matter."

"I've told you before, Pete, I'm not going to spend an unlimited amount of my own money like Cross. It's not that I'm cheap. I just feel strongly that a candidate for president should be judged on his ideas and leadership ability—not on his ability to accumulate personal wealth. The business world and the political world are apples and oranges. Success in one does not necessarily translate to success in the other. If I'm to lead this country successfully, I have to demonstrate that the average citizen has faith in me. One way to do that is to show people I am not just relying on my own money to finance my campaign."

"I agree. It's just that it would be a lot easier if I didn't have to also worry about raising money," replied Sawyer.

"Anyway, as I was saying, Prescott and his money don't worry me. His problem is that everyone is expecting him to perform miracles . . . frontrunners often don't finish the race that way. The commercials that Cross just started airing here in Iowa are going to inflict some damage," continued Colfax, referring to Stanley Cross' ads that demanded to know where Prescott stood on the issue of abortion. "And Dick Graham is going to kick Prescott right where it hurts in New Hampshire. His fiery 'isolationist' rhetoric will always find a small but enthusiastic crowd among the blue-collar Republicans and conservative Democrats."

"Graham," said Sawyer, referring to the former nationally syndicated talk radio host, "will also benefit from the fact that many of the true believers in the Republican Party perceive Prescott as being an elite, East Coast, Republican establishment candidate, and they'll vote against him on principle alone."

"Cross and Graham will have to fight for the same voters," said Colfax. "My money is on Graham in Iowa and New Hampshire, but after that, Cross' money kicks in, and he becomes Prescott's main challenger. He's the only one who can compete with Prescott's money, which is too bad because Jack Quinn is actually the Republicans' most competent candidate," continued Colfax, referring to the stubbornly independent Republican senator from Montana. "But he's pissed off too many of Washington's money boys—they hate his positions on campaign finance reform. In fact, I'm sure they're the ones behind the ads distorting his position on tax increases for tobacco."

"I agree," said Sawyer, "but that's good news for us."

"Maybe, but it's bad for the country."

"I meant that he'd be our toughest competitor."

"I don't know," said Colfax. He knew Quinn was honorable and would play by the rules. That was something that could not be said of the other candidates.

"Anyway," said Sawyer, getting the conversation back to the original issue, "Graham and Cross are both going to force Prescott to move to the right to appease the ultraconservatives in the party. It's my job to keep him painted in that corner once he moves in that direction to secure the nomination."

"What about Byrne?" inquired Colfax, referring to Vice President Martin Byrne.

"His situation is a little different. I think he can use the power of his office to crush Gordon and Greene," said Sawyer, referring to the vice president's two challengers. "However, if Greene gets some traction with his message that the blacks and the poor citizens of Appalachia are being left out of the Byrne's 'Grand Vision for the Twenty-first Century,' he could cause Byrne some problems. In that case, Byrne will be forced to run to the left to secure the Democratic nomination. If that scenario plays out, with Prescott moving to the right and Byrne moving left, then I just might be able to get you elected as we sweep up the vast majority of voters who are put off by extremists in both parties."

"And if Greene decides to sell his soul for a cabinet position and withdraws? Then what?"

"Then we'll simply let Byrne hang himself," replied Sawyer. "So far, he has tried to be all things to all people, and in the process he hasn't uttered a new idea in three years. He lacks energy and intensity. His super-safe approach and his fear of alienating anyone isn't going to cut it this campaign. The people want ideas and leadership. You're the only candidate offering that."

Colfax pondered Sawyer's remarks for a moment. He never spent much time on the insider political analysis, but Sawyer's comments affirmed his own gut feelings. He knew he could win the presidency.

"You're right. The public is tired of blow-dried candidates without ideas, being managed by professional pollsters without convictions, running campaigns without content. The public is hungry for real leadership. But I think we also have one other advantage. The way to win is not just to convince the Republicans or Democrats to switch votes. It is to get the fifty percent of people who don't vote to vote for the first time. That's our bread and butter—the first-time voter."

Switching gears, Colfax began reviewing the notes that his staff had readied for him for his speech to the Burlington Women's Group. Sawyer was intensely aware of Colfax's need to prepare for any speaking engagement and left him alone for the last few minutes of the trip. Colfax scribbled a few notes, digested the names of the key women in the group and committed the bulk of the briefing paper to memory.

Inside the turn-of-the-century hotel, where the Burlington's Women's Club had been meeting every month for the last one hundred years, the mayor of Burlington, Jane Olive, graciously welcomed the governor of Minnesota and independent candidate for president.

Twenty minutes into his speech, Colfax had the rapt attention of the 150 women in the audience. "Why are we subsidizing a company like Holten, Incorporated, with more than a billion dollars a year when we could better invest that money in small businesses? Women like you are creating more than half of all new small businesses in this country. Why aren't we helping you?" asked Colfax. "I'll tell you why—because our current crop of leaders are beholden to people like Win

Murdock. And why," continued Colfax, "are we continuing to give massive tax breaks to multimillion-dollar corporations like Philson Gas & Oil and Wextron BioTech when we know that five million women are working every day just to pay for health and medical insurance for themselves and their families? Why don't we provide more tax breaks for woman like you? I'll tell you why—because you don't write big, fat campaign checks."

The women were on their feet.

"As president," Colfax continued, "I pledge to you that I will eliminate corporate welfare. It is time we stop the outrageous giveaways to wealthy corporations and start serving people like you. As businesswomen, as members of your communities, wives, sisters, mothers, and daughters, you are giving everyday. It is time we recognize your contributions and start working with you rather than against you."

Jane Olive had never seen a politician receive a more enthusiastic response. Later that afternoon, the mayor collected $1,900 from a half-dozen businesswomen. She also referred another twenty friends to the Colfax for President web site where they could access the "women's issues" link. Many of these women, in turn, referred other women to the site. The proliferation of chain e-mails triggered a sizeable reaction of interest in the Colfax campaign. The same site had a video clip of an emotional Colfax describing his experience of losing his mother to lung cancer. The painful encounter, he said in the video, explained his commitment to regulating the tobacco industry and increasing the federal excise tax on tobacco.

* *

Sean McGowan looked out his window and admired the Minneapolis skyline as he pondered his first case as a "street guy." He knew that his friends on the presidential detail would find his new job amusing. The "Golden Boy," as he was called behind his back, was now "chasing P-notes." McGowan didn't care. Tracking counterfeiters as a field agent got him out of Washington. He had to get out not just because of his reservations about the current occupant of the White House but for health reasons. It was said within the Secret Service that for every year an agent served on the presidential detail, he aged two years. The Secret Service had medical evidence backing up the claim.

Turning from the window, McGowan admired the counterfeit bills on his desk and marveled at the skill with which the yellow, magneta, cyan and black toners were mixed to produce the fake money. Rapid advances in low-cost, high-quality computers and ink-jet printers were making life difficult for the Secret Service. He studied a map of the city and placed pins at the locations where the phony bills had turned up. They were all within a three-mile radius of the University of Minnesota. McGowan knew there was a better than even chance that the perpetrator was a student at the university.

As he was studying the bill, a young agent, Julie Brix, knocked on his door. Brix was a lean, athletic woman who had been an academic All-American at St. Olaf College in Northfield, Minnesota. She had graduated with degrees in physics and ethics and was the captain of her college basketball team. McGowan was aware of her can-do attitude. She reminded him of himself ten years earlier.

"Come in," McGowan said. "What do you have?"

"It looks like your first case will be an easy one," said Brix, flashing an easy smile and turning to the map. "Not only did he leave a trail of crumbs leading to his neighborhood, our man used a color printer that uses tracer dots. I tracked down the printer. It was purchased at a computer store over by the university." Smiling at McGowan, she continued, "And, bless his heart, he paid for it by check."

"Are you serious?" said McGowan, "I'm always amazed at how some of these counterfeiters can be so smart in one area and so goddamn stupid in another."

"Kind of like some of the politicians we protect," replied Brix, with a mischievous expression. McGowan didn't smile back; he thought it would be unprofessional. But he instantly liked the young agent. Brix then added, "I once caught a graduate student at the university who produced a beautiful counterfeit fifty-dollar bill using a PC, a bubble printer, and bamboo parchment. His only mistake was that he used the same serial number for every bill. Guess what numbers he used."

"His birthday?"

"Exactly. A quick search of the university's records revealed five potential candidates. Based on the areas of academic study, only one seemed to fit the profile of a potential counterfeiter, and sure enough, he was our man."

"It seems as though you have some experience in this area, Agent Brix."

"I do," she responded with a little bit of an attitude.

"Good. Then why don't you go and round up our man."

Just then the phone rang. McGowan answered it on the first ring. It was the assistant director of the Secret Service. McGowan listened for a minute.

Brix noticed McGowan's attitude change immediately. He was not happy.

"Yes, sir," said McGowan, hanging up.

"Trouble?" asked Brix.

"No," replied McGowan turning back to the window and rubbing his temples, "The boss would like our office to develop a tentative security plan for Colfax. He will be eligible for Secret Service protection if he reaches five percent in the polls."

Brix had heard the rumor that McGowan had come to Minneapolis to get away from politics.

"It looks like I might also have to go to Iowa for a short while to assist with the protection of Congressman Greene."

"Nothing like Iowa in January. Greene will be tough. I've heard the death threats have already started—but I also think Colfax will be an interesting candidate," said Brix. "His approval ratings as governor have been hovering around seventy-five percent."

"I know—but can he make it on the national scene?"

"I wouldn't underestimate the guy. He's an incredibly hard worker. He starts with a five-mile run every day before sunrise and doesn't stop going until after midnight."

"You're the second person in the last few days who's said the guy is for real."

"Oh? Who was the first?"

"My girlfriend," replied McGowan.

Brix didn't display any emotion. The Secret Service code of honor prevented agents from being involved with one another, but she was still slightly disappointed. She had always been attracted to intelligent, athletic men.

* *

The apartment of the United States ambassador to the United Nation was a spacious 2,500 square feet of expansive good taste. Despite its size, comfort, and beautiful early twentieth-century French antiques, Elizabeth Vandiver only slept in the apartment. When she was awake, the fifty-three-year-old diplomat was working at her office or attending meetings. She had immersed herself in her work following her highly publicized divorce two years earlier.

The latest crisis to occupy her time was the festering situation in Kosovo. The Albanian refugees, who had been so brutalized by the Serbian Army the year before, were slowly making their way back to their homes under the protective eye of NATO forces.

The problem was that Serbian paramilitary forces, lead by Zeljko Seselj, a pistol-waving Serb nationalist and a wealthy businessman from Belgrade who had his eyes on the Serbian presidency, were still conducting clandestine raids on Albanian towns. Seselj's forces had done the same thing in Bosnia in 1991 and Croatia in 1993. His reputation was well established and his methods universally despised. He was known as "The Hyena" throughout Yugoslavia. His continuous attacks were straining NATO's alliance.

Since the horrible atrocities of the spring of 1999, most Western governments had presented a united front against Serbia. A year later, the strain was beginning to show. The governments of Greece, Turkey, and Italy had never been comfortable with the NATO operation in Kosovo. Now the French government was beginning to get cold feet. Certain leaders within the French government felt the conflict in Kosovo was centuries old, and there was little they could do to help heal the wounds. The French wanted to cut their losses and get out.

The task of informing the United States government of their growing reservations fell onto the large, tapered shoulders of Colonel René DeBrentanga, a strikingly handsome twenty-three-year veteran of the French Army. His tall and imposing manner reminded many of a young DeGaulle, only he was neither aloof nor arrogant.

Ambassador Vandiver was immediately struck by DeBrentanga's intelligence, candor, and wit. What had been scheduled to be a half-hour meeting lasted almost two. The colonel had conveyed his government's unease over Kosovo to the ambassador, and Vandiver, in return, asked that the colonel relay the United States government's grave concern and disappointment with France's shift in policy. Not willing to accept France's position, she requested an official meeting with the French ambassador. DeBrentanga said he would relay the message to his ambassador.

The last fifteen minutes of their conversation turned to French art. Briefed in advance on Vandiver's interest in twentieth century French antiques, the elegant colonel commented on a cast-iron art deco lamp on the ambassador's desk. An animated discussion ensued.

"It isn't often that I meet someone with an interest in, let alone a knowledge of, such things," said Vandiver. She noticed he wasn't wearing a wedding band and took a calculated risk. "If you and your wife are free this weekend, I would like to show you my modest collection."

"Thank you, Madam Ambassador, I would very much enjoy the opportunity. From what I have seen so far, though, it is not very modest," said DeBrentanga, looking the ambassador in the eyes. "Unfortunately, my wife will be unable to join us. She has returned to Paris to care for an ailing aunt," DeBrentanga lied. He and his wife were estranged.

Vandiver's risk had paid off. "I'm sorry to hear that," she replied. "Of course, you are still welcome to come. Are you free this Saturday evening? I will be attending a holiday party at the German Consulate, but I'll be free after nine."

"That is very gracious of you, Madam Ambassador. I would be honored."

* *

The second meeting of the Coalition for a Prosperous New Millennium took place in the same stylish conference room of the law firm of Lawrence, Mance & Scott. The only difference was that David Luther had been replaced by Jacob Mance, the managing partner of the law firm and one of Washington's most powerful lobbyists. He commanded a team of 142 lobbyists, most of whom either had at least ten years' experience on Capitol Hill or had served in the current or a former White House administration. The firm did everything from lobbying to conducting political campaigns to strategic planning, polling, consulting and opposition research. The latter was a firm specialty. If there was dirt to be found, the law firm of Lawrence, Scott & Mance found it. And if there wasn't any dirt, it created some.

Sitting behind the curved table in leather high-back chairs were six middle-aged white men. Represented at the table were the top lobbyists for Philson Gas & Oil, Wextron BioTech, the American Gas Association, Vanderbilt & Sampson Tobacco, and the National Biotechnology Council. Preston Briggs, a junior partner at the firm, was also in attendance. It was his job to operate the audio-visual equipment. Holten, Incorporated, was billed $400 an hour for his services.

Jacob Mance quickly welcomed the group. No introductions were needed— everybody knew one another. With no other remarks, Briggs dimmed lights in the room and made two large TV screens appear on each side of Jacob Mance. On the screens was projected the smiling image of Robert Colfax. It was a video clip from Colfax's Burlington speech. It was less than four hours old. Everyone in the room instantly knew the purpose of the meeting: Jacob Mance and his firm had been retained to derail Colfax. For the next few minutes, the group listened as Colfax railed against their companies or their industry. When the clip ended, the video faded and the screens receded back into the wall. The lights came on, and Jacob Mance stood before the group.

"I recognize that Governor Colfax is only at two percent in the polls," said Mance, referring to the latest poll, "but I hope you agree that the public has a right to know where he stands on certain key issues." Everyone in the room understood that the phrase "right to know" was Washington-speak for negative campaigning.

Howard Kelso, senior vice president of public affairs for Wextron, spoke first. "I agree. The public must be informed of Colfax's positions on various issues." Wextron was anxious to keep its hefty tax breaks as quiet as possible. Walter Johnson, executive director of the American Gas Council, spoke next. "Howard is right. Colfax's proposal to require that contributors of independent political expenditures be made public would undermine our ability to advance our causes. I mean, sweet Jesus, if the public knew how much Murdock contributed to all of our organizations, the press would have a fucking field day. We can't afford to let the public know how much we are spending to protect our interests." Alexander Tennesan, Vanderbilt & Sampson's chief counsel and top lobbyist, said nothing. He was well aware of Colfax's anti-tobacco sentiments. He had secretly committed one million dollars to Mance in advance of the meeting. With the promise of more, if necessary.

"Exactly," said Mance, "and that is why we can ill afford to allow Mr. Colfax to continue."

"What do you need, Jacob?" asked Kelso.

"A half million from each of you." The men at the table didn't blink at the figure. "The organization you will be contributing to is called the Coalition for a Prosperous New Millennium, and it already has three members," said Mance.

"And the money will be used exclusively to attack Colfax?" asked Johnson.

"Exclusively," replied Mance.

By afternoon, the Coalition for a Prosperous New Millennium had grown to eight members and its coffers by three million dollars.

* *

The following day another 1.6 million dollars were added to the coalition's treasury after every one of Holten's fifteen executive vice president's received a confidential memo informing them that they would submit a personal check for $100,000 to the Coalition for a Prosperous New Millennium.

David Pollard of the National Small Business Coalition received a similar message, via Jacob Mance, that Holten, Incorporated, in return for continuing to be a platinum associate member of his business group, was requesting that he contribute to the coalition. Mance assured Pollard that he would be reimbursed. He provided Pollard a limited sketch of the purpose of the Coalition for a Prosperous New Millennium and shared with him the names of a few of the other businesses and associations that had already joined. Although it made him feel physically ill, Pollard signed the check that night. He knew in Washington that, in order to get along, you had to go along.

CHAPTER SIX

Lee Manning held the rifle and admired its beauty. It was a perfect combination of advanced technology and craftsmanship. From the first time Jeremiah Manning had placed a rifle in the hands of his only child, the young marksman had savored the power of the rifle. It was the only time Manning felt in total control. The U.S. Marine Corps later instilled an even greater respect for the power of a sniper's rifle. In the hands of a skilled and properly trained Marine, Manning's first gunnery sergeant had said, a sniper could pin down a platoon of enemy soldiers for days, exact tactical damage by killing a high-level military officer, or inflict strategic damage on a nation by assassinating a prime minister or president. It was a belief that Manning now held as gospel.

The MA40A1 rifle felt like a natural extension of Manning's body. The even distribution of its fourteen pounds made it feel much lighter than it was. Manning admired the crown of the barrel and the hex screws that torqued the rifle to perfection. The only disappointment was that the weapon was not a bolt-action rifle. Manning preferred single-action rifles, a taste instilled by Jeremiah Manning, who felt that single-action weapons fostered a strict shooting discipline. Every shot had to be carefully considered because a second shot was not always possible.

Manning cradled the rifle and recalled being given only three bullets for a day's worth of hunting and being told to come back with three kills. Anything less than perfection usually resulted in Jeremiah Manning administering a severe beating—or worse. Manning learned early in life never to miss.

Next, Manning examined the bullets. According to Baptista's note, all 4,000 of the M118LR bullets were manufactured at the same plant, loaded into the cartridge by the same machine, with the same gunpowder and stored under the same conditions.

Manning was impressed with Baptista's attention to detail. It was further proof that he was a professional. If every bullet was manufactured by the same machine, under the same conditions, chances were that each would perform the same way every time.

Still, every day before heading out to practice, Manning would select the twenty bullets to be fired during the day's practice round and weigh each one separately. Even a slight deviation in weight could cause a bullet to fly wide by six inches at a distance of one kilometer. It was a deviation Manning could ill-afford. Manning diligently noted the weight of every bullet in a logbook with a mechanical pencil.

At the firing range, the actions of the bullet were recorded in the logbook along with distance, time of day, temperature, wind, barometric pressure, humidity, elevation, and anything else that could possibly affect the trajectory of the bullet. With $100,000 riding on a successful shot, Manning made it a point to know as much as humanly possibly about how any bullet would operate under any condition. Out of the 620 shots Manning took over the course of the month, only three deviated more than three inches from the target.

When Raphael Baptista showed up on January 12, Manning was ready. What the sniper was not ready for was the job that Baptista had in store.

"Have you ever heard of Zeljko Seseji?" asked Baptista.

Manning thought about the name for a minute. "It sounds familiar," replied Manning, trying to associate the odd-sounding name.

"Are you familiar with Kosovo?"

"Yes, sir."

"Have you ever heard of a man called 'The Hyena?'"

"Is he the one still terrorizing people over in that hellhole?" said Manning.

"That's him."

"That's my target?"

"It is." Baptista watched Manning's face light up. It was the opportunity the sniper had always dreamed of.

*   *

The low-pressure system made its way across the Pacific Northwest, turned south over Montana and headed toward Colorado before taking a brief break over the Oklahoma panhandle, where it soaked up a massive amount of moisture from the Gulf of Mexico.

The weather forecasters had predicted the storm and tracked its progress over Kansas and Iowa, where it dumped an inch of rain. But they seriously misjudged how far the low-pressure system would push the warm, wet Gulf air north and how far south a second system, a cold Arctic Canadian front, would drop.

By the time Colfax left the governor's mansion for the state capitol in the relatively warm December temperatures, the misty rain was just beginning to turn to sleet. By 8:00 A.M., the sleet had turned to snow. The Minneapolis-St. Paul airport shut down two hours later.

By noon the storm had dumped six inches of snow in the Twin Cities. In the western and northern parts of the state, twelve inches had fallen, with more accumulating at a rate of two inches an hour.

Of more concern to Colfax were the rapidly dropping temperatures and increased wind speeds. The state meteorologist reported that blizzard conditions could be expected across the state by late afternoon. Colfax immediately ordered all schools in the state closed, sent all state employees home and encouraged the private sector to do the same.

At 1:00 P.M., the first reports of stranded vehicles started to come in from the worst hit areas. Colfax conferred only briefly with his commissioner of public safety before ordering the state's interstate highways closed.

The next visitor to the governor's office was the head of the Minnesota National Guard, Brigadier General Dusty Larson. As the two reviewed the state's emergency blizzard plan, more reports of stranded vehicles trickled in, including the first reports from the metropolitan area. Cars had begun to stall as they ran out of gas in slow-moving traffic. Within an hour, the trickle turned into a deluge. Soon the major artery connecting Minneapolis and St. Paul came to a complete standstill, and an hour later, the interstate ring around the Twin Cities looked like a parking lot.

The situation became more critical because of the temperature. Since dawn it had plummeted from forty-three degrees to near zero. With the wind, it felt like thirty below. Few people were prepared for the storm, and it was expected to get worse.

"I authorize you to activate the National Guard," said Colfax to the general. "And I'll call Governor Wood to see if Iowa's National Guard can provide any help to the motorists stranded in the southern part of the state." Turning to his press secretary, Colfax asked that all the radio and television outlets be contacted. "Tell them I will make a critical announcement on the current situation in half an hour. It affects the health and well-being of the citizens of this state, and I am asking for five minutes of uninterrupted time. If anyone resists, let me know."

The press secretary began to speak, "Governor—"

"Do it," barked Colfax. "The situation is only going to get worse. We have to act now." Colfax then turned to his chief of staff, "I want to be on the air ASAP."

Colfax then retired to his office and called his wife to check whether their two daughters had made it safely home from school.

Poking her head into his office, the press secretary said, "Governor, channel three is refusing your request."

"You're kidding me," said Colfax, genuinely shocked. "Get the station manager on the phone—now." A minute later, Kent Zender was holding for the governor. "This is Governor Colfax. With whom am I speaking?"

"Hello, Governor. This is Kent Zender, I am—"

"I don't care who you are," said Colfax, cutting him off mid-sentence. "What I want to know is why you feel a goddamn soap opera is more important than the health of the citizens of Minnesota. In case you haven't looked out the window, we've got the worst blizzard in the last fifty years out there. People are leaving their cars on the freeway and trying to get to safety on foot, for Christ's sake. And they can't even see ten feet in front of them. Do you think they're going to make it home, Mr. Zender?"

Zender said nothing.

"Well, do you?" demanded Colfax, "I don't. And I think the people of Minnesota will have to open their doors to strangers if we are to survive this situation with a minimum number of causalities. And, if they are to open their doors, it would be best if they first heard from the governor explaining the seriousness of the situation."

"I agree," said Zender, meekly.

"Good, my press secretary will explain how you are to assist us," replied Colfax, handing the phone over to his aide.

At precisely five minutes after two, every radio and television station with a feed into the state capitol aired Colfax's plea to the citizens of Minnesota. Replayed every half-hour, the governor's calm, reassuring speech was heard by an estimated three-fourths of the state's citizens. How many stayed in their cars, followed his instructions and survived was unknown. Anecdotally, the numbers were impressive. Even more impressive were the stories of how the citizens heeded Colfax's plea and let strangers into their homes.

Colfax's immediate dispatching of the National Guard and his request for assistance from the Iowa National Guard further limited the fatalities. Experts agreed his quick and effective response saved the lives of an untold number of people. The following day, as Minnesota dug out from twenty-nine inches of snow, the *Washington Post*'s senior political columnist wrote a story about Colfax's decisive actions and argued that it provided further proof that he was of "presidential timber." He also wrote that Colfax was "the most legitimate, and most serious third-party candidate since Teddy Roosevelt ran as a progressive in 1912."

* *

Stephanie Freeberg was so busy with her new responsibilities as the director of research for the Center for Ethical and Responsive Politics that she hardly missed the reassuring presence of Sean McGowan. When she did find a minute to reflect on their budding relationship, she admitted to herself that she would have liked to accept his invitation to go to Minnesota over the Christmas holidays. But her student loans and relatively low salary precluded any trip. She had to settle for a phone call.

". . . I wish you were out here," said McGowan, "I could use a little comfort in this Minnesota weather."

"Believe me, I'd love to, but my dad is still in the area and none of my other sisters can make it home for the holidays."

"What's your sister Lisa doing? I thought she went to school in D.C.?"

"She does. She's at Gallaudet," said Freeberg, referring to the prestigious university for the deaf in Washington. "But she's spending the holidays over in Vienna."

"Nice—what's she doing?"

"Studying German—she wants to be a diplomat. But, knowing her, she's probably also doing her fair share of partying."

"That's an important skill in diplomatic circles. So how's your job going?"

"Great. I feel like I did when I first started with the Secret Service—like I can make a difference. Plus, things are really starting to heat up, so I'm busy as hell. Trying to track how money flows in a presidential campaign isn't easy."

"Don't the campaigns have to report all their contributions?" asked McGowan.

"Yes, but there's a huge loophole in the campaign finance laws. Groups can raise unlimited amounts of unregulated money for issue advocacy. There are no limits on the level of contributions that individuals, businesses, or associations can make to these groups, and the groups are not required to make public their list of contributors. I'm talking about millions of dollars—all unregulated."

"And no one knows where the money is coming from?"

"Exactly."

"But the money can only be used to promote issues, right?"

"Legally that's true, but they have become so sophisticated at blurring the lines between issues and candidates that they've made a mockery of the current system. If something isn't done, I fear our government will be sold to the highest bidder."

"So how does it work?" asked McGowan.

"The most common ploy is the negative TV ad. The commercial will usually begin with a distorted and unflattering picture of a politician, and then the announcer, usually a male with a deep baritone voice, will intimate that the target of the ad, who is usually 'dangerously liberal' or a 'coldhearted conservative,' wants to 'slash Medicare' or 'raise taxes.' The commercial will then end with something like, 'Please call your senator and ask him not to slash Medicare,' or 'Call candidate Jones and ask her not to raise taxes.' As long as the commercial doesn't specifically advocate voting for or against a particular candidate, it's all perfectly legal."

"Unbelievable. So, as long as they don't use the words 'vote for' or 'vote against,' they're pretty much free to say anything they want?"

"Exactly."

"So, even if Robert Colfax begins to do well, he'll probably get whacked."

"Absolutely. I'm sure Washington's most skilled character assassins are already sharpening their knives and drawing him into their sights."

* *

Stephanie Freeberg usually had no problem figuring out the true agenda of most political-action committees. Conservative groups often used such words as "freedom," "faith," or "family" somewhere in their name, and Democratic groups used "community," "progress," or "children" somewhere in theirs. Issue-advocacy groups were even easier to track because they were up front with their motive, even if whoever was paying for the motive was not so obvious.

So when Freeberg came across a new organization called the Coalition for a Prosperous New Millennium, she was a little perplexed. Her first reaction was that it was probably a front group for the high-tech industry. That the group already had 6.5 million dollars in contributions seemed to fit her theory. Only software companies and the rapidly growing Internet industry could contribute that much money in so short a period of time, she thought. It also seemed reasonable because Washington was increasingly trying to regulate the industry.

Freeberg powered up her computer and logged on to the Internet. Searching for the phrase "the Coalition for a Prosperous New Millennium" yielded only one hit, and that came from the Federal Election Commission web site. As she stared at the computer screen, contemplating her next step, her boss, Ira Bernstein, a crusty fifty-five-year-old Jewish New Yorker who favored rumpled suits and scuffed shoes, poked his head into Freeberg's paper-strewn office.

Bernstein was the reason Freeberg had accepted the $29,000-a-year job. For the last twenty-five years, he had been the Washington political establishment's resident pain in the ass. He started his career by advocating for changes to the campaign finance system in the wake of Watergate and then moved on to the struggle for a nuclear freeze in the mid-1980s and health care reform in the early 1990s. He remained passionate and free of cynicism. Bernstein, whom Freeberg had met when he taught a course in her graduate program, had shown her that the current campaign finance system had been so mangled by lawyers and special-interest groups that it no longer represented the spirit of the changes he helped usher in years before. He wanted to reform the system and convinced Freeberg that it would be possible with her help.

"How's it going?" Bernstein asked in his thick Brooklyn accent, which had somehow not been diminished by almost three decades in the nation's capitol.

"What do you know about the Coalition for Prosperous New Millennium?" asked Freeberg.

"Never heard of the group. Sounds like a front for the pharmaceutical industry— you know, promoting new drugs for old men like me so that we can recapture our lost youth. That's what I think of when I envision a prosperous new millennium," said Bernstein with a smirk. "How much does the group have in their coffers?"

"Almost seven million dollars—and they were just created this past November."

Bernstein's smile disappeared. "Have they spent any money yet? That might help us figure out who they are."

"Nothing yet."

"Where are they located?"

"The address listed is 1701 K Street."

Bernstein considered the address for a moment. "That's the address of Lawrence, Mance & Scott," Bernstein said with a tinge of concern in his voice. "Those son of a bitches are the sleaziest lobbyists in town. I don't know what they are up to, but it can't be good. I want you to give this a high priority. Find out everything you can about the group and keep me updated. You might also want to contact our friend at the *Washington Herald* and alert her to the existence of Washington's newest special interest group," Bernstein said, referring to Anne Strong, the *Herald*'s most aggressive political reporter.

*　*

Ambassador Vandiver had rarely drunk more than a glass of wine in an evening, but, since her divorce, she had begun to drink more. She needed a glass or two to help her sleep, she told herself, and it never affected her work.

Perhaps it was her excitement at seeing the aristocratic-looking French colonel again that led her to have three glasses of wine at the German delegation's holiday party. She had another when she returned to her apartment to prepare for DeBrentanga's visit.

By the time the colonel arrived, Ambassador Vandiver was drunk. If DeBrentanga was aware of it, he was too diplomatic to say anything.

"Would you like a glass of wine, Colonel?" asked Vandiver, after taking his coat.

"Thank you, Madam Ambassador."

"Please, call me Elizabeth. May I call you René"

"Of course, Madam—I mean, Elizabeth."

Handing him a glass of wine, Vandiver began describing a wrought iron and gilt art deco table located just off the foyer. For the next half-hour, she escorted him on a tour of her apartment and her antiques. Another glass of wine followed.

The last destination was the bedroom. Vandiver guided the colonel to a beautifully handcrafted iron table lamp that sat next to her bed. As he admired the craftsmanship, Vandiver slid closer to DeBrentanga. So close that their hands touched.

DeBrentanga only temporarily paused before leaning over and giving the Ambassador a deep, solid kiss. Vandiver responded by pulling herself closer. The bed was only five feet from where they were standing.

A miniature camera, secretly installed by a Holten technician, captured the whole scene.

* *

John Gordon, the only other announced challenger to the vice president, besides Congressmen Reginald Greene, for the Democratic endorsement, was preparing to announce his withdrawal from the presidential race in his hometown of Tampa. He was surrounded by his wife and a group of loyal supporters who were doing their best to look upbeat.

"It is with great sadness and reluctance that I stand before you today," Gordon told the room full of reporters, many of whom had been merciless in their reporting of him and his campaign. "Martha and I have enjoyed these past eleven months travelling across America. We have met so many wonderful people and made so many new friends . . ." Gordon's voice trailed off. Looking up at the room full of reporters and with conscious deliberation, Gordon crumpled up the graceful exit speech that his speechwriter had prepared for him and handed it to his wife. She smiled. She told him earlier in the day to speak from his heart.

"I got into this race eleven months ago because I had a vision for America—but I was unable to have my vision heard because I wasn't able to raise twenty-five million dollars. Twenty-five million dollars is supposedly the magical number that a candidate needs in order to be considered a contender—a contender by you, the media." Gordon said, glaring at the reporters. "If someone can't raise enough money, that is all you ever report. You don't talk about their ideas. You just tell the public that we are not competitive because we don't have money. End of story! What ever happened to ideas? Since when did raising money become more important than raising ideas or raising the level of political discourse in this country?" Gordon looked out at the crowd of reporters in front of him. It was the largest group for a news conference that he had been able to attract since he entered the race. He knew they were there because they smelled blood—it had been leaked that he was pulling out of the race.

No one in the media returned his stare. "I still believe ideas are more important than money, and I would love to stay in the race to prove that point—but you have so tarnished me with the loser label that my ideas can't even be heard. You have so polluted the public's mind with your assessment that I can't win that the voters tune me out before I even begin to speak."

The room was strangely silent except for the whirring and clicking of cameras. "Let me conclude by saying that I accept some responsibility for my low poll numbers. I know I'm not the most exciting speaker and that I can appear wooden at times, but my vision lies in my ideas. I wish you would have reported on those ideas in greater depth, and I ask that you afford the few remaining candidates in the presidential race that courtesy. The country will be a better place for it. Thank you."

With that, the former senator and his wife left a room full of stunned reporters without answering any questions. The next day, in an effort to appease their guilt, many of the reporters wrote glowing articles about Gordon's "integrity," his "substance," and even, ironically, his "ideas." Another wrote that if he had displayed the same passion in his campaigning that he did in his withdrawal speech, he would have been a legitimate contender.

Fifteen hundred miles away, Colfax watched on C-SPAN II as Gordon withdrew. Later that evening, he reached Gordon, and the two old friends talked for over an hour. Colfax was the only candidate to congratulate Gordon on his campaign.

CHAPTER SEVEN

Z eljko Seselj had been responsible for the deaths of 5,000 Kosovars in the last six months, and before that he had ordered the deaths of more than 20,000 Bosnian Moslems. Baptista's employer considered Seselj a butcher and feared that if he became the next president of Serbia, as was expected, the severity of the situation in the Balkans would grow exponentially. Baptista explained to Manning that the sniper's own government viewed Seselj as the primary obstacle to peace in this troubled region of the world and would not be displeased if he were mysteriously expunged from the face of the earth.

Manning, after reading the materials that Baptista provided, came to the same conclusion: too much money and too many resources—including thousands of Marines—were being put in harm's way because one madman had grand visions of a Greater Serbia.

It was the kind of mission about which Manning had always dreamed—putting an end to senseless killings and in the process serving the United States of America. The former Marine would have preferred to terminate Zeljko Seselj under the official auspices of the United States government, but that was not possible.

Ironically, Manning's particular skill was the only kind of international diplomacy that Seselj understood. In fact, it was a skill the fifty-five-year-old Serbian nationalist respected so much that he ordered his troops to employ it indiscriminately against innocent Bosnians and Kosovars, including women and children, during his seven-year reign of terror.

* *

Calvary Baptist church was located in central Des Moines' worst neighborhood. But the area was making a comeback, in large part due to the efforts of the Reverend Nathaniel Abercrombie. As part of his normal Sunday services, he often invited in outside speakers. He was also trying to get his community more active in the political process. Abercrombie was thrilled when Robert Colfax immediately accepted his invitation to address his six-hundred-member congregation.

"Education is a monopoly," began Colfax as he peered down from the pulpit that towered above the congregation, "and nothing will change until that is changed." A few heads nodded. "African-American and Hispanic kids are getting shafted. Is it right that only a quarter of your children can pass a basic reading test? I can no longer accept the status quo—and neither should you. Too much is at stake. The education professionals will tell us that they need more money or smaller class sizes. Well, we've tried that, and it hasn't worked. It is time to shake up the system—we need competition in our public schools. I want to give you the power to send your children to the public school of your choice.

"The education establishment will say it can't be done. They'll say it'll wreck the system. Well, my friends, this is not about the system, it's about your kids. Who knows what's best for your children—you or some bureaucrat? I think you do, and, as president, I'll work to see that you have that choice."

Nathaniel Abercrombie was not disappointed. It was just the message that he wanted his congregation to hear.

* *

The rustic chalet was just as Baptista described it. Tall pines and a ten-foot security wall surrounded it, accessible only through a well-guarded gate, approximately six hundred yards from the nearest road. Except for the guards at its entrance, the chalet didn't really appear to be an environment where one of the world's most brutal man would spend a great deal of time.

Seselj didn't, in fact, visit the chalet much. He preferred instead to stay in Belgrade, where the economic sanctions didn't limit his access to fine wine, scotch, and cigars.

Inside the chalet, which Seselj's grandparents owned before it was confiscated by Albanian Muslims after World War II, three soldiers stood watch over the three young women who rotated in and out on a schedule known only to Seselj. They ranged in age from eighteen to twenty-three. Seselj knew that once a Muslim Albanian girl was raped, she was not welcomed back into society. That was why he raped as many as he could.

Psychologists working for the CIA speculated that Seselj's behavior had its roots in his witnessing the death of his parents at the hands of Albania partisans when he was only four. The same psychologists theorized, based on Manning's history, that the sniper would welcome the chance to kill a rapist. They were right.

* *

Blanketed by a new moon night, Manning easily blended in with the trees on a knoll overlooking the chalet. The earthen pit was located just where Baptista had said it would be. For the next sixty-eight hours, the sniper waited in near-freezing temperatures. An insulated sleeping bag and protective clothing allowed Manning to get some sleep. Otherwise, the sniper just waited.

All Manning had been told was that Seselj frequented the chalet on rare, unscheduled occasions. When he did show up, Manning was told, he often smoked a cigar on the veranda on the south side of the chalet after he finished violating his victim. This usually occurred somewhere between the hours of 11:00 P.M. and 1:00 A.M.

Manning marveled at the planning that had gone into the shot. The earthen pit provided what every sniper needed—a place to see without being seen. Manning had also been given an escape route, a vehicle, and a sophisticated tracking device to be activated only upon the completion of the mission or in case of an emergency. The mission seemed to be wired for success. It was just a matter of patience.

* *

Josh Parker finished studying at Meredith Library about midnight and went back to his fraternity house. His roommate was not around, so he powered up his computer and began going through his e-mails. There were the standard jokes that circulated through the Internet, a message from his father and one from his little sister. He deleted the chain e-mails and was responding to his sister's message when another e-mail appeared. It was from the Colfax campaign.

Parker couldn't believe what he read in the campaign update. Colfax was coming to Drake on January 10 for the sole purpose of discussing Social Security reform.

Parker quickly tapped out a reply asking what he could do to help. He wrote that he had an e-mail list of 230 students at Drake and would be happy to do whatever he could to generate a large crowd for Colfax. He also offered to start linking up with the other colleges in Iowa in anticipation of the caucuses on January 24. Parker hit the enter key, and, seconds later, the response was back at the Colfax campaign headquarters, a large brick warehouse on the west side of the Mississippi River in Minneapolis.

Inside the warehouse, which glowed eerily from the numerous computer stations dispersed throughout the large open space, sat three young Colfax campaign volunteers. A twenty-five-year-old graduate student at the University of Minnesota received Parker's e-mail and instantly recognized its value. He took it to Pete Sawyer, who had just finished tallying the contributions Ed Kielty had collected from his friends and acquaintances in the software world and was about to start on the checks that Jane Olive, the mayor of Burlington, had forwarded to the campaign.

"How's it going?" asked the graduate student.

"Not bad. We've collected close to $19,000 in Internet donations in the last two days."

"That's great. Does that mean I can start getting paid?"

"Paid? Hell, we're going to make history. You should be paying me for the opportunity to work on this campaign," replied Sawyer with a wink. "What's on your mind?"

"Look at this e-mail," replied the student, handing Sawyer a printed version of the message. He watched as Sawyer read it. "I'm going to e-mail him back and tell him he has our approval. "

"If he can get even fifty students to attend, that'd be great," said Sawyer.

"I also like his idea of connecting with the other colleges and universities down in Iowa—creating e-campus coordinators. We've only got two weeks to make an impression before the caucuses, and if we can do that by getting young people to turn out in record numbers for Colfax, that'll be the story of the night."

"Let's do it," replied Sawyer. "E-mail him back and let him know he is now our official Drake University connection for the event on the tenth. Tell him that if he can guarantee at least fifty students, I'll guarantee him a one-on-one visit with the candidate." Sawyer was already thinking about how scenes of Colfax talking to a large audience of students would play on the nightly news in Iowa.

Parker was checking out the official Super Bowl web site when he was alerted he had mail. A live online discussion ensued.

"We appreciate your offer," typed the Colfax volunteer. "You're our main man for the speech on the tenth."

"Excellent. What do I have to do?" responded Parker.

"Guarantee at least fifty students attend."

"No problem," Parker wrote back, "I'll drag my sorry-ass frat brothers there if I have to."

"Bring any sorority sisters you know, too."

The next day Parker drafted an e-mail that briefly outlined who Colfax was and why he thought his online friends should come hear him speak. To the e-mail, he attached a copy of the term paper he wrote two months earlier and added a "hot link" to the Colfax web site. He encouraged everyone to check out the financial calculator so that they could see for themselves how much they would benefit from

Colfax's plan to allow people to invest a portion of their Social Security contributions in a personal retirement account. Parker was so excited about the visit that he even used traditional methods of communication: he made announcements at his fraternity's all-member meeting and before his political science class. He also posted flyers all over campus and sent notices to the local media.

By the time Sawyer had arrived in town, the *Des Moines Daily Tribune* and all the local television affiliates were covering Colfax's visit to Drake. Sawyer smiled to himself at the young student's initiative and called campaign headquarters for Parker's local telephone number. The two met at a McDonald's just off campus. After finding out a little about Parker's background, Sawyer asked, "So, are we set for tomorrow?"

"I think so. But we've got a problem," said Parker to the suddenly nervous campaign manager.

"What kind of problem?" asked Sawyer. "Does it have to do with the numbers?"

"Yes."

"Shit, don't tell me that no one is going to show up. The media is already coming." Sawyer ran his hand through his hair, which seemed to be getting thinner every day of the campaign.

"Oh, that's not the problem," said Parker, sheepishly. "It's just that the room Governor Colfax has been scheduled to speak in can't possibly hold all the students who have said they'll be coming."

"Are you sure, Josh?" asked Sawyer, with more than a little skepticism. "I've been in politics a while, and if you get half the people who promise that they are coming to an event, you're doing well."

"Even if we get half, the room is still going to be too small," replied Parker.

Sawyer looked into Parker's eyes and knew he was telling the truth. "Is there anyway we can get a bigger room?"

"I thought about that," said Parker. "I didn't want to make a decision without you, but I have spoken with the student body president, and she said she would talk to the administration and see if the main auditorium could be made available. She confirmed about an hour ago that we could have it."

"How many can the room hold?"

"350."

"You do good work, Josh."

"Thanks. But there is one small problem—the student body president asked if she could sit on the stage with Governor Colfax."

"Jesus," laughed Sawyer, "politicians are the same regardless of age, sex, race, or creed. If there is a stage, they want to be on it."

* *

Win Murdock rarely came to New York City, and then only to exert a little pressure on the ambassadors of those countries where Holten, Incorporated, had facilities. When he was in the city, he stayed at his Park Avenue apartment. It was three floors above Ambassador Vandiver's apartment.

"Your little project has paid off," said Luther, handing his boss his favorite drink. Luther always did the advance work for Murdock's trips and insured that his apartment was prepared for his arrival.

"What do you mean?"

Luther flashed a copy of the key Murdock had ordered to be stolen during Vandiver's trip on his private jet. He then popped the video into the VCR of an obviously drunk Vandiver making love with Colonel DeBrentanga.

Murdock was speechless but could not bring himself to pull his eyes from the screen. After watching the whole episode, he asked, "Who is he?"

"Colonel René DeBrentanga, chief military liaison to the French ambassador to the U.N."

"I never . . ." stuttered Murdock. "All I wanted was some inside information on the upcoming negotiations with China. I never expected this."

"I also have the information on China. I just thought you might find this more interesting. You know—just in case we have to make sure that Holten's interests are fully protected in the upcoming negotiations with China."

"Oh," said Murdock, "I'm sure we'll be well represented. I think I'll save this little tidbit for a really special occasion. Maybe if we need help stopping the FBI's investigation of our little price-fixing adventure."

"That won't be necessary. Geary," said Luther, referring to the FBI director, "has agreed to stop the investigation. Wiley has taken care of it. He's billing us $300,000 for his services, however." Murdock rewound the tape and watched the scene between the two lovers again.

* *

The main auditorium of Drake University was filled to capacity with over 400 students. Outside the auditorium, Sawyer and Parker waited for Colfax to show up. He had just arrived at the airport a few minutes earlier.

Parker immediately recognized Colfax as he stepped out of the car. Colfax headed straight for the pair.

"Hi, Pete," Colfax began, then turned to face the young student. "And you must be Josh Parker. Pete has told me all about you. I can't thank you enough for all your hard work. I understand that as a result of your efforts, we had to move to a larger room."

"It's a pleasure to meet you, Governor," said Parker, still shaking the candidate's hand. "I'm just happy I could help."

"You did more than help. You made this event a success. I have one more favor to ask," said Colfax, who made it a habit to recognize—and reward—hard work.

"Sure. Anything, Governor."

"Would you do me the honor of introducing me today?" The surprised look on Parker's face caused Colfax to offer him a graceful way out. "If you're not comfortable with public speaking, I certainly—"

"No—it's nothing like that. I just wasn't prepared for something like this."

"Pete told me the story about your term paper. Why don't you just retell that to the audience. Explain how you came to support me and then say, 'And now I would like to introduce to you, Governor Colfax.'"

"I can do that."

Josh Parker's introduction was flawless, and Colfax's speech was perfect. He was funny, educational and motivational. Then, near the end of his speech, he dropped a political bomb that went virtually undetected by the students but was picked up by every political reporter in the audience. The story led the nightly news and made the front page in the *Des Moines Daily Tribune* the next day.

"I need you," Colfax bellowed at the students, "to become more involved. Change will only happen with your support. You are the future—and you have to get involved. The first thing I need you to do is to attend your precinct caucuses next Monday. You can only go to the Republican or the Democratic Party caucus. There is no independent caucus. But don't worry. Once inside a caucus, you can support any candidate you want—including me. Now," said Colfax pausing, trying to assess if the students were tracking with his request, "my goal is not to win any delegates to either political convention. I simply want to show people that I have the support of Republicans and Democrats alike. More important, I want you—the young people of this country—to attend the caucuses to send a loud signal to both political parties that you are dissatisfied with their candidates and with business as usual. You can do that by supporting me. Together," Colfax concluded, "we can change the country. Thank you."

Without thinking, Parker, who was seated next to the student body president on the stage, jumped to the microphone and thanked the candidate. Then, turning to address the students, he said, "If you're interested in attending the precinct caucuses—and you should be—but don't know how, please contact me." Parker then scribbled his e-mail address on the board behind the podium. The information was also posted on the Colfax web site.

That night, Parker received over a 150 e-mails, mostly from Drake students. The numbers grew the next day when he was quoted in the *Des Moines Daily Tribune*. The paper, in its lead editorial, decried Colfax's meddling in the caucuses as "a serious threat to democracy."

*   *

Since 1972, when the Secret Service began providing protection to presidential candidates, no candidate had received as many threats in as short a period of time as had Congressman Reginald Greene. A majority of the threats made either direct or passing reference to his African-American heritage.

Greene's entrance into the presidential sweepstakes placed an additional burden on the already loaded shoulders of the Secret Service. They were presently protecting the president and the First Family, the vice president and his family, plus six Republican presidential challengers. Colfax was also on the verge of receiving protection. The first poll of January 2000 showed him at four percent.

Under normal circumstances, Sean McGowan would not have been called down from the Minneapolis office to help oversee a candidate's visit in Iowa, but the tone of some of the threats against Congressman Greene required that the Secret Service send an experienced agent to help manage the candidate's first visit to that state.

McGowan arrived in Ames a day and a half in advance of Greene. The Iowa State University's farm extension service was hosting a forum on the prospects of the family farm. McGowan was briefed on all the security arrangements that had been made. Greene's hotel had been swept and searched; the entire hotel staff had been interviewed; the elevators had been secured; even a backup ventilation system had been installed in the candidate's room.

McGowan was reasonably satisfied with the work the advance team had done. The main and alternate travel routes were scouted and assessed for vulnerabilities, and every medical facility was identified and mapped. McGowan was also comfortable with the local enforcement officials. Due to the sheer number of presidential contenders that visited Iowa every four years, most local police were well trained in protective services. They were a valuable addition to the Secret Service's team.

After finishing his preliminary work, McGowan sat down with the entire protection team and reviewed the comprehensive security plan for Greene's visit. Every possible contingency was covered in the 110-page classified briefing book. Near the end of the two-hour briefing, McGowan rose up from his chair. Looking out over the room of twelve agents—a lot, given that Greene was far behind Vice President Byrne in the polls—McGowan began to speak. "I don't think I have to tell anyone that Deacon is not your average candidate," said McGowan, using Greene's codename, which was given to him because his father was a well-know minister. "Every candidate receives exactly the same level of protection from the Secret Service, and that is perfection. The challenge comes in the form of Deacon's opponents. Racists are a motivated group, and it is abundantly clear that a number of people—and or groups—do not wish to see him survive this campaign. It is our job to see that he does."

McGowan then turned the briefing over to one of the Secret Service's leading experts in the science of profiling. "Deacon has received some very threatening letters recently. Three letters in particular have caught our attention. All three, it has been determined, were written by the same individual."

The profiler distributed copies of the letter for all the agents to read. When everyone was finished, she asked for the letters to be returned to her for shredding. "Based on our analysis, the author of these letters is male, thirty-five to forty-five years old, educated at less than a tenth-grade level, is an only child and works in a menial job where he reports to a supervisor whom he considers inferior—either a minority, a woman, or, possibly, a Jew. The letter writer suffers from low self-esteem and probably lost a parent early in his life. It is also highly likely he belongs to a racist or militia-type group."

McGowan added, "And based on some idiosyncrasies, we think the person comes from either the southern part of Iowa or northern Missouri. Therefore, it is important that everyone keep this profile in mind as you go about your job."

"I know a lot of people will fit this description, but keep your eyes open," said the profiler, "because our analysis also suggests that the person is methodical and is likely to scope out an attack in advance."

* *

The Family Farm Forum held in the fieldhouse at Iowa State University attracted almost 2,000 people—mostly farmers. Elroy Jarvis politely listened to Reginald Greene rail against the evils of corporate farming and international trade. It was almost the same message that Dick Graham, the conservative former television talk show host, espoused. Jarvis liked the message. In fact, he liked it a lot. He just detested the color of Greene's skin.

From the middle of the packed fieldhouse, the Missouri native did not stand out in the crowd of farmers that night. Jarvis' position also made it difficult for any of the twelve Secret Service agents to notice that he spent an inordinate amount of time looking at them instead of the candidate. But even if they had, they likely would not have detected that the right-hand pocket of his wool-lined denim jacket bulged slightly more than the left. Inside the pocket was a glass vial containing battery acid.

Jarvis didn't plan to use the acid that night. He was more interested in finding out if the security forces surrounding Greene had systems that could detect its presence. They didn't.

High above Jarvis and the rest of the crowd, a Secret Service camera in the rafters scanned the fieldhouse floor. Hours later, the video was downloaded into a sophisticated software program in the technical branch of the Secret Service's headquarters in Washington, D.C. The tape was scanned for any familiar faces already in the Secret Services "Hot Faces" database. Elroy Jarvis was not in the database.

* *

Since breaking the presidential scandal back in 1998, the *Moriarty Minute* had become the most reviled and criticized Internet news source in the country. The mainstream media consistently downplayed its significance and criticized it "as tabloid journalism of the worst kind." But they also read it—because Moriarty had sources they didn't.

The *Moriarty Minute* had also become a fashionable way of filtering tabloid-like stories into the mainstream media. It was an increasingly common trick. The major networks would lament the move toward sleazy news stories and harshly criticize the low ethical standards of the *Moriarty Minute* in the first paragraph of their version of the story and then report on its contents in the next. In this way, the story was considered "cleansed"—they weren't the ones responsible for stooping to the new low standard; they were only "reporting the story."

The January 12th edition of the *Moriarty Minute* did not, on first glance, appear to offer any earth-shattering news. It began with a story about the rocky relationship between the president and the vice president. Moriarty reported that Vice President Byrne was attempting to distance himself from the president and First Lady Judy Butler. Sources close to the vice president said that their candidate's association with the president was hurting his efforts to court female voters, and his close relationship with the more liberal and opinionated first lady was hindering his ability to reach out to the blue-collar independent voters.

The second story speculated that Governor Prescott of Pennsylvania was considering naming Elizabeth Vandiver, the United States ambassador to the United Nations and the former pro-choice Republican governor of Maryland, to be his running mate. Dick Graham's campaign manager was quoted as saying, "If Prescott names that Dragon Lady to be his v.p., he can kiss the Republican nomination goodbye. The activists will crucify him and so will Graham. There is no room on the Republican ticket for a pro-choice woman who served in a Democratic administration. The Republicans need conservatives in the number one and number two spots. There is too much riding on the next election to pick someone of Vandiver's ilk. The selection of three or four Supreme Court justices hinges on the next election."

It was not until the second-to-the-last paragraph that one of the day's two most important news items was reported for the first time. Moriarty wrote that sources close to former Democratic challenger Senator John Gordon were claiming that he was not going to endorse the vice president and was considering endorsing Robert Colfax in return for a cabinet position.

The second key item came, almost as an afterthought, in the last paragraph, which announced the creation of Washington's newest issue advocacy group, the Coalition for a Prosperous New Millennium. The report did not speculate on the purpose of the organization but noted that it had raised $6.4 million and was being run by Lawrence, Scott & Mance, Washington's most sophisticated and notoriously nasty law firm.

* *

The knock on the door was almost indistinguishable over the loud hissing of the turn-of-the-century radiator. "Come in," said Colfax, setting down a report on the affordable housing crisis facing many lower- and middle-income citizens.

"Sorry to bother you, Dad."

"Pumpkin," replied Colfax, taking off his reading glasses and facing his ten-year-old daughter, "you could never bother me. What's on your mind?"

"Nothing," replied Colleen, moving closer. Colfax knew the more quiet and reserved of his two daughters was not being entirely truthful.

"Come here," he said, motioning for her to sit on his lap. "I've really missed you."

"I've missed you too, Dad. You're never around anymore. When will the election be over?"

"Not soon enough," said Colfax, gently pushing a strand of hair out of her eyes.

"We don't dance anymore," blurted Colleen. Colfax now knew the real reason for the visit. From the time of her birth until she was eight, Colfax made a point to dance with her for a few songs every night. He thought she had outgrown this.

"Oh, Pumpkin, I've always got time for a dance with you." He got up and put a Louie Prima CD in the stereo, and the two danced. He knew she would again quickly outgrow the ritual. "When you're smilin', when you're smilin' and the whole world smiles with you. . . ."

*   *

Of the half million people who regularly accessed the *Moriarty Minute*, only four assigned any importance to the creation of the Coalition for a Prosperous New Millennium. David Luther was concerned enough to call Jacob Mance and suggest that his firm's opposition research team find out where the report came from. He also ordered the public relations people to begin working behind the scenes to deflect any scrutiny that might result from the story.

Two blocks down from David Luther, on Connecticut Avenue, Stephanie Freeberg smiled as she read the story. Her off-the-record conversation with Moriarty had paid off. In Minneapolis, Pete Sawyer downloaded the report, highlighted the last paragraph and sent a note to a campaign volunteer asking her to find out who was behind this group and how it might be neutralized. The volunteer, a low-paid informant for Jacob Mance, never followed through on the request.

The fourth reader sent Ellen Moriarty an e-mail from the CyberCafe in Georgetown, informing her that the Coalition for a Prosperous New Millennium was more than just the average political action committee—it had been created for the sole purpose of derailing Robert Colfax's candidacy.

CHAPTER EIGHT

T he cold, shallow pit provided minimal protection against the harsh Balkan winter. The sixty-eight hours since Manning's helicopter drop had passed slowly, and the sniper bided time by estimating the distance of the shot, assessing the wind from the swaying of the pines, recaliberating the rifle scope, calculating the adjustments needed to place the bullet through the target's head and, when possible, sleeping. Manning considered every possible scenario and prepared for every contingency. What the sniper did not think about was the person or organization on the other end of the bank account. The chance to assassinate a known terrorist—an enemy of the United States—was the fulfillment of a lifelong dream. The money was frosting on the cake. The sniper would have done it for free—something Manning's new employers knew but chose not to exploit.

* *

The interview was almost over when the reporter for the *San Francisco Chronicle* flipped through her notebook to confirm that she had asked the independent candidate for president all of the questions she wanted answered. The word "moratorium" jumped out at her. "One last question, Governor Colfax. The citizens of California are very concerned about the long-term impact of offshore oil drilling along the state's coast. Do you favor a moratorium?"

"I do," responded Colfax without hesitation. "But even more, I favor a permanent ban over a moratorium. Not only can such a position be justified on both environmental and economic grounds, it is the right thing to do for our children and our grandchildren."

The reporter was jotting down his words, when Colfax started speaking again. "You know, Prescott and Byrne will talk about protecting the environment, but the fact is they won't do anything about it because the big oil and chemical companies don't want them to do anything about it. I mean, just look at Holten. They own fifty-five oil refineries. Do you really think Prescott or Byrne will have the courage to demand that Murdock stop spewing his millions of tons of toxic emissions into the air? I don't . . . and it's a crime. Murdock drops a few million dollars into the hands of his Republican and Democratic pals, and we, the taxpayers, are stuck with the bill for cleaning up his multibillion-dollar mess."

* *

Manning felt the rumbling of the caravan before seeing the first headlight. Suddenly, five official-looking cars roared down the narrow road and straight toward the chalet.

Inside the second and most heavily secured car was a very drunk General Seselj. "Are we almost there?" he slurred to the driver. "I haven't had a piece of ass in over a week!"

"We are just now arriving, General," replied the driver as the two heavily armed guards outside the chalet waved the first of the cars through the gate.

"Excellent. Radio the captain and tell him that I want that whore Anna to be in my room with legs her spread by the time I get upstairs."

The driver did as instructed. A minute later, the captain was informing the eighteen-year-old Kosovar woman that it was her lucky night. "The general has requested your services tonight," he said, laughing. For good measure, the captain told the other two women to keep their thighs moist in the event the general was in an energetic mood.

After the captain left, the selected victim began quietly weeping. The other two women, relieved that they were not the ones being called into service, tried to console her. Each knew that if the general was drunk—and he usually was—the first woman took the brunt of the physical beating that so often accompanied his sexual activities. They also knew that if he was drunk, the odds of his calling for another victim were remote. He usually passed out after he was finished with his business. The young woman ignored her companion's sympathies and began trying to disassociate herself from the experience that she was about to encounter. If she could have committed suicide, she would have.

The long walk down to the master bedroom seemed to take an eternity. Entering the bedroom, the woman flicked on the overhead light. A kilometer away, Lee Manning spotted the light and thought, "Show time."

If Seselj came out on the veranda, the shot would be incredibly easy. The light from the room would frame the target nicely, and the lack of wind reduce the chance for complications. Even the temperature was perfect—twenty-five degrees Fahrenheit—well within the range at which the rifle had been "zeroed." The selection of Colorado Springs could not have been more perfect for training. The climate and elevation were almost identical to those of Kosovo, meaning that a bullet fired in either location would perform exactly the same.

Manning just had to wait and hope that the rapist would cooperate and place himself in a location where a bullet could reach him. As Manning was adjusting the beanbag under the stock of the rifle, Anna was surveying the master bedroom when she decided that an outside view might have a soothing effect on Seselj and opened the curtains.

Thinking it was Seselj, Manning quickly brought the rifle up and sighted the target. Instantly, the sniper saw the fear in the young woman's deep brown eyes. It was a fear borne of a private hell.

Downstairs in the chalet, Seselj poured himself another glass of scotch as he phoned Belgrade and spoke with the man he one day hoped to replace. "Mr. President," Seselj said, "NATO and KLA forces continue to pose some problems, but we are reasserting control in the hills outside of Pristina."

"I want as many of those fucking swine eradicated as possible," screamed the president, a man well known for his temper. Seselj realized the president was drunk and wouldn't remember a word of their conversation in the morning. Hanging up, he turned to the captain and asked if Anna was ready. The captain responded in the affirmative.

Seselj bounded up the stairs with his glass full of scotch and began undressing even before he entered the bedroom. From Manning's hard, shallow hole in the ground, Seselj's entrance went unnoticed.

"Come here, you Muslim whore," Seselj bellowed at the young woman. As she made her way over to the aging and fleshy Seselj, she made her mind go blank. When she approached Seselj, he grabbed her and violently thrust her onto the bed.

Pinning her down by her silky black hair with one hand and taking a gulp of scotch with the other, Seselj mounted her. When it was over, the woman lay bleeding and bruised on the bed, an exhausted Seselj collapsed next to her. For forty-five minutes, she didn't move. She didn't want to rouse the sweaty, naked monster next to her. When she finally heard him snore, she grabbed a loose sheet and wrapped it tightly around herself and made her way to the veranda. Once outside, she silently prayed to her deceased father for forgiveness and began to cry.

Manning saw the woman on the veranda and froze. The sniper had seen the look years before. It was the same look Maggie Long had worn after being brutally raped.

An hour earlier, the young woman had been frightened but had maintained a certain innocence. Now the same face looked years older. As tears continued to stream down the bruised face, Manning patiently waited for the rapist to appear.

The cold air from the open veranda door aroused Seselj. He was slow to get up but eventually made his away to the bathroom, adjacent to the bedroom. After relieving himself, Seselj downed the remnants of the eighteen-year-old scotch.

As he savored the single malt whisky, he noticed Anna out on the veranda and made his way toward her. As he stepped outside, the cold breeze instantly reinvigorated him, and he placed his arms around his victim, who stood frozen with horror.

"This cold air is just what I need to get it up," he said, laughing. "Why don't you get yourself ready for some more fun?" Slapping her on the ass, Seselj ordered her back inside and turned his face toward the open field. He lit up a big Cuban cigar.

Sweat began dripping from Manning's forehead. Quickly, the sniper assessed the wind, double-checked the scope and selected a spot on Seselj's head just above his right ear. The weeks of training instantly kicked in. Manning pulled the trigger taut so that there was no slack, instinctively drew a breath and ever so gently pulled back on the trigger.

The small piece of hot lead exited the barrel and sliced through the cold winter air, well ahead of its sound, and closed in on Seselj's neural motor strip. He never heard the shot. Upon impact, the bullet sprouted open like a miniature umbrella, ripped his brain apart and instantly incapacitated Seselj. The Hyena's reign of terror was over.

The man who had been responsible for thousands deaths and even more rapes and other atrocities was now dead. Thousands of lives would be saved as a result of a single bullet, and the Balkan peace process would gain new momentum. This fact would not be known for another six hours.

* *

Josh Parker spent the week after Colfax's visit to Drake organizing students to attend precinct caucuses. All told, his efforts produced a list of 253 first-time volunteers. Parker dubbed these his e-precinct leaders. He then reported, via the Internet, his progress to the Colfax campaign headquarters in the Minneapolis warehouse.

"Pete, check this out," said Barb Hoppe, a Colfax field organizer, to Sawyer, who was seated at a gray metal utility desk that had been purchased at a garage sale for five dollars. The campaign manager was eating a reheated burrito and drinking a stale cup of coffee from a giant plastic mug. "Our man Josh Parker claims to have lined up almost two hundred and fifty students for Tuesday's caucuses."

"No shit? That's fantastic. Tell him he needs to reconfirm his list on Monday. Students aren't particularly reliable."

"Already done," replied Hoppe, who at twenty-five was a veteran of two congressional campaigns. "I was thinking we should use Parker to help mobilize every college and university in Iowa. What do you think?"

"It's a great idea. Why didn't you think of it two days ago?" replied Sawyer. "You know I'm swamped. I'm relying on you to be proactive. If you think something will benefit the campaign, go ahead and do it."

"All right," said Hoppe, who knew that Sawyer was feeling the stress of his first presidential campaign.

"That directive comes from the governor himself. He has said that he trusts all of us implicitly. If we're going to win, we need to remain flexible and take calculated risks. As he always tells me, it's easier to apologize than to ask for permission."

"I'll e-mail Parker right now," said Hoppe. Eyeing Sawyer's burrito, she added, "Is there any food left?"

"Do you consider day-old coffee sludge, food?" replied Sawyer.

* *

Jacob Mance handed the *San Francisco Chronicle* article to the man seated across the table. The section on Colfax's position on offshore oil drilling was highlighted so the vice president of government affairs for California's largest oil and chemical company could not miss it. Mance explained the purpose of the Coalition for a Prosperous New Millennium over a lunch of grilled sea bass and a glass of Chardonnay. By the time the waiter presented the bill, Mance had received a commitment for an additional one million dollars in funding for Win Murdock's pet project.

* *

Josh Parker was busy retrieving the few e-mails still straggling in when he received Hoppe's response with a list of e-mail addresses for contacts at the University of Iowa, Iowa State, Grinnell, Coe, the University of Northern Iowa, Spirit Lake Community College and a dozen other colleges throughout the state.

Instead of attending his three-hour finance class, Parker began contacting student leaders at each college. In his lengthy e-mail, he outlined his success at Drake and asked each one if they would take the lead at their school for organizing caucus attendees. He also referred them to the web site that he had created. On it was both a printed version and a five-minute video clip of Colfax's impassioned remarks at Drake. It also linked back to Colfax's main web site.

Within twelve hours, sixteen of the nineteen contacts had agreed to organize their campuses. In less than a week, Josh Parker had gone from being a political unknown to one of the most successful and sophisticated political operatives in Iowa.

He had accomplished for Colfax in a few days what paid political consultants for the vice president and Governor Prescott had been unable to do in fifteen months: set up a process for delivering people to the caucuses. And he had done it at no cost to the campaign.

Hearing of Parker's success, Sawyer sensed a story and was quickly on the phone with Gerry Malcolm, the *Des Moines Daily Tribune*'s senior political reporter.

"Gerry, this is Pete Sawyer, Governor Colfax's campaign manager."

"How are you?" said Malcolm, "I'm sorry I didn't get a chance to meet you when you were at Drake last week. Our editorial board is interested in sitting down with Governor Colfax prior to the caucuses next Tuesday. Any chance a visit could be arranged?"

"Absolutely," replied Sawyer. "The governor will be participating in a two-man debate with Congressman Greene before the Indianola Chamber of Commerce on Friday. Could we meet later that afternoon, say at three o'clock?"

"I'll check with my editor, but that should work. Since you called, I presume you have something else on your mind."

"I do. I want to give you a heads-up on an emerging story. I know you're aware that the governor has asked his supporters to attend either the Republican or Democratic caucuses but to caucus for him."

"I am," said Malcolm with no inflection in his voice. "I think it sets a dangerous precedent and places our position here in Iowa at risk." Malcolm felt that if Colfax was successful, future candidates would not take the Iowa caucuses seriously, costing the state the financial and media benefits that come from hosting the nation's first presidential event every four years.

Ignoring his comment, Sawyer continued, "You saw the enthusiastic support the governor received at Drake. If you send a reporter to some other campuses across the state, I'm certain you'll find similar support."

"Go on," said Malcolm.

"The amazing thing is that this support has been generated almost entirely through the Internet."

"Thanks for the tip," responded Malcolm with what sounded like a tinge of annoyance. "Anything else?"

Sawyer said there wasn't.

Not willing to give up on the story, Sawyer worked the phones for another half-hour and left messages for every reporter covering the Iowa caucuses. Knowing that most were terminally bored and looking for a new angle, he figured at least one would return his call.

Sawyer was surprised when reporters from the *New York Times*, *Wired*, *George*, and *The Economist* called back. He would have been even more surprised if he knew that Malcolm had assigned two of his more experienced reporters to the University of Iowa and Grinnell College to investigate the lead.

*   *

Sean McGowan was happy that he didn't have to convince either Congressman Greene or his campaign manager, Terrell White, a brash, opinionated lawyer in his late thirties, of the necessity of wearing a bulletproof vest. Deacon was going to be difficult enough to protect. McGowan didn't need him taking foolish risks.

As McGowan and Deacon waited in the holding area for the debate to begin in the gymnasium of the Indianola high school, White fumed. "Why the hell can that SOB Colfax glad-hand with the crowd while the congressman is stuck sitting in here with you?" asked White.

"Mr. White," said McGowan, "we've been over this before. Governor Colfax is not under the protective service of the Secret Service. His campaign has not yet requested it, and Congress has not yet authorized it."

"That's bullshit," said White as he paced the room. McGowan ignored him and continued to monitor, through the molded earpiece in his right ear, the discussion among the other Secret Service agents working the gymnasium floor

At precisely one minute before noon, McGowan asked Greene if he was ready to make his entrance. Putting down his notes, he looked at McGowan and said he was.

"Deacon is ready," whispered McGowan into his left sleeve. Outside, the faces of the five Secret Service agents didn't show any reaction to the announcement, but mentally, each one stepped up his powers of observation a notch. The lead agent responded to McGowan, "The area is secure."

McGowan walked through the door of the staging room and onto the gymnasium floor. Greene and White followed directly behind him. Two additional Secret Service agents took up positions on Greene's right and left flanks. Behind the congressman was Tom Miller, a local cop who had helped protect three different presidents and numerous other candidates during his seventeen years on the force. Miller closed the door to the staging area and positioned his massive six-foot-four-inch frame right in front of it. No one was going to get in or out.

The crowd went wild when they saw Greene. It was not the reaction that Tom Miller had expected the black congressman from Texas to receive from the all-white crowd. The enthusiastic applause was in response to Greene's recent calls for an end to the Freedom to Farm Act, a bill that had been passed by the Republican Congress in 1996. He had also called for an additional thirteen-billion-dollar grant program to aid family farmers.

A number of the farmers at the debate had arrived hours earlier and had bided their time by reading the newspaper. Sixteen-year-old Gordon Campbell, there with his father, was almost finished with the sports section when Greene entered the gym. But it wasn't the candidate that caught his attention; it was Sean McGowan.

Campbell saw McGowan speak into his sleeve and knew immediately that he was a Secret Service agent. It was then that the idea hit him. Campbell knew that Greene had been threatened, and he wanted to see how close he could get to Greene if he pretended like he had a gun hidden in the newspaper. Campbell figured if anybody stopped him, there was nothing they could do to him because he was a minor, and he didn't have a weapon.

On the stage, Colfax warmly greeted Greene. The two had served together briefly in Congress. Both badly needed exposure prior to the caucuses on Monday, and if the other major candidates wouldn't debate them, they agreed they could both benefit by staging their own debate. Based on the crowd in the auditorium, they were right.

The hour-long debate, which was broadcast live on Iowa Public Radio, focused primarily on farm issues, and Greene seemed to be winning in terms of applause from the audience. He received a very appreciative roar when he proclaimed his undying support for ethanol. Colfax's denunciation of the subsidy drew complete silence.

What surprised Colfax during the debate was Greene's support for school vouchers for poor urban children. Like Colfax, he reasoned that it was wrong to keep poor, mostly black children condemned to the worst schools. He demanded that parents be given the opportunity to send their kids to good schools—like most middle-class Americans. Colfax agreed.

Greene also argued that Social Security was a rip-off for male African Americans—and hard-working farmers—whose average life expectancy was well below sixty-five years. "Hell," he said, "the average black man—and the average farmer—don't even live long enough to receive back the money they put into the system. Why not let them invest a portion of their own money and pass it on to their families." Again, Colfax agreed, saying, "It is time that we let people accumulate wealth."

As the two were agreeing on education and Social Security, Gordon Campbell continued to edge closer to the front of the stage. He was almost directly in front of

Tom Miller when McGowan and another agent noted his movement. McGowan was about to take action when Miller also picked up on Campbell's movement. Seeing that the newspaper covered the young man's right hand and that the young boy was exclusively focused on Greene, Miller decided to act. With catlike quickness, the large cop reached out with his large arms and squeezed Campbell's arms to his side so the boy couldn't move. The vice grip caused Campbell to drop the newspaper and exposed that he was holding nothing other than the paper.

Miller wasted no time pulling Campbell into the holding room. McGowan noted Miller's action and sent one agent to cover Miller's spot and detailed another to help Miller in the holding room.

Within minutes, Miller and the Secret Service were certain that Campbell was simply a prankster. Taking no chances, they detained him until a complete investigation could be conducted.

While Campbell was testing the Secret Service, a far more serious threat lurked in the front row of the gymnasium. Elroy Jarvis, with his glass vial of acid, had been one of the first to arrive at the auditorium that morning. He had shaken hands with Colfax before the debate, but it was Greene who he wanted. The Secret Service agent protecting the congressman's left side had shielded the candidate from Jarvis and his acid when he first approached the podium. Jarvis was hoping for a second shot when the debate concluded.

McGowan had noticed the middle-aged Jarvis immediately upon entering the auditorium. He recognized the face from the videotape of the farm forum, which every agent had reviewed prior to the debate. It was too much of a coincidence. He radioed an agent in the front to move toward Jarvis, and before Jarvis knew what had happened, the Secret Service agent had bumped into him and quickly and efficiently frisked him for weapons. The agent missed the small, thin vial strapped midway up his right arm.

The agent signaled back to McGowan that he was clean. Still, McGowan didn't like the looks of Jarvis and made a mental note to investigate him.

As the debate ended, Greene and Colfax shook hands, and Greene, with McGowan in the lead, headed to the holding room. As McGowan approached Jarvis, his sixth sense went off and he decided to "freeze" him. The agent stared directly at Jarvis, and he froze. As McGowan drew closer, he said in tones that only Jarvis could hear, "Whatever you're thinking of doing, don't." He didn't take his eyes off Jarvis.

Jarvis was completely rattled, and McGowan, without knowing it, saved Greene from being blinded by battery acid. An ensuing investigation, initiated by McGowan, revealed the plot. Jarvis was quietly arrested—just another unpublicized victory for the Secret Service.

* *

As Sawyer and Colfax rode to Des Moines for the editorial board visit, they discussed Greene's surprising positions.

"He's certainly not your typical Democrat, is he?" asked Colfax.

"No, he's not."

"What if I were to offer him a position in my cabinet—something like secretary of Education. Do you think he'd take it?"

Sawyer turned his head, lifted his right eyebrow and smiled. "Not right now. I think he wants to be a pain in Byrne's ass until the Democratic convention in Los Angeles. He'll then negotiate for whatever he can from the vice president. If it's not enough or if he gets the cold shoulder, then he might be open to an approach."

"Just thinking out loud, Pete," said Colfax. "I'd really like to offer the American people a picture of what my cabinet would look like before the election. It'd be a powerful campaign tool."

"I agree. The problem is that no one is exactly jumping on our bandwagon at this point," laughed Sawyer.

"They will," responded Colfax, matter-of-factly.

Sawyer turned on the radio, and the pair headed east toward Des Moines. On the outskirts of town, they heard the first radio ad blasting Colfax for his position on ethanol. The tag line, read by a man with a deep, serious-sounding voice was: "Robert Colfax. Wrong for Iowa farmers. Wrong for Iowa." A softer female voiced then added, "Paid for and prepared by the Coalition for a Prosperous New Millennium."

"The coalition for what?" asked Colfax. "Who the hell are they?" Sawyer shrugged his shoulders and said he would look into it.

CHAPTER NINE

Win Murdock had been explicit: stop Colfax. Jacob Mance knew his most powerful client didn't care how he did it—he just wanted it done. Mance figured adding two of Washington's largest and most influential lobbying organizations to the coalition would be a good place to start.

The scene in the tastefully decorated boardroom of the law firm of Lawrence, Mance & Scott was exactly the same as the month before. The only difference, besides the expensive suit, tie, and cuff links Jacob Mance was wearing, were the two people seated before him. Mance's junior partner, Preston Briggs, was seated far off to the side.

Replacing the leaders of the oil and chemical industry were Judy Forsythe, an immaculately dressed, iron-willed woman in her late fifties and the executive director of the Committee to Protect Social Security. Next to her was Joseph Leider, a cautious, calculating political animal who had methodically risen to his current position as the president of the Federated Teachers Council. Together, the two organizations represented more than seven million members and possessed annual political action committee budgets in excess of ten million dollars.

Forsythe and Leider were aware of Mance's well-established reputation of winning at any cost. It was the reason both had agreed to attend the hastily arranged meeting. They were intrigued by Preston Briggs' call. A partner in Mance's law firm, Briggs had informed the pair that the meeting was of "a vital, but sensitive, nature."

"Why are we here?" asked Forsythe in her direct, no-nonsense style.

"It's good to see you again, too, Judy," said Mance.

Forsythe was not amused.

"Would you like a cup of coffee?"

"No. Why am I here?" repeated Forsythe.

"I'd like to talk with you about the 2000 presidential campaign."

"What's so goddamn vital or sensitive about that? Everyone knows it's going to be a race between Byrne and Prescott."

"Really?" replied Mance in condescending tone. "I'm concerned the race may be significantly different than past presidential campaigns. Let me explain."

"Please do," replied Forsythe.

"As you just said, you are relatively sure that Byrne and Prescott will be their respective party's nominees. Is that correct? Do you agree with that assessment, Joe?" Leider nodded his head in agreement at the prevailing political wisdom.

"And it can be assumed that both Prescott and Byrne will spend a good deal of their time trying to define the other. Byrne will say Prescott is a cold-hearted conservative. Prescott will respond that Byrne is a typical Yale-educated, tax-and-spend liberal. Do you agree?"

Unaware of where Mance was heading, both nodded their agreement.

"As it currently stands, neither has taken a position on Social Security or education to which you or your members are vehemently opposed. Correct?"

Forsythe and Leider again nodded affirmatively.

"And it is safe to assume that your members support Byrne and Prescott in roughly equal numbers?"

"Actually," Forsythe volunteered, "our latest poll shows Byrne ahead fifty-four percent to forty-six percent."

"Our numbers are about the same," guessed Leider, who didn't want to appear to be less informed than Forsythe.

"Have you conducted any polls describing a hypothetical race between Byrne, Prescott and Colfax?" asked Mance. Silence. "Perhaps you should," continued Mance. "In the last two months, Governor Colfax has gone from two percent in the polls to five percent." He signaled to Briggs, who flipped a few switches.

The room darkened and a projection screen rolled down from the ceiling. On it was a graph with approval ratings along the vertical axis and dates along the horizontal axis. The graph was constructed to make Colfax's gains seem more impressive than they actually were. The graph faded from the screen and was replaced with the image of 400 cheering Drake University students packed into an auditorium. It was a video clip of a local Des Moines television reporter describing the students' favorable reaction to Colfax's calls for allowing citizens to invest a portion of their Social Security contributions in personal retirement accounts.

Forsythe, who was aware of Colfax's position on Social Security and had read his remarks at Drake University, was alarmed by the chord Colfax had struck with the students.

The next clip, which was videotaped by the lone black associate at Lawrence, Mance & Scott, showed Colfax in the pulpit of the Calvary Baptist Church in central Des Moines, speaking to an all-black congregation. Colfax clearly had the attention of his audience.

"The schools in urban America are a disgrace," Colfax said as the congregation voiced its agreement. "They are more than a disgrace, they are a tragedy," he continued as a few more people added their voices to the approval. "It is time to change the system."

"Amen," responded a few parishioners.

"But more money isn't the answer," continued Colfax. "We have tried that approach before and it hasn't worked. And the longer it doesn't work, the more our children—your children—are being deprived of a quality education. It is time we let the money follow the student. I want you, as parents, to be able to send your children to the public school that you feel will best educate your child." Colfax stopped and drew in the audience in. "Now, myself, the vice president, and Governor Prescott can all afford to spend our children to private schools. And many upper- and middle-class Americans can move to a better school district if they feel their children aren't getting the education they deserve. But can the average poor or lower-income family do that?"

"No!" was the resounding answer from the congregation.

"Can a single mother who is working two jobs to make a better life for herself and her family afford to do that?" asked Colfax.

"No!"

"Is it fair that only lower-income families be stuck in the worst schools?"

"No!"

Pausing, Colfax lowered his voice and asked the congregation how many remembered the day George Wallace stood outside the school in Birmingham and didn't let black students enter. "How many of you are familiar with that particular bit of history?" asked Colfax as he raised his hand to show that he wanted those who recalled the incident to also raise their hands.

Most raised their hands.

"Well, just as it was wrong for Governor Wallace to stand outside those doors and block black kids from entering, it is wrong for the professional teachers unions to stand outside the doors of the worst schools in America and not let your children leave!"

More and louder amens followed.

Colfax went on to praise the teachers who worked in inner-city schools, but Mance turned off the videotape before Leider could hear those remarks. He also did not hear Colfax's proposal to use the money saved from eliminating the oil, gas and ethanol subsidies to help increase pay for inner-city teachers. Nor did he hear how Colfax's own experience of receiving a hardship scholarship after his father's death shaped his thinking on this issue. Such information did not suit either Jacob Mance's or Win Murdock's purposes.

"Judy, Joe," said Mance, who now had their complete attention, "I trust you agree that Colfax is not only growing in stature but he also poses a potentially significant threat to your two organizations. If Byrne and Prescott direct all their ammunition at each other, the only beneficiary is Colfax. If Colfax is the beneficiary, your groups lose." Leider and Forsythe looked at one another. Mance's reasoning made sense.

Mance proceeded to outline the other organizations that belonged to the coalition and how the campaign to educate the public about Colfax would be conducted. After he was done, Mance requested—and received—$500,000 commitments from Forsythe and Leider. Each promised to provide more if necessary. They also agreed they would activate their members against Colfax at the appropriate time.

Satisfied with the additional one million dollars he had raised for the coalition, Mance returned to his spacious, Capitol-view office where his executive assistant handed him a note saying that Stephanie Freeberg of the Center for Ethical and Responsive Politics had called twice. She wanted to ask him a few questions about the Coalition for a Prosperous New Millennium. He smiled. He had no intention of returning her call.

* *

The scene would have looked ridiculous if the outcome that it sought to settle were not so serious. Six Republican candidates, all in crisp blue suits and solid red ties, nervously chatted with one another as they waited for the start of the only scheduled debate before the Iowa caucuses. This would be most Iowans' only opportunity to see and hear all the candidates. The political pundits were predicting that only the top three finishers would survive and move on to the New Hampshire primary.

Last-minute makeup was being applied to the foreheads of the candidates, and those with thinning hair had a little applied to their pate so as not to draw unwanted attention to this unpresidential characteristic. A few reviewed note cards, mostly on obscure farm policy.

Governor Prescott was present, as was former Senator and Ambassador to India Benjamin Walsh. Senator Jack Quinn, a decorated Air Force pilot; Ryan Glynn, a boyish-looking congressman; Stanley Cross, the multimillionaire; and Dick Graham, the arch-conservative former television talk host, were also on stage.

Unbeknownst to Prescott or his campaign, the campaign managers of other participants had secretly gathered on the fourteenth floor of the Marriott Hotel the night before and devised an orchestrated strategy to focus all attacks on Prescott. Quinn's campaign manager had declined to attend—and then only on specific instructions from his candidate, who did not believe in negative campaigning. The strategy was not unexpected by the Prescott campaign, but the level of its sophistication and its mean-spiritedness were.

From the opening question, Prescott was on the defensive. Benjamin Walsh, a thirty-year veteran of the Washington establishment, questioned Prescott's experience, noting that Prescott had only been the governor of Pennsylvania for five years. Dick Graham, playing to the cultural conservatives, hammered away at Prescott's comment about "the Supreme Court already settling the abortion debate." The others also chimed in on this point, hoping to curry favor with religious conservatives.

Congressmen Glynn attacked Prescott for "a lack of boldness" in his call for a ten-percent tax cut. Stanley Cross criticized as "squeamish" Prescott's unwillingness to privatize Social Security and went on to deride the governor's call for "common-sense conservatism" as an affront to every conservative in America.

Only Quinn refused to attack Prescott and instead chose to use his few minutes to focus on campaign finance reform, a strong national defense, and an open policy on immigration and trade. The other candidates ignored him.

When the debate concluded at 8:00 P.M., Prescott was like a prizefighter who had withstood fifteen punishing rounds: bruised and bloodied but still standing. All the candidates shook hands and smiled until the camera lights faded. The only one to shake Prescott's hand after the lights went off was Senator Quinn. "Are you still enjoying your status as frontrunner, Elliott?" he asked with a slight smile.

"Wouldn't have it any other way," responded Prescott. Quinn knew he was telling the truth. Being the frontrunner had some downsides—like being ganged up on—but the upside was that raising money was a hell of a lot easier. Everyone loved to back a winner.

"Well, by Wednesday, I suspect you'll only have two of us attacking you instead of five."

"Small comfort," said Prescott. "By the way, Jack, I want you to know that I noticed that you took the high road tonight. I appreciate that."

"You're welcome," said Quinn, who had a reputation as one of the Senate's true gentlemen. "Good luck on Tuesday."

As Quinn was walking away, Prescott called out to him. "Jack?"

"Yes?"

"If things don't work out for you on Tuesday, I'd like to sit down with you afterward and talk about how we might be able to work together. I'd like to ask for your endorsement. In return, I'm sure my finance people would be happy to discuss ways I might be able to help you retire the debt your campaign has accumulated." Quinn's face went blank. "I know you're close to one million dollars in the red," added Prescott. The message was perfectly clear to Quinn: support me and I'll take care of your debt. Stay in the race—and I'll make your life hell.

Appalled by Prescott's thinly veiled bribe, Quinn repressed his anger. He knew how the game was played, but he was surprised that Prescott thought that he, of all people, would play it. Instead, Quinn graciously replied that there were still significant areas of disagreement between themselves. He decided right then that he could never support Prescott.

* *

For thirty-five straight years, Colfax had spoken with Father Otto Wilhoit on January 21. Wilhoit always expected the call. It was the anniversary of the suicide of Colfax's father.

"How are you, Robert?"

"I've been better. I'm sitting in a small, grimy hotel a thousand miles from Linda and the girls, and I'm exhausted. The campaign is grueling. I've been in either Iowa or New Hampshire seven of the last ten days. At least the hard work is beginning to show results."

"But you're not calling to discuss the campaign," said Wilhoit.

"No," replied Colfax, letting out a sigh. "Even after all of our discussions and all the books I've read, I can't help but feel as though I was partially responsible."

"Robert, your father was depressed. He was also sick. Gambling is an addiction. Nothing you did or didn't do could have contributed to his death, despite what his note said. Truth be told, if he would have just said that he was having difficulty paying your tuition, the school would have worked something out. But he didn't."

"I know. He was too proud to ask for help."

"Well, you finally have the opportunity to do something about it."

"What do you mean?"

"You're running for president, right?"

"I'm glad you noticed," deadpanned Colfax.

"Why are you taking on the tobacco industry?" asked Wilhoit.

"Because I saw what their product did to my mother—and millions of others."

"Right. Why don't you do the same thing with the gambling industry?"

"They call themselves the 'gaming' industry," replied Colfax, with more than a touch of sarcasm.

"Whatever—the gaming industry is wreaking havoc on untold numbers of families. The government shouldn't be in the business of gambling. You have the chance to do something about it, Robert."

Colfax knew he was right.

The following day, with no polls or advice from his staff, Colfax outlined his anti-gambling initiative. In addition to increased regulations on the industry and a complete ban on gambling advertising, he proposed an extensive counseling program financed through higher taxes on gambling.

* *

The escape had been easier than Manning had expected. The sturdy Jeep was right where Baptista said it would be. It helped that Seselj's body wasn't found for six hours. The young Kosovar woman had not checked on Seselj when he didn't come in from the veranda for fear that he would rape her again. Eventually, she fell asleep.

When it was finally determined that the shot that killed Seselj had been the work of a sniper, Manning was 150 kilometers away from Pristina in a remote and uninhabited section of northwestern Kosovo, waiting to be evacuated.

The sun was just rising on January 23, 2000, when Manning activated the radio and established a link with Baptista informing him through a code that the mission was accomplished. Baptista received the news around 10:00 P.M., Washington, D.C., time. Immediately, he informed the team leader of the Balkan Office of the Central Intelligence Agency, who in turn chose to confirm the news before notifying his boss, Jeffery Payne, the deputy director of the CIA.

An hour later, the CIA's best informant in Pristina, the one who learned that Seselj liked to frequent the chalet during his visits to the region, confirmed that Manning had been successful.

For the next ten hours, Manning waited in near-freezing temperatures to leave Kosovo. When the sun finally set, the former Marine activated a remote sensing device. In twenty minutes, a sleek black helicopter landed a football field's length away from where Manning was hiding.

The hundred-yard dash strained Manning's legs, still stiff from staying motionless for nearly three days in subzero temperatures. Under the cloak of darkness, Manning was hoisted aboard by a man dressed in dark camouflage, and the helicopter departed war-torn Kosovo as secretly as it arrived.

Half a world away, Robert Colfax was responding to a seemingly harmless question from the editorial board of the *Des Moines Daily Tribune*. His answer would trigger a chain of events that would ultimately bring Lee Manning's rifle scope to bear on his head.

* *

The first fifteen minutes of the editorial board did not go well. The focus had been on ethanol. Colfax was vehemently opposed to the continued subsidization of the product and tried to convince the four members of the editorial board that the elimination of the subsidy would not wreak havoc on Iowa's economy. Colfax used his own experience in eliminating ethanol subsidies in Minnesota three years earlier to demonstrate that the product could become competitive without government money. He also emphasized that he was not just opposed to ethanol subsidies, he was opposed to all corporate subsidies.

"Look, you heard the debate between the Republican candidates yesterday. Everyone of them except Senator Quinn supported ethanol. Why? I'll tell you why," said Colfax, taking time to look at each board member. "Because they know that if they are to have a snowball's chance in hell of surviving the Iowa caucuses and moving on to the New Hampshire primary, they have to pay homage to ethanol. Why else would three of them have changed their position on the subsidy since they decided to run for the White House?" asked Colfax. "Do you really believe that they think we should be supporting huge conglomerates like Holten, Inc.? Or are they supporting ethanol because it's the politically expedient thing to do?"

The board members knew what Colfax said was true; they had just never heard a candidate say it so plainly. "The problem," Colfax continued "is that once they support ethanol in Iowa, they will feel obliged to support subsidies to the defense industry to win California, and gas and oil subsidies to win Texas, and protective tariffs for oranges and tomatoes to win Florida. The list goes on and on. Ultimately, it's the American consumer who loses. Each time we support a subsidy, the American consumer ends up paying more money. It doesn't make sense. It's not good policy, and it's not good for the American people."

As the board listened to Colfax's reasoning, at least two of its members began to detect the leadership qualities that had been missing in the other candidates they had already interviewed. An endorsement of Colfax, reasoned Daniel Steward, the publisher, might push the two leading candidates, Prescott and Byrne, to take more substantive positions.

The interview continued along with questions about tax policy, crime, gun control, domestic abuse, immigration policy, Social Security and Medicare reform, and education policy. The board, while not sympathetic to all of Colfax's positions, came away impressed with his level of understanding about each issue and the conviction and passion he brought to the issues.

The interview next turned to foreign affairs. Colfax answered questions about the United Nations, the North Atlantic Treaty Organization, the International Monetary Fund, the World Trade Organization, and the North American Free Trade Agreement. Eventually the conversation moved to defense spending.

"Governor Colfax, you have said that there is still room for the defense budget to be squeezed. Could you elaborate?" asked Gerry Malcolm, the senior political reporter and twenty-one-year veteran of the *Des Moines Daily Tribune*.

Nodding his head in an indication that Malcolm had asked a good question, Colfax responded. "For the last few minutes, I have been answering questions about the U.N., NATO, WTO, IMF, NAFTA—seemingly every possible acronym. What has made answering some of the questions difficult is our lack of quality information. For example, without good intelligence, how can we know if the U.N. is effective in Baghdad? How can NATO be effective unless we know if Serbia is taking our threats seriously—without good intelligence? And how, without good intelligence, can we be sure that economic resources being sent to China or Pakistan are being used in ways that are not detrimental to the security of the United States? We can't," continued Colfax. "It seems to me that we need fundamental reform of our intelligence community. We must start with the CIA. Despite spending billions of dollars, the CIA did not foresee the collapse of the Soviet Union; it did not predict Iraq's invasion of Kuwait; it let Aldrich Ames roam around for almost a decade before it discovered him; and it was caught completely unaware by India's nuclear detonation in 1998."

The board signaled their agreement with Colfax's remarks by scribbling furiously in their small handheld notebooks. Colfax then proceeded to outline his proposal to consolidate the Central Intelligence Agency, the Defense Intelligence Agency and the intelligence branches of the Army, Air Force and Navy under the auspices of the National Security Agency.

The proposal struck Daniel Steward as a good one and, ignoring the former-congressman-turned-lobbyist's request to write a stinging editorial against Colfax in return for a large under-the-table bribe, he used the idea in the paper's lead editorial to highlight the kind of fresh thinking that a Colfax presidency would bring to the country.

*   *

The first edition of the Sunday, January 23, 2000, *Des Moines Daily Tribune* hit the street around 1:00 P.M. on Saturday. Within minutes, news of the editorial was being reported on CNN. Minutes after that, David Luther, Murdock's top lieutenant, was on the phone to Jacob Mance, screaming, "Why the fuck are we paying you so goddamn much money if you can't even deliver a simple editorial for us?"

Mance had no response but offered to fire the former congressman who had been given the responsibility for ensuring Colfax was treated harshly in the *Des Moines Daily Tribune*.

Win Murdock was concerned by the editorial after reading it, but not being a man to anger easily, instead picked up the phone and called a man with whom he had established a friendship years earlier at Washington's annual Gridiron Dinner. At the time, Jeffery Payne had been an obscure assistant secretary of Defense. Today, he was deputy director of the CIA, the number two man. He hoped to be number one in the next administration.

"Jeffery, this is Win Murdock," he said after being patched through on a direct line on which only select individuals, including the director of the CIA and the president, could reach the deputy director.

"How are you, Win? To what do I owe the pleasure of your call?"

Murdock didn't waste any time. "Have you seen the lead editorial of the *Sunday Des Moines Daily Tribune?*"

"No," replied Payne thinking that at seventy-seven years of age, Murdock's legendary mental acuity had finally begun to slip.

"Do you have access to CNN or the Internet?"

"Both," replied Payne.

"Then access CNN's web site and download a copy of the editorial."

"What's this about, Win?" asked Payne with more than a hint of annoyance in his voice.

"It's about you and me both being screwed if Colfax becomes a legitimate candidate for the presidency. That's what this is about."

"Let me put you on speaker phone," said Payne, accessing the Internet and trying to figure out what Colfax had to do with his position at the CIA.

"Do you know Colfax very well?" asked Murdock, as Payne was locating the editorial.

"We had a few run-ins when I was an assistant secretary of Defense and he was secretary of Navy. He could be a real pain in the ass. Even back then, his reputation as a maverick was well-established." Finding the article, Payne said, "I've got it."

"Read it."

Payne quickly absorbed the article and softly said, "I see your point."

"Jeffery, it appears Governor Colfax is extremely critical of your agency and, if he has his way, he'll put you out of a job."

"And I assume it is Colfax's position on ethanol and oil subsidies—and not the CIA—that has your attention," said Payne.

"Among other things," replied Murdock. "I think it would be in our mutual self-interest to get together to discuss this matter. Does Tuesday at ten o'clock work for you? No, let's make it Wednesday. I want to see how Colfax fares in Iowa."

"That would be fine," said Payne, knowing full well that he would make whatever time Murdock selected. Payne was not about to slight the one man who could help him achieve his lifelong dream of becoming director of the CIA.

"Good. I'll have my assistant, David Luther, arrange the time and place. Have a good day, Jeffery." Payne would have had a good day—if not for Murdock's phone call. In the moments preceding the call, he had been savoring the news that his assistant, Raphael Baptista, had provided him minutes earlier: Seselj was dead and the CIA's newest asset, Lee Manning, was being extracted safely from the region.

CHAPTER TEN

The mild, almost springlike temperatures had given way to a cold front overnight. The result was a thick, heavy blanket of wet snow that covered most of Iowa. The combination of weather and a relentless barrage of negative advertising for almost forty days resulted in a near record low turnout for the Iowa caucuses.

Still, thousands of farmers, housewives, mechanics, accountants, retirees, and students trudged to schools, churches, libraries, community centers, and firehouses all across Iowa for the purpose of supporting a particular candidate for the presidency of the United States of America.

Four years of campaigning, four years of speaking to small groups, four years of bad chicken dinners and traveling to Iowa at least once a month for most candidates was about to come to a head. Benjamin Walsh had been campaigning almost nonstop since 1992; a second-place finish in Iowa in 1996 had only fueled his ambition and caused him to redouble his efforts. He would end the night bitterly disappointed by his poor performance, cursing the influence of big money or at least his inability to raise it.

As seven o'clock rolled around, each campaign was still desperately calling their respective precinct captains trying to gauge the effectiveness of their turnout efforts. The wet snow was causing many voters to stay home. As expected, each campaign was experiencing a significantly lower level of success than desired. There were two exceptions: the campaigns of the archconservative activist Dick Graham and Governor Robert Colfax.

Graham, as he had in 1992 and 1996, used his skills as orator and his unique brand of prairie populism to fire up his supporters through fear, bigotry, and raw emotion. Colfax, through the help of Josh Parker and his network of college students, was getting a very strong turnout of supporters around the campuses of Iowa's universities and colleges. Most of the students were so close to their precinct caucus location that weather was not a factor.

Since the governor had announced his candidacy in October, the Colfax campaign had also been extremely busy identifying people throughout Iowa who would participate in caucuses. Most supporters had volunteered through the Internet. A few had watched Colfax make his announcement at the Headwaters of the Mississippi. Some had seen his remarks before the National Small Business Coalition on C-SPAN II, and an even greater number had volunteered within the last few days as a result of the editorial endorsement. Colfax's few television commercials had also succeeded in driving people to his web site.

The end result was that Colfax had a functional campaign organization in every one of Iowa's ninety-nine counties and at least one supporter in 2,056 of Iowa's 2,142 caucus meetings. In terms of raw numbers, Colfax was only outdone by the vice president's well-oiled machine and Elliott Prescott's impressive organization, which was the best money could buy.

Ultimately, the Iowa caucuses had become a game in which the goal was to meet or exceed the expectations that the media placed on a campaign. A candidate's standing at the end of the night bore little resemblance to his actual numbers. If a candidate received more support than expected, the candidate was deemed a winner and allowed to proceed to New Hampshire. If the candidate fell short of the expectation, he was placed in the loser category and treated harshly by the media. Raising money also became more difficult. It was widely assumed in political circles that only three of the six Republican candidates would advance to New Hampshire.

The expectations game required that campaign managers assess their candidate's prospects such that they would finish better than expected by the media.

Pete Sawyer played the game as well as any. He had spent the days preceding the caucuses working the phones. To the *Washington Post* reporter, to whom he had only days earlier been talking about the campaign's use of the Internet, he now downplayed the reports that Colfax was doing well on college campuses by reminding him that college students were notoriously bad about getting engaged in politics—especially in the dead of winter. To the *New York Times* reporter, he spun the tale that the *Des Moines Daily Tribune* editorial endorsement was meaningless, reminding her that other thoughtful candidates had received important endorsements only to lose to less honest and less thoughtful, but better financed, opponents.

Both reporters, and most others with whom Sawyer spoke, agreed that Colfax's odds of defying political convention were minimal. Most accepted at face value Sawyer's comment that if Colfax could garner five percent in either the Republican or Democratic caucuses, that would be a significant victory.

* *

Josh Parker finished the lasagna dinner with twenty-three of his fraternity broth-ers and reminded all of them of their earlier promise to attend precinct caucuses. Only one excused himself from his democratic duty professing he had to fulfill his student-worker obligation at the university athletic center, where he handed out bas-ketballs and towels.

Parker thanked his brothers again, quickly ran over the basic rules governing a precinct caucus and concluded with a short, fiery speech about why Robert Colfax would make an excellent president. He then asked if anyone had a preference for attending either the Republican or Democratic caucus. Almost three-fourths chose to attend the Republican caucus. The figure was about what Parker had expected from his mostly white, suburban fraternity brothers.

En masse, the men of Theta Chi trudged over to the small church directly behind the fraternity house and presented themselves in unequal numbers to the chairs of the Republican and Democratic caucuses. Fifteen minutes later, aided by scores of other students from Drake, Parker had organized the Colfax caucus for the Democratic Party and his best friend, Steve Bell, did the same at the Republican cau-cus. It wasn't even eight o'clock before the first caucus, from the small church behind the Theta Chi fraternity house, was reporting to the Republican and Democratic headquarters in downtown Des Moines the first victories for a person who didn't even belong to their parties—Robert Colfax, the independent governor of Minnesota.

The scene soon replayed itself in Ames, Iowa City, and Cedar Falls. Unexpectedly, Colfax picked up caucuses in Dubuque, Indianola, Mason City, and a host of communities close to the Minnesota border. By nine o'clock, the major tele-vision anchors, who had made their quadrennial pilgrimage to Iowa's capital, had begun reporting on the "Colfax factor."

By 9:30, two political pundits from NBC were suggesting that any candidate who failed to get a higher vote total than Colfax in their own party's caucus could kiss goodbye the prospects of becoming president in 2000. One pundit went so far as to speculate that any candidate incapable of beating Colfax could never sufficiently recover from the humiliation to ever again be considered a legitimate presidential contender.

By ten o'clock, the prospect of not beating Colfax was becoming a distinct possibility for three of the Republican candidates. Former Senator and Ambassador Benjamin Walsh, who had been running for presidency nonstop since 1992 and had made over two hundred visits to Iowa in the last fourteen months, garnered only three percent of the vote. Senator Jack Quinn, the only candidate besides Colfax to abstain from negative campaigning, did only marginally better at four percent. Congressman Glynn was barely a factor receiving only one percent.

Shortly after ten o'clock, the ABC affiliate was the first to declare Governor Prescott the winner of the Republican caucuses with a projected thirty-five percent of the vote. Dick Graham received twenty-nine percent—attributed largely to his campaign's massive get-out-the-vote effort among religious conservatives. Millionaire Stanley Cross came in third with eighteen percent of the vote. His last-minute barrage of positive ads talking about his simple flat tax proposal resonated with a certain segment of the Iowa population. But at $350 a vote, this third-place finish was hardly an exercise in fiscal prudence—a trait Cross claimed to advocate. Colfax later joked that Cross' $350-a-vote effort made the old stories about the Pentagon paying $800 for a toilet seat look like a bargain.

But the story of the night was Governor Colfax's astounding fourth-place finish in the Republican caucuses. The pundits, all of whom had questioned the wisdom of the Colfax campaign engaging in such a risky strategy at the beginning of the night, were hours later praising the strategy, claiming in retrospect that he had little to lose. If the numbers didn't materialize, his campaign could say that they never expected to do well. But if he did do well, he could declare victory, say that people were dissatisfied with the two-party process, skip the rest of the caucuses and primaries, and move on to the general election. The pundits also speculated that Colfax benefited from the minority pro-choice block within the Republican Party that had no place to go with the all-male, pro-life slate of candidates. In truth that was only half the story. Colfax also did surprisingly well among religious conservatives, who liked his strong anti-gambling position.

The story only got bigger when the Democratic numbers began to take shape. The vice president easily won the Democratic caucuses, but, from the perspective of the media, he lost the all-important expectations game. Vice President Byrne was expected to receive over two-thirds of all delegates. His inability to meet that number was being portrayed by one political analyst as the "first serious chink in the Byrne armor." Another claimed that the "Byrne juggernaut has experienced a serious assault on two—possibly three—different fronts." The anchor asked the analyst if the evening's results might cause John Gordon, the cerebral former senator, to consider reentering the race.

"David," replied the analyst with a serious, foreboding tone in his deep voice, "that must be going through Senator Gordon's mind as we speak. As you recall, he withdrew from the race a few months ago, citing his frustration with his inability to raise money. By virtue of the vice president's less-than-stellar performance, those money gates may now open a little easier."

"Does the vice president also now have a problem in the form of Congressman Reginald Greene?" asked the anchor. "Do you think the thirty-one percent he received represents a strong statement for him, or is it more of an anti-Byrne vote?"

"That's the question, David," replied the analyst. "One school of thought says that Greene is now the vice president's top challenger by virtue of his strong showing. The other school says that, given Governor Colfax's strong performance in the Democratic caucuses, Gordon probably would have picked up many of those Colfax supporters. A strong argument could be made that had Gordon stayed in the race, a lot of Greene's supporters would have gone with him. Using that reasoning, if Gordon chooses to reenter the race, I think he'll become the top challenger to Byrne."

"I'd like to go back to your comment about Governor Colfax," said the anchor. "The Republicans are still trying to figure out his fourth-place finish in their caucuses, and I suspect the Democrats are trying to do the same with his third-place finish in theirs. But you said earlier that a lot of Colfax's supporters would have gone to Gordon. Why?"

"I based those remarks on the assumption that Senator Gordon's slightly more fiscally conservative positions and his position on campaign finance reform more closely mirror those of Governor Colfax," replied the analyst. "Therefore, those Colfax supporters who liked his positions on those issues would probably have gone with Gordon."

"It appears that many of Colfax's supporters were first-time caucus attendees. Reports from the colleges and universities are showing record numbers for Colfax. Do you really think those students would have supported Gordon?" asked the anchor in a tone that was meant to convey his own superior political instincts.

Ignoring the snub, the analyst tried to recover by saying that a portion of Colfax's support may have gone to Gordon.

"Well, what looked like was going to be a quiet night for both the vice president and Governor Prescott has turned into quite a night," said the anchor, wrapping up the interview. "It is now a seven-day sprint to New Hampshire."

* *

Jacob Mance never liked Tony Costello. His flashy style, large gold jewelry, perennial tan and sleek coiffure rubbed him the wrong way. Mance especially hated having to pay a $500 bar and restaurant tab and listen to Costello brag about all the jobs being created by the gambling industry.

"It's true, Jacob," said Costello, taking a long drawn out drag on his obnoxious Indonesian clove cigarette. "My industry has created over a million jobs in the last fifteen years. No politician is going to fuck with us."

"That's where you're wrong," replied Mance. "If Colfax keeps gaining in the polls, the gambling industry is going to start taking some hits. His proposal to ban all gambling advertising helped him in Iowa."

"Iowa is filled with a bunch of backwater hog farmers, and Colfax is a cock-sucker. The odds of that douche bag actually getting to the White House are a hundred to one."

"He's more serious than you think. We've done some polling—he's catching on with women and younger voters," said Mance, handing Costello a copy of the poll results.

"Are these numbers for real?"

"They are."

"Well, what the fuck are you doing about it?"

Four drinks and an expensive meal later, after he explained the coalition to Costello, Mance received a personal commitment for one million dollars, plus Costello's promise to get another dozen gambling executives to contribute $100,000 each to the Coalition for a Prosperous New Millennium.

* *

The television ad grossly distorted Colfax's limited tax on gambling to help finance counseling. The viewer was led to believe Colfax wanted to raise all taxes. The thirty-second piece urged its listeners to "Call Robert Colfax and tell him we don't need higher taxes." They were informed by a tiny line at the bottom of their television screen that the commercial was paid for and prepared by the Coalition for a Prosperous New Millennium. Most viewers paid no attention to the source of the commercial.

* *

The morning following the Iowa caucuses, Congressman Glynn made his expected departure from the race, declaring that his campaign had not been in vain because his call for a fifteen-percent, across-the-board tax cut was now being championed by Governor Prescott, whom he was proud to endorse. The real reason he endorsed Prescott was that he harbored a dream that he could be the governor's vice presidential candidate. It was, in fact, the only reason he had entered the race in the first place—to raise his political profile.

Later that afternoon, Benjamin Walsh also withdrew from the race. Unlike Glynn, he did not endorse Prescott; instead, he chose to stay in attack mode and declare the governor to be "the wrong man, with the wrong message, at the wrong time." He surprised many by endorsing Stanley Cross. Pundits speculated that Walsh, who had spent six years chasing his dream, was jealous that it was Prescott and not himself whom the Washington establishment had selected as the man to recapture the White House for the Republicans.

Only Jack Quinn, among those who didn't fare better than Governor Colfax, stayed in the race. A political maverick, the former Air Force pilot who had been shot down over Vietnam and survived three months on his own in the jungle, decided to press on to New Hampshire. He did this against the advice of his wife, campaign manager, and top campaign supporters.

Robert Colfax spent the next morning being interviewed by the *Today Show*, *Good Morning America*, and two other television programs—one in Manchester, New Hampshire and the other from a station in Boston that covered a large portion of the New Hampshire market. Later in the afternoon, Colfax and his small campaign staff sat down for a teleconference call with his top two hundred supporters, who were listening in from various locations around the country. In the call, Pete Sawyer outlined the strategy for New Hampshire, and Colfax reiterated that because he had committed to only matching the money that individuals sent in, it was imperative that he continue to raise money to show his campaign was being supported by the public. Colfax concluded by asking all two hundred supporters to raising a thousand dollars apiece before the New Hampshire primary. Ed Kielty, the software developer, and Jane Olive, the mayor of Burlington, were among those who began working the phones immediately.

Sawyer added that the money was necessary to counter a barrage of negative television and radio ads that had already begun to inundate the airways of New Hampshire. "It is unclear to us who, exactly, is sponsoring the negative ad campaign. The organization goes by the name of the Coalition for a Prosperous New Millennium. All we know is that it is being run by a Washington law firm with a long history of engaging in nasty, negative political warfare."

"Can you speculate?" asked Lance Williams, who made his fortune in the pharmaceutical industry by developing databases that mined genetic information. Williams was backing Colfax because the candidate mirrored his free trade and libertarian beliefs.

"I can't really," responded Sawyer. "Under current Federal Election Commission guidelines, the organization is under no obligation to report their contributors."

"You mean any asshole off the street could contribute a million dollars to this coalition and there is no way for the public to find out?" asked Williams.

"That's right."

"And this group—or coalition—can run as much negative advertising against Governor Colfax as it wants?" asked Erica Yeager, a financial planner who liked Colfax's position on allowing people to invest a portion of their Social Security contributions in personal retirement accounts.

"That's right, Erica," said Colfax, recognizing the distinctive nasally tone of her voice.

"Well, you've got my support, Bob," she said, referring to Colfax by the name only his closest friends used. "In fact, I'll commit to raising $10,000 before next Tuesday. Damned if I'm going let a group of spineless and faceless weasels engage in political character assassination."

"So will I," added Williams. "I'm so sick and tired of the all this Washington bullshit. We've gotta change things."

"I agree," said Colfax.

"The momentum you created in Iowa is fantastic," added Kielty, "I have no doubt you will now become a target for a lot of people and organizations. I'll do whatever I can to help you."

"Thank you," replied Sawyer. "As campaign manager, I am sensing that we haven't pushed all of you to do enough. Let's raise the goal. If the campaign can do anything to help you raise the money, please contact us through our web site, and we'll respond within an hour."

After the teleconference broke up, Sawyer said to Colfax, "Erica's comment about character assassination reminded me: the Secret Service contacted me this morning and requested a meeting. Based on your performance in Iowa, they are recommending that you accept their protective services."

"It was our performance, not my performance, Pete," replied Colfax. "Regarding Secret Service protection, I guess it's inevitable, but I'd prefer to wait until after New Hampshire."

"Are you sure that's wise? I mean you're now a legitimate threat to a lot of people."

"Yes," replied Colfax matter-of-factly.

That afternoon, Sawyer informed Colfax that Secret Service Agent Sean McGowan would be coming to the governor's mansion the following Wednesday, the day after the New Hampshire primary, for a preliminary briefing.

* *

Scheduling Win Murdock's luncheon meetings in Washington, D.C., had always been one of David Luther's easier jobs as Holten's top lobbyist. He would either use Murdock's assigned table at the Monocle restaurant near the Capitol or the more secluded dining facilities at the Congressional Country Club, just outside Washington, for more discreet meetings. Murdock's meetings with Jeffery Payne, deputy director of the CIA, always fell in the latter category.

Payne arrived at the restaurant five minutes before the appointed meeting time, as was his custom, and was escorted to the back room by the elderly maître d' who had seen enough power players during his forty years in the business to be thoroughly unimpressed with the deputy director of the CIA. Win Murdock, whom he had been escorting to the same back table since Lyndon Johnson was Senate majority leader, was an entirely different matter. The maître d' knew that his cherished position, along with the handsome tips that had paid for his three daughters' college educations, would be gone in a heartbeat if Murdock was in any way displeased with his service. So when Murdock was seated at his table, his usual drink and salad already awaited him.

"Good afternoon, Jeffery," said Murdock, gesturing to Payne not to get up.

"Good afternoon, Mr. Murdock," replied the ambitious Payne. "It appears that you again were prescient in your estimation of Minnesota's governor."

"Indeed. But not even I could have predicted that the son of a bitch would do so well in both the Democratic and Republican caucuses," said Murdock in a tone that revealed how concerned he was about Colfax. "Add up his combined votes, and he came in a solid third—behind only Byrne and Prescott."

"What do you think his strategy is?" asked Payne.

"I think he's made his point. He wanted to be recognized as a legitimate contender," replied Murdock, adding, "And now he is, thanks to the incompetence of the Republican and Democratic parties and the media."

"Why is he campaigning in New Hampshire then?" asked Payne.

"He's got a hell of a lot of momentum coming out of Iowa. I think he's going to try to parlay the free media exposure into another successful showing in New Hampshire so that he can say that Iowa wasn't some sort of fluke based on his being a governor of a neighboring state."

"And then if he does well," suggested Payne, "he'll stop playing the presidential primary game, say he's proved himself a contender and just move on to the general election?"

"Exactly," said Murdock. "It's a brilliant strategy. He uses the smaller 'retail' politic states, where his brand of campaigning is effective, to prove his mettle, then he skips the bigger states like New York and California where he doesn't have the money to compete." Murdock added, "The beauty of his plan is that he will just sit back and let the Republicans and Democrats kick the shit out of themselves as they all chase the endorsement. I mean Cross, with his millions, is going to bombard Prescott with negative ads, and Graham and his band of right-wing fanatics are going to beat the bushes for supporters. While Greene, with his focus on the poor and disaffected, will likely find a sympathetic home among the lefties in the Democratic primary."

"Jesus Christ, you're right. Graham and Cross are going to force Prescott to cater to the far right, and Greene could make the vice president kneel before the altar of every liberal special interest group there is."

"All the while, Governor Colfax will be sitting on the sideline, picking up the disaffected moderate members of both major political parties," added Murdock. "Moderate Republicans already like his socially liberal views, and centrist Democrats like his positions on controlling government spending, free trade, and immigration. If Byrne goes too far left, they'll abandon him for Colfax in the bat of an eye. Same thing happens if Prescott decides to give social issues too much prominence is his campaign. They'll win the fringe vote but lose the center."

The maître d' broke up the conversation when he entered the room to serve the lobster bisque. He then took the orders and cleared off the salad plates.

"Well, I assume you didn't come here to discuss the campaign strategy of Bob Colfax," said Payne.

"You're right. As we discussed earlier, I believe we would both mutually benefit from Governor Colfax's prompt departure from the presidential race," said Murdock as he stared at the deputy director squarely in the eye and sipped a spoonful of soup.

"We would," replied Payne.

"The purpose of this meeting, then, is to brief you on an organization that is dedicated to that mutually shared goal." For the next ten minutes, Win Murdock outlined the strategy the Coalition for a Prosperous New Millennium was employing against Colfax. By the end, Payne was convinced that Colfax had no chance of escaping the barrage of negative advertising that was on the horizon.

"Impressive," said Payne when it was clear that Murdock was done.

"However," continued Murdock, "you know that I am a man of caution and I value planning. That leads me to how I believe you can help us in our shared effort."

"Continue," said Payne, seeing that the old man was trying to get a read on his reaction.

"For the last thirty years, Holten and the CIA have enjoyed a mutually beneficial relationship. Our facilities in over a hundred different countries have served your agency and the interests of the United States government very well." Payne was well aware that Holten had always been willing to provide cover to the CIA's economic and espionage officers, and he was also aware that Murdock was not above calling on the agency to return the favor. This was clearly one of those occasions. Payne also knew that if he wanted to become the next CIA director in the new administration of either Martin Byrne or Elliott Prescott, it would be in his interest to accommodate Murdock.

"I would like to ask two things," said Murdock. "First, I would like your agents currently working on our payrolls to channel some financial contributions to the coalition. This will allow the coalition to claim even wider support." Murdock then listed the companies and organizations already members of the coalition.

"Consider it done," replied Payne after he received assurances from Murdock that the funds would be reimbursed. "And the second item?"

"As I said, Jeffery, I'm a man who values planning—particularly contingency planning. I rose to my current position because of my skills as a commodity trader, where I learned to hedge my bets—both business and political." Murdock paused to again gauge Payne's reaction, which was receptive. Murdock knew how much he wanted to be the next CIA director.

"My political instincts tell me Colfax can be stopped through our orchestrated advertising campaign. But my instincts also tell me that Colfax is a smart political animal, and he won't easily be defeated—especially since he is independently wealthy. This concern, together with my penchant for hedging my bets, necessitates a contingency plan."

"And this is where I come in?" asked Payne.

"Your agency," Murdock corrected him. "I don't think I have to remind you that if Mr. Colfax becomes our forty-third president, the Central Intelligence Agency will not exist in its current form."

"I'm aware of his consolidation plan."

"Good," said Murdock, steering the conversation in the direction that he wanted. "I read with great interest about the assassination of General Seselj the other day. The circumstances surrounding the assassination are very mysterious but seem to have all the signs of a classic agency operation."

Smiling, Payne responded, "Win, as you are well aware, a great many people—and countries—wanted Seselj dead." Murdock knew by Payne's reaction that the CIA was behind Seselj's assassination.

"Of course."

"And you are also aware that it is the official policy of the United States government not to engage foreign targets," replied Payne, repeating the standard line that all intelligence experts use when dealing with the public.

"Of course. I'm merely suggesting that whoever assassinated Seselj had a contingency plan."

"And you would like my agency's help in developing a contingency plan for Robert Colfax?"

"Precisely," said Murdock, signaling to the maître d' who was waiting by the door to deliver the grilled swordfish.

* *

Forty-five minutes later, Jeffery Payne left the restaurant. Win Murdock stayed behind and enjoyed a rare afternoon glass of port and a good Cuban cigar. His exit would not have been noticed except for the fact that Ellen Moriarty was eager to find out with whom the deputy director of the Central Intelligence Agency had been having lunch. She had been expecting to see someone like the chairman of the Senate Select Committee on Intelligence. She was surprised when she saw the legendary Win Murdock leave the same room. He walked by her without so much as a glance. Even if he had noticed her, he would not have had any idea who she was, what she did for a living, or why his lunch with the deputy director of the CIA might soon be a subject of interest in an Internet newsletter.

CHAPTER ELEVEN

The coalition's anti-Colfax attack strategy was orchestrated with military efficiency. The residents of nursing homes and assisted-living apartments began receiving brochures in the mail declaring, in big bold letters, that "Bob Colfax wants to invest your Social Security check in risky stocks!" Every New Hampshire teacher received a similar brochure proclaiming that Colfax's "destructive policies will destroy America's public education system." The farmers of New Hampshire were warned that he was not interested in saving the family farmer. Pro-life organizations were warned that a Colfax administration would mean another four—and possibly eight—years of "unfettered abortions." Their members were also told that the Colfax's libertarian views on gay and lesbian rights would throw the Supreme Court into "dangerously liberal waters." Union members received literature proclaiming that Colfax "was more interested in sending jobs to Mexico" than protecting their rights as American workers.

All of these actions were taking place below the radar screen—away from the watchful eye of the media. But they were having the intended affect on Colfax's popularity. In the air, the television stations of New Hampshire and the greater Boston area were bombarding the citizens of New Hampshire with an endless barrage of anti-Colfax ads. More often than not, a male announcer with a deep, serious voice would distort Colfax's position on a particular issue, while a grainy black-and-white photo of Colfax glared out from the screen. The commercials would then end with a colorful picture showing a vivid fall foliage and the announcer saying, in a more optimistic tone, "On Tuesday, February 1, remember to vote. New Hampshire needs someone who will represent New Hampshire values."

Like the direct mail pieces and the paid telephone calls, the television commercials were tailored to the demographics of the time slot and the show. In mid-morning, when a number of stay-at-home mothers were watching television, the commercials labeled Colfax "an anti-education advocate." During the nightly national news, when more seniors were likely to be watching, the ads proclaimed Colfax wanted to "cut Social Security and slash Medicare."

On the radio, farmers heard anti-Colfax commercials from 5:00 to 7:00 A.M. On progressive radio stations and around the universities and colleges of New Hampshire, students were told that Colfax wanted to raise the eligibility age for Medicare—"so that you might never get it!" They were exhorted to "Vote on February 1. Don't get ripped off." For four straight days, the ads and brochures were aimed with laser-like precision at their intended target groups.

"Jesus Christ, Governor" said Pete Sawyer, who never called the candidate anything other than 'Governor,' "we have got to respond to these ads. The polls are showing they're having a serious impact."

"Positive or negative?" asked Colfax with a sarcastic smile.

"This is serious, Governor. The bump we got from Iowa is gone. We're barely registering. Let me commission a poll to find out what kind of damage they're doing with certain voting groups and how we can best respond."

"No," said Colfax with a definitiveness that told Sawyer he would not reconsider the idea. "When I said that I wasn't going to conduct polls, I meant it."

"Did you also say that you were also just going to let special interest groups kick the shit out of you?" challenged Sawyer.

"I'll have to reread my speech," said Colfax, flashing his crooked smile. "I think I might have." Sawyer, who had always enjoyed Colfax's dry humor, cracked a smile.

Switching back to campaign manger mode, Sawyer said. "These ads have been airing since we arrived on Wednesday. And now we've got people showing up at forums with these brochures." Sawyer held up copies of the anti-Colfax pieces on Medicare and education for Colfax to see. "We can't just sit back and take this shit. Half of what they are saying are outright lies."

"I agree. It is almost time to go on the offensive."

"What do you mean, almost?" shot back Sawyer.

"Let's give the ads one more day. We'll begin responding tomorrow night."

"I'm not sure if there is any air time left between now and Tuesday. It seems as though the Coalition for a Prosperous New Millennium has purchased every last second of TV and radio time to proclaim to the citizens of New Hampshire that you are the Antichrist."

"See what you can find. I'm sure there must be some time on a few Boston stations," said Colfax.

* *

That afternoon, Sawyer purchased a few slots during the *Saturday Night Live* show and some more time during the highest rated sitcoms on Monday night.

Early the next morning, Colfax and Sawyer went into a recording studio in the Boston suburb of Braintree.

"I've got a script for you," said Sawyer, handing it to Colfax, who was deeply absorbed in an article in *The Economist* about the ramifications of the death of Serbian General Seselj.

Looking up, Colfax said, "It's too bad this son-of-a-bitch Seselj wasn't brought to trial and tried and convicted as a war criminal. I don't even think his own people knew the atrocities he was committing in their name." Almost in passing, Colfax added, "I can't understand how people like Dick Graham and Reginald Greene can honestly believe that America has no interest in preserving peace in Europe. Trying to close our eyes to the world's problems has never worked and it never will."

Sawyer, trying to get Colfax focused on the commercial, said, "I think you'll like the script."

"I've already got the commercial in my head," responded Colfax, who then turned his attention back to the article. Sawyer just shook his head incredulously.

"You mean you're not even going to read what I wrote? You're just going to wing it?" After a few seconds, Sawyer added, "I'll keep it handy just in case."

In the studio, a young man who had no idea that Colfax was a serious candidate for president applied makeup to the older man's forehead and touched up his hair. A few minutes later, Colfax was sitting on a tall, wooden stool about fifteen feet in front of a camera. Behind him was a gray screen that would later allow editors to insert graphics and other visual cues into the final version of the commercial. Looking into the camera with his warm and trusting eyes, Colfax began speaking.

"Hi, I'm Governor Robert Colfax, and I'm running for president. For the last few days, you have been hearing and seeing a lot of commercials about me. In fact, they are so numerous that even I can't avoid them," said Colfax, "and believe me, I try." The camera then panned out, which allowed for editors to later insert clips of the coalition ads. "Pretty scary stuff, those accusations. I'm not even sure I'd vote for myself—if they were true." Colfax paused and made a mischievous face. "Actually, I just wanted to come on TV and show you I don't have horns. I also wanted to announce that on behalf of you, the citizens of New Hampshire, I'm filing a restraining order against the Coalition for a Prosperous New Millennium. I believe they are unnecessarily harassing you. I mean, their brochures fill your doorways at home, they speak to you in your car on your way to work, and they broadcast their way into your home in the evening. Hell, if they could figure out to get into your dreams, they'd do it," deadpanned Colfax. "I'm joking, of course. I'm not going to file a restrain order. I can't. I'm not a lawyer—I promise." Colfax did not hold lawyers in high esteem. "I am, however, a candidate for president—which means I do want your vote. Unlike my opponents, however, I'm not going to barrage you with misleading ads or attack their motives. In fact, this will be my only commercial. I only ask that you visit my web site and find out where I really stand on the issues that are important to you. The future of this country is too important to be influenced by faceless special interest groups running misleading and distorted ads. You deserve better. Thank you and remember to vote this Tuesday." The screen then changed to the Colfax for President logo, and the address for his web site appeared.

By Sunday morning, the television stations in New Hampshire were running clips of the commercial on the local news. Even CNN ran a cut on its half-hour news segment. By noon, the Colfax campaign had put a copy of the commercial on its web site. By late Sunday night, the link had over 100,000 hits, many from residents of New Hampshire. The ad was so popular that those who hadn't yet seen it were calling the television stations asking when it was scheduled to air.

"Jacob," said David Luther, "you know that Mr. Murdock is not one to take chances. He likes to cover all his bases. In that vein, he asked that I ask you to use your influence with the members of the debate commission to effectively preclude Colfax from participating in the debates—just in case he is still in the race this fall."

"That's easier said than done."

"Don't bullshit me, Jacob. I know the Republicans and the Democrats have got the commission stacked. And I know that they'll will make it hard for Colfax to get into the debates anyway. Mr. Murdock wants you to make sure that they make it as difficult as possible. He is very interested in ensuring that Colfax does not receive a national platform on which to espouse his ideas, and he is especially interested in seeing that Colfax doesn't appear as an equal to either Prescott or Byrne. Mr. Murdock is willing to give you a bonus of a million dollars if you can influence the commission to set the hurdle for Colfax's entrance to be at least fifteen percent in a national polls. Make sure that the national polls listed as qualifying polls are all ones that we can influence. I think it would also be wise if the commission specified that the fifteen percent must be achieved among 'likely voters.'"

Mance smiled at the last suggestion. He knew "likely voters" tended to be established Republicans or Democrats—making it just that much harder for Colfax to gain entry into the debates.

Lee Manning spent the first few days back in the United States holed up in a comfortable hotel in the Washington suburb of Great Falls, Virginia. With little to do except read and watch television, the former Marine devoured every newspaper available at the hotel's small store. The *Washington Post* and the *New York Times* did an adequate job reporting on the mysterious circumstances of General Seselj's death, but the *London Observer* and the more conservative *Washington Times* provided Manning the most insightful reporting.

The *Observer* said that the Kosovo Liberation Army was taking credit for the assassination and warning other top Serbian officials that if they continued to harass and occupy portions of Kosovo, they would meet the same fate. The Serbs responded by stepping up their attacks against civilians, including children.

The *Observer* also reported that Seselj's death had shuffled the deck in terms of who was going to be Serbia's next president. Seselj's law-and-order policies had been gaining in popularity not only with the armed forces but also with the citizens. His death left no clear successor and set back Serbia's ambitions throughout the region. An editorial in the *Washington Post* called on America, Great Britain, and NATO to use the opportunity to their advantage and create a coherent strategy to bring peace to the region.

Manning reread the editorial and felt an immense amount of pride. A single bullet had stopped a number of horrible atrocities and created an opportunity for peace.

The *Washington Times* provided no more information about Seselj's death than the other papers; however, an article by a columnist unknown to Manning had a very intriguing idea about Seselj's death. The columnist speculated that any number of Western governments—including the United States, France, Great Britain and Germany—benefited from the assassination and should be considered as possible sponsors of the act. The writer suggested that Turkey was the main suspect because of that nation's large Muslim population and the strain that the government had felt at NATO's inability to bring Seselj and other Serbian war criminals to justice. Manning reread the article and wondered if Baptista's employer was the government of one of the European countries mentioned.

After finishing all the newspapers and scanning the news stations for more information about the death of Seselj, the sniper dialed the toll-free number to the Navy Federal Credit Union to check on the status of the growing bank account listed under the name of R.E. Lee Manning. Manning listened in amazement as the automated voice stated that the account held $126,000. The former Marine grabbed a cold beer from the wet bar and laughed out loud. "One hundred fifty-six thousand dollars richer and changing the world—I love it." The pain of the North Carolina trial had completely faded. "The Lord works in mysterious ways," thought Manning.

Just then the telephone rang. Manning immediately recognized Baptista's voice.

"Congratulations, Sergeant Manning. You do excellent work," said Baptista.

"Thank you," replied Manning, who been expecting the call—but not the praise—from the stoic Baptista.

"My employers are most pleased with your professionalism. They have asked, after a proper rest period for you, that we discuss a future assignment."

Manning said nothing, still unsure for whom Baptista worked.

"You will, of course, be compensated accordingly."

Once again, thought Manning, *The Lord works in mysterious ways*, adding out loud, "I'd be happy to talk with you."

* *

Josh Parker had been so thrilled at Colfax's astounding showing in Iowa that he asked his father what he thought about him taking the semester off and working full-time for the Colfax campaign. The campaign had offered him a job as the "Colfax campaign college coordinator," or "C4" for short. He told his father that he would be paid a small salary and that he could stay in Sawyer's apartment in Minneapolis until he could find his own efficiency.

His father agreed that it was a once-in-a-lifetime opportunity. A formal college education could be postponed a few months, he said. He even offered to pay for the apartment in Minneapolis. Parker declined, saying that he wanted to do it on his own.

* *

Parker's first full day on the job was Thursday, January 27. Immediately, he set about contacting students at the colleges in New Hampshire. The job was easy because in the last forty-eight hours, students from the University of New Hampshire, Daniel Webster College, Hesser, White Pines, Keene State, and Franklin Pierce had inundated the campaign office with e-mails, almost begging to get involved.

After cataloging the names and e-mail addresses of those who said they were students, Parker fired off a generic e-mail outlining the role they could play in the Colfax campaign. The task was simple and straightforward: they should e-mail as many of their friends and family members as possible and encourage them to write in Robert Colfax in the primary election of their choice. Colfax could not, according to New Hampshire law, appear on either the Republican or Democratic ballot.

By mid-afternoon, Parker had finished the listserv for New Hampshire college students when he decided to take a break and run down the street to the

SuperAmerica to get a super-large container of Mountain Dew. He needed the caffeine. As he approached the convenience store, he noticed a sign offering a free car wash with a full tank of gas. He recalled how much he hated having to hold the sign for his Little League baseball team car washes when the idea hit him. Without the benefit of the extra caffeine, he sprinted back to the campaign headquarters.

"Barb," he yelled, quickly catching Barb Hoppe's attention. "I've got an idea. Tell me if it's fucked up."

"Oh, I'll tell you," replied Hoppe.

"I've been getting a lot of e-mails from students—even some high school students—asking what they could do for the campaign. I haven't asked them to do much beyond e-mailing their friends and encouraging them to vote," he said excitedly, "but I know they want to do a lot more. That's when it hit me."

"What hit you?"

"My idea: why don't we put the Colfax campaign logo on the web site in a way so that people can download it and create their own Colfax hand signs, lawn signs or posters?"

"What are you talking about?" asked Hoppe.

"Did you ever have to wash cars for your Little League team or your school?"

"Yeah, didn't everyone?"

"And how did you get customers?" asked Parker. Not waiting for a response, he answered his own question, "You waved them in with a homemade sign, right?"

Hoppe nodded her head, beginning to see where Parker was going with his idea.

"Well, we've got a lot of young people who are Internet savvy and want to do a lot more. But for the governor to do well, we also have to reach those people who still aren't connected."

"Brilliant," replied Hoppe. "If we can get hundreds of students and other people to hold up signs they can easily download from our site, not only can we demonstrate strong grassroots support, we can also ensure that the signs are consistent and professional." She added, "It's new-age technology combined with old-fashioned politicking. The people of New Hampshire and the media will eat it up. Pete told us a few weeks ago that if we ever had a good idea to run with it. This sounds like a good idea. Do it."

Working with another campaign volunteer proficient in graphics, Parker modified the Colfax2000 web site to include an image that could be downloaded and printed into campaign signs. People were urged to use color printers if possible. The site even had an option for those wanting bigger signs. The image could be divided into smaller sizes, which could then be printed and pasted together to make a much larger sign.

By six o'clock that evening, only five hours after coming up with the idea, Parker was e-mailing the New Hampshire listserv and encouraging students to download the signs so that they could post them in their dorm windows and hold them up on busy street corners. By seven o'clock, the first signs began springing up in windows on college campuses. By ten o'clock, Julie Romero and Mardi Arbeit, juniors at St. Anselm College, had put together a five-by-eight-foot sign with which to welcome Colfax when he came to speak at the college the next day.

Parker was about to call it quits around midnight when he was struck by another idea. This one was aided by a giant-sized Mountain Dew. Why not tap into the massive student population at the Boston-area colleges and universities: Harvard, Boston University, Boston College? Acting on his own initiative and without seeking permission from anyone—per Sawyer's instructions—Parker proceeded to carry out his idea.

* *

In David Luther's seventeen years of working for Win Murdock, he had never seen his boss so concerned. "David, I want you to find out everything you possibly can about Robert Colfax. I want you and your investigators to crawl up his ass and find even the tiniest piece of shit."

"I understand," replied Luther.

"Do you?" responded Murdock, "I want to know everything there is to know about the son of a bitch. I want to know if he was ever caught stealing as a little kid. I want to know if any of his business partners ever cheated the federal government. I want to know if he ever hit on his secretary, or if his wife ever had an affair. I want his phone records scrutinized to see if he's ever dialed a 900 number. I want his past job applications and military records reviewed for accuracy. I want his tax records scrutinized so thoroughly that if he underpaid the government so much as a dime, we know about it. I want to know how he voted and where he stood on every issue as a congressman, secretary of the Navy, and governor. I want you to review every article ever written about him—and I don't care about the source. The more obscure, the better."

"I understand, Mr. Murdock."

"Good. I want it done in three days. No expense is to be spared."

"Yes, sir."

Minutes later, Luther was on the Holten Lear jet flying to Washington for a meeting with Jacob Mance. During the two and one-half-hour flight, Luther wrote over four pages of questions that he would pose to Mance.

* *

Luther arrived in the mahogany-paneled lobby of Lawrence, Mance & Scott's Washington office and was promptly escorted up to the eighth floor by an imposing private security guard. Even though it was after 8:00 P.M., the office had the feel of a newsroom rushing to meet a deadline.

Luther wasted no time in sharing the massive list of questions he had prepared for Mance, who added two additional pages of questions in the first half-hour of their meeting.

"I have three opposition research experts I can recommend for this project. Two are located here in Washington. The other, T.J. Hannon, offices out of Atlanta," said Mance.

"Why the one in Atlanta?"

"Hannon has a number of connections to the current administration, and, if he were located here in Washington, his presence would raise too many questions. In Atlanta, he is, as the old saying goes, out of sight, out of mind."

"Good. It sounds as though he might be valuable," said Luther.

"He is. Based on Colfax's resumé, I think it best that we have one researcher concentrate on Colfax's seven years in Congress and another on his three years as secretary of the Navy."

"What's Hannon's role?" asked Luther.

"Hannon will go to Minnesota to investigate Colfax's life there and his time as governor. He has a small but capable staff. If past history is any gauge, he will bring a few of his staff to Minneapolis and dedicate a least one person to each significant phase of Colfax's life—childhood, high school, college, marriage, business career," said Mance. "And for those miscellaneous aspects his life, such as officer candidate school, time in Vietnam, and travel abroad, my opposition research staff will fill in the rest."

* *

For the next seventy-two hours, four opposition teams, each consisting of three to seven members, scoured every newspaper article, phone record, tax filing and credit history report that mentioned Robert T. Colfax. Criminal records in every town where Colfax had ever lived or visited were reviewed. The backgrounds of his parents, wife, brothers and even his two young daughters were reviewed. Old employees, teachers, neighbors, and acquaintances were contacted and discreetly interviewed. The researchers usually posed as friendly reporters claiming to be doing background research for an article on Colfax.

Jacob Mance received the detailed reports from every team and then condensed the 472 pages into a three-page memo. The summary highlighted a thirty-year-old military report citing Ensign Colfax for disorderly and drunken conduct in Subic Bay in 1972. But it went on to say that Colfax had frequently and publicly referred to the incident as the reason for his twenty-eight years of sobriety and was, thus, not a good prospect for "candidate profiling." The summary also mentioned that a few employees of the high-tech start-up Colfax headed as CEO were aggrieved, but none was willing to go public with their complaints. The report identified two employees who might make some noise if the price were right. Overall, the bulky report was as dry as toast and lacking in any real damaging information. Mance forwarded the 472-page confidential report to Luther, who read it and passed it on to Murdock.

*   *

Murdock retired to the plush, darkly paneled office in his spacious estate located outside Omaha and read the entire document in one sitting. He did not make a single mark on any page. Murdock just digested its contents and went to bed for the night.

After his customary five hours of sleep, he arose at 5:00 A.M. and was served a cup of tea, a croissant and fresh fruit. By 7:00, he had reread the whole report. This time, he highlighted three small passages. When he was finished, he called for Luther.

"David, I've read the report. Please get me a copy of Mr. Colfax's high school yearbook. I need a copy of the 1983 article in *Runner's World* and the profile that Northwest Airlines did on Colfax in its in-house magazine in the spring of 1985. I also want copies of both the Minneapolis and St. Paul papers for the day after his 1982 congressional win and his 1996 gubernatorial victory."

Luther obtained the requested documents and made an extra copy of each for himself. That evening, he read the 1967 St. John's Prep School yearbook, the *Runner's World* article, the Northwest Airlines profile, and the old newspaper clippings. He paid scant attention to Colfax's victory as state cross-country champion on page seventeen of the yearbook, found the magazine articles to be fluff and saw nothing of interest in the clippings. The only common theme Luther saw was that Colfax was an accomplished and avid runner.

Murdock, however, saw a more important thread running through all three. The thread would not be useful for political character assassination. It would be useful for assassination, period.

CHAPTER TWELVE

Pete Sawyer knew his candidate had regained the momentum when he and Colfax drove through the main entrance of St. Anselm and were greeted by a huge "Colfax for President" sign held up by two energetic students, Julie Romero and Mardi Arbeit.

"Stop the car, Pete," said Colfax, upon seeing the huge sign. With his dark-blue wool overcoat unbuttoned and his gray silk scarf draped elegantly around his neck, Colfax swung his lean frame out of the car and into the cool February air. With steam emanating from his cup of coffee, Colfax approached the young women.

"I couldn't help but admire your sign," said Colfax, smiling as he thrust his right hand in the direction of Julie Romero, who was speechless. "I'm Robert Colfax."

"It's an honor to meet you, Governor Colfax," offered Arbeit, who was never short for words, as she shook the candidate's firm hand. "I'm Mardi Arbeit and this is Julie Romero."

"The pleasure's all mine, Mardi. I can't tell you how much it means to me to have supporters standing out here in this cold. It's going to be because of people like you two that we'll win this election."

Romero just smiled. She still hadn't sufficiently recovered from being face-to-face with the man for whom she intended to cast her first vote in a presidential election.

"Would you like some coffee?" asked Colfax, motioning to Sawyer to grab the thermos from the car.

"Yes, please," said Arbeit. "Would you take a picture with us?" she asked, reaching into her pocket to pull out a camera.

"Absolutely. Pete, would you please take a photo of Julie, Mardi, and me?" said Colfax, displaying his skill of remembering people's names. Posing in front of the sign between the two women, Colfax asked where they got the sign. He was told they downloaded it from his campaign web site. He then asked them what their top priorities were in this campaign.

"I support a woman's right to choose," offered Arbeit quickly.

"I guess Social Security and the environment are my top two concerns," replied Romero.

"They're all important issues. Do you have any specific questions or concerns on those or any other issues? I want you to continue to support me all the way through November."

"I know you're pro-choice," said Arbeit, "but do you also support funding for birth control?"

"I do," said Colfax, succinctly. "As president, my administration's top priority in this area will be to reduce the number of unintended pregnancies. The tough reality is that in half of all abortions performed neither the woman nor her partner used birth control. We must better educate young people, and this includes making sure that men understand that they are equally responsible for the pregnancy. Let me be honest, though," said Colfax, looking directly at Arbeit, "I'm pro-choice but I believe the whole pro-choice, pro-life debate has endured too long. Whenever I talk about rights, you'll also hear me talking about responsibility."

"Governor, we're going to be late," said Sawyer, referring to the speech Colfax was to give in five minutes at the commons area of the college.

"Thank you again, Julie, Mardi," said Colfax. "Remember to stay involved. Get your friends and family involved. It's the only way we can win."

"By the way," Arbeit yelled as Colfax was getting back into the car, "I liked your commercial."

Inside the car, Colfax turned to Sawyer and said, "I love that kind of stuff. It fires me up."

"I can tell."

"Unfortunately, once I start receiving Secret Service protection, these encounters will disappear. How do you feel about Secret Service protection?"

"I know you won't like it. I don't think any candidate does. But your showing in Iowa and the momentum you are gaining here in New Hampshire makes the prospect that someone will try to kill you more likely." Sawyer purposely used the word "kill" to drive home the reality of the situation. "I mean, I even got nervous when that young girl—."

"Young woman," said Colfax, correcting his campaign manager.

"—when that young woman pulled her camera out of her pocket. For all I knew, it could have been a gun."

"So you think we should accept protection?"

"I do," said Sawyer without hesitation as he pulled the car in front of the main hall. Sawyer immediately noticed the colorful "Colfax for President" signs posted on the doors of the building and in most of the windows. Colfax and Sawyer were even more surprised when they entered the hall and 200 boisterous students began waving similar signs as soon the candidate came into view.

"Now, this really gets me fired up," said Colfax, turning to Sawyer.

* *

". . . It is not enough for candidates like me to say to you—the young people of this country—that you are the future of this country. Of course, you are," said Colfax, as he looked over the throng of St. Anselm students. "You deserve a candidate—and a president—who will turn that rhetoric into specific actions. It is not enough for me to say I want to be the 'education president.' I must show you how I intend to make good on that promise —and that is just what I intend to do.

"As president, I am fully prepared to devote an additional twenty billion dollars a year to students to pursue educational opportunities in specific fields of study—such as science and technology—that will shape this country in the twenty-first century. And I will get that money by stopping the production of the F-22 fighter.

"The question is: what is more vital for the future of this country—three hundred jet fighters that even the Pentagon experts agree are not needed or providing 20,000 students four-year scholarships to the schools of their choice? To my way of thinking, it's a no-brainer—I'm going to place the money with you."

* *

Half an hour later, on seeing Arbeit and Romero standing in the back of the room and being unaware of Parker's plans, Colfax exhorted the students to show their support on Tuesday by putting the signs to use. "Put those signs in your windows, in your cars, hold them on street corners. Let's show Prescott and Byrne that they can't just buy support through radio and television ads. More important, let's show New Hampshire and the rest of the world that Iowa wasn't a fluke and that the young people of this country care enough about their future to vote in record numbers. After all, it is your future," said Colfax to the boisterous crowd. "Thank you," he said, although none of the cheering students could actually hear him. He then jumped down from the stage and into the audience to begin shaking hands. Sawyer knew that Colfax understood that his days as a freewheeling campaigner were rapidly coming to an end and that he was savoring the feel of "retail politicking." At one point, Sawyer watched nervously as the students tried to touch, feel or shake Colfax's hand from every direction. He knew that anyone with hostile intentions could easily kill the man he wanted to see become president. He was looking forward to Secret Service protection, even if his candidate wasn't.

* *

It was the easiest million dollars Jacob Mance ever made. Kevin Haver, chair of the debate commission, a former head of the Democratic National Committee, and now the president of his own lobbying firm—whose clients included the tobacco, gambling, oil and defense industries—had already convinced a majority of the debate commission to limit the presidential debates to those candidates receiving at least fifteen percent in a nationally recognized poll.

"Do you think your coalition can keep Colfax from reaching the magical number?" asked Haver.

"I think so. It would be helpful, however, if you would let me know in advance of when the polls will be conducted. I can make sure that we inundate the airwaves in an attempt to drive his numbers lower—assuming he's still in the race by then. It would also be helpful if you would only allow polls among 'likely voters.' We have been noticing that Colfax is doing substantially better among first-time voters."

"No problem. I've already worked out those details."

"Do you think the media will complain that the standard is too high? Too anti-Colfax, too anti-third party?" asked Mance.

"Fuck no. If we do it early enough, no one will even notice, except Colfax and the reformers. Then the trick is just to ignore them or use our media contacts to spin the situation to our advantage."

* *

Everywhere Colfax and Sawyer went, they saw signs of Josh Parker's work. Hundreds of students from the Boston area and many others from as far away as Philadelphia had come to New Hampshire to support Robert Colfax.

When the volunteer coordinator for the state had run out of spots in the telephone bank, and, when the literature drop coordinator had run out of neighborhoods to paper, the volunteers were sent into the small towns to demonstrate Colfax's growing grassroots support the old-fashioned way—by waving hand-made signs. Wherever possible, Colfax stopped to personally thank the sign holders.

The Colfax supporters began drawing supportive honks from passing cars and people giving the thumbs-up. Many of the more reserved at least made note of the prominent web address and went home or to work and accessed the web site to find out more about the independent governor of Minnesota. Once at the web site, most viewed a video clip of the commercial. The commercial had also begun to run again on Monday and fueled many of the appreciative honks and waves.

As one balding man in greasy mechanic's coveralls told Romero and Arbeit, "Any candidate for president who doesn't take himself so goddamn seriously has got my vote." Arbeit replied that Colfax was also a candidate of substance. "Whatever," he said, "the guy's got a sense of humor. That's enough for me at this stage."

Later in the day, when Colfax left for Dover to address a Chamber of Commerce audience, he invited Sandra Griffith, a hardened and cynical *Time* magazine reporter, who was recently assigned to cover the Colfax campaign, to ride along. Her editor told her that Colfax would be on the cover of the magazine if he received more than ten percent in either the Republican or Democratic primary.

As Dover came into sight, Griffith asked Colfax about his political philosophy. "You describe yourself as being fiscally responsible and socially liberal. Does that make you a libertarian?"

"No," replied Colfax. "Unlike the other candidates for president, with perhaps the exceptions of Jack Quinn on the Republican side and John Gordon on the Democratic side—if he decides to get back in the race—my positions do not easily fit into some neat prescribed box. My mission is simple: I want to leave this country a freer, healthier and more productive place for my children. I kind of view myself like a kickoff return specialist in the NFL. His goal is simple: improve his team's field position. To achieve that goal, he sometimes runs right, other times left. And if something isn't working, he isn't afraid to change direction. Neither am I. If a policy helps me achieve my goals of making this a freer, healthier, more productive country, I'll consider the idea. Also, I won't be afraid to abandon ideas that aren't working."

"Okay—"

"If I could take the analogy one step further—and I apologize for the excessive sports analogies. Sometimes, a kickoff return specialist uses his teammate's blocking. Other times, he runs free. That's kind of how I see government. Sometimes it is helpful. Other times, it's a hindrance and should get out of the way."

"What exactly do you see as government's proper role?" pressed Griffith.

"I'll answer that by way of personal experience. I believe in individual responsibility. But I also believe in the power of government to improve people's position in life. I'm the product of an upper-middle-class background. My father owned and operated a handful of successful grocery stores in southern Minnesota when I was growing up. Financially, this afforded me the opportunity to attend a college prep school. Unfortunately, for my family and me, the larger grocery chains soon began delivering more goods at lower prices to my father's customers. By my sophomore year, my father had to declare bankruptcy. He committed suicide shortly after that. It was only through the help of a priest that I was able to continue going to the prep school—my family couldn't afford it. It was at this stage that my view of government began to take shape. Because I had studied hard and worked hard, I was accepted to a number of prestigious colleges. But I was only able to attend my top choice because I received a federal grant and was a recipient of government-backed student loan. Were it not for the federal government, I wouldn't be where I am today.

"Note, however, that I did not—and do not—believe government had any role in trying to protect my father's business from the competitive pressures that forced him out of business. My father could not compete and he was fairly forced out of the business." Griffith was both surprised and impressed by Colfax's candor. "I should add," said Colfax, continuing, "that my father also suffered from depression. If you wonder where some of my anti-libertarian positions come from—such as my positions on tobacco, guns, alcohol, and gambling—they were all borne of personal experiences."

"Gambling?" asked Griffith.

"My father's bankruptcy was partially attributable to his gambling."

"Tobacco?"

"Watching my mother suffer the last six months of her life hooked up to an oxygen tank."

"Guns?"

"Watching nine good men torn apart by AK-47s in Vietnam."

Griffith wanted to probe further but knew time was running short. Switching gears, she asked one last question. "Why did you leave the Republican Party?"

"I don't think I left the Republican Party. The Republican Party left me. In 1996, I wanted to run for governor as a Republican. But many of the conservative delegates to the state convention couldn't or wouldn't accept my position on abortion. Now, I respect those who disagree with me on the issue, but what troubled me was the hatred that many of the party activists expressed toward me and my wife."

"And that was because of her position as a board member of Responsible Choices?" asked Griffith, referring to Linda Colfax's position on the nation's leading provider of health-care information to low-income women.

"Yes. Many of the party activists portrayed the organization as nothing but a government-sponsored front for unlimited abortions. Nothing could be farther from the truth. Responsible Choices is singularly dedicated to education, birth control, and prenatal care. In short, it is dedicated to preventing abortions."

"So you left the Republican Party over the abortion issue?"

"Not entirely. In 1996, the endorsed candidates for both the Democratic-Farmer-Labor Party—that's what the Democratic Party is called in Minnesota—and the Republican Party both supported public financing for a new baseball stadium. The DFL mayor of Minneapolis supported it because the unions wanted to build and operate the stadium. For them, it was a matter of jobs. And they contributed heavily to her campaign. On the other side, the endorsed Republican candidate supported it because the wealthy owner of the team contributed heavily to his campaign. The owner would have stood to rake in millions of dollars in profits from the new stadium. No one was representing the taxpayers. That's really why I ran as an independent. Because in today's era of special interest money, no one represents the people," Colfax said, before pausing. "That's why I'm running for president as an independent."

"One final question: Can you win?"

"Absolutely," said Colfax who purposely chose not to elaborate too much on the remark. "And I will."

"Thank you for the interview," interjected Sawyer, signaling to Griffith that the interview was over and that no follow-up questions would be allowed.

*   *

Samuel Metzen, chief lobbyist for the Alliance of Defense Manufacturers, stared at the video. "Colfax wants to kill the F-22?"

"I can replay the video," said Jacob Mance.

"I'm not entirely surprised. He was a thorn in our side when he was secretary of Navy, always questioning the need for every new piece of equipment. Luckily, he doesn't stand a chance—"

"He won't—with your help," replied Mance. "A half million dollars is a small premium to pay to ensure your industry is able to retain that twenty billion dollars for the F-22 fighter."

"I don't know . . ."

"It's not just the F-22. Colfax is on record for unfunding every defense-related project that Admiral Sewell recommended cutting before he retired as chief of naval operations. That means the Navy's LHP-8."

"I guess you're right. Even though I don't think Colfax stands a chance, I don't want him out there raising these issues to the broader public."

"Can I put you down for $500,000? You're in good company."

"The contribution won't be made public?"

"Absolutely not. Under federal law, I'm under no obligation to provide that information," said Mance, smiling.

Metzen smiled back. Both knew how the game was played.

* *

The momentum was palpable. The second wave of Colfax commercials began airing on Monday, the eve of the primary election. Not since Eugene McCarthy, another maverick politician from Minnesota, stunned Lyndon Johnson in February 1968 had New Hampshire seen so many people engaged in a campaign.

The experienced political operatives were nervous, and it didn't matter whether they were Democrats or Republican. The coalition ads were reaching their intended targets—seniors, teachers and various other special interest groups—but Colfax continued to gain in the polls. His campaign was reaching young voters, independents and a great many first-time voters, none of whom cared what the coalition ads said about Colfax. The voters who were influenced by the ads were already predisposed to vote for another candidate.

It was about noon on Monday when Earl Glenn, the twenty-nine-year-old *wunderkind* of the Democratic National Committee, placed an unprecedented call to his equally precocious counterpart at the Republican National Committee, Paul Sutton. According to federal election law, the call was illegal. Neither was concerned with being caught. No one had ever been prosecuted for the crime.

"Paul, this Earl Glenn," said the chair of the DNC, quickly adding, "We've got problems, and I suspect the polls that you took last night show the same thing ours do."

"What's that?" asked Sutton coyly. He knew full well that his party's latest polls showed Colfax's momentum growing to dangerous levels.

"You can play stupid, you arrogant asshole, but if we don't stop Colfax, he's going to fuck us both before we can even begin to fuck with one another," spat Glenn, who had minutes earlier received a memorable ass-chewing from the president of the United States. Donald Butler had wanted to know what Glenn was doing to help his vice president win New Hampshire by such a healthy margin that Congressman Greene would drop out and John Gordon wouldn't consider getting back in the race.

"I was just yanking your chain," said Sutton, switching into business mode. "We're very concerned about Colfax. In fact, I'm just about to have a meeting here in my office to discuss how we can thwart his progress."

"Good. I was hoping I wasn't too late," said Glenn. I've scheduled a similar meeting at my office for one o'clock. What I would like to do is find out if we can find some mutual ground upon which to coordinate our activities." Sutton knew what Glenn was proposing was illegal and momentarily paused. Sensing Sutton's hesitation, Glenn added, "Paul, certain situations require strong responses."

"What do you have in mind?" responded Sutton cautiously.

"We've done extensive push polling," said Glenn, referring to the political tactic of asking respondents politically charged questions with the intention of negatively influencing the way people think about the candidate in question. "The one question that elicited a favorable response for us—among both likely Democratic and Republican voters—was the wasted vote question. We asked: 'Because a vote for Robert Colfax will have no consequence in determining who the Republican or Democratic nominee will be, who are you most likely to vote for in Tuesday's primary?'"

"Go on," said Sutton, scribbling notes furiously onto the legal pad on his desk.

"Among those most likely to vote, if they can be convinced that their write-in vote is a 'wasted' vote, sixty percent are less likely to vote for Colfax."

"What's your strategy?" asked Sutton carefully so as not to convey a sense of commitment to Glenn.

"I would like to propose to my executive committee a last-minute ad campaign that emphasizes the wasted vote syndrome."

"And your idea is too risky to conduct alone?" volunteered Sutton.

"Yes," responded Glenn in a rare display of candor. "If both parties were to conduct similar but separate ad campaigns, the approach would have a better chance of succeeding."

"I see," said Sutton.

"I think it's too risky for the national committees to conduct. What do you think if we have our respective state parties pay for the ad? You know, something along the lines of: 'The nation is counting on you, New Hampshire. Don't throw away your vote.'"

"I like it. But if we're seen as outsiders, it could backfire," said Sutton. "Let me discuss it with my executive committee," he added, referring to the party's top legislative leaders and biggest donors.

By three o'clock that afternoon, the Republican Party of New Hampshire was producing an ad along the lines Glenn had sketched. The Democratic Party of New Hampshire taped a commercial that noted New Hampshire's near perfect record of voting for the candidate who went on to become president. The tag line said: "Make sure New Hampshire's right again. Don't waste your vote on a write-in candidate."

The Federal Election Commission would later look into allegations made by the Colfax campaign that the ads were a coordinated effort. The commission, made up of three Republican and three Democratic members, found no abuse to have occurred. The decision, which received no media coverage, didn't surprise Pete Sawyer, who had filed the compliant.

* *

By eight o'clock, the ads were running side-by-side with Colfax's ads and having a demonstrable effect. It was not, however, the effect for which the parties had hoped. Independent voters who saw the ads were infuriated and became more committed to vote for Colfax. And a number of independent-minded voters who had planned on either voting for Jack Quinn or casting a write-in vote for John Gordon, who had not explicitly ruled out getting back into the race, decided to vote for Colfax. Ironically, the ad convinced many Quinn and Gordon supporters that their votes would be better directed toward Colfax.

* *

All the campaigns, Republican and Democrat alike, were aware of Colfax's rising poll numbers. They were not aware of the strategy that their respective state parties had instigated. Accordingly, each campaign came to roughly the same conclusion: if they were to survive New Hampshire and make it to the general election, they had to finish in either first or second place and receive more votes than Colfax.

This scenario forced each campaign to target the most likely primary voters. For the Republicans, this meant the very conservative Republicans, and for the Democrats, seniors, union members, and liberals. The strategies of the remaining candidates could not have worked any better to Colfax's benefit.

Graham, the bomb-throwing, red-meat-eating, lock-the-doors-to-foreigners, former talk show host, directed all his venom at the Republican frontrunner, Elliott Prescott. In his well-attended stump speeches and in his ads, he pilloried Prescott for being "mushy" on the abortion issue, looking the other way as the media continued to impose its "liberal and homosexual agenda" on an unsuspecting populace, and ignoring the dire effects that free trade and open immigration policies were having on blue-collar workers. His message was finding a small but enthusiastic home.

Stanley Cross, the wealthy cable and television magnate, attacked Prescott along similar lines. Any candidate worthy of upholding the Republican Party banner in November, he said, "must surely be an unabashed and unequivocal supporter of the rights of the unborn."

The cumulative effect of the Graham and Cross ads was that they forced Prescott to abandon his cautious, middle-of-the-road approach. As his campaign manager told him, "Unless we shore up the Republican base, we aren't going to survive to the general election." This political calculus moved Prescott further to the right as he sharpened his position on abortion, saying that the issue would be a litmus test for his Supreme Court appointments. He also began advocating a thirty-percent, across-the-board tax cut and took a much harder line against trade with China, claiming, "It is time human rights supplant economic rights."

A similar scenario was being played out on the Democratic side. Congressman Greene was furiously trying to expose the vice president's weaknesses and, in the process, drive a wedge between Byrne and some of his more hard-core Democratic supporters by advocating for universal health care coverage. Like Graham, Greene was striving for the disaffected blue-collar worker. He felt he had a better chance at the group because he was a Democrat and some of those voters couldn't bring themselves to go for a Republican no matter how much they liked his positions. Greene also knew that he would also lose some voters simply because he was black.

The populist congressman also chastised Byrne for the size and variety of campaign contributions he accepted. He cited the huge contributions the vice president had taken from large corporations and used it to question Byrne's commitment to labor. He wondered in one commercial how the vice president could accept hefty campaign contributions from the tobacco industry and make good on his claim to reduce underage smoking.

Greene, despite repeated pleas from Earl Glenn, the Democratic National Committee chair, also chose to run a series of commercials showing the vice president meeting with foreigners. The ad left the distinct impression that foreigner's access to Byrne was purchased through campaign contributions and unbecoming of a man who aspired to represent the American people. An emphasis was placed on the phrase "American people" in the commercial. Glenn and the vice president had both expected the commercials—just not so soon, and not from a member of their own party.

Greene even challenged Byrne in areas where he was perceived as being strong. On the environment, the congressman again sounded the theme of campaign contributions and asked voters if they trusted the vice president's commitment to protecting the environment when he "accepted hundreds of thousands of dollars from America's largest corporate polluters?"

The end result was that Byrne, like Prescott, had to temporarily abandon his centrist-sounding policies. He moved left to placate the more liberal members of the Democratic base. The vice president promised labor that he would review all free trade agreements to ensure "the rights of every American worker are protected."

* *

With every new promise Byrne and Prescott made, Pete Sawyer smiled. The road—the middle road—to Colfax's victory was being paved by the major candidates needing to placate their bases. It was Sawyer's job to make sure that once they moved to the fringe, they stayed there. His first effort toward achieving that goal was to send two campaign volunteers to every place Prescott and Byrne were speaking to video-tape their remarks. The purpose was to record for posterity the very conservative remarks of Governor Prescott and the very liberal utterings of Vice President Byrne. Sawyer hoped the remarks would later come back to haunt them in the general election.

* *

Tuesday, February 1, was a picture-perfect day in New Hampshire. The Colfax campaign knew before sunrise that, regardless of the weather, it was going to be a good day. At precisely one minute after midnight, the residents of Hart's Location cast the first votes of the primary. Among their twenty-seven votes, Governor Prescott received eight; Vice President Byrne, seven; Governor Colfax, six write-in votes; Stanley Cross, three; Dick Graham, two; and Reginald Greene, one. Neither Senator Quinn nor John Gordon received any votes. Upon hearing the news, the editor of *Time* decided not to wait for the final results and put Colfax on the cover of the magazine. *Newsweek* made the same decision later in the day.

The excitement was evident at voting booths all across the state from Nashua to Manchester and Dover to Concord. Voter turnout surpassed record levels. In many places turnout had exceeded 1996 figures by 10:00 A.M.

Thousands of students manned the busiest street corners in the state to wave signs and urge people to write in Colfax. The night before, many of the students had combed the state and posted flyers urging a vote for Colfax on the windshields of every parked car. By mid-morning, those same students were driving voters to the polls and encouraging them to vote for Colfax. Later, they worked the phones, urging people to get out and vote for Colfax.

While this was going on, the opposing campaigns were frantically mobilizing their supporters. In the end, however, the yearlong efforts of the Byrne and Prescott campaigns couldn't stop the hemorrhaging that Colfax's late surge produced.

In the Republican primary, Governor Prescott came in first place with forty-three percent of the vote; Cross came in second with twenty percent; and Colfax's write-in campaign yielded a surprising third-place finish with thirteen percent of the vote. Graham and Quinn finished with twelve and ten percent, respectively.

On the Democratic side, the vice president finished solidly in first place with fifty-five percent. Colfax bested his numbers on the Republican side and but still came in third with fifteen percent of the vote, and Greene was a disappointing second with twenty-two percent. John Gordon received write-in votes totaling eight percent.

The national media had already written their stories by the time the polls closed. Colfax was the clear winner. He had won the expectations game again. Never had a candidate attempted a write-in campaign against both major parties and done so well. The conclusion was clear: Colfax was a legitimate candidate. A few media elite speculated on what a three-way race might mean in terms of an Electoral College scenario.

Pete Sawyer, now the hottest political commodity in the country, attributed his candidate's strong showing to a number of factors: his message, the strong independent streak in New Hampshire voters, the youth factor, and the relative weakness of the two major parties. Sawyer was careful not to play up Colfax's surprisingly strong showing too much. He was well aware of the pleasure the media took in building up a candidate only to tear him down later. He concluded every interview by saying that Colfax was running like he was behind by thirty percent because he was behind by thirty points in the most recent nationwide poll.

At ten o'clock, after learning that the vote totals were not expected to change appreciatively, Colfax and his wife, Linda, went down to the main ballroom of the Holiday Inn and made their way through the massive crowd of mostly young people—many of whom were going strong on nothing more than a few hours of rest and massive amounts of caffeine and adrenaline. The candidate stood in front of the large Colfax 2000 banner until the crowd quieted down.

"Thank you, New Hampshire!" bellowed an excited but haggard-looking Colfax into the microphone. "A special thanks to the young citizens of New Hampshire. This is your victory. We would not have been able to do as well as we did if you hadn't gotten involved."

The crowd erupted with whoops, yells, and chants of "Colfax, Colfax."

After quieting them down, Colfax continued. "We did well tonight. In fact, we did really well. But I don't need to remind you that we still came in third. And in this game, second or third place doesn't do you—or me—any good. I need you to stay involved through the general election in November. Will you do that?"

"Yes," screamed the crowd back.

"Will you get your friends involved?" Colfax asked with great emphasis.

"Yes!"

"Your brothers and sisters?"

"Yes!"

"Your parents?" Colfax asked, raising his voice.

"Yes!"

"Your neighbors?"

"Yes!"

"Strangers?"

"Yes!" responded the crowd of people who probably would have said yes to anything Colfax asked at that moment.

"Well, that is what it will take. I'm asking for everything you can give me over the next eight and a half months. In return, I will commit the same to you—and then give you four years on top of that." Colfax paused before adding, "After I am elected the next president of the United States."

With that, the crowd erupted again with the chants of "Colfax, Colfax."

As the crowd was still chanting, Colfax thanked them and departed. As he made his way back through the crowd with the assistance of two local Manchester police officers, he passed within three feet of a discreet, gray-haired gentleman. The man looked like a middle-aged policy wonk, but he was Jeffery Payne's most trusted assistant at the Central Intelligence Agency. He was known to some as Raphael Baptista.

CHAPTER THIRTEEN

By virtue of receiving more than five percent of the vote in the New Hampshire primary, Robert Colfax was entitled to Secret Service protection. Special Agent Sean McGowan was given the responsibility of describing to the candidate, his family, and his campaign staff how this protection would alter their lives.

"Governor," said Jenny Walters, Colfax's executive assistant, "Mr. McGowan of the Secret Service is here for your two o'clock meeting."

"Thank you, Jenny. Please let Pete and Annette know that I would like them to join me," said Colfax, referring to his campaign manager and his chief of staff, Annette Christianson.

McGowan was escorted into the Treaty Room, which was situated in the southwest corner of the Capitol. The formal meeting room was decorated with five large paintings depicting famous scenes of Minnesota regiments in the Civil War, each in a heavy gilded oak frame. McGowan had already introduced himself to Sawyer and Christianson when Colfax entered the room through a side door.

"Good afternoon, Governor," said the thirteen-year Secret Service veteran as he stood up and extended his hand to Colfax. He was surprised by the strength of Colfax's grip.

"You have been introduced to my campaign manager and chief of staff?" asked Colfax as he signaled McGowan to take a seat. "Would you like a cup of coffee?"

"That would be nice," said McGowan, who was surprised when Colfax poured the cup himself. McGowan couldn't remember someone under his protection ever doing that.

"I was hoping my wife would be able to join us for meeting," said Colfax, handing the cup to McGowan, "but she is volunteering at our daughter's school this afternoon."

"That's fine, Governor. It may work better if we discuss some of the more personal aspects of Secret Service protection with you and your family in private," said McGowan.

"I understand," replied Colfax. "I'll have Jenny arrange a time later this afternoon for that discussion."

"Thank you, sir," said McGowan. All business now, the Secret Service agent quickly dispensed with the formalities and provided Colfax and his assistants with a short history of the Secret Service's protection of presidential candidates. He explained that the need for protection was born of Robert Kennedy's assassination in 1968, although protection for candidates was not formally instituted until 1972. McGowan also informed the three that the agents who would be protecting the governor were trained in a variety of areas, including state and federal law, biological and chemical hazards, evasive driving, fire fighting, repelling hand grenades, "ten-minute" medicine, and the art and science of physical personal protection.

"Repelling hand grenades?" asked Christianson.

"The Secret Service must be ready for anything," replied McGowan. "In fact, we're trained in a great many other areas, but I needn't bother you with them all."

"What exactly is 'ten-minute' medicine?" asked Sawyer.

"Simply put, it's the art of keeping someone alive for ten minutes," replied McGowan.

"Enough time to get me to the hospital," offered Colfax.

"Yes, sir," said McGowan looking at Colfax without emotion. He knew Colfax had been on both ends of the technique while serving in Vietnam. It had all been outlined in the file the Washington office had provided on Colfax.

"Let's hope you won't get an opportunity to practice either your grenade repelling or medicinal skills during your time with me," said Colfax with a smile. "Please continue, Agent McGowan."

McGowan went to explain the extra physical security measures that the Secret Service would implement at both the State Capitol and the governor's mansion. "As we speak, a team of experts is reviewing all electrical wiring, outside telephone lines, cables, exhaust ducts and underground pipes for exposed weaknesses. If any problems exist, they will be taken care of immediately. Passive motion detectors and cameras are also being installed in bushes, trees, lanterns and other obscure places. And control rooms will be established here at the Capitol and at your residence to monitor all activity."

"I don't want either place looking like a goddamn fortress," said Colfax in a tone that sounded like an order.

"I understand, Governor. The Secret Service shares your concern," replied McGowan, unfazed by Colfax's direct manner. He had survived the temper tantrums of the current president, and from what he had read about Colfax—and he had read a lot—the candidate seemed like someone who had complete control of his emotions. "We are trained to minimize the appearance of security equipment—without compromising its effectiveness. We also strive to minimize our presence. Given your heightened profile," said McGowan, glancing at the freshly printed copies of *Time* and *Newsweek*, "this may be a little difficult."

"I understand," said Colfax.

"Your increased visibility will also make you a more tempting target, Governor. The closer people perceive you to reaching the presidency, the more attractive a target you become."

"Will the governor receive additional protection based on his strong performance in Iowa and New Hampshire?" asked Sawyer.

"Normally, I would say yes. But this year is not a normal year. The president and vice president are already afforded protection. So are Governor Prescott, Congressman Greene, Stanley Cross and Dick Graham. What I am about to tell you is classified information so I ask that you not repeat it to anybody—especially the media."

"You have our guarantee," said Colfax, looking at both his chief of staff and campaign manager. Both Sawyer and Christianson knew that if they ever purposely violated an agreement that Colfax had personally guaranteed, they would lose their job in a heartbeat.

"The Secret Service is presently stretched to the limit. Presidential election years are always difficult for our agency, but the sheer number of viable candidates this year make it that much more difficult. Add the Summer Olympics in Sydney, the pope's visit and a host of other special events for which we provide protective services—and you begin to see how stretched we are."

"I wasn't asking for more protection," said Sawyer. "I merely—"

"I know, Mr. Sawyer," said McGowan, cutting him off, "I just wanted you to know that the number of agents assigned to a particular candidate is based on a number of factors. Governor Colfax and every other candidate will receive the highest level of protection, period," said McGowan, knowing that many high-level Secret Service officials were, in fact, very nervous about their ability to meet the extremely high standards that the agency set for itself.

"Tell me what I will and won't be able to do, Mr. McGowan," said Colfax adding, "Do you prefer being called Mr. McGowan or Agent McGowan?"

"Either is fine, sir."

"Very well, Agent McGowan it shall be."

"In response to your first question, I can tell you this, now that you are accorded Secret Service protection, you will feel like you are living in a bubble. The only way to get out of the bubble is to lose or die."

"It's nice to have options," said Colfax, grinning at McGowan, who smiled back.

"I have provided Mr. Sawyer a briefing book on the procedures that the Secret Service would like you, your campaign personnel, and your family to follow. After you have had a chance to review the document, I'll be happy to answer specific questions. But the book covers policies on handshaking in public, when and where you should wear your bulletproof vest, and our involvement in selecting the venues you appear at."

"I'll review it this evening," said Colfax.

Sawyer and Christianson knew that this meant that they were also to read and familiarize themselves with the book.

"We also have specialists available to help you and your family make the transition to Secret Service protection. It has been our experience that children sometimes have difficulty adjusting to the idea that their parents are in danger," said McGowan.

"Linda and I have tried to prepare Catherine and Colleen for this eventuality. But your offer of assistance is welcome," said Colfax.

"Governor," interrupted Sawyer, "you're scheduled to speak at the U of M Law School at three. If we are to be on time, we should get going."

"Thank you for your time, Governor Colfax," said McGowan.

"Thank you, Agent McGowan. I know you have a difficult task, and my staff and I will work with you in every possible way. I don't mind being told when I'm being a horse's ass. I trust you will tell me when I'm acting in a manner that you deem unwise."

"Thank you, sir. I'm sure that won't be necessary," replied McGowan.

"And if you are wondering when I'm acting like a horse's ass, just follow my wife's lead," said Colfax, with a wink. "She usually knows—and isn't afraid to share that information." McGowan laughed.

As McGowan was walking out the room, Sawyer threw one last question at him. "What's the governor's codename, Agent McGowan?"

Turning around, McGowan replied, "Gibraltar."

"I like it," said Sawyer. It was every campaign manager's wish to have his or her candidate be given a strong sounding codename. Some campaign managers even lobbied the Secret Service to change their candidate's codename if they felt it somehow portrayed their candidate in a less-than-macho light.

"How did you choose it?" inquired Christianson.

"The Secret Service conducts an extensive background review of every candidate we protect. The codename is often based on some personal factor that relates to the candidate's background."

"I don't see the connection," said Colfax.

"It was learned during the course of our review that you work out everyday. I understand you run five miles a day—even do some speed work—and do 250 sit-ups, 250 push-ups and 100 pull-ups everyday," replied McGowan.

"Not every day," said Colfax. "I still don't see the connection."

"Well, we also reviewed your medical records and found out that you have only five percent body fat. One agent said you're hard as rock. Gibraltar is a hard rock."

"I love it," said Sawyer excitedly. He was already scheming how to get the story behind the name out to the media.

"One more question, Agent McGowan. Will I still be able to run?"

"Of course. We'll just have to be very careful and vary where you run every day."

* *

This time, no one from the media saw the two having lunch together. Jeffery Payne was the first to arrive. Win Murdock arrived a few minutes later. Both were escorted to the private room in the back of the restaurant by the maître d'.

"Your concerns about Governor Colfax were well founded," said Payne, beginning the conversation as soon as the maître d' left.

"I wish they weren't. I was hoping by this time that he would have returned to Minnesota permanently and left the presidency to more suitable individuals," replied Murdock. "But those idiots at the Republican and Democratic committees tried to tell the voters of New Hampshire not to waste their vote. Jesus Christ, how fucking stupid! I could have told those assholes that the ads would backfire. No one, particularly the citizens of the 'Live Free or Die state,' like to be told that their vote doesn't matter."

"So, you weren't behind that effort?" asked Payne.

"Hell no! In fact, I'm so pissed off that I'm thinking of withholding the money I usually give each party every year." Payne knew the figure easily exceeded a million dollars a year. "I might not even underwrite their conventions this year. I'd like to watch 'em squirm as they try to find some other large corporation pay for their lame three-day paid television commercials that masquerade as political conventions."

"Where are the conventions this year?" asked Payne.

"The Republicans will be in Philadelphia and the Democrats in Los Angeles."

"I never understood why you sponsored those things anyway. Nobody watches them anymore," said Payne.

"That's true, Jeffery. But Holten doesn't view our contributions as benefiting the democratic way of life. We pay so we can have unlimited access to the entire political establishment for three days. Every representative and senator attends their party's convention—and those politicians not angling for a position in the cabinet of the new administration are usually bored out of their minds and want to be entertained," said Murdock. "Holten is only too happy to occupy their time."

"The conventions might not be so lame this year if Graham or Cross is able to challenge Prescott, and Greene can scrape up enough delegates to be a presence at the Democratic convention," said Payne.

"That's what I am afraid of. If the conservative wing of the Republican Party gives Prescott problems at their convention, and the unions and minorities do the same at the Democratic convention, Colfax is going to look more and more reasonable to most Americans," said Murdock.

"Do you have anything in mind to prevent this from happening?" asked Payne.

"Yes. The coalition is going to concentrate on helping Prescott and Byrne become their party's nominees. We are going to do it by directing our resources, for the time being, at Cross, Graham, and Greene," said Murdock.

"The strategy being that if they are out of the race, Prescott and Byrne can take more moderate positions and deny Colfax the middle ground?" asked Payne.

"Exactly. Plus, by going after candidates other than Colfax, the coalition becomes more legitimate in the eyes of those good-government groups trying to monitor our activities."

"You're referring to the Center for Ethical and Responsive Politics?"

"Yes. Those self-righteous assholes have been snooping around, asking questions about the coalition. That obnoxious Jew, Bernstein, has apparently hired a new bitch to track soft money and independent expenditures. Of course, Mance is stonewalling her. By law, he doesn't have to tell anyone who contributes to the coalition. But these self-righteous good-government pricks think that the public has a right to know." The conversation stopped as the maître d' brought Murdock and Payne their drinks.

"Well," said Murdock, "tell me what your moles have learned."

"I sent my top guy up to New Hampshire—he's the same one, if you recall, who wrote the report on Colfax for you last fall." Murdock recalled the report.

The brief mention of the old priest had served as a focal point for his plot. Payne continued, ". . . and he reported that Colfax was currently unprotected. We have since learned that Secret Service coverage was started on Wednesday, the day after the primary."

"That's what I suspected. I have some ideas for our contingency plan," said Murdock as he handed Payne a packet of information containing old newspaper articles and photocopies of some pages from Colfax's prep school yearbook.

"What's this?"

"You'll see," replied Murdock. He then described in great detail how Colfax's high school athletic exploits and his relationship with Father Otto Wilhoit might be used to successfully complete the contingency plan.

"Interesting," said Payne. "I will make arrangements to have our newest asset redeploy to St. Paul. After spending time in Kosovo, Minnesota might look pretty good."

"What can you tell me about your newest asset, Jeffery."

"Very little—a former Marine, a sharpshooter."

"And one confirmed kill?" asked Murdock, hinting at the assassination.

"For political reasons, I choose to limit my knowledge," said Payne, with a grin. "You know—just in case Congress decided to take its oversight responsibilities seriously."

"Excellent," said Murdock, taking a bite of his salad. "Remember, we have plenty of time. Your man should only attempt a shot if it is a sure thing. We can change our plans later, if necessary."

With the discussion finished, the two completed their lunches and left separately. The maître d' thanked Murdock after receiving his customary fifty percent tip.

* *

The senior senator from California, Jack Quinn, announced his withdrawal from the race at two o'clock Central Standard Time. His thirteen-minute announcement was upbeat, optimistic and humorous. He told reporters he was disappointed by his numbers. But he remained convinced that his foreign policy expertise and his willingness to tackle difficult issues such as campaign finance reform and corporate welfare would have made him a good president.

The next day, the political pundits, as they did when John Gordon withdrew, praised Quinn's principled campaign and inveighed against the influence of money on the political process. Senator Jack Quinn, they all agreed, would have made an excellent president. A few speculated that he would make an outstanding choice for Elliott Prescott's vice president. One even speculated that despite being a

Republican, Quinn would be a good choice for secretary of Defense if the vice president should win the election.

Only one candidate still in the race took the time to call Quinn and congratulate him on his campaign. It was not until almost midnight that Colfax reached the straight-shooting former Air Force pilot.

"How are you, Jack?" asked Colfax who had served in Congress for two years with Quinn before Quinn was elected to the Senate. They had continued their relationship when Colfax became the secretary of the Navy and Quinn served on the Senate Armed Forces Committee. Both had served in Vietnam.

"Tired. I don't envy the schedule you'll have to keep up for the next eight months," replied Quinn.

"Neither do I," said Colfax. "I just wanted to call and congratulate you on a well-run campaign."

"Thank you," said Quinn, "I have admired yours as well."

"Thank you. Your positions on entitlements, campaign finance reform, corporate welfare, school choice, and more open immigration were very courageous."

"They're the same as yours, Bob."

"I know—that's why I admire them so much," said Colfax with a hearty laugh. Quinn returned the gesture. "Seriously though, your no-nonsense, no bullshit approach to the issues facing this country elevated the level of debate. You should be proud of your campaign."

"I am. And I'm happy that you're doing so well. At least our issues will continue to be addressed. I just hope you get in the debates. That fifteen-percent requirement the debate commission announced last week is bullshit. It is specifically designed to keep you out."

"I know."

"It's the same old crap, Bob. They're scared shitless of you. They'll do anything to keep you from reaching that level. I hope you and Linda are prepared for what's ahead."

"I am."

"I hope so. Because we can't afford another four years of meaningless rhetoric, political partisanship and inaction."

"I agree, Jack. And that's why I would like to ask you to consider something."

"You're not thinking of getting out the race and throwing your support to me, are you?" said Quinn lightheartedly.

"Now that I've got Secret Service agents outside my door," said Colfax, "the idea has a certain amount of appeal." Colfax then paused and said, "I would like you to consider being part of my administration when I'm elected."

"Pretty confident, aren't you?" said Quinn, who had always liked Colfax's confidence and directness. He had become familiar with his style during the many meetings the two had to work out legislation that closed over fifty unnecessary naval bases and facilities.

"Like you said, we can't afford another four years of inaction. We need someone with real leadership skills in the White House. With you out of the race, I have to win," replied Colfax.

"I appreciate the offer, Bob. I'll think about it. But I am, after all, still a Republican."

"So was I—until four years ago. I'm proof that there is life after the Republican Party, Jack. And I must say, it's pretty liberating."

"It's only a temporary life, Bob. If I understand my religious conservative friends within the party correctly, you're going to hell," said Quinn with a big laugh.

"They thought I was going to hell even when I was in the party," said Colfax returning the joke.

"I appreciate the offer," said Quinn, "and I'll give it serious consideration. Can I ask what you had in mind?"

"I would like to have you serve as my secretary of Defense. Your credibility in defense matters is impeccable, and I think we both agree on which weapons systems must be eliminated and where money must be reallocated. In fact, I will be giving a major speech in a few days outlining why the F-22 fighter is not appropriate to build at this time." Colfax paused, then added, "If you are interested in being vice president, I would also be comfortable offering you that position."

"No thank you," said Quinn. "You know the old joke about the mother who had two sons. One went into the Navy and the other become vice president and she never heard from either again."

"It wasn't meant as an insult," replied Colfax with a twinge of humor in his voice. "It would, however, be reassuring to know that if anything ever happened to me, someone of your stature and caliber would assume the office."

"Thank you. Can I ask if you have given any thought to Admiral Sewell as a potential running mate?" asked Quinn referring to the former chief of naval operations and the architect of the successful naval blockade of Iraq.

"I haven't yet spoken with him. By all indications, he intends to remain nonpolitical."

"I suggest that you do. Elizabeth Vandiver would also be an excellent choice," said Quinn. "She has foreign policy experience and would also offer you gender and geographic balance."

"I agree, but she's on Prescott's short list of candidates."

"She is," replied Quinn, "but there is no way the conservatives are going to let Prescott nominate a pro-choice woman who is presently working for a Democratic president."

Colfax thanked Quinn for his suggestions and again congratulated him on his campaign. The conversation ended with the two agreeing to stay in touch.

* *

Lee Manning had never been so happy. The former Marine had over $125,000 in the bank and was fulfilling a lifelong dream of using the skills God had provided for the benefit of the United States. How the skills were being employed wasn't exactly the way the sniper would have preferred, but it beat the alternative, which Manning figured was working at some menial job in a restaurant in North Carolina. Sniping was the only marketable skill Manning possessed.

Baptista and Manning met at the restaurant across from the hotel where the sniper had been staying. At seven o'clock, it was crowded with business executives flying in or out of Dulles Airport. Baptista was almost indistinguishable from the majority of men in the restaurant, and Manning simply looked like a young graduate student being interviewed for a job. Manning, who had been told to dress professionally for the meeting, had purchased a blue suit for the occasion. It was the first suit the sniper had ever owned.

As was his custom, Baptista approached Manning from behind and slid into the booth so that he was facing the door and the rest of the restaurant.

"Did you enjoy your R and R?"

"Yes, sir," said Manning who wasn't accustomed to having friendly conversations with Baptista.

"What did you do?" asked Baptista, who knew exactly what Manning did.

"I visited Antitiem Battlefield one day. I was hoping to find some interesting reading material on Civil War snipers. I also visited the Smithsonian, the monuments, and some of the other attractions," said Manning.

"Did you visit Ford's Theater?" asked Baptista.

"I wanted to but didn't have the time," replied Manning.

"What do you think of John Wilkes Booth?" asked Baptista, rather awkwardly redirecting the conversation.

Manning paused a few seconds, trying to size up the thin man sitting across the table before answering. "I think Lincoln changed the North's aim during the middle of the war. The assassination, from the perspective of a Southerner, was justified."

Baptista was aware of Manning's background and knew that Manning's father was not only an abusive alcoholic but a racist as well. The latter was a trait he had passed on to his only child.

"If you felt an American president was unfit for office or was known to be conducting business in a manner inconsistent with the United States' best interests, would you consider using your skills to affect a positive change?"

Manning looked at Baptista as though it were a trick question. But the sniper focused on the phrase "affect a positive change."

"I guess that would depend on your definition of 'positive change.'"

"I'll let you be the one who defines it. If it met your definition, would you do it?"

"Yes."

"Excellent," responded Baptista who was ninety-five-percent certain that Manning would answer in the affirmative. He had already had a team of CIA psychologist's review Manning records for personality traits that would help determine the likelihood of the sniper being comfortable with such an assignment.

"Do you have a new assignment for me?" asked Manning, wondering if the man sitting across the table was considering having the president of the United States assassinated.

"Yes and no," said Baptista. "I have an assignment, but the details will not be made clear to you for a few more weeks. It seems as though my employer is uncertain of whether or not the target is enough of a threat to be terminated."

"Can I ask who the target is?"

"No," responded Baptista sharply. "It is not the president—in case you were wondering."

"Can I ask how much I'd get paid?" asked Manning, who was quickly growing accustomed to the idea of being rich.

"Yes. My employer is willing to pay you three million dollars for the successful completion of the job. You will receive $500,000 upon acceptance of the job and the other 2.5 million dollars after you have achieved the objective."

Manning sat in stunned silence.

Baptista continued, "The figure reflects the importance my employer attaches to the job. It is also a reflection of the difficulty of the job. If you are successful, you will never be able to work as an assassin again."

"I won't have to," replied Manning, who liked being described as an assassin. "How difficult is the job?"

"I can't give you specifics at this time. But I do know that the target will be protected by professionals whose skills match your own."

"I like a challenge," said Manning.

"Can I assume that you are interested?" asked Baptista.

"I am. Of course, I'll need to know a lot more about the target—and the protective forces around the target."

"You will, in due time." Baptista then handed Manning a packet of information similar to that which the assassin received prior to the Seselj assassination. In the packet was a one-way ticket to the Minneapolis-St. Paul airport, directions to an address in St. Paul, keys to an apartment, and a fake Minnesota driver's license and University of Saint Thomas student I.D. bearing the name Lee Murphy. The packet also contained a deposit slip showing that $500,000 had already been placed in Manning's account.

Manning arrived in St. Paul that evening. During the flight, the sniper was trying to figure out if the target was located in the area or if the environment of the area was similar to that of where the target was living—like the Seselj assassination.

CHAPTER FOURTEEN

The February air was perfectly still. It was four degrees below zero and pitch dark at 4:45 A.M., when Father Otto stepped out of the monastery and began running. It was the same routine he had followed all his adult life. Early mornings were when he was most at peace with himself and the world.

The packed snow crunched under his feet as he made his way down the solitary road and into the pine forest that surrounded the Abbey of St. John. As he gazed across the frozen waters of Lake Sagatagan, he thought of his former student Bobby Colfax and smiled. He recalled the day he first met Colfax and remembered thinking, even in the fall of 1963, that the skinny, shy kid possessed a certain quiet strength that would take him far in this world. Father Otto, now in his fifty-first year of serving the Lord, had assumed that Colfax's quiet strength would be employed as a priest. But Colfax was not even fifteen years old when he stunned Father Otto by telling him that he did not hear the calling. Wilhoit replayed the conversation, now more than thirty years old, in his mind as he continued to make his way through the forest. The year was 1964 and Bob Colfax was a sophomore at St. John's Preparatory School.

"Bobby, have you given any thought to what I asked you yesterday after practice?" asked Father Otto as they stretched out for their early morning run—a ritual that had begun Colfax's freshman year as he was struggling to make the varsity cross-country team.

"I have, Father," said Colfax as the two began running side by side. "I've prayed, and I am not meant to be priest." The directness of Colfax's statement stunned Wilhoit. What Colfax said next was even more of a shock.

"I continued praying last night, and my future path is clear. I'm meant to serve the Lord—but in other ways," said the boy.

"In what ways, Robert?" asked the priest.

"I am meant to serve my country. First, as a naval officer and then in politics," replied Colfax with utter confidence.

Father Otto pondered Colfax's words and debated whether or not he should push the boy on the matter. President Kennedy, the country's first Catholic president, had been assassinated the year before, and Father Otto understood that he had become a hero to a number of boys at the prep school. He also knew that Eugene McCarthy, a fellow prep school graduate and Minnesota's junior United States senator, had followed a similar path. "Politics is a noble calling," replied Wilhoit. "If that is what the Lord is telling you to do, then you must follow His command. I just remind you that the Lord often works in mysterious ways and the path that seems so clear today may not be so clear tomorrow. You must have faith."

"When did you know that you were meant to be a priest?" asked Colfax.

"I didn't really know until I was almost through with college."

"But I thought you joined the monastery right after you graduated from the prep school?"

"I did," said Father Otto, "but I only came to learn that it was the right decision during my last year of college. As you may know, I was a wrestler throughout high school and college. My senior year of college, I was training for the Olympic trials. I had set my eyes set on winning a medal in the 1948 Summer Olympics. Two weeks before the trials, I broke my left arm in practice."

"You must have been devastated," said Colfax, who had not known that his mentor had been a world-class wrestler.

"I was," replied Wilhoit, "at first."

"At first?" asked Colfax as he strained to keep up the pace.

"That night I prayed and asked God why He let this happen to me. I asked Him if I had done something wrong, something to displease Him. The answer I received was that I had done nothing wrong. I was simply meant to serve Him completely—and immediately."

"And that was it? You were okay with not going to the Olympics?"

"I was. That's not to say that it wasn't hard on me. I cried when I read about the Olympics in the newspaper that summer—but I wasn't jealous. I had complete faith in the path God chose for me."

"So do I," said Colfax forcefully, as he surged ahead of his running partner with a sudden burst of energy. Wilhoit remembered that it was at that moment that he knew Colfax was not only going to be a good runner but was destined for great things.

＊　＊

The second Republican debate, held in Phoenix on February 20, two days before the Arizona primary, appeared to be yielding no new insights when, out of the blue, Dick Graham asked Prescott whether he was considering selecting Elizabeth Vandiver as his running mate. As was his custom, Prescott avoided a direct answer. Graham went on the attack.

"I think the people of Arizona have a right to know for certain whether or not Elizabeth Vandiver will be one heartbeat away from the Oval Office if you are elected president," said Graham, practically spitting out the name of Vandiver as though it were some form of bile that had to be immediately expelled from his mouth.

"As I said, Dick," replied Prescott in a cool but condescending tone, "I have not yet had time to consider who my vice president will be. I must secure the nomination first, something I'm working hard at doing," continued Prescott in an obvious effort to demonstrate to the viewers of the debate that he had not grown overly confident in his lead over his two remaining Republican challengers.

"Well, let me rephrase my question, Elliott," replied Graham, who usually referred to Prescott by his first name, "since you are apparently incapable of answering a simple question with a simple yes or no answer. Will you select as your vice president a candidate who is committed to overturning the Supreme Court's *Roe* vs. *Wade* decision?" Graham purposely let the question linger before continuing. "Will you select someone who will not coddle Chinese dictators by opposing free and open trade to China? Will you select someone who is a committed Republican and has never served in a Democratic administration? Can you answer those three questions, Elliott?"

Annoyed at the continued use of his first name, Prescott grew flush. He was suddenly very aware that he didn't have a quick, straightforward answer to Graham's line of questioning and that the in-house audience, the television audience and, most important, the media were expecting an immediate response. He temporarily froze and muttered an inaudible reply. After what seemed like an eternity, Prescott elaborated on his meek answer and said that he and his team of advisors would vet all prospective candidates to make sure they "adhered with the principles of the Republican Party."

Wanting a piece of the action, Cross chimed in and asked, "Is it the opinion of your team of advisors that protecting life from conception to birth is a Republican principle? After all, it is in our party's platform."

Recovering somewhat, Prescott responded that reasonable Republicans could come to different conclusions over the question of abortion. The supporters of Graham and Cross, and even some of Prescott's own backers in the audience who were pro-life, audibly moaned. Polls would later show that his response was well received by a majority of television viewers—especially independent voters. But Prescott's advisors knew that those voters could not help their candidate secure the Republican nomination. In Prescott's mind, he had already crossed Elizabeth Vandiver off his short list of prospective running mates.

* *

Prescott's campaign manager, Dan Miller, made the official announcement minutes after the debate, declaring that his candidate had never actively considered Elizabeth Vandiver for the vice presidency. A news release was sent out shortly after and was immediately picked up by all the major media outlets. Prescott and Miller conferred and agreed that they had to put some distance between himself and Vandiver—quickly. In a state as conservative as Arizona, the prospect of "the Vandiver albatross," as Prescott privately referred to it, was something they had to get rid of immediately.

The news release stressed that while Governor Prescott had an immense amount of respect for the former Republican governor of Maryland and current United Nations ambassador, her positions on a range of foreign affairs issues were fundamentally in conflict with the candidate's own, and, for that reason, she was not on the short list of prospective vice presidential candidates. The release did not focus on any of the specific issues Graham raised during the debate. It was classic Washington spin: the Prescott campaign distanced itself from Elizabeth Vandiver by claiming that she had never been considered for the position—but for reasons wholly unrelated to the issues Graham had raised. It even tried to gain a few points by praising Vandiver before tossing her overboard.

* *

Vandiver referred all media inquiries to her press secretary at the United Nations and instructed him to tell the reporters that she was surprised at the attention. He was to say that the ambassador had never actively expressed interest in the position, nor would she have been interested had she been offered it. Privately, Vandiver was crushed. She had known her acceptance of the ambassadorship with a Democratic president was a risky one, but she had always felt that her bipartisan profile, along with her pro-choice position and foreign policy experience, would have made her a legitimate candidate for vice president. Robert Colfax held the same opinion.

* *

Stanley Cross had already spent over twenty-five million dollars of his own money in his quest to become president. Another two million dollars meant nothing to the cable television magnate. Air time in the Phoenix and Tucson markets was relatively inexpensive, and he was able to saturate the airways with what would later become known as the "deer-in-the-headlight" commercial.

Cross, seeking to highlight Prescott's unwillingness to commit to other specific policy positions, posed a series of direct questions to Prescott. After each question, the video clip of Elliott Prescott's frozen response to Dick Graham's question about Elizabeth Vandiver was used as his response. The commercial hit its mark. Prescott looked like a fool, and Cross received points for injecting some humor into the campaign. Stanley Cross won the Arizona Republican primary with forty-five percent of the vote. Prescott came in second, and Robert Colfax, running as an independent and without campaigning, tied Dick Graham for third place with seven percent of the vote.

* *

Secret Service protection for Gibraltar commenced immediately. Colfax and Sawyer left the meeting with Sean McGowan and were met outside by Luke Parish, a young Secret Service agent who appeared to have come straight from central casting. He had short hair, a square jaw and wore a crisp blue suit. His face was expressionless except for his alert eyes. A third agent, Julie Brix, was waiting next to the Lincoln Continental to escort the governor to his three o'clock speaking engagement at the University of Minnesota.

"Are you sure you want to go ahead with this?" Sawyer asked the candidate, referring to his upcoming speech.

"Absolutely. I'm not going to start playing it safe just because I'm considered by the media to be a legitimate presidential contender," replied Colfax.

"I know. It's just that the trial attorney lobby is so goddamn powerful."

"All the more reason to take them on," said Colfax.

"I just think you have to choose your battles," replied Sawyer carefully.

"Dammit, Pete," said Colfax, turning quickly toward Sawyer. "I can't afford to have you thinking like a typical politician. The trial attorneys are going to oppose me regardless of whether I piss them off or not. So I might as well tell the truth. Remember, I'm not running for the presidency just to top off my resumé. I'm running because I want to fundamentally change the way this country operates. If I can't win by telling the people what I want to say, then I don't want to be president—nor do I deserve to be president."

"I understand," said Sawyer, although he was not thoroughly convinced that Colfax had fully considered the entire political equation. "It's just that what makes for good policy might be disastrous for your campaign. Sometimes it's necessary to suppress your ideas until you get in office."

"That's bullshit. That's the problem with politics. That's why people are so cynical and voter turnout is so low. Everyone feels that politicians are always hiding something from them. I'm not going to play that game."

Sawyer could see the passion in Colfax's eyes. It was moments like these that he relished working for the man.

"I'm not doing this on a whim, Pete. I truly believe the legal system has to be reformed, and I intend to reform it here in Minnesota first.

"And I'm certainly not going to let my presidential ambitions cloud what I believe is best for the citizens of Minnesota." Colfax was on his soapbox now, and Sawyer knew better than to interrupt him. "I mean, it's ludicrous for a person or corporation to be found fifty-percent liable—or less—for an accident but still be required to pay one hundred percent of the damages just because they have the deep pockets. That's wrong, and I want to change it. It's also wrong that people can file frivolous lawsuits and not have to pay the consequences for wasting the time of the defendant—and the legal system. If you bring a lawsuit to court and you lose, you should be required to pay for the other party's costs. Why should innocent people have to pay to protect themselves from these Armani-wearing, Lexus-driving, Merlot-drinking, lawsuit-happy leeches called lawyers?"

"Tell me how you really feel," said Sawyer, knowing that Colfax had almost been put out of business in the late 1970s by a frivolous lawsuit that had consumed a year of his life and drained all of his company's profits. "As your campaign manager, I feel I should caution you to tone down the rhetoric about lawyers," added Sawyer.

"You think? I kind of like the ring of 'lawsuit-happy leeches,'" laughed Colfax, knowing full well that he would never use such language in public. "But seriously, Pete, don't you find the fact that this country has ten times more lawyers per capita than the Netherlands a tad bit disturbing? And aren't you concerned that we graduate more lawyers every year than are currently working in all of Japan?"

"I am," admitted Sawyer.

"Then don't you think that I, as both the governor of this state and as a candidate for the presidency of the United States, have a responsibility—a duty—to bring this issue before the American people?"

"Of course, I do. I just think that if you do it now, the trial attorney lobby will do everything in their power to defeat you."

"You're probably right, but our legal system is choking our economy. Lawyers add little to our economy. They simply fight over the existing pie—unlike small businessmen and women who help expand the pie. That's why we need legal reform."

* *

As Colfax, now under the protective eyes of the Secret Service, approached the law school, Sawyer reminded him that his speech was to be broadcast live on C-SPAN II and repeated later that evening on C-SPAN I.

"In other words, no comments about Armani-wearing, Lexus-driving, lawsuit-happy leeches," said Colfax, winking at Sawyer.

"I'd shy away from it. You might get sued," said Sawyer with a laugh.

Minutes later, Colfax was before a group of 200 law students, outlining many of the points he had made to Sawyer only moments earlier in the car. He was just as passionate—if not as colorful in his description of the legal profession. As he was nearing the end of his speech, he added, on a whim, a new paragraph.

"Have you ever considered the economic cost of our legal system? Some will say that it is a ludicrous thought because you cannot put a price on justice. They are, of course, right. But as a policy-maker who is responsible to all the citizens of this state, it is a dereliction of duty to not consider these costs. For example, did you know that one-half the cost of certain medically necessary procedures can be attributed to the cost of medical malpractice insurance? How many people are being denied life-enhancing services because our legal system has priced them out of reach? As a public official, I have a responsibility to weigh those costs. It is time to restore some balance to the system, and that is why I am proposing major legal reform in this legislative session."

* *

In Washington, D.C., Jacob Mance watched Colfax's performance on C-SPAN II and laughed out loud. Within minutes of the end of Colfax's speech, Mance had a team of his legal secretaries calling his entire Rolodex of legal colleagues and old law school friends. Early the next morning, he would be making his pitch to his largest group yet. Twenty hours after Colfax's speech, the Coalition for a Prosperous New Millennium had an additional three million dollars, compliments of a cadre of Washington's highest paid lawyers, to direct against the independent candidate for president, Robert T. Colfax.

✳ ✳

Win Murdock was in a foul mood. "David," he screamed at his trusted assistant, "what the hell is Mance doing?"

"I don't understand," said a genuinely confused David Luther. "Mance just told me he showed Colfax's C-SPAN clip on legal reform to a group of Washington's top trial attorneys and they pledged over three million dollars on the spot—with commitments to raise an additional two million dollars from their various chapters across the country."

"What good is the fucking money if he doesn't use it?"

"I don't understand, sir. Colfax isn't campaigning in any of the primary races anymore. He proved he was a contender in Iowa and New Hampshire, and now he's indicated that he's going straight to the general election," replied Luther.

"I know that! But the end game is to defeat Colfax. If the Arizona primary was any indication, and Cross and Graham continue to push Prescott to the right and Greene—and his call for universal health care—is able to do the same to Byrne on the other side of the spectrum, the only beneficiary is Colfax." Before Luther could even say a word, Murdock continued, "I want the coalition to use the upcoming primaries in California, New York, and the other states to get Graham, Cross and Greene out of the race. I want ads targeted against them starting tomorrow!"

"Yes, sir."

"And David," said Murdock, "I also want to confirm that we are making it as difficult as possible for Colfax to get on the ballot in every state."

"Yes, sir."

That afternoon, Luther flew out of Omaha to Washington. By evening, he and Mance had devised a strategy to achieve Murdock's wishes. One and a half million dollars was committed to getting the other Republican and Democratic candidates out of the race. Television and radio commercials were readied the next day, and Murdock's private army of lobbyists were dispersed to key states, where talk radio hosts and editorial boards were briefed on the weaknesses, vulnerabilities, and human faults of Dick Graham, Stanley Cross, and Reginald Greene. Win Murdock even personally called the owners of the networks that ran the Sunday morning talk shows—all of whom were well-aware that Holten, Inc., almost single-handedly sponsored the programs—and demanded that the shows attack the three candidates he wanted out of the race. Another two million dollars was allocated to bribe various state officials to throw additional barriers up to deny Colfax ballot access.

* *

Sean McGowan and Stephanie Freeberg lay exhausted next to one another on the rumpled sheets. "I am glad the Secret Service still requires refresher courses," said Freeberg referring to the agency's policy of requiring every agent to return to its state-of-the-art facility in Beltsville, Maryland, every few months to become familiar with the latest threats and enhance their protective skills. "You're certainly in no need of a refresher course in one area," she added as she crawled out of bed. "I'm so sorry I couldn't make it out for Christmas."

"That's okay. The wait was well worth it," said a tired but appreciative McGowan.

"Are you enjoying your new job?"

"I am. I'm even excited about protective services again," replied McGowan. Freeberg was disappointed and surprised by his answer, but she didn't signal this to McGowan.

"I thought you had had enough of that crap after you left the White House."

"So did I. But Governor Colfax is the kind of person I envisioned protecting when I joined the service."

"Really," said Freeberg, who was becoming more intrigued with the Colfax candidacy and was happy to hear her lover intimating that Colfax was as honorable in private as he appeared to be in public.

"I met with him, his staff, and his family. He's extremely sharp but also down to earth," said McGowan, revealing more than a Secret Service agent normally would to a loved one. But since Freeberg was a former agent herself, he figured that he could speak in generalities. "His staff also has great respect for him. If what I saw when I was with his wife and two daughters is any indication, they're a real family."

"Unlike the current occupants of the White House?" said Freeberg. McGowan didn't offer a response. It was unprofessional.

"How was Beltsville?"

"Same old, same old. You know the routine."

"I sure do. I don't miss it at all. All those instructors always yapping away about the technique of taking a bullet for another human being a perishable skill. I mean, of course it is, the natural instinct is to always protect yourself first."

"It's true, though. Otherwise the techniques won't be used when they're needed."

"You're starting to sound like an aspiring director of the Secret Service, Sean. Anything new?"

"Not really. The usual—a lot of running and shooting. We got an update from the 'Fantasy Farm,'" said McGowan, referring to the Secret Service's team of experts whose sole purpose was to dream up potential threats to the president and then figure out how to thwart that threat. "We spent a good deal of time reviewing a new internal document called the Exceptional Case Study. It's a comprehensive review of all the people who have tried to assassinate a president this century. It also has a few isolated cases of other assassins who tried to kill famous people."

"I remember hearing about the project just as I was leaving. It sounds interesting," said Freeberg.

"It is. The book extensively profiles eighty-three different assassins. It starts with Ruth Ann Steinhagen."

"Who?"

"Have you ever seen the movie *The Natural?*"

"The baseball movie with Robert Redford?"

"Yeah. Steinhagen is the woman who shoots the character played by Robert Redford. In real life, the player was Eddie Waitkus. He played for the Chicago Cubs. The case studies end with the nut who tried to fly his light plane into the White House a few years ago."

"I remember that. I was on duty when it happened."

"So how's your job going?" asked McGowan in effort to change the subject. He didn't feel comfortable talking about sensitive information—even with a former Secret Service agent.

"Frustrating. I'm trying to find out more about a new organization that has suddenly appeared out of nowhere and is now a major player in the presidential campaign. The group is called the Coalition for a Prosperous New Millennium."

"I reviewed some of the commercials that they ran against Colfax," said McGowan. "They were included in the background file the service put together to help us develop a security plan for him."

"Yeah, well, I can't find out a thing about the group. Under current law, the organization is not required to provide a listing of who its contributors are," said Freeberg. "I've tried every possible way to get the information but I always run into the thorough work of Lawrence, Mance & Scott. They're the shysters who are operating the group, and they're stonewalling me."

"Our files indicate that they are a legitimate political organization. They're nonpartisan and dedicated to providing voters information. From their commercials—and some of the literature pieces I saw—I can't tell what exactly they stand for," said McGowan.

"That's just it. They're all over the board on the issues. At first, I thought they were simply an anti-Colfax group, but now they have taken after Greene and Graham. Go figure. They go after the Greene on the left, Colfax in the middle, and Graham on the right."

"Whoever they are, it appears that they're interested in maintaining the status quo. All three of those guys, despite their vastly different politics, would shake up Washington," said McGowan.

"You're right," said Freeberg. "Maybe the group hasn't attacked either Byrne or Prescott because they know that neither is going to rock the boat very much."

"Hell, neither one will rock the boat at all."

CHAPTER FIFTEEN

Carroll Avenue looked like any number of streets in the American Midwest. The middle-class homes were well maintained but had small yards. In recent years, a few of the homes had been converted into apartments to accommodate the growing number of students attending nearby St. Thomas University.

The third-floor apartment, which Baptista had rented for Manning, crowned just such a house. An elderly couple who wintered in Florida and spent their summers at their lake cabin in northern Minnesota owned the home.

The apartment was more spacious than Manning had imagined it would be. It had a living room and dining room, kitchen, bedroom, and a very comfortable bathroom. The hardwood floors and large windows on three sides made the apartment seem much larger than it was.

The southern windows in the living room looked out over Carroll Avenue; the eastern window in the kitchen gave out to the roof of the neighboring house; and the western window in the bathroom framed a view of the houses on the other side of the block. Beyond those houses was Cretin Avenue, on the other side of which lay the Town & Country Club golf course. From the window, the course was only visible from late October through mid-May, when the large white oak, maple, and elm trees that lined the avenue were leafless.

After settling into the apartment, Manning explored the city and proceeded to find the nearest grocery store, bookstore, gun shop, hardware store, and sporting goods store. Manning purchased some food from a local supermarket, a handbook on sniping techniques from the bookstore, some Nomex gloves from the gun shop, one sandbag and a box of alcohol wipes from the hardware store, and a couple of magazines on deer hunting from the sporting goods store. Everything was paid for in cash.

*   *

Annette Christianson, Colfax's chief of staff, and Pete Sawyer arrived at the governor's mansion at the same time. Agent Parish momentarily detained both and described the new security procedures. Even key staff members, he said, would have to be searched before meeting with the governor.

"Good Morning, Governor," said Christianson, somewhat crankily. She had never grown accustom to Colfax's preference for early morning breakfast meetings.

"Good morning, Annette. Would you like a cup of coffee?" said Colfax warmly, as he began pouring her a cup in anticipation of her response. "How about you, Pete?"

"That'd be great, Governor."

Sitting down at his large oak desk, upon which was a framed copy of Teddy Roosevelt's "The credit belongs to the man in the arena" speech, Colfax motioned the two to have a seat on the other side.

Christianson and Sawyer looked at one another and knew that whatever Colfax was about to tell them was going to come in the form of an order rather than a request. They had both learned that whenever he had made up his mind, he issued his orders from behind his desk. When he wanted their advice, he joined them at a conference table on the other side of the room and solicited their opinions. Colfax was more than aware of the habit—it was something he had consciously done since he was a young naval officer.

"It is time," Colfax said simply. Sawyer and Christianson again looked at one another. This time, they smiled.

"Are you suggesting what I think you're suggesting?" asked Christianson.

"Yes. It is time that I put my full weight behind the effort to enact a unicameral legislature here in Minnesota," said Colfax. The merger of the two chambers of the House and Senate into a single legislative body had long been his dream.

Christianson, who no longer needed coffee, was ecstatic. "The timing is perfect! Your tort reform effort has obviously hit some resistance from the legal community and is quickly becoming the primary focus of this legislative session. An initiative for a single-house legislature will divert that emphasis and engage the public. The public will be overwhelmingly on your side. Plus, you'll have the lobbying community so scared that they'll drop everything—including fighting your tort reform bill—to defeat you."

"They'll go ballistic," said Sawyer.

"For sure," replied Christianson, "it will definitely make their job harder. Under the new system, every bill would get a hearing, and it would be defeated or passed on its merits. No longer could a bill be killed in committee by a powerful committee chair or, alternatively, slipped into a conference committee report. That's how lobbyists currently do most of their work. Under a single legislative body, they'd actually have to get to know every legislator. That's more work for them. More work means that they can handle fewer clients—and few clients means less money."

"That's right," said Colfax. "The current system favors the career politicians and the lobbyists. A single body will help restore power to the people. Imagine a legislative system so simple that anyone could follow it."

"It's also perfect timing from a political perspective," added Sawyer. "It will continue to give you a lot of exposure in your presidential campaign. Also, if you announce your plan on March 7, you can divert some exposure from the mega-primaries in California, Ohio, New York, and Illinois that day."

"I'm glad you agree. But I want you to know that I'm doing it because I think it will benefit the citizens of Minnesota." Smiling, Colfax added, "Although I'm not unaware that the issue might prove useful in my bid for the presidency."

"You're damn right it will," said Christianson. "While all those other lame-ass candidates are talking about reform, you are actually trying to achieve it. The media will eat it up."

"Of course, the political and lobbying community won't," volunteered Sawyer.

"I know," said Colfax. "But that's what makes this job so much fun. Plus, I figure since I already have the trial attorneys gunning for my head; what are a few extra shots in the grand scheme of things?" Colfax paused and looked at both Christianson and Sawyer. "My question to the two of you is, can we do it?"

"Absolutely," said Christianson.

"Without question," responded Sawyer.

"Good. I agree. Let's hold a news conference at ten o'clock tomorrow morning on the steps of the Capitol. I want all the media invited, and I want every legislator who has ever gone on record as saying he or she supported a unicameral legislature to join us. I also want to meet with the co-sponsors of the bill. If memory serves me correctly, we have an equal number of Republicans and Democrats—in both the House and the Senate—sponsoring the bill."

"That's correct, Governor. The speaker of the House and the Senate minority leader both support the idea. Of course, I think, their support has been contingent on the fact that they figured they would never actually have to vote on the issue," said Christianson with a smirk.

"You're right, Annette. They've always publicly supported the idea because they know it's popular. But they've never pushed for it because it would diminish their power. They've had the best of both worlds. Well, now is the time for them to put their money where their mouth is," said Colfax. "Invite them to lunch today. It's time we force them to take a stand. Also, contact my database of campaign volunteers and supporters. I want the Capitol steps filled with supporters for tomorrow's event."

By mid-morning, Christianson had contacted all of the major media outlets. By mid-afternoon, after the lunch with a dozen nervous legislative leaders, a full-scale offensive was set in motion to make Minnesota the first state in over seventy years to fundamentally reform the way its government operates.

Pete Sawyer, in the meantime, had gone back to the campaign headquarters on the other side of the Mississippi and briefed his growing campaign staff. He called on Josh Parker to head up the twenty-four-hour effort to generate a huge turnout for the next day's event.

Parker, who was beginning to be seen as something of a miracle worker by Sawyer, immediately posted an urgent e-mail to every college and university contact in Minnesota, asking them to attend the rally. He listed the date, time and location. He also provided a brief explanation of how this issue fit into Colfax's presidential campaign. By late afternoon, leaflets announcing the event began to spring up all over town, including at St. Thomas University.

* *

Lee Manning immediately spotted the leaflet with the large photo of Colfax. The sniper suddenly recalled Baptista's strange line of questioning about assassinating a president. The trip to St. Paul was beginning to make sense. Manning smiled. The sniper was glad Baptista didn't say in advance that Colfax was the target. If he had, Manning might have taken the job for free.

* *

Dick Graham wanted to keep running. He was a professional presidential candidate. It was his reason for living. He knew he could never win, but he loved the attention. Graham was also a realist. He knew a continuation of low vote totals would hurt his ability to augment his income during nonpresidential years by giving speeches to various conservative organizations. He knew the times had passed him by. Stanley Cross had co-opted his message, and Cross had the money to keep going. With great reluctance, Dick Graham withdrew from the race and from presidential politics forever. The Republican establishment and Elliott Prescott, with the help of the coalition, breathed a collective sigh of relief. Now they just had to focus on getting Stanley Cross out.

* *

David Pollard, the executive director of the National Small Business Coalition, was a political junkie. Politics was his life—and the reason his first two wives had left him. It was well past midnight when he flicked on C-SPAN II and caught Colfax's speech on legal reform. He was captivated. He absorbed every word.

"You tell'em, Bobby," he screamed at the television. "You're the fuckin' man!" he said as though Colfax had just sunk a last-minute basket in a crucial basketball game. Although Pollard was trained as a lawyer, he had little respect for the profession. After the rerun was over, Pollard watched as the camera continued to linger on the scene at the University of Minnesota law school. He watched as a few students asked Colfax for his autograph and a third, a young woman in a Smith College sweatshirt, asked Colfax a pointed question. Pollard couldn't hear what was being said because the melodious voice of an anonymous C-SPAN announcer was informing viewers that a subcommittee hearing on transportation funding would follow at 2:00 A.M. and Colfax's presentation would be replayed again at six and eight o'clock. Pollard grabbed a beer out of his nearly empty refrigerator and set his video recorder. He wanted to show some of his members Colfax's speech. He was confident that he could get a few to contribute to Colfax's campaign.

It was only after his third beer that he settled on a course of action. Having been an early contributor to the Coalition of a Prosperous New Millennium, Pollard was aware of the group's game plan. His conscience, as well as everything he had heard Colfax say, told him that he should resign from the coalition and try to influence his organization to become the first major business group to support Robert Colfax. But Pollard, who had two monthly child support payments, also knew that such a step would ruin his career in Washington. Jacob Mance would make sure of it.

In his heart, Pollard knew Colfax would make an excellent president, and he was determined to help the Minnesotan in some way. Then he remembered meeting Ellen Moriarty at the Mayflower Hotel in November. She had told him then that if he ever had any interesting information, she wanted to be the first to hear it.

Pollard went to his computer files, pulled up his automated Rolodex and scribbled down Moriarty's e-mail address and telephone number. He pondered sending an e-mail but decided against it. They were too easy to trace. Instead, he dialed her number and was stunned when she answered the phone.

"Moriarty," she said as though it was not at all unusual that she would receive a call at 2:30 in the morning.

"Hi," said Pollard, cautiously.

"Can I help you?" said Moriarty, impatiently.

"Yes—ah—you and I have met before, but I can't tell you who I am. I run a trade association here in Washington, and I'm aware of a massive conspiracy against Robert Colfax."

"Go on," said Moriarty, quietly turning on her tape recorder.

"The law firm of Lawrence, Mance & Scott is a front for a group of Washington insiders who want to ensure Robert Colfax's defeat."

"You mean, the Coalition for the . . ." said Moriarty, unable to recall the entire name of the group.

"That's right. The Coalition for a Prosperous New Millennium," said Pollard.

"Who's behind the group?" said Moriarty, getting right to the heart of the matter.

"I've given that a lot of thought and have an educated guess. I don't yet have proof but . . ." said Pollard, pausing for a moment, "I think it's Win Murdock."

"The head of Holten, Inc?" asked Moriarty. "Really? Why do you say that?"

"Just a hunch," said Pollard, suddenly questioning the wisdom of contacting Moriarty. He feared he might be wrong or worse—that the people at the coalition would find out he was the source of the leak.

"I need some proof before I can run a story," pressed Moriarty. "What's your hunch based on? Who else is involved? Can we meet to discuss this?"

The flurry of questions and the Moriarty's offer to meet in person spooked Pollard, and he wanted to hang up. "I've got to go."

"Wait," demanded Moriarty, "how large is the conspiracy?"

"I don't know, but I suspect it's growing. Colfax is threatening a lot of powerful groups—lawyers, lobbyists, defense manufacturers, the gambling industry, the education establishment, Holten—and they'll stop at nothing to derail his candidacy. They view him as a real threat. I think it's Murdock because Colfax is the one candidate who won't take his money, and he is the only candidate espousing the complete elimination of all gas, oil and ethanol subsidies. Without those subsidies, Murdock's out over a billion dollars a year. Murdock also has enough clout to get a lot of legitimate Washington players to the table. It's easy for him to hide his involvement by working through those other groups." Suddenly, Pollard realized he had said too much said. "Really, I've got to go"

"How can I get a hold of you?"

"You can't."

"Will you contact me if you have any more information?"

"I don't know—I'll contact you from the CyberCafe," said Pollard as he hung up.

He was more nervous than he realized. But there was no real danger, he kept telling himself.

* *

That same morning, at a more reasonable hour, Pete Sawyer called Ellen Moriarty.

"Good morning, Ms. Moriarty. This is Pete Sawyer, Robert Colfax's campaign manager."

"Well, good morning. What a coincidence. I was just thinking about the distinguished governor from Minnesota. To what do I owe this pleasure?"

"Just a courtesy call. I have a little insider information for you. Nothing major—just something to help keep you one step ahead of the competition," said Sawyer.

"Let's have it," said Moriarty with more patience than she really felt.

"Would you like to know Colfax's Secret Service codename?"

"I didn't know he was getting Secret Service protection."

"Well then, I've just given you another first."

"Okay, I'll bite. What's his codename?"

"Gibraltar."

"As in the Rock of Gibraltar?" asked Moriarty

"Exactly."

"Why?"

"Because he's so solid," joked Sawyer. "The Secret Service said they had never seen a more sturdy candidate in their 135 years of protecting presidents."

"I think I'll report that they are calling him Gibraltar because they think he's as dense as a rock," countered Moriarty, who was just toying with Sawyer.

"Seriously, the reason the Secret Service gave him the name is because he has only five percent body fat. Someone at the agency apparently likened him to the Rock of Gibraltar in a staff meeting, and the codename stuck."

"What else is new in the campaign?" replied Moriarty in a bored manner.

"You know about his recent major speech on legal reform?"

"Yeah, I read about it. Pretty ballsy. Those are the kinds of things I'd like you to give me a heads-up on. No offense, but my readers could give a shit about his Secret Service codename. Anything else?"

"As a matter of fact, there is. The reason for the news conference he called for today will severely test his skills as a political reformer. He's going to announce his unilateral and unconditional support for a single legislative house. He wants to entirely eliminate one chamber of the Minnesota legislature. If you think lobbyists don't like him now, just wait until this hits the fan. He's prepared to go to the wall on the issue."

"No shit?"

"No shit."

"Now, this is the kind of stuff I want to know. I don't know if your man can make it to the White House, but he's going to make this election year the most fascinating in recent memory."

"He'll make it," replied Sawyer.

Moriarty then proceeded to grill Sawyer about the issue for several minutes.

"I have another question for you," she said after a while. "What do you know about the Coalition for a Prosperous New Millennium?"

Sawyer paused, then replied, "Not much, other than they appear to be some front group for the status quo. I originally thought they were just out to get Colfax. But I've heard that they have been running ads against Greene, Cross, and Graham."

"Why the status quo?"

"It's the only thing that makes sense. Greene, Graham, Cross, and Colfax share one thing in common, and that is they're not part of the Washington political establishment—at least not the way Byrne and Prescott are."

"Interesting. Do you think Win Murdock could be behind the coalition?"

"You know, you're the second person to ask me that in the last few days."

"Who was the first?"

"Governor Colfax."

"Really?" said Moriarty.

"That last comment was meant to be off the record," said Sawyer, trying to backtrack.

"Sure," replied Moriarty, more easily than Sawyer would have expected. "Of course, in return, I'll want you to continue to feed me inside information throughout the campaign."

"I think we can come to some sort of mutually beneficial agreement."

"Okay, off the record, tell me why Colfax thinks Murdock might be behind the coalition."

"When Colfax was running for governor in 1996, he publicly renounced Murdock's offer of a campaign contribution. And he did it in a highly visible fashion. He called a news conference and tore up an unsolicited check from Murdock. At the time, he called Murdock's willingness to contribute to every candidate in the race 'legalized bribery.' Colfax also vetoed a fifty-million-dollar state ethanol subsidy in the 1997 session that would have greatly benefited Holten. He repeated those vetoes in 1998 and 1999—much to the consternation of Murdock and his team of highly paid lobbyists."

"What about Cross, Greene, and Graham? What does Murdock have against those three?"

"Nothing, other than this: the longer they stay in the race, the more it benefits our campaign."

"How so?"

"All three, in one way or another, force Prescott and Byrne to abandon their centrist themes. Once they do, they'll alienate moderate, middle-of-the-road voters. Colfax is, then, the most logical alternative for them."

"Plausible," said Moriarty as though she was generally satisfied with Sawyer's line of reasoning. "I've got a deadline. But I appreciate the info. Stay in touch."

* *

Moriarty, seeking to shake up the major media—which were focused on the primary races in California, Ohio, Illinois, and New York—decided to lead her daily Internet report with Colfax's effort to push for a unicameral legislature under the headline "COLFAX TO PUSH BOLD REFORMS: LAWYERS AND LOBBYISTS TARGETED." The opening line of her report read: "While Prescott and Byrne seek to cinch their respective party's endorsement by promising reform, only one candidate for president is actually trying to deliver it. That candidate is Robert T. Colfax." Satisfied that her work for the day was done, Moriarty grabbed a beer from her refrigerator. She began reviewing her notes from her earlier conversation with Sawyer. She wrote down one word: "Gibraltar." She also reviewed her notes from the mysterious caller of the night before. Next to the word, she scribbled another word: "conspiracy." The Gibraltar conspiracy.

* *

Alone in his office, Sean McGowan poured over a list of activities that the agents in the Minneapolis office had completed in the last week. Included were a number of standard Secret Service activities. One agent had interviewed a handful of local retailers who had been victimized by counterfeit bills. Another was busy tracking down the mastermind behind an elaborate food stamp fraud. Another had interviewed three local citizens—all psychotics—who had recently threatened President Butler.

161

Agent Luke Parish, however, had the week's most interesting and disturbing case. He reported on his visit to a suburban home to investigate the origins of e-mail expressing a desire to kill the president in a very vivid and graphic fashion. Parish was stunned when he found that a seven-year-old boy was the author of the e-mail. After extensive discussions with the boy's parents Parish determined that the boy had a personality disorder but, in the words of his report, "posed no realistic threat to the president." The two-hour interview left Parish troubled. The Secret Service drilled into its agents heads from their first day that a threat to the president could come in any form—including a nun, a pregnant woman, a girl scout, or even a seven-year old boy. This was the first time that that lesson had really hit home for Parish. Parish also included in his report a brief analysis on the protection being accorded Gibraltar. As McGowan finished reading Parish's report, the phone rang.

"What?" he said incredulously after listening to the caller, Agent Brix. "You've got to be kidding me. I specifically told Sawyer that we need at least twenty-four hours—preferably forty-eight hours—advance notice of any public event that Gibraltar was going to attend!"

"I thought I'd tell you as soon as I found out, boss," said Brix.

"Thanks. I'm going to call Sawyer right now," replied McGowan as he hung up and immediately dialed the campaign manager's cell phone.

"Sawyer here," replied the campaign manager on the first ring.

"This is Agent McGowan," said McGowan coolly. "I was just informed of the governor's scheduled appearance on the steps of the Capitol tomorrow."

"That's right."

"I thought I specifically asked that you give at us least a day's advance notice of any event. And if the event was going to take place in a public forum or before a large audience, we would need at least two days."

"I know," said Sawyer sheepishly. "But once the governor is committed to something, he's very hard to dissuade."

"I know that," replied McGowan. "Every candidate is. It's your job as campaign manager to do just that. If the Secret Service is going to provide the level of protection the public expects—and we expect of ourselves—I need your full cooperation."

"I understand," said Sawyer.

"I'm not sure you do, Mr. Sawyer. I would like you to postpone tomorrow's event. I cannot guarantee the governor's safety."

"Christ, Agent McGowan, the governor's not going to go for that. He has already made commitments to various legislators and a media announcement is scheduled for 3:00 P.M. today."

"I need you to postpone the media announcement—at a minimum. And, I would like to ask you to reconsider the whole event. Colfax is now a serious contender for the presidency and if it is known that he'll be on the steps of the Capitol at ten o'clock tomorrow, any number of scenarios could be constructed that will place him in harm's way."

"I'll postpone the media announcement," said Sawyer, forgetting that he had already leaked the information to Moriarty. "I'll also speak with the governor, but I don't think he'll go for any major changes."

"Thank you," said McGowan. "It is simply not possible to secure the entire grounds of the State Capitol and search every possible venue that surrounds it with our small staff within the next twelve hours."

"I understand," said Sawyer.

McGowan knew that it was probably too late to convince Colfax to reschedule the event so he ordered an emergency staff meeting of the Minneapolis field office and informed them that they would all be working nonstop until the event was over and Gibraltar's safety was guaranteed.

CHAPTER SIXTEEN

T he wide stone steps of the State Capitol were wet with melting snow. Hundreds of students from colleges and universities in the Twin Cities area had responded to Josh Parker's urgent e-mail. Some of the students came from as far away as western Wisconsin, northern Minnesota, and Iowa. A few hundred more people came to the Capitol when they learned of the rally on the news the night before or read about it in the morning papers. The crowd was even larger because close to half of the one thousand state government employees working in the buildings surrounding the Capitol had also come to watch the announcement. The most interested observers, next to the seventy legislators who stood to lose their jobs, were the almost 200 legislative staffers who would also be out of work if Colfax was successful in consolidating the two legislative bodies into one. It was these staffers who most worried Sean McGowan. He knew that all it took was one disgruntled employee with a gun to place Robert Colfax in the same what-could-have-been category as Robert F. Kennedy.

In the hours preceding the event, a team of Secret Service agents had scrambled to review the background of every government employee who could possibly lose his or her job under Colfax's plan. They also closed all the windows overlooking the Capitol steps and limited access to those windows that presented a direct line of fire to where Colfax would be standing.

German shepherds from a local Air Force Reserve unit had been borrowed to help sniff out any potential bombs or explosives. Scores of extra St. Paul police had been called in that morning to assist with the event, as had a number of Minnesota Highway Patrol officers. Sean McGowan organized the entire operation and saw to it that at least six plainclothes police officers—three men and three women—were dispersed into the crowd to help identify potential troublemakers.

Colfax's limousine arrived from the rear of the Capitol and parked on the east side, next to the Supreme Court building. It was a mild day for early March, and Colfax didn't wear a coat. At the suggestion of the Secret Service, he did wear a bulletproof vest. The speaker of the House, the Senate president and three other high-ranking state officials escorted him to the podium. Sean McGowan proceeded him by two steps, and Luke Parish was two steps to his rear.

It was from the podium—overlooking a crowd of more than a thousand people—that Colfax announced his intention to create a single legislative body. Many were holding "Colfax for President" signs. Some of the students were handing out copies of signs that they had downloaded from the Colfax web site.

"Good afternoon," Colfax began, "It's a pleasure to see so many people here on this beautiful March day. It is especially nice to see so many young people."

The students in the crowd roared back.

"I can see from many of the sweatshirts that some of you have come a great distance," Colfax said, as he listed off the names of Midwestern colleges—Bemidji State, Mankato State, St. Cloud State, Grinnell, River Falls, Carleton—to the delight of the contingent from each school. "I'm here today to announce my unconditional support for the effort to create a single legislative body in the state of Minnesota. The time has come for this common-sense initiative. It is time that we again make the legislature the people's house."

The audience erupted.

"Our current system of having a Senate and a House no longer makes sense at the state level. Our representatives and our senators represent the same people and work on the same issues. It is time to end the duplication and send half of them back home to become productive citizens." More hoots and hollers followed.

"It is my belief that with a single assembly, the people will know who exactly to hold accountable. No longer will our elected officials be able to hide from their actions. A single house will also make politics more understandable to the average citizens. It will be more open, responsive and accountable." Colfax then added, "And it will save thirty-five million dollars each year!"

The crowd began to chant, "Let the people decide! Let the people decide!" Colfax watched with pleasure as the chant took on a life of its own. It slowly died down and Colfax continued.

"To those who oppose a single legislature, I ask them this: How is it possible that city councils, county boards, and school boards can operate with a single governing body but the state cannot? And why is it that Minnesota has twenty-six million fewer citizens than California but eighty more legislators? Are we that much better governed?"

The crowd answered Colfax's question with a resounding no.

"You're right," said Colfax back to the crowd, "and that's why I need your help. I need each and every one of you to contact your legislators and tell them to put this issue on the ballot this November. Will you do that?"

"Yes" was the loud response.

"The choice is yours. It is only fair that you—the citizens of this state—vote on this issue."

The crowd began to chant, "It's only fair, it's only fair."

Colfax sensed that if he had asked them to storm the Capitol at that particular moment, they would have.

The rally went on for another fifteen minutes as each politician took the opportunity to share the limelight with the governor. Throughout it all, Sean McGowan and Luke Parish continually scanned the crowd for sudden hand movements and the rooftops and windows for rifle barrels. McGowan's sixth sense told him there was a threat lurking somewhere nearby.

Far behind Colfax and the Secret Service agents, on the roof of the Capitol, a Secret Service cameraman clandestinely captured the entire crowd at the rally on video. Every three minutes, the cameraman scanned the entire crowd. In between scans, he zoomed in on individual people in the audience. He was told to spend no more than a few seconds on each person.

Just as the rally was concluding, the cameraman directed his lens to the far back right of the crowd and recorded a few seconds of what appeared to be a bored young student in a University of St. Thomas sweatshirt staring off into oblivion.

What Lee Manning was actually doing was looking for Secret Service sharpshooters on the roofs of the buildings and committing to memory every detail about the men and women protecting Governor Colfax.

* *

From California to Ohio to New York, farmers, teachers, and seniors were inundated with anti-Colfax mailings. That he wasn't even going to be on the ballot in those states made little impression on the citizens of those states or the media. Simultaneous with the targeted attacks, Jacob Mance was cutting $25,000 checks to a variety of professional political operatives who were successfully working their connections throughout the media to plant anti-Colfax stories.

* *

Martin Byrne had been focused on March 7, 2000, since election night 1996. Elliott Prescott had been similarly focused on the same date since he entered the race in April 1999. Both candidates felt that the seven primaries on that date would determine who would win the right to represent their party in the general election. Because California and New York offered the largest potential block of delegates, both contenders chose to focus their efforts in those two key states.

The lack of time between primaries—the New Hampshire primary was only four weeks earlier—gave those candidates with the most money and the best organization the greatest odds of winning. Dark horse candidates, such as Stanley Cross and Reginald Greene, couldn't compete in the large states because of the need to purchase massive amounts of television time. It was possible that an outside candidate could do well if he was riding a wave of momentum that had carried over from an earlier victory in a smaller state. Robert Colfax would have had that momentum had he chosen to seek the endorsement of one of the major parties. But neither Greene nor Cross had the benefit of any significant momentum. Instead, they opted to bypass the large states where they knew they couldn't compete and instead focus on trying to win in one or two smaller states. The victories would not help them secure enough votes to wrestle the nomination away from the front runners, but they would prove useful in helping them limp along until their respective party's conventions in mid-summer— where they hoped to either pull off a miracle or extract some type of political buyout.

In the case of Cross, he wanted veto power over the vice presidential candidate and a guarantee that the anti-abortion plank of the Republican Party would not be diluted to make it more palatable to moderate voters.

Of the seven primaries that day, only two offered Cross or Greene much of an opportunity for success. Greene felt he could do well in Rhode Island, and Cross organized an all-out effort to win in Georgia. Both knew a victory, however small, would keep them alive.

As expected, Byrne's and Prescott's overwhelming financial and organizational advantages produced significant victories in California and New York. Ohio, Maryland, and Missouri went for the favorites. Cross eked out a victory in Georgia, and Greene won an equally close race in the Democratic primary in Rhode Island and finished a close second in Massachusetts. The night's only other surprise was Stanley Cross' decisive victory in Connecticut.

Despite the surprises, the political pundits for NBC's *Decision 2000* were calling it "a good night" for Byrne and Prescott. The anchor for Fox's *Campaign 2000* declared that "barring a miracle, the Prescott and Byrne juggernauts are unstoppable and headed for their party's nominations." The sheer magnitude of the frontrunners' victories in the large states made the whole evening so anticlimactic that each network, independent of the others, devoted portions of their broadcast to Colfax's controversial announcement to create a single house in Minnesota.

Experts explained what a unicameral legislature was, and a team of hastily gathered academics listed the potential benefits and pitfalls of a single legislative body.

This discussion inevitably led into discussions about the "Colfax factor." Pollsters for NBC's *Decision 2000* showed that if the election were held today with a three-way race between Vice President Byrne, Governor Prescott, and Governor Colfax, Prescott would win with forty-three percent, with the vice president receiving forty-one percent and Colfax holding eight percent. Eight percent were undecided. The ABC/CNN poll showed similar numbers. None of the pundits speculated on how much the Coalition for Prosperous New Millennium ads were hurting Colfax. An unpublished excerpt from the same poll, one that sampled all voters—not just "likely" voters—showed Colfax receiving twice as much support—seventeen percent. Jacob Mance had used his connections to make sure that those numbers remained unpublished.

The poll numbers led a few pundits to speculate about the possibility of a deadlock in the Electoral College. Because none of the experts or reporters in the television studios was knowledgeable about the intricacies of the Electoral College, the topic wasn't discussed in any meaningful way.

* *

"David," said Murdock to his senior vice president for public affairs and Holten's top Washington lobbyist, "Colfax's strategy is clear. He's going to use the next few months to prove to America that he's presidential timber by passing some significant political reforms in Minnesota. If he's successful in passing legal reform and creating a single house, the American people might very well reason that he could reform the federal government. It is your job to see that this doesn't happen."

"I've already scheduled a meeting with Mance. We're going to discuss how the coalition can work behind the scenes to defeat Colfax in his home state. If we can make him appear ineffective in running a small state like Minnesota, we can easily paint him as not being ready for prime time on the national stage."

"I agree," responded Murdock. "Keep me informed of your progress. It appears that we now have the luxury of focusing exclusively on Colfax—although Cross and Greene still bother me a little."

"Me too," said Luther. "Greene's win in Rhode Island and his strong finish in Massachusetts demonstrate that his call for universal health care is finding a receptive audience. Cross is also a concern. His deep pockets mean he can hang around until the convention."

Murdock wasn't listening to Luther's political analysis. "Tell Mance that he can expect a bonus in next month's retainer if he can defeat Colfax's legislative initiatives in Minnesota," said Murdock matter-of-factly. "And I'll double it if he's out of the race all together by May 1."

"I'll inform him."

"I would think that he would definitely want to work through the trial attorneys in Minnesota. They have to hate Colfax's proposal," said Murdock.

"They do," replied Luther.

"Also tell him that he's authorized to spend up to a million dollars assisting the trial attorneys in their lobbying effort, and he's free to spend another half million working to defeat Colfax's dumb-ass unicameral idea."

"Are there any restrictions on the money?" asked Luther.

"No. I trust the two of you will spend it wisely. Just make sure that it's properly laundered through legitimate organizations—and that it can't be traced back to the coalition. If Colfax were to find out that an outside group was working to defeat an issue specific to Minnesota, he'd have a field day in the media. I can hear him now, 'Why are these out-of-state special interest groups spending millions of dollars in Minnesota?' It would make him look like some goddamn, squeaky-clean saint. Make sure it doesn't happen."

"Yes, sir."

* *

Sawyer's leak to Ellen Moriarty paid off. The major newspapers picked up on Moriarty's story and had reporters in St. Paul covering the event. A majority of the papers gave Colfax's announcement coverage equal to that of Prescott and Byrne's victories on the front page. The *Wall Street Journal* went one step further and ran a glowing editorial praising Colfax's leadership style—specifically, his willingness to push ahead with bold and controversial positions in the middle of an election year. The editorial suggested that if Byrne and Prescott didn't begin to define themselves as sharply as Governor Colfax, they risked losing a sizeable chunk of the voting population that was hungering for real leadership—the kind of leadership Colfax was offering.

* *

That afternoon, a team of former congressmen who had connections to Win Murdock and were on retainer to the coalition pulled a few strings and began visiting editorial boards of the *New York Times* and the *Washington Post*, subtly suggesting that they tell their readers about Colfax's "irresponsible" positions on legal reform and a unicameral legislature. They came to the meeting armed with a handful of papers, produced by credentialed academic experts, documenting their case against Colfax's proposals. What they didn't say was that the research had been paid for with Win Murdock's money.

Next, the team of lobbyists scheduled a round of breakfast, lunch and dinner meetings with a number of Sunday morning talk show producers and asked that Colfax's ideas be given higher visibility. They followed up by visiting with the participants in the shows and providing them with detailed talking points designed to skewer Colfax or anyone supporting his positions. The hosts didn't find anything unethical about receiving the information from a third source. After all, in Washington, it was only fair to tear someone down after they had been built up. It was the American way.

* *

Moriarty quickly scanned the major papers and smiled when she saw that they had followed her lead and run stories on Colfax. The hypocrisy of the media elite calling her a tabloid journalist and then shamelessly using her stories never ceased to amaze her. She also thought Pete Sawyer owed her a favor for running the story.

After grabbing a light lunch at a sushi place just off Dupont Circle, Moriarty went back to her apartment and began calling her regular list of contacts. She touched base with the press secretaries for every presidential candidate. On their private voice mail systems, she left a short message telling them the exact time she would be available to take their phone call. She informed each one they would have ten minutes to "spin" their candidate's performance in yesterday's primary elections. Each press secretary called at the allotted time. Dan Miller, Elliott Prescott's campaign manager, was the first.

Moriarty, who was wearing a headset with a microphone that allowed her to listen, type and talk simultaneously, listened to Miller intently for about a minute before she swung her chair around to face her computer and began reading some of the 500 e-mail messages that had been sent to her the previous night.

It had been over a year since she had actually read all her incoming messages. If the subject line didn't interest her, she simply deleted it. Her method meant that she sometimes missed important information, but the benefits outweighed the costs.

She was almost through her conversation with Miller, who was suggesting that Prescott's message of lower taxes and less government was the reason for his overwhelming victories last night, when she spotted the e-mail.

"You don't think that maybe it was your massive spending advantage—rather than your message—that accounted for your victory?" she asked distractedly. Miller responded, but she wasn't paying attention to his mindless political spin.

She opened the e-mail, marked urgent, with the subject line that read "the CyberCafe connection." She quickly read the message and rudely told Miller she had to go. The message originated from the CyberCafe, a coffeehouse in Georgetown. Whoever the sender was, he didn't want to use his own computer.

* *

Moriarty marveled at the level of political insight contained in the e-mail message. The writer was obviously an insider knowledgeable in the ways of Washington politics. The first three paragraphs outlined the threat that Colfax posed to Win Murdock. The writer also indicated that a partner in the law office of Lawrence, Mance & Scott had personally solicited him for a $500,000 contribution for the coalition.

"The Coalition for a Prosperous New Millennium is a rapidly growing organization," read the message. "I am personally aware of a variety of organizations, including Philson Gas & Oil and Wextron BioTech, plus my own, that have contributed to the group. Based on the latest figures posted on the Center for the Ethical and Responsive Politics web site, I believe a significant number of other organizations have done the same." The e-mail concluded with a warning that Moriarty should not be dissuaded from monitoring the organization just because it had recently run ads against candidates other than Colfax. "The end game of the coalition is the complete and utter destruction of Robert Colfax. The group has the means and the wherewithal to achieve this goal—even if it means that they must tap into resources at the highest level of government."

Moriarty desperately wanted to respond, but she knew it would be useless. The sender would not still be at the CyberCafe. Instead, she began writing her regular report by dissecting the recent events of the primary elections. She speculated on possible running mates for both Prescott and Byrne—names that the campaign managers had planted with her in expectation that she would float them as trial balloons.

The presidential campaigns could then run polls to see which of the potential candidates added the most value. It also allowed the media—and others—to begin searching for skeletons. If any were found, the person could be easily dropped from consideration and dismissed as have never been seriously considered—all with no damage to the presidential candidate.

The remainder of the *Moriarty Minute* speculated on a few key U.S. Senate and congressional races across the country, with the exception of the last paragraph.

Under the heading, "The Gibraltar Conspiracy," she reported Colfax's Secret Service's codename, noting that it was another Moriarty scoop, along with the rationale for the conspiracy that "her exclusive inside source" had outlined.

By the time she was done with the report, it was still relatively early in the evening. Often she wasn't finished until well after midnight. Moriarty decided to visit the CyberCafe to make some discreet inquiries of the staff about their clientele. As luck would have it, one of the clerks behind the counter, Troy Hall, was an aspiring journalist doing his undergraduate work at the American University. For the prospect of a possible internship, the eager young man agreed to remain extra vigilant and promised to report back to about certain clientele.

"Are you looking for a particular person? An administration official? A congressman?" asked the young man hopefully.

"I don't know who I'm looking for—other than he is a man. Probably a white, middle-age, professional, somewhere in the neighborhood of thirty-five to fifty years old."

Disappointed at the level of intrigue that a middle-aged man suggested, Hall was still able to offer Moriarty a ray of hope. "Our customers are primarily students from either American University or Georgetown. Most just want some caffeine to pull an all-nighter. Others come to use a computer because they have to share one with a roommate."

"So, you might notice an older man if he came in here at two or three in the morning?" asked Moriarty.

"Yeah, probably. But there are still a fair number of middle-aged losers who use these public cyberplaces to try and pick up co-eds."

"Thanks. Keep your eyes open. I'll be back," said Moriarty, who only intended to return if she received another e-mail from the late-night caller.

"Are you serious about the internship thing?" asked the young man to Moriarty as she was heading out the door.

"Absolutely," she lied.

* *

Two hours after Moriarty posted her March 8 report, a printed version of it lay on Murdock's desk. Having throwing the paper down on his desk, Murdock turned to Luther and said, "Arrange a secure phone call with Payne for first thing tomorrow morning. We may require some of their technical assistance to find out from whom Miss Moriarty is receiving her information."

172

CHAPTER SEVENTEEN

J effery Payne had finished reading the *Washington Post*, the *New York Times*, and the *Wall Street Journal* and was midway through his agency's internal intelligence briefing when his secure personal telephone rang. It was 5:55 A.M.

"Payne," he said gruffly, reaching for his coffee.

"We've got a problem," said Murdock without bothering to introduce himself.

Payne immediately recognized the voice on the other end of the line. "What kind of problem?"

"Media."

"I've already read the papers and didn't come across anything—other than Colfax's initiatives in Minnesota, which you should be able to use to your advantage."

"Are you familiar with the *Moriarty Minute*?" asked Murdock.

"The Internet rag?" replied Payne.

"Yes."

"Of course, I am. What about it?"

"Can you access your computer?" asked Murdock. "Pull up last night's report." Murdock waited while Payne powered up his computer and searched for the report.

Seconds later, Payne was scanning the document. It took him a minute to reach the headline: "The Gibraltar Conspiracy."

"How the fuck did Moriarty get the names of the contributors?"

"I don't know," replied Murdock, "but it concerns me."

"It should. If the major media smell a story, you and the coalition could get some heat. In fact, it could get ugly."

"I know," said Murdock. "That's the purpose of my call. I've got Mance working on controlling the situation, but I'd like to ask you to dedicate some resources to help track down the leak."

"Sure. What did you have in mind?" asked Payne.

"I suspect whoever is talking with Moriarty is from the Washington area and that they are probably talking with her over the phone or by e-mail."

"And you would like me to help determine who the leak is."

"Yes."

"I'd be happy to do it," lied Payne, who knew that Murdock's connections with both the Prescott and Byrne campaigns would help him secure the top position at the CIA in either administration. After his time at the CIA, Payne also knew Murdock could line him up with a prestigious well-paying position in corporate America.

"Let me know as soon as you find out anything."

"You'll be the first to know, Win."

Payne took another sip of his coffee and considered the situation. The operation was relatively low-risk—anyone, especially the CIA, could do it. He considered telling Murdock that using the CIA to conduct a simple surveillance operation was like using a Stealth bomber to attack Haiti, but he decided against it.

＊　＊

Payne reread the *Moriarty Minute* and called his assistant into his office. Although it wasn't yet six in the morning, Payne knew Baptista would be at his desk scouring the nightly cable traffic and recording to memory an endless list of minutia on the theory that one never knew when it might come in handy.

The deputy director briefly summarized the situation for Baptista, who was the only other CIA official to know of Payne's involvement with the coalition. Baptista instantly recognized the danger. "I realize that this task is well below your capabilities," said Payne almost apologetically, "but the sensitive nature of the project does not lend itself to delegation."

"Of course, sir. A little field craft would be good for me," replied Baptista. "It's important to stay fresh on the tricks of the trade."

"Thank you. I'd like a preliminary report by tomorrow," said Payne, indicating that their brief conversation was over.

"Can I anticipate that once it is determined who the leak is, appropriate steps will be taken to eliminate the source, sir?"

Payne shrugged his shoulders, although the expression on his face suggested that that was a distinct possibility.

"Just let me know, sir," said Baptista as he exited the office.

* *

Robert and Linda Colfax left the deserted state Capitol at 1:30 P.M. Under the watchful eyes of Luke Parish and another Secret Service agent, the pair drove an hour and half north of the Twin Cities to the Abbey of St. John for Good Friday mass. As they pulled off I-94 onto the road that connected the Abbey and the campus to the interstate, Colfax stared at the massive modern bell tower that loomed in front of him. He was suddenly reminded of all the anxieties he had felt when he arrived at St. John's as a young, scared boy who was moving away from home for the first time. It was Father Otto Wilhoit who first welcomed him, and it was Father Otto whom he was returning to see again. Colfax had made an annual ritual of attending the veneration of the cross at St. John's ever since he left the prep school. He had only missed a few years—the four years he was in the Navy and one when he was secretary of the Navy and living in Washington, D.C. The year was 1991, and he was busy dealing with the consequences of America's massive naval build-up in the Persian Gulf and the aftermath of America's rapid victory over Saddam Hussein.

The black Lincoln Continental, the governor's official car, stopped directly under the hulking bell tower and in front of the massive oak doors to the church. Agent Parish got out first and surveyed the area. The Secret Service had searched the church a few hours earlier, and a team of local police had subtly checked the sparse crowd for any unwelcome visitors.

Parish radioed Joe Lefebvre, the Secret Service agent responsible for maintaining the security of the church prior to Colfax's arrival. Receiving confirmation that the church was secured, Parish surveyed 360 degrees around the car one more time, looking for any suspicious behavior. Seeing none, he opened the passenger door and indicated to Colfax and his wife that it was safe to exit. At the same moment Parish opened the car door, Lefebvre opened the door to the church. Parish efficiently whisked the pair into the church. They were exposed to the open environment for less than two seconds.

Once inside, Agent Lefebvre escorted the pair up to the balcony of the church, another security precaution. Alone, with the exception of Parish and Lefebvre protecting both the north and south entrances to the balcony, Colfax and his wife settled in for the two-hour Good Friday mass. They left the balcony only for the veneration of the cross and communion. After the latter, the pair returned to the balcony and silently prayed for a few minutes.

Alone now in the empty church, the pair went down to the basement chapel and lit a candle in memory of their deceased parents. From out of the back of the church,

Father Otto suddenly appeared, escorted by a Secret Service agent. Colfax embraced the priest.

"It's good to see the two of you," said Wilhoit. "I didn't know if I could expect you this year—with the campaign and all."

"I wasn't sure myself, but Linda convinced me this morning that I needed some time away from the campaign — some time to reflect," said Colfax.

"Smart woman," replied Wilhoit, smiling at Linda.

"I also needed some time alone with my husband," said Linda, adding light-heartedly, "It's a sad commentary on our life when we count as our only private time an hour and a half drive to church."

"It must be tough. How are the girls handling the campaign?" asked Wilhoit.

"It is difficult," said Colfax. "But we knew what we were getting ourselves into. All in all, they're doing well."

"They were a little scared when they were briefed by the Secret Service, but they're taking it better than I expected. And they're certainly handling it better than I am," added Linda.

"The security is definitely discreet," said Wilhoit, nodding his head in the direction of Agent Parish, who was standing in the shadow of a concrete pillar, guarding the back entrance of the chapel. "I didn't even know you were here until I saw you at communion. I hope you make more of an entrance during your campaign events."

The three departed the church and continued their conversation over a simple meal of soup and bread in a private dining room off the monastery. The three talked nonstop about the campaign for the first half-hour. Eventually, the conversation turned to other subjects as they started dessert.

"You won't believe who I heard from last month, Robert," said Wilhoit, returning to the table after getting a cup of coffee."

"Who?"

""Peter Kulas."

"Are you serious? I haven't heard from him since prep school. I thought he had dropped off the face of the earth," said Colfax.

"So did I," replied Wilhoit.

"Who's Peter Kulas?" asked Linda.

"Peter Kulas was the best cross-country runner in the state in 1966," said Colfax.

"Second best," said Wilhoit, interrupting Colfax. "Remember, you won the state meet."

Linda, with a mild look of confusion, raised her eyebrows at her husband. "How come I've never heard of this mysterious Peter Kulas?"

"It's not a big deal," said Colfax.

"But I think it is, Robert," replied Wilhoit, winking at Linda.

"Well, if Bob won't tell me the story, why don't you, Father?" said Linda directly to Wilhoit, who looked at Colfax as if to ask permission. Colfax shrugged his shoulders in tacit approval.

"The story actually begins well before the 1966 state cross country championship meet. It began in the fall of 1963, when a then very skinny Bobby Colfax decided he wanted to be the best runner he possibly could. First, though, he had to make the cross-country team."

"This is where you two started your early morning runs?" interjected Linda.

"Yes. Your husband was very persistent—I don't think he ever missed a run. Well, young Bobby made the team as a sophomore. He was the number five runner."

"A polite way of saying that I was the worst on the team," said Colfax.

"But your husband continued to practice. As he did, he silently focused on his fellow classmate Peter Kulas, a gifted athlete for whom running three miles came as easily and naturally as breathing."

"By his junior year, Bobby had moved up to the third spot, and by his senior year he was number two, just behind Peter."

"Well behind," added Colfax.

"Although number two, your husband was still elected captain," said Wilhoit, looking at Linda. "Even back then, he had strong leadership skills. He had a way of encouraging everyone on the team to excel."

"Except Peter Kulas," said Colfax.

"That's true," said Wilhoit. "Peter didn't think he needed to improve. Throughout the season, Peter won all of the individual meets, but Bobby was consistently finishing an impressive second. But unlike Peter, your husband continued to improve his times with each meet," said Wilhoit. "The combination of their one-two finishes guaranteed our team a spot at the Catholic state championship meet down in St. Paul at what we refer to as the 'Tommie Loop.'"

"The Tommie what?" asked Linda.

"The Tommie Loop. It's really the Town and Country golf course," said Wilhoit, "We just call it that because it's where the St. Thomas Academy and St. Thomas University host their cross-country meets. Anyway, as I saying, back then, cross-country was a big deal and St. John's was competing against much larger schools. The race was well covered by the local sports media."

"And Peter Kulas was the center of the pre-race attention?" asked Linda.

"Yes," replied Wilhoit. "But the entire week before, Bob remained focused on the goal at hand—winning the team championship. It was all he talked about on our morning runs. When the race started, Bobby knew he would have to finish somewhere in the top five if St. John's was to have a chance of winning the team championship. It was expected that the individual championship would be a fight between Kulas and St. Thomas' top runner. Coming in at anything lower than fifth place would mean that the combination times of St. Thomas' other top runners would edge us out.

"Two miles into the race, Kulas and Bobby—along with two runners from St. Thomas—were packed together. Suddenly, St. Thomas' top runner pulled ahead, forcing Kulas and Bobby to react. Kulas took it as challenge and pulled even with him. Bobby stayed behind and drafted in their wake. Slowly, he and the other runner fell farther behind, and it began to look like a two-way race between Kulas and the boy from St. Thomas. Then with about 400 yards to go, Bobby kicked it into high gear.

"Never before in my forty years of coaching have I ever seen such a kick. In the course of 200 yards, Bobby made up the thirty-yard difference. He left the number two St. Thomas runner in his dust and eventually pulled even with Kulas and the other runner. Both were stunned by his appearance. And just when I thought he couldn't possibly have anything left in him, he reached a little deeper and surged ahead of both runners. I still remember his metal cleats kicking up the cold November mud onto Kulas and the other boy. Every stride was a thing of beauty—his lead just kept growing.

"At the finish line, your husband collapsed. But he did so as the individual state cross-country champion and, more important to him, the captain of the state champion cross-country team. The next day, your husband was quoted as saying, 'As captain of the team, I had a responsibility to give one-hundred percent. I did that and the Lord blessed me.' I still have the article. I keep it with my copy of the 1967 yearbook." The yearbook contained two photos, side-by-side. One was taken of the entire St. John's team. Colfax was holding the team championship trophy. The caption under it said, "How about we call it Johnnie's Loop? 1966 Catholic champions." The next photo was just of Colfax, he was holding his individual state championship trophy. The caption beneath the photo read, "—or Bobbie's Loop. 1966 individual champion."

"I've never heard that story, Bob," said his wife, slightly surprised.

"Sure you have. Maybe not the exact way Father Otto tells it, but I know I've told you about it. In fact, I'm sure there was an article—maybe ten or fifteen years ago in *Runner's World*—about it. It was one of the first stories written about me after

I was elected to Congress. I recounted what a life-altering event that was for me. It was on that day that I first lived up to my leadership potential and, more important, I really began to believe that I could accomplish anything if I set my mind to it."

✳   ✳

Anne Strong, the *Washington Herald*'s most promising political reporter, had spent the last few months in a series of dumpy hotels and loved every minute of it. But now that the March primaries had given Governor Prescott and Vice President Byrne what appeared to be unstoppable momentum, her political editor, Charlie Demming, called her back to Washington.

"Anne, your coverage of the Iowa caucuses and the New Hampshire primary was outstanding. I was particularly impressed with your reporting on the consequences of the Arizona primary and your political instincts in California," said Demming.

"Thank you. I hope you didn't call me back here to tell me that I'm off the presidential campaign," said Strong, who was not someone to mince words—a trait her editor appreciated.

"Not at all, Anne. It's just that the campaign trail is going to go a little cold for the next few months," said Demming.

"I disagree," replied Strong hurredly. "Colfax is still raising hell in the flatlands of the Midwest. I can cover him. I want to cover him." *I need to cover him,* she thought.

"Hold on, Anne. If you slow down a bit, I think you'll find that we're thinking along the same lines," said Demming calmly. "Colfax apparently is using his legislative initiatives before the Minnesota legislature to garner national media attention. It's a smart strategy. It helps him push his reforms in Minnesota, and it helps bolster his image on the national stage."

"I know. That's why I want to go to Minnesota. His strategy is fascinating. I can get into the nuances and subtleties better than any other reporter. Can I go?" begged Strong.

Demming laughed, "Slow down, Anne, you'll get there. But first, I need you to do some work here in Washington."

"Shit," muttered Strong softly but loud enough for Demming to hear.

"What I want you to do is a little investigative work on a new issue advocacy group."

"A what! Goddammit, Charlie, I'm above that. Can't you get some green reporter just out of college? It's a good way for them to cut their teeth."

"I agree, Anne. But I don't think this is your run-of-the-mill political group. In my twenty-four years of covering politics in this town, I've just never seen a group spring up so quickly. What makes it interesting is that they claim to have no political agenda. Even more interesting, the group is run by Lawrence, Mance & Scott, and they won't reveal any of the contributors."

"What's the name of the group? Citizens for the Next Millennium or something like that?"

"Close. They call themselves the Coalition for a Prosperous New Millennium," said Demming.

"They're the group that ran a few ads against Colfax in Iowa and New Hampshire, aren't they?

"They are."

"I've also heard they're doing some low-key negative campaigning elsewhere."

"More than that," said Demming, "there are rumors that people are being paid to manipulate the media. I've heard from a reputable source that for every anti-Colfax article they successfully plant, they're receiving a $25,000 bounty."

"No shit! Didn't Moriarty just report on the group?"

"They've also run some ads against Greene and Cross," answered Demming, who chose to ignore Strong's question about the Moriarty report.

"I had a call from someone at the Center for Responsive and Ethical Politics a few months ago," said Strong. "She left me a message about the group—but I can't recall her name."

"Stephanie Freeberg," replied Demming. "Her boss, Ira Bernstein, is an old friend of mine. He called and asked that I look into this matter."

"Why?"

"Because in the last two months—since Freeberg called you—the organization has raised an additional eleven million dollars—with no signs of slowing up."

"Even in this year of soft money, that's a shitload," said Strong, incredulously. "You still haven't answered my question about whether Moriarty reported on this. Are we just trying to cover our asses so that we don't get burned by the bitch again?"

Smiling at her directness and her vulgar language, Demming again ignored her question. "Are you interested in the job, or do you want to cover Capitol Hill?"

"Are you threatening me with a boring assignment, Charlie? You still haven't answered my question."

"Yes—to your first question. The answer to your second question is also yes. We are reacting to the *Moriarty Minute*. Jesus Christ, you're persistent."

"Thank you, Charlie. I'll get to work immediately. Do you have Freeberg's number?"

Demming handed her Freeberg's card.

"Great. But I want your assurance that as soon as I finish the article, I'm free to cover Colfax. Promise?" she demanded, staring him in the eye.

"Promise," said Demming.

* *

Sean McGowan was thinking about how much he missed Stephanie Freeberg's long, toned legs when the telephone jolted him back to reality. "This is McGowan," he said into the phone.

"Sean, this Bob Dupont." McGowan immediately knew that the outcome of the call would result in more work for both him and his office. The only reason the Secret Service director of operations ever called a field office was to inform them—usually only a few days in advance—of some major project.

"Yes, sir. How can I help you?"

"McGowan, I know you left Washington to get away from the White House and the stresses of pulling protective duty." McGowan was about to protest that he left because of his personal reservations about the person whom he was charged to protect, but he decided against it. Dupont was old school and would not tolerate any talk, even if it were private, that sounded like disrespect for the office of the president. "But we've almost reached a breaking point. Our protective services are stretched pretty thin, and I'm going to have to order you to return to protective duty full time."

"Sir," said McGowan with an edge of annoyance in his voice, "who's going to run the Minneapolis office?"

"For the time being, Tom Cheney in the Chicago office is going to take over the day-to-day operations of both the Minneapolis and Madison offices."

"May I ask what prompted this transfer of responsibilities?" asked McGowan.

"As you know, for the first time ever, Congress pared back our budget request this past fiscal year. We informed them that the large number of presidential contenders in the 2000 campaign was going to place great stress on our services, but our concerns fell on deaf ears. They said they needed to keep the budget balanced."

"I guess it would have been hard to predict that five major candidates would still be requiring protection this far along in the campaign," said McGowan as a way of defending Congress, an institution that he didn't normally feel inclined to defend. "Is there any chance that Greene or Cross will drop out of the race soon?"

"The team leaders for both campaigns are reporting that they both intend to stay in the race through the conventions, even though they have no chance of winning."

"And that's why you're calling me back to protective duty full time? Surely, there are other young field agents who are clamoring at the chance to get out of the field offices in Des Moines or Kansas City. You don't really need me."

"Agent McGowan," began Dupont, "I'll be honest with you. There are a few good young agents who I could have called upon, but the situation is a little more serious than that." McGowan didn't say anything and let Dupont continue. "Our computer models are suggesting that Gibraltar has a very high assassination potential. He's a third-party candidate, he's growing in the polls, a good many of his positions are extremely controversial, and he is beginning to draw some attention from those segments of society that we consider to be the most dangerous."

"I'm aware of those threats, sir. The governor's office has been receiving a substantial number of threats, but I feel comfortable that we have the resources to deal with the threats here in the Minneapolis office," replied McGowan.

"Perhaps I haven't made myself clear, Agent McGowan. Our models suggest that Gibraltar has crossed a threshold that indicates that for every one verbal or written threat that you receive in Minnesota, another twenty threats exist but do not appear on anyone's radar screen."

"You're kidding me?"

"No, I am not, Agent McGowan. Gibraltar was on the cover of *Time* and *Newsweek*, and he has been appearing in greater frequency on television and in papers all across the country. That makes him a much more attractive prospect for some individual seeking to leave his or her imprint on history."

"When do my new responsibilities begin?" asked McGowan, knowing there was no way out of his new assignment.

"They are effective immediately upon your return from Beltsville."

"I was just at Beltsville on refresher training," said McGowan. "I'm quite sure I haven't lost anything in the few weeks."

"We are ordering the lead agents for every presidential candidate back to Beltsville for enhanced training. The service is going to extensively review the Exceptional Cases Study. It is our belief that the stars are aligning in 2000 for a rash of assassination attempts. Class begins Monday at 7:30 A.M. sharp," said Dupont.

At least, McGowan figured, his thoughts of Freeberg's long, lean legs being wrapped around his body would become a reality—if only for a day.

CHAPTER EIGHTEEN

I t was Friday night and most of Washington's policy wonks and political nerds had called it quits. David Pollard, however, was still at his office on Seventeenth and L Street, watching *Washington Week in Review* on public television while simultaneously reviewing CNN online. At eight o'clock, he turned off both the computer and the television, read the latest *Cook Report* and skimmed through a few back copies of the *New Republic* and *Congressional Quarterly*. At nine, he turned the television back on for *Larry King Live*. The guest was Governor Robert T. Colfax. For the next hour, Pollard marveled at Colfax's grace and the easy manner with which he answered every question King threw at him. Pollard was most intrigued about Colfax's willingness to try to fundamentally reform politics in Minnesota by creating a single legislative body.

"Governor, isn't your legislation to create a unicameral legislature just election-year posturing?" asked King.

"Absolutely not, Larry. I outlined for you earlier the reasons why this is a legitimate issue. I can honestly say that regardless of whether or not I was running for president, I would have placed this issue on the top of my agenda this year. I campaigned on the issue in 1996 and I intend to fulfill my promise. If anything, this issue puts my campaign in jeopardy. If I fail, my opponents will question my effectiveness—and rightly so."

"Does the same go for your legislation on reforming the legal system in Minnesota?" queried the show's host as he placed his elbows on the table and leaned toward his guest.

"Yes. If I'm an effective leader, I should be able to pass both bills—despite the large number of trial attorneys who are opposing me on legal reform and the vast number of lobbyists who view a single house as a threat to their way of doing business. I welcome the challenge, Larry. I do not shrink from it."

Pollard leaned back in his chair and contemplated asking his employer for a leave of absence so he could volunteer for the Colfax campaign. He had no social life—he was watching *Larry King Live* on a Friday night in a town with one of the highest female-to-male ratios in the country. He was a political junkie. He might as well give in to his vice, he thought. And at least working for Colfax, he reasoned, he could feel good about himself in the morning—unlike he did now, working for an organization that was secretly supporting an effort to defeat the one person he thought could really lead this country. Was his six-figure salary worth selling his soul? he silently asked himself as he left his office.

Pollard was about to jump on the Metro and retire to his shabby little apartment in Alexandria when he opted instead to grab a beer at the Black Crow Bar. What the hell, he thought, he might get lucky.

Once inside the dark and crowded room, Pollard elbowed his way up to the bar and ordered a Rolling Rock. He was quickly pushed to the edge of the bar by other aggressive Washington types looking to get drunk after another week of fighting to grab hold of the proverbial brass ring.

Pollard was trying to catch the eye of a woman half his age and probably an intern up on Capitol Hill when he heard someone shout his name.

"David? David Pollard? Is that you?" said a large, perspiring, overweight man wearing a stiff, white monogrammed oxford shirt and a silk tie that still hadn't been loosened. It took Pollard a few seconds to recognize his old law school classmate, Preston Briggs.

"Preston?"

"Goddamn right, Davey boy," said Briggs, obviously drunk.

"How are you?" said Pollard, who was actually relieved to know someone in the bar. He was conscious of looking like a lonely middle-aged man in a bar full of young, beautiful people.

"Great. Fucking great. I'm pulling in $500K and I finally made partner at Lawrence, Mance & Scott," said Briggs in a tone loud enough to impress the young women standing nearby.

"Congrats—that's fantastic," said Pollard, studying the bags under Briggs eyes and the graying hair around his temples.

"How about you?" said Briggs, who wasn't really interested and had already begun to scan the bar to see if any of the women were expressing an interest in him based on his income.

"Still with the National Small Business Coalition," replied Pollard, taking a sip of his beer.

"Oh, you must be working with Mance on the coalition project," said Briggs, spilling a few drops of his large martini, his fourth of the night.

"You know about that?" responded Pollard, lowering his voice and looking around to see if anyone heard Briggs' comment.

"I'm a fucking partner," said Briggs loudly, "I know everything."

"Then you know about Murdock?" asked Pollard on the chance that it would confirm his suspicions.

"I know about Murdock, I know about the trial attorneys, the Social Security Group, the gambling industry, the education group—I know about everything. I even know about the chemical, oil and ethanol industries."

On a professional level, Pollard was disturbed by Briggs' knowledge. But on a personal level, he wanted to know who else was involved in the coalition. "Is Mance bringing all these groups in?" he asked.

"Jacob isn't doing shit—other than picking up thirty-three percent of everything the group collects. Which, at last report, was a cool fourteen million dollars."

"I can't believe Colfax is that big of a threat to Murdock."

"He isn't. The old man's buying a little insurance on his billion-dollar oil and ethanol subsidies. Can I get you another beer?" said Briggs, gulping down the last of his drink, "I'm going to have another martini."

"No thanks, Preston. I've got to get home. Let's get together for lunch sometime."

Briggs just smiled and turned his glassy eyes toward the bar.

Pollard left the bar and started walking toward the Metro station when he stopped and considered placing a call to Ellen Moriarty from the pay phone inside the station. Instead, he hailed a cab and told the driver to take him to the CyberCafe. He had one more e-mail to write.

*   *

The waiter and aspiring journalist hardly noticed Pollard when he took a seat behind the computer terminal. The time was 11:12 P.M. Friday, April 28. The subject line read "The CyberCafe connection." The message text read: "Murdock is definitely behind the coalition. An old friend of mine works at Lawrence, Mance & Scott and confirmed my theory. He also indicated that Murdock is the force behind the fourteen million dollars in contributions." Pollard then listed all the organizations that Briggs had cited. "In the words of my friend, Murdock is funding the coalition as insurance for his billion-dollar oil and ethanol subsidies." He then signed off by saying, "Eagerly awaiting the next *Moriarty Minute!*"

Ellen Moriarty never received the electronic message. Baptista had techicians at the CIA secretly diverting select e-mail messages to Moriarty. If the message included certain words such as "Murdock," "coalition," or "Colfax," it was routed to his computer. He reviewed each message, and, if it was irrelevant, it was forwarded without any electronic fingerprints to Moriarty's e-mail server.

Almost as soon as Baptista saw the subject line, he knew he had his man. He quickly read the message and copied it to a disk. He efficiently traced the message back to it origins. The code imbedded in the message stated that it was sent from the CyberCafe on Wisconsin Avenue in Georgetown. He quickly deleted the message from his server, grabbed a few items from his desk and left his office on the seventh floor of an office building near the Clarendon Metro stop in Arlington, Virginia. In ten minutes, he was outside the coffee shop. Baptista had earlier been given photos of every person who was aware of the coalition. He instantly recognized the ordinary, nondescript features of David Pollard.

Pollard loitered in the coffee shop for another twenty minutes and made a lame attempt at flirting with his waitress, an older graduate student at Georgetown. Troy Hall, the aspiring journalist, just shook his head at the middle-aged loser until he remembered Moriarty's request of a few weeks earlier. Hall made a mental note of the man's features.

When Pollard left, rather than catching a cab back to his apartment, he decided to save a few bucks and ride the Metro. He walked the few blocks to the nearest station since it wasn't quite midnight and he still had time to catch the last Metro to Alexandria. If he had bothered to look back, Pollard would have noticed that someone was following a block behind him.

Before he jumped on the Metro, he grabbed a copy of the *Washington Times*, a paper he usually didn't read. He immediately turned to the opinion page. Pollard was so engrossed in an article trying to debunk global warming that he never noticed the gray-haired man get on the Metro with him. Pollard frowned when he finished the article. He knew the piece, written by a scientist from a reputable East Coast university, had been commissioned and paid for by the oil industry. He frowned because he knew the oil industry was spending millions of dollars trying to downplay global warming so they could avoid any new government policies that might erode their profits. It was standard Washington bullshit, and Pollard hated it.

For the next few minutes, Pollard thought of his two daughters. He knew the oil industry never thought of them—or, more important, their generation—when contemplating their profits. He was happy that at least one candidate for president, Robert Colfax, did. As he stared out the window of the Metro, he knew he did the right thing by sending the e-mail. He still did not notice the other man on the Metro with him.

At the last stop on the blue line, Pollard finally rose from his seat to get off. "May I have your paper?" asked the gray-haired man behind him.

Pollard jumped. "I didn't hear you," said Pollard, relaxing when he saw the clean, professional appearance of the man.

"Thank you," replied Baptista as the two stepped off the Metro car together. "You know it's been a long day when you're bumming the morning paper off a stranger."

Pollard laughed, and the two continued past the security cameras and walked out into the dark parking lot.

"Do you live close by?" asked Baptista.

"Yeah, just down the road," said Pollard, nodding his head toward his apartment.

"Me, too," said the man who went on to explain that he was coming home so late because he was a lobbyist for the chemical industry and was working on a bill in the Senate. It was times like these that Baptista's appetite for minutia came in handy. Talk of lobbying consumed the two for a few more minutes until they were well away from the Metro. The street was dark, and Pollard didn't notice when Baptista dropped slightly behind him. Pollard never saw the knife. He only felt the air escape from his lungs as Baptista expertly twisted the razor-sharp knife in his back. His last thoughts were of his daughters.

The *Washington Post* reported the death and robbery of David Pollard on the front page of its metro section the next day. It received more attention than most murders in the greater Washington area because the victim, a divorced lobbyist with a law degree from the University of Virginia, was a successful white professional from the suburbs. The story hit very close to home for a large number of the *Post*'s readers.

*　*

Stephanie Freeberg and Anne Strong met at the designated Thai restaurant in the trendy Adams Morgan neighborhood of Washington. Strong selected the restaurant because it had recently been written up in the *Washingtonian* as the latest hot spot in the city. It was also reported to have the best coffee in town.

In many ways, Anne Strong and Stephanie Freeberg were very similar. Both were young and attractive, disciplined, motivated and dedicated to their respective professions. It wasn't until their early evening conversation was almost an hour old, however, that Strong learned that Freeberg was on her second career.

"You were a Secret Service agent?" said Strong with surprise in her voice.

"For six years."

"No kidding," said Strong, taking a sip of her dark coffee. "Why did you leave?"

"A number of reasons—mostly personal."

As a reporter, Strong was intrigued. "Care to elaborate?"

"I could, but I won't."

"Oh, right—the Secret Service code of silence."

"Something like that," responded Freeberg, looking around the restaurant.

"You left because the president hit on you, didn't you?"

"No."

"Bullshit! That sleaze bag hit on you," said Strong, trying to elicit a reaction out of Freeberg.

"Honestly," lied Freeberg with a straight face, "that wasn't the reason."

"You left for some reason that had something to do with the way Butler treats women. I've heard the rumors. You must have seen the ugly reality and decided you couldn't take it any longer."

"Really, Anne, I can't—and I won't—discuss it," said Freeberg.

Strong's reporter instincts told her that she had hit on the reason. Freeberg's body language told her she was right. Her instincts also told her that she would file away this tidbit of information for future reference. Maybe, she thought, if she ever did an exposé on the issue of sexual harassment in Washington, she could get Freeberg to at least provide her background information about what really went on in the White House during her tenure.

"Let's get back to the purpose of our meeting—the Coalition for a Prosperous New Millennium," said Freeberg in a clipped tone that told Strong she had pushed the issue as far as possible.

"What about the speculation that Win Murdock is behind the organization?" asked Strong.

"I can't confirm that. The Federal Election Commission doesn't require these groups to make public their contributors. But it wouldn't surprise me. Murdock contributes to every politician, regardless of party affiliation. And if he doesn't contribute directly, either his wife or one of his hundreds of minions at Holten write the check for him. He's also an associate member of about ten different trade associations. They carry a lot of his heavy baggage for him, too. Where did you hear that Murdock might be behind the story?" asked Freeberg.

"The *Moriarty Minute.*"

"Really? I don't read her report. Maybe I should start. From what I've heard, her reporting was very objective about what went on in the White House," said Freeberg, smiling at Strong as if to confirm the reporter's earlier speculation. "Why don't you just talk with Moriarty?"

"Professional reasons. My paper still looks down on her tactics and methods."

"They can't be that different from your own. Your paper is always quoting unnamed sources and 'sources close to the president.'"

Strong recognized the double standard but chose not to respond directly to Freeberg's point. "If I were to go to Moriarty, she would probably report it in her Internet newsletter and, in turn, my paper, my boss and myself would be extremely embarrassed and held up for ridicule among our peers for months. Furthermore, in the midst of a presidential election, I can't afford the luxury. If people knew that I was talking with Moriarty, they might expect to see some of the quotes they gave to me off the record reported in Moriarty's rag with their name attached to them. My credibility would be shot."

"I had no idea the world of reporting was so filled with intrigue and Machiavellian maneuvering," said Freeberg.

"About as Machiavellian as the world we cover," responded Strong. "Well, I hope you'll let me know first thing if you are able to find out any information—however small or insignificant—about the coalition. If it's true that Murdock is behind the group, I want to nail his slimy ass to the wall."

"I will," said Freeberg. "I want the same thing."

"What else is the Center for Responsive and Ethical Politics following these days?"

"I'm tracking all the contributions flowing into the presidential campaigns."

"Interesting. Didn't the FEC quarterly report just come out?"

"It did—earlier this month. Byrne and Prescott continue to roll. Now that it appears they have a lock on their party's nomination, the special interest money is just pouring into their coffers. What always amazes me is that so many of the special interest groups contribute to both candidates. They don't care if the winner is Republican or Democrat. They just want access to the office."

"Like who? Which special interests contribute to both sides?" asked Strong.

"Let's see," said Freeberg, rattling off each industry on her fingers, "the construction industry, the airline industry, the chemical industry, the petroleum industry, the agriculture industry, the telecommunications industry, the banking and financial services industry, the broadcast industry—do you want me to go on? The list is endless. These groups don't give a shit who becomes president. They just want to make sure that whoever it is, he doesn't go after their industry."

"How are these groups responding to Colfax's insurgent campaign?"

"That's the sixty-four million dollar question. Anyone can channel money to be targeted against Colfax through the loopholes in 'soft money' and independent expenditures. It's impossible to say how they are responding—if at all."

"Maybe it's not a sixty-four million dollar question. Maybe it's a fourteen million dollar question. Moriarty's theory about Murdock is plausible."

"I agree. Unfortunately, there are a lot of other people and groups that would hate to see an independent president. Especially if that candidate were Robert Colfax."

The waiter was refilling their coffee cups for the third and final time, and they were discussing the murder of the lobbyist, when Freeberg spotted McGowan's large angular frame ease into the restaurant. She had only learned that he was coming to Washington the night before and had asked him to meet her at the restaurant at 6:00 P.M. The Secret Service often ended its Saturday classes at Beltsville a little early. The time gave McGowan an opportunity to shower and change into some casual clothes.

"Sean," she said with great excitement as she gave him a passionate kiss and a big hug.

"Aren't you going to introduce me to your friend," said McGowan, somewhat embarrassed.

"Of course. I'm sorry. Sean, this is Anne Strong. Anne, this is my friend Sean McGowan."

"Nice to meet you, Sean," said Strong shaking McGowan's solid hand. "Stephanie, I appreciated your time. I don't want to get in the way of your dinner plans, so I'll let you two enjoy each other's company. It looks like you have some catching up to do."

"You're welcome to stay," said McGowan. "I'm only going to have a beer and then we're off to dinner." With a subtle flick of his hand, McGowan caught the eye of the young waitress, who rushed over to take his order.

"Thanks for the offer," replied Strong, "but I should be going. I just have to ask you one question; I'm a reporter you know. What brings you to Washington? Stephanie says you're from Minneapolis."

"Training," said McGowan nonchalantly, hoping that would be the end of the conversation.

"What kind of training?" asked Strong. It was a natural question for a reporter.

"Secret Service training," said Freeberg, jumping into the conversation.

"You're a Secret Service agent, too?" said Strong, suddenly wishing that she had taken him up on his offer to stay for a beer.

"I am."

"You must be assigned to Colfax—or Gibraltar?" said Strong, adding, "God, I love that codename—it's so macho." McGowan was a little startled to hear the codename. He knew it would get out into public—they always did. Still, he was surprised to hear it so soon after it was assigned to Colfax.

"If you don't mind me asking, what kind of training?"

"It's classified," replied McGowan with a wink.

"Come on—"

"It's not nearly as exciting as you might think—I spent an hour getting tailored."

"What?"

"It's true," said Freeberg. "The weapons and communication gear Secret Service agents wear have to be concealed yet easily accessible. It's not an easy thing to do."

"What else?"

"Reaction tests," said McGowan.

"Like those cop simulators where you're shown a video of a hostage situation and you have to react?"

"Exactly. Only ours are a little more intense."

"Describe them."

"I can't—but I can give you an idea of how fast we have to react."

"Okay."

"Pull out a few coins, a matchbook, business cards or whatever else you might have in your purse. Don't let me see them." Strong did as asked and added a key chain, a health insurance card and a bank receipt from a cash machine. "Now cover them with a napkin." Strong again did as requested. "On the count of three, lift the napkin off, but just for one second."

"One, two, three . . ." Strong lifted the napkin.

McGowan's eyes quickly scanned the contents before Strong recovered the items. "The quarter was minted in 1972 and the penny was minted in 1988—at the Denver mint. The telephone number on the matchbook is 202-555-3489. The business card is from Seth Weinstein. He's a legislative assistant for Senator Lewis. I could also tell you his fax number, your insurance policy number and how much money you have left in your bank account."

"How much?" asked Strong, who didn't even know what her bank account read.

"$322.69."

"That's amazing," replied Strong, lifting the napkin and studying the details of the pile of items. "Can all Secret Service agents do that?"

"To a degree," said Freeberg. "Sean is a little more skilled in that department than most."

"Maybe we should skip the beer if we're going to catch both dinner and the movie," said McGowan, diplomatically ending Strong's questioning and indicating to her that they were leaving. "It was nice to meet you," said McGowan, placing a five dollar bill on the table to pay for the beer he never received.

"Nice to meet you, too," replied Strong. "Stephanie, please let me know if you hear anything more."

McGowan meant to ask Freeberg about the comment but never got around to it. They also didn't make it to dinner or a movie. They spent the next four hours in bed. McGowan then caught the red-eye out of Dulles to Minneapolis.

* *

The Cathedral of St. Paul sits on top of a hill overlooking downtown St. Paul and the Capitol. It is a magnificent structure that seems to offset the Capitol in size, style and substance. It is as though the Irish Catholics who built it purposely put it close to and above the Capitol in order to thumb their noses at the Lutherans who seemed to run the place for so long.

Colfax and his family had traditionally attended Easter Service at the Basilica of St. Mary in Minneapolis, Colfax's hometown, but he had opted for the St. Paul Cathedral for the last few years because of its proximity to the governor's residence.

"Let's go, girls," said Linda Colfax, calling to her two daughters. "We're going to be late." She knew it wouldn't look good if her family were late for Easter service.

Colleen, age ten, and Catherine, age sixteen, were the pride of their father. With their jet-black hair, fair complexions and vivid green eyes, they were the spitting image of their mother. They also had her slender build. Only Colfax's sleek, angular nose made it visibly into their genetic code.

"You look beautiful," said Colfax to his youngest daughter as she scrambled down the stairs after her mother's admonishment. "Where's Catherine?"

"Putting on eyeliner."

"Eyeliner?" said Colfax, turning and giving his wife a quizzical look.

"She's growing up," replied his wife.

"She thinks Jeremy Welsh might be at church," said Colleen, offering some clarification.

"And who is Jeremy?" asked Colfax.

"Her boyfriend."

"He's not my boyfriend," yelled Catherine from the top of the stairs.

"He's not? Good, then you won't mind if I instruct the Secret Service to arrest him if he so much casts an eye your way," said Colfax with a mock stone face.

"Dad," drawled Catherine as she came down the stairs. She had grown accustomed to her father's sense of humor over the years.

"Let's go," said Linda, ordering everyone into the car. As the family piled into the black Lincoln Continental, Colleen and Catherine both greeted the Secret Service agent assigned to chauffeur the First Family of Minnesota. "It's a gorgeous day, isn't it?" said McGowan, who, despite a lack of sleep, was feeling refreshed from his time with Freeberg.

On the way to the Cathedral, Colfax probed Catherine about her new romantic interest. How old is he, where does he go to school, does he play any sports? Catherine politely answered all the questions. He asked Colleen about her softball team's latest game and apologized for missing it. Colleen said she understood but proudly reported her two hits and, in her words, "an awesome catch" from her position at third base.

The trip to the Cathedral took less than three minutes and only an observant person would have noticed the cars in both the front and back of the Lincoln Continental. Since Friday, Colfax had been assigned two additional Secret Service agents.

Once at the Cathedral, the family entered the church through the attached rectory. The entrance allowed the family to remain unseen by the general public. It also got them to their reserved seats in the front row of the church without being gawked at by the entire congregation.

Colfax used the few minutes before the service started to quietly pray. His wife and daughters did the same, although Catherine first scanned the crowd, looking for Jeremy. Colfax prayed for continued strength to follow his conscience, he prayed over the abortion issue—his position stood at odds with the Church. He prayed, too, that his decision to run was the right thing for his family. The three-minute conversation with his daughters on the drive over to the Church had left him feeling that his run for presidency was a greedy and selfish thing to do. He continued to pray until his thoughts began to drift to brunch after Mass—and talking further with his daughters. There was so much he wanted to ask them, so much he had to catch up on in their lives.

The mass was only slightly longer than usual due to Easter. Many politicians would have lingered afterward to show their constituents that they were devoted parishioners. Colfax never did, feeling that religious services were private, and it was in poor taste to mingle the two.

Only·a few parishioners beyond the first few pews even knew Colfax and his family were in the church. Even fewer would have recognized the governor and his family had they been watching the mass on the public access station.

Despite Colfax's low profile, the Secret Service had taken the precaution of stationing an agent in the choir, located on the left side of the altar, so that at least one person would have a bird's-eye view of any possible danger lurking in the crowd of nearly two thousand people.

This responsibility fell to Luke Parish who, because of his height and the need to keep the microphone inside the right arm of his robe hidden, was positioned in the middle of the choir. He made a valiant attempt to mouth the words to every hymn but his real purpose was to constantly monitor the congregation for any possible assassins. He didn't see any. And if he had paid any attention to the parishioner who seemed somewhat confused by the Catholic rituals of when to stand, sit or kneel, he wouldn't recall it months later.

CHAPTER NINETEEN

J effery Payne sat in the comfortable den of his secluded suburban house and sipped his coffee as he read the story of the tragic death of David Pollard, aged forty-one, executive director of the National Small Business Coalition and a 1984 graduate of University of Virginia Law School. Nowhere in the story was there any indication of Pollard's death being anything other than a case of being in the wrong place at the wrong time.

The *Post* story had not come as a surprise to Payne. His assistant had briefed him on all the activities of the preceding night, from the murder to the contents of the e-mail. It was the latter that most disturbed Payne. If one lawyer at Lawrence, Mance & Scott knew about Murdock's involvement in the coalition, how many others did? And if more than one knew, how long would it be before a reasonably competent reporter began creating trouble. Payne picked up the phone and called Murdock.

"Good morning, Win. This is Payne," said the deputy director of the CIA.

"Good morning, Jeffery. How are you?"

"I've been better. Did you see the story about David Pollard in today's paper?"

"David who?" said Murdock, trying to place the familiar-sounding name.

"Pollard. He was the head of the National Small Business Coalition."

"Oh, yes—no, I haven't seen the paper. What happened?"

There was a rather lengthy pause before Payne spoke. "Mr. Pollard was a contributing member of the Coalition for a Prosperous New Millennium. He was killed last night."

This time it was Murdock's turn to pause. He checked to confirm that he was speaking on a secure line. "How was he killed?"

"The papers are saying it was a crime of opportunity—a case of a white suburban professional being the victim of a random, drug-related crime."

"The papers often exaggerate the truth," said Murdock in a manner meant to elicit more information from Payne.

"Yes, they do. There is more to this case than meets the eye."

"Go on," said Murdock impatiently.

"What is not reported and what is not known by anyone other than myself, my assistant, and now you is that Mr. Pollard visited the CyberCafe in Georgetown last evening around 11:00 P.M. From there, he accessed a computer and sent an e-mail to Ellen Moriarty."

"What did the message say?" asked Murdock hurriedly.

"The contents were alarming, Mr. Murdock. Pollard listed a number of contributors to the coalition. Worse, he indicated that he had learned of these members from a school friend who worked at Lawrence, Mance & Scott."

"Jesus Christ," yelled Murdock into the phone. "Was the message received by Moriarty?"

"No."

"Are you sure?"

"Positive."

"Have all possible traces of the message been erased? Electronic correspondence makes me extremely nervous," said Murdock. Holten, Inc., had once been found guilty of scheming to fix prices because a few employees had incorrectly assumed that once they deleted a file from their computer, it was gone forever.

"Yes. My assistant assured me that it is gone—forever. We're very proficient in these technical areas," said Payne, confidently.

"Excellent. Now," said Murdock, "tell me what we know about the leak within Mance's firm."

"We know that he is a school friend of Pollard's and that he knows who has been contributing. Pollard's e-mail gave no indication of how exactly his friend obtained the information."

"This is serious. If one person knows, it's possible others know as well."

"I agree. And if that is the case, there is no way the contingency plan can go forward."

"Let me do this," said Murdock, not willing to abandon the contingency plan so fast. "I'm going to call Mance and demand a full accounting of the situation. In the meantime, I would like you to cross reference Pollard's undergraduate and law school classes with the list of lawyers employed at Lawrence, Mance & Scott."

"It's being done as we speak."

"Good. I'll get back to you in an hour," said Murdock before hanging up the phone.

For the next ten minutes, Murdock yelled, screamed and chastised Jacob Mance. On numerous occasions, he threatened to not only take away Holten's business but also use his power to influence other businesses to stop using the services of Lawrence, Scott & Mance. It was a threat Mance knew Murdock could make good.

Jacob Mance gave every assurance that the only person at the law firm beside himself who could possibly be aware of the contributors was J. Preston Briggs, a partner who had been asked to sit in and record the proceedings. It was a job that normally any qualified secretary could have done but, ironically, for security purposes, a partner—at the rate of $500 an hour—was used.

"Are you absolutely sure, Jacob? If you are wrong—or worse, if you are lying—you can kiss your sweet little retainer goodbye—forever. Do you understand me?"

"Yes," replied Mance, who was astounded at Briggs' lack of discretion and was already formulating in his mind the ass chewing he was going to give the junior partner.

"You better—because I can't afford another fuck-up of this kind."

"I understand, Mr. Murdock."

Minutes later, Murdock was back on the phone with Payne, telling him that he had been assured that the only person besides Mance who knew about the Coalition was a lawyer by the name of J. Preston Briggs. Payne confirmed that Briggs had graduated from the University of Virginia Law School with Pollard.

The sun had not yet risen when the plan to remove J. Preston Briggs from his earthly existence was finalized. Briggs himself was still in a deep, drunken sleep. The seven martinis from the night before had not worn off.

* *

Trial attorneys from all over America poured money into the campaign to defeat Governor Colfax's legislation requiring that a person or corporation be found at least fifty-percent liable for an accident before they could be required to be paid one hundred percent of the damages. Simultaneously, massive amounts of money flowed into the state to defeat his single-house initiative.

"Jesus Christ, it's like we're being tag teamed by two 800-pound gorillas," said Annette Christianson, Colfax's chief of staff, in response to the latest slate of television and radio ads running against the governor's proposals.

"I knew we'd face some stiff opposition," said Pete Sawyer, "but I thought we could expect a little help from Republicans. After all, they campaigned on these issues."

"Those sons of bitches are the biggest wussies I know," said Christianson. "I'm sure they're getting pressure from the national Republican Party to back off. They know that if Colfax is successful, it will make Elliott Prescott look like a candy ass in comparison."

"That's a good point," said Sawyer, "but I think the Republicans are also scared by the polls. They're heading south pretty fast—which isn't surprising, given that the special interest groups have pumped in nearly a million dollars to cast the two proposals as the end of motherhood, baseball, and apple pie." Just then the phone rang. It was Colfax. The chief of staff simply listened, but the look on her face told Sawyer it wasn't good news. She hung up without saying a word.

"The governor just informed me that the Senate majority leader is confident enough with the poll numbers that he is going to refer both bills to the rules committee. Apparently, he has also received assurances from the Republican minority leader that they will not make it a campaign issue," said Christianson.

"You mean he's going to try to kill both bills in committee?"

"Worse," said Christianson, "He's so confident about the polls that he's not even going to allow them to get to a full floor vote."

"I can't believe the Republicans are going along with it," replied Sawyer.

"It just goes to show you that at the end of the day, there isn't much difference between Democrats and Republicans. It's the special interests that run the show."

"How's the governor?" asked Sawyer.

"You know him. He never loses his cool, but it sounded as though he was channeling his anger toward some defined action. I think the editorials in the *Minneapolis Star Tribune* and the *St. Paul Pioneer Press*—both of which panned his ideas today—really pissed him off. When he told me about the Senate majority leader, I could almost hear the steam coming from his ears."

"Good. That's when he's at his best," offered Sawyer.

* *

Within minutes of entering the State Capitol complex, Colfax had his entire staff assembled. "I feel strongly that both of these initiatives are in the best interest of the citizens of the state of Minnesota," said Colfax, turning slowly to look into the faces of each and every one of his staff. "I know you have all seen the polls showing that there is dwindling support for these initiatives. I also know most of you have seen the clever ads running in opposition to my plans. Maybe some of you have even been convinced that the ads are right—and I'm wrong." He paused to let this comment sink in before he began again. "Well—I am not."

The resoluteness in his voice surprised even Christianson who had been with Colfax since he was a congressman in the early 1980s.

"Damn the polls, I intend to shape them. If the special interest groups, the trial attorneys and the Republicans and Democrats want a fight—they've got one!" said Colfax, hammering his fist on the giant oak table.

"Kick ass," came the surprised response from the corner of the room. Everyone, including Colfax, turned and looked in the direction of Josh Parker, who had driven Pete Sawyer over to the Capitol and had been invited into the room—past the Secret Service agents—by the campaign manager.

"Kick ass is right," said Colfax smiling. "It's nice to know that someone here is as excited as me. It's Josh, right?" he asked, recalling Parker's boyish face and his enthusiasm from the Iowa caucuses.

For the next half-hour, with no notes, Colfax barked out orders to individual staffers. He ordered the press secretary to arrange a one o'clock news conference. He wanted every television, radio and newspaper reporter working the Capitol beat to attend. He sent two of his government relations staff to shore up the wavering Republicans on the rules committee. He sent two others over to the Senate with specific instructions that they were to inform whomever would listen that he was more than willing to engage in political hardball to get a full vote on this issue. "You tell anyone who is opposed to this bill that I'm going to go through every appropriations bill with a fine-toothed comb to sift out every little piece of pork that they've put in for their district and I'm going to veto it! Also tell anyone who opposes these issues that I'll make it my business to see to it that they aren't re-elected."

To another staffer, he dictated a letter and ordered it sent to the Senate majority leader. The letter demanded that both bills be released from the rules committee and be given an up or down vote by the full house. When he was done, he again looked over the entire staff and said, "We've got less than twenty-four hours before tomorrow's committee hearing. Damned if I'm going to let a bunch of powerful special interest groups deprive the citizens of this state of good public policy. I'm counting on you. Now, let's go do it."

What Colfax was not counting on was the skill of Josh Parker to exhort the campaign's thousands of "netizens" to leave their computer terminals on short notice and show up at a support rally for the two initiatives.

* *

Like Win Murdock, Raphael Baptista was a man of meticulous planning. As a precaution after David Pollard's death, he had CIA technicians place a few additional word filters on Moriarty's incoming e-mails. Any messages containing the words "Pollard," "murder," "stabbing," or "lobbyist" were to be screened out. Troy Hall, the aspiring journalist, unfortunately, used two of those words in his e-mail.

Hall posted his e-mail minutes after seeing the photo of David Pollard in the *Washington Post* and reading the account of his death. In addition to sending a copy to Moriarty, Hall sent a copy to his home computer—he wanted to retain a record for his electronic journal. He was positive Pollard was the man he saw in the CyberCafe the previous night.

Hall's e-mail never reached Moriarty. And his death, unlike Pollard's, received little attention. Baptista knew that the heroin overdose of a young black male would garner little media attention.

*   *

J. Preston Briggs was still sleeping off the effects of his seven-martini evening when the phone in his chic Georgetown apartment began ringing. His head was throbbing and his mouth was dry, and he tried to ignore the incessant ringing. He hoped it would stop so he could return to sleep. It didn't. Briggs finally picked up the phone on the thirteenth ring. "What?" he yelled into the phone.

"Mr. Briggs?" came the soft reply.

"Yes! Who is this?" demanded Briggs, rubbing his temples.

"Mr. Briggs, this is Jackie—Mr. Mance's assistant. Please hold for Mr. Mance. He wishes to speak with you." Briggs felt his stomach get a little queasy. Mance wouldn't call unless something very important was happening or someone had fucked up.

"Briggs, you fucking dumbshit," screamed Mance. Briggs pulled the phone back from his ear—the yelling hurt his head. "I don't know what the fuck you've said— or to whom—but because of you, Win Murdock just ripped me a new asshole!"

"What—ah—I don't understand—" said Briggs lamely, trying to figure out what he had done.

"You don't have to understand, Briggs. What you have to understand is that your position as a partner in this firm is in jeopardy. Get your fat ass down to the office immediately. I want a full accounting of everyone you met last night and everything you said."

"Jacob—" Briggs pleaded.

"Now," said Mance, hanging up.

Briggs strained his hungover mind, trying to recall what he could have possibly said or done last night that could have jeopardized his entire career—and his lifestyle—with Lawrence, Mance & Scott. He was still struggling with that question in the shower when last night's dinner decided to revisit him. For the next several minutes, he knelt on the tile floor of the shower and vomited.

Whether it was the running water, the insulation of the walls or his preoccupation with his rebelling stomach—or a combination of all three—Briggs never heard the door to his apartment open and close.

Baptista heard Briggs retching and surmised that he had had too much to drink the night before. If he played it right, his task would be even easier than he had anticipated.

Finally, the retching stopped and Briggs continued to let the hot water cascade down his flabby body in an attempt to revive himself. It wasn't working. The phone began to ring again, and Briggs, thinking that it might be Mance, grabbed a towel and ran into his bedroom to answer the phone.

"Hello? Hello? Shit," said Briggs, thinking he missed the call. Hanging up the phone, Briggs began to towel off his wet hair, which was dripping onto his bed and the floor. Briggs never heard Baptista approach from behind.

With violent quickness, Baptista yanked Briggs' left hand from the towel. Briggs, still drunk from the night before and numb from Mance's call, had no idea what was happening and put up little resistance. Using his left hand, the trained murderer rapidly placed the silencer flush against J. Preston Briggs' left temple and fired a single bullet. The towel conveniently held by Briggs' other hand contained the contents of his brain.

Baptista deftly touched up the limp body and the placement of the gun. He was careful not to leave any fingerprints. Baptista then returned to the closet, picked up the cell phone that he had used only a minute before to draw Briggs out of the shower and left the apartment.

Briggs' sister would later say that her brother was remarkably neat and that limiting the physical presence of his own suicide was completely in keeping with his character. Jacob Mance would also report that Preston Briggs was under great pressure at work and his suicide, while unexpected, was not entirely surprising.

A more thorough investigation by the Washington police may have yielded some interesting information, but no such investigation regarding J. Preston Briggs' "suicide" ever took place.

CHAPTER TWENTY

The gentlemanly maître d' escorted Murdock to the Congressional Country Club's private dining room. Jeffery Payne was already waiting. "I had hope it wouldn't come to this," said Murdock, starting the conversation as soon as the maître d' left the room.

Payne stared back at him in silence, not knowing whether the seventy-seven-year-old billionaire was referring to murders of Pollard and Briggs or the sudden re-emergence of Greene and Cross.

"It appears that Stanley Cross and Congressman Greene stole a page from Colfax's book and used the Internet to turn out their supporters last Tuesday in South Dakota. Their success, however, still would not have been possible without the incompetence of the other campaigns. I swear, when Prescott or Byrne wins the general election, it won't be because of their tactical or strategic brilliance," said Murdock. "It'll be because of me."

"You're right, Win. All they had to do was put together a halfway decent field organization in South Dakota and they could have finished their opponents off," offered Payne.

"Instead, the cheap bastards assumed that because they had their nominations locked up, they didn't have to bother campaigning. They wanted to save a measly million dollars. Their fuck-up is going to end up costing them a lot more than that."

Payne nodded in agreement.

"We've got to a lot to discuss, Jeffery. But let's order first," said Murdock, glancing in the direction of the maître d', Sam Matheny, who was positioned on the far side of the room—well out of hearing—where he always patiently waited until beckoned. Although it was not his responsibility to wait on customers, Matheny always made an exception for Win Murdock.

Matheny listened to each man's order, committed it to memory, and silently slid away. When he returned a few minutes later with their salads and iced tea, the two were deep in conversation. They stopped when he approached. Matheny cracked some fresh pepper on both salads and again silently departed.

"As I was saying," continued Murdock, "I appreciate the efficiency and effectiveness of your team."

"It is only one person," said Payne, correcting him.

"I appreciate it even more. The fewer people involved, the better the prospects for success. That is a lesson Mr. Mance has recently had to learn the hard way."

"That concerns me, Win. Does he really believe that Briggs committed suicide?"

"No," replied Murdock, pausing, "he doesn't. But don't be alarmed, Jeffery. Jacob has been around long enough to know that he is playing a high-stakes game. His silence is ensured. If anything, I fault him for Briggs' death. He was responsible for letting the young man know the need for complete discretion."

"You're right," said Payne, who wasn't particularly troubled by Briggs' death.

As they ate their salads, the discussion returned to the presidential campaign and the relative merits of a Prescott or Byrne presidency. When they were about finished with the entrée, Murdock brought up the real reason for the lunch.

"Jeffery," he began, looking Payne squarely in the eyes, "it is time to implement the contingency plan." Payne said nothing as he tried to calculate, in political terms, what this meant. "Colfax's path is widening. He has to be stopped—and he has to be stopped now," continued Murdock. So focused was Payne on what Murdock was saying that he didn't notice the elegant, but unobtrusive, Matheny approach from behind Murdock.

"May I take your plates?" asked Matheny softly.

"Please, Sam," replied Murdock, who was not perturbed by Matheny's sudden appearance.

"Would you care for coffee or dessert?"

"Coffee, please," said Murdock.

"Sir?" said Matheny, looking at Payne.

"Coffee for me as well," replied Payne, who was still surprised that Matheny had been able to approach the table without his knowledge. When Matheny departed, Payne whispered, "Do you think he heard anything?"

"Sam? No," laughed Murdock. "I've known him for close to thirty years, and I have dined in these rooms with all kinds of noteworthy people—and have said outrageous things in his presence. They have never been repeated."

"Still—"

"We didn't say anything anyway, did we?" asked Murdock.

"No, I guess not," replied Payne, figuring that the phrase "We've got to stop Colfax" was harmless.

"I appreciate your sensitivity to the possible risks, Jeffery. That's why I'm comfortable delegating this delicate project to you."

"Thank you."

"Your contact is aware of the contingency plan?"

"Only part of it."

"It's time to tell him the rest of the plan," said Murdock. "I want the plan implemented—the sooner, the better. If successful, I'll personally guarantee that the next president will remove the 'deputy' from your title."

Payne smiled. He had dreamed of being the director of the CIA for the last twenty years. Now, he could almost taste it.

* *

"How much does she want?" asked Colfax.

"One-hundred K," replied Sawyer.

"For six months' work? Is that the going rate for a web master?"

"It is, if you want a good one."

"Is she good?"

Sawyer nodded his head.

"Does she want the job?"

Again, Sawyer nodded. "I want to meet her," said Colfax.

Sawyer left the room and brought back Stacy Arbuckle, a freelance web designer who had learned about the opening through a friend of Sawyer's. After the standard pleasantries, Colfax got down to business.

"I understand you want the job," said Colfax, staring at Arbuckle. His face showed no emotion.

"I do," replied Arbuckle, who was pleased that she was meeting with the candidate. It told her he valued her work.

"Why should I hire you?" asked Colfax.

"Because I can help you win the election," responded Arbuckle with equal frankness.

"How?"

"By this November, seventy-eight million people will be on the Internet. Eighty-six percent of those users will vote. Of those eighty-six percent, I'd say roughly three-fourths are aligned with your political philosophy—independent, fiscally responsible, socially tolerant. They hold the key to your victory, and I can deliver them."

"How?"

"By designing a web site that gives them what they need—while also portraying you in a way that is most favorable to you."

"Go on."

"Internet users aren't like TV viewers. They are not passive—they don't respond well to negative attacks. You have to give them a reason to vote for you. They need to know who you are, and why you have taken the positions you have. I can do that for you. I'll also give them constant updates, online conversations, community action kits, letters to the editor. Whatever they want, I'll get it to them. They will be some of your hardest workers.

"I'll also improve your current site. We need to keep surfers' attention. The political cartoons are a good start, but they have to be updated constantly. I want people, especially young people, coming back to your site everyday."

"I'm impressed, Ms. Arbuckle. I understand you want $100,000."

"Correct," replied Arbuckle, maintaining eye contact with Colfax.

"Let me ask you," said Colfax, "how much do you think I can raise over the Internet?"

"From what Pete has told me, you're off to a good start. But I think you can realistically raise five million dollars between now and November."

"Really?"

"Really."

Colfax pondered her response for a moment. "Well, if that's the case, I want to make you a counter offer. The job is yours. But instead of a flat salary, I'll give you a percentage of everything the campaign brings in over the Internet."

Arbuckle's eyes lit up.

It was the reaction Colfax wanted.

"What's the cut?" she asked.

"Two percent of the first five million dollars, and three percent of everything above that."

"Done," said Arbuckle extending her hand.

By the end of her first week, Arbuckle had created three new links: a daily top-ten list, a link showing gaffes that Prescott and Byrne uttered on the campaign trial, and a third entitled: "Tired of soundbites? Check out this site." The link showed video clips of Colfax outlining, in depth, his position on various issues. Arbuckle also collected over $75,000 in Internet donations her first week on the job.

* *

"You wanted to see me?" said Baptista, standing in front of his boss' desk. He remained standing until the deputy director swung his chair around to face him and motioned for him to have a seat.

"The contingency plan is a go."

"When is it to be executed?"

"Immediately," replied Payne.

Baptista smiled. He was aware of Colfax's plan to eliminate the CIA and shared Payne's desire to see that that did not become a reality. "Yes, sir."

"I want you to go to extraordinary lengths to protect our newest asset. Eluding the Secret Service will be difficult—and not without risk."

"I understand. Do you have something specific in mind?"

"I do," said Payne, handing Baptista a thin, sealed folder. "Inside is the psychological profile of a person likely to try killing Governor Colfax."

Baptista pulled a small ivory pocketknife from his pocket and expertly sliced open the envelope. He quickly digested the information.

"I shouldn't have much trouble finding a suitable candidate. I can access the Defense Department's personnel database and have a list of five potential candidates within the hour."

* *

Rudolph Emerson Bradford, a former Army clerk, had not held a full-time job since his wife divorced him in 1996. He didn't need to—his part-time job at the gun shop in Fayetteville, just outside Fort Bragg, coupled with his extracurricular trading and selling of illegal guns, allowed him to spend most of his time pursuing his real passion—hunting and fishing in the backwoods of North Carolina.

Raphael Baptista deliberately chose the timing of his pitch. He knew Tuesday was the slowest day of the week at the gun shop and that Bradford worked alone in the afternoons.

A loud chime announced Baptista's entrance into the store. Bradford looked up from the gun magazine that he had been reading and watched the slender, well-dressed man approach the counter. The man did not bother to look at any of the guns displayed in the store.

"I need a Barrett .50 caliber," said Baptista, staring directly at the clerk. "And I need it ASAP."

"Can't do it," replied Bradford in his thick backwoods accent, "It's illegal." He was nervous about being directly approached by stranger for an illegal purchase. Baptista was unfazed. He had expected this response.

"If you're worried that I'm a cop or a member of ATF, I'm not. If you don't want to deliver, I understand. I'll take my business elsewhere. But I want you to know that I'm willing to pay $4,000 up front for a Barrett .50 caliber and another $4,000 upon delivery. If you secure the rifle within twenty-four hours, I'll pay you an additional $2,000 bonus." Baptista slid an envelope of forty crisp $100 bills across the counter. He watched as the young man counted the money. "Can you deliver?"

Bradford sized up the man standing before him. "Yeah, I've got some contacts who can help arrange that," replied Bradford. In fact, Bradford knew it would be relatively easy, especially for the price the man was willing to pay. He knew a lot of soldiers at Fort Bragg, especially those with families who were scraping by on the low Army pay and food stamps, who would be happy to supplement their income by selling one of the military's most potent long-range sniper rifles.

"Good. When can I pick it up?"

"Meet me at my trailer at noon tomorrow," said Bradford, writing down the address of the trailer park. "I'm in lot 317."

*   *

A beat-up 1983 Ford pickup, with a shotgun rack and large Confederate flag visible from the back window, was parked on the small patch of dirt in front of the trailer. Baptista knew he was at the right address.

Before Baptista could knock on the tattered screen door, Bradford pulled open the inside door and motioned for him to enter. The CIA operative glanced around quickly and stepped inside. "Do you have the rifle?"

"Yeah."

"May I see it?"

"What's your rush, pal? Would you like a beer?" asked Bradford, who was holding a Budweiser long neck in his hand. It obviously wasn't his first.

"No, thanks. I'm on a tight schedule. I'd like to inspect the rifle."

"Whatever," said Bradford going into the bedroom and pulling out a large plastic case. Setting it on the floor of the living room, directly below a Molly Hatchet poster, he opened the case. Securely surrounded by foam cushion were the rifle, a tripod, and a scope.

Baptista picked up the rifle and felt its heft. For the next five minutes, he examined every aspect of the rifle. Bradford stood over his shoulder, drinking his beer. "You've done a good job," said Baptista, flashing a rare smile. "Here is the remaining $4,000 plus the promised $2,000 bonus." Bradford counted the money.

"Thank you, sir. It's been a pleasure doing business with you. If you ever need anything else, just let me know—I can deliver it." Bradford was about to ask what the man intended to use the rifle for but decided against it. Better not to know, he thought.

"I will," replied Baptista. "I think I'll take you up on that beer now." Bradford smiled and rushed to the kitchen to get his new acquaintance an ice-cold beer. As he did, Baptista surveyed the small interior of the trailer home. It was perfect. The interior reeked of a good-ole-boy redneck. It would not be a far stretch for anyone to imagine that someone like Rudolph Emerson Bradford might plot to kill a politician like Robert Colfax.

After Bradford returned with the beer, he and Baptista talked about hunting and guns for almost twenty minutes. Another beer followed, and eventually Bradford offered to take his new friend to his favorite hunting spot. It was about forty miles away, said Bradford, and in the middle of a swampy forest. Even in the best of weather, it was difficult to reach. With all the rain the area had received during the past year, it was even more inaccessible.

Bradford talked almost nonstop from the time they left the trailer to when they pulled up at the end of a dirt road that disappeared into the swamp. Baptista was thankful for the constant chatter because it allowed him to concentrate on the twists and turns Bradford was making. The last thing he wanted was to get lost in the backwoods of North Carolina for the better part of a day.

"Do you take a lot of friends hunting out here?"

"Fuck no. This is a great spot. I wouldn't let any of my shit-bag buddies anywhere near here. They'd be back the next day, fuckin' everything up. I figure since you're not from around here, chances are you ain't coming back."

"I don't think I could find my way back."

Bradford laughed and pulled a beer out of the cooler behind the front seat. He offered Baptista one.

"I'm afraid two is all I can have before my shot begins to go a little wild," Baptista said. Bradford shrugged at the man's excuse.

"I've got an extra pair of boots in the back. You might want to put 'em on. It's a little muddy."

"Thanks, I appreciate that."

208

The pair both slid on the long boots and began walking toward a dry piece of land between two good-sized swamps. Bradford never heard his companion take the pistol from his coat pocket. Baptista fired point blank into the back of Bradford's head. The divorced twenty-four-year-old former Army private crumpled to the ground, dead. Reaching down, Baptista lifted the key from the dead man's pocket.

Baptista rolled the limp body up in an old tarp he took from Bradford's pickup and dragged it to the edge of the swamp. Unrolling the tarp, Baptista pushed Bradford face down into the thick, muddy bottom of the swamp. With any luck, Baptista thought, the body would begin decomposing immediately and Bradford would be unrecognizable long before he was found.

* *

Baptista waited until it was dark before returning to Bradford's tiny trailer. He turned the headlights off well before he parked. He didn't want any unwanted attention. Using the keys he lifted from Bradford, Baptista entered the trailer. He knew exactly what he needed. He grabbed a one-piece camouflage hunting suit and some leather boots. He also left three clippings; one from *Time* and the other two from the *Charlotte Observer*. Robert Colfax was the subject of all three and each highlighted a different policy position. The *Time* article drew attention to Colfax's liberal gun control positions. One of the newspaper pieces highlighted his willingness to allow gays and lesbians to serve in the military. The third was a passage from an interview with Colfax outlining why the candidate did not support a Constitutional amendment prohibiting the burning of the American flag. The passage read: "To me, the issue is not about protecting the symbol of freedom, it is about protecting the principle of freedom." The sentence was highlighted, and Baptista, forging Bradford's writing, scribbled next it, "This is fucked up!"

CHAPTER TWENTY-ONE

J esus Christ! Every television station in the state is leading their six o'clock with Josh's e-mail. They're setting the stage as if it was a gun fight at the OK Corral," complained Sawyer.

"Calm down, Pete," replied Colfax in a soothing tone.

"Calm down. Governor, your candidacy is hinging on tomorrow's vote, and we don't have the votes to pass it. We've done a hard count, and most of the Republicans are flaking off, and the Democrats are holding firm against us. They're going to screw us. And Josh has painted us into an untenable position with his e-mail by saying that you have to win tomorrow to be considered a contender."

"But I do, Pete."

"Not necessarily. I can spin the situation . . . minimize the damage. I can talk to my media contacts, downplay the significance of the vote, and play up your willingness to go to the mat against special interests. Win or lose, you should be complimented on your willingness to lead."

"No," said Colfax, in an even, measured way, "that's not my idea of leadership. We've still got fourteen hours until the vote. It's up to me to find a way to win. If I'm going to be president—and I am—it's imperative that I demonstrate my ability to lead."

"Governor—" pleaded Sawyer.

"Goddammit, Pete. We are going to win. If you don't believe that, then I need to get a new campaign manager. Are you up to the challenge?" asked Colfax, staring intently at his campaign manager. "Yes or no?"

"Yes."

"Good. Go get Annette and let her know that I want interviews with any television station willing to grant me one."

Beginning at 9:00 P.M., Colfax started one-on-one interviews with the lead reporters for every major television station in the Twin Cities area. Together, the stations covered the entire state. In each interview, Colfax let it be known that the vote was all-or-nothing. When asked if his presidential campaign rested on the outcome, Colfax didn't hesitate; he simply answered, "Yes, it does." He then used his limited time to explain his position and implored the viewers to contact their representatives and urge them to support his position. He also encouraged people to attend the hearing.

At 11:30 P.M., Colfax left the Capitol after a short meeting with his gubernatorial staff and was driven to his campaign headquarters in Minneapolis. Inside the old warehouse, forty young workers were still answering phones—telling callers why tomorrow's vote was so important and how they could make a difference. Colfax looked over the room of mostly volunteers, who hadn't even noticed his arrival, and cracked a smile as he observed the discarded pizza boxes and plethora of Diet Coke cans scattered around the office. The office was humming with activity.

Slowly, one by one, the workers noticed him. As they did, he motioned each one over to him. Within a minute, the entire campaign staff was gathered around him.

"First, let me say thank you to each and everyone of you," said Colfax to the group—many of whom were new and he didn't recognize. "I appreciate your hard work. With your help, we're going to win tomorrow and both bills are going to sail through the Senate—and I will sign both into law!"

A loud bout of cheering erupted.

"I would also like to thank Josh Parker. Where are you, Josh?" said Colfax, his eyes searching through the crowd. From the very back of the room, the young man raised his hand. "Come up front, Josh." Colfax waited as Parker made his way through the throng of campaign volunteers. "I want to recognize Josh because his actions today represent what this campaign is all about. After a meeting with me earlier today, Josh promptly acted in a manner that he felt was in the best interests of this campaign. His e-mail generated a great deal of interest and coverage. I want to applaud him for his initiative and encourage all of you to do the same. Take the initiative. We're not going to win this election by being a top-down organization. I want—and need—all of you doing just what Josh did today. We will sometimes make mistakes—everyone does—but I will never—I repeat, never—criticize or fault anyone for doing what they genuinely thought was in the best interests of this campaign.

"Now, we all have a long road before us. But I'm confident that tomorrow's vote is going to be a defining moment—not just for the state, but for our campaign. It's going to send a powerful message to the status quo—here in Minnesota and in

Washington—that we don't just talk about reform, we deliver it. There's still a lot to do before tomorrow's vote, so let's get back to work."

The room again erupted. The few workers who were planning to go home stayed on and helped answer the phone calls that were still coming in. As the phones died down, the volunteers worked at answering every e-mail query, and around 3:00 A.M., a group of about twenty began dropping literature on cars in the Twin Cities. Those who stayed in the office made signs to be used at the rally.

* *

The committee hearing didn't start until 8:00 A.M., but people began arriving at the Capitol at 5:30 A.M. Many had left their homes at two or three in the morning to make the hearing. Others had left the night before—minutes after receiving Parker's call to action. The subject line had read: COLFAX CANDIDACY AT RISK! The message was marked "urgent." The text outlined how a defeat at the hands of the obscure committee would kill Colfax's two biggest legislative initiatives.

A little before eight, the members of the Rules Committee began to arrive at the usually deserted Capitol. Most had expected a larger-than-normal crowd for the hearing—but no one had anticipated a crowd that the Capitol police later estimated at 10,000. People were lined up outside the Capitol trying to get in. Those who had arrived by 6:30 A.M. were able to get in the building, but only those who were there at 5:30 were able to get a seat in the hearing room.

Security guards had to clear a path for the twelve members of the committee. By the time they got to their seats in the hearing room, the majority had changed their minds. Even the Senate majority leader, the man who had just the day before confidently predicted the death of Colfax's bills, conceded defeat before he even brought the two issues up for a vote. He had received over 200 phone calls from constituents and twice as many e-mails demanding that he support Colfax's position. He also knew by the looks on his colleagues' faces that none wanted to risk the wrath of 10,000 people outside the Capitol and explain why they voted against the people's will.

The two bills cleared the Rules Committee on a voice vote and later that afternoon went before the full Senate. By that time, every senator was aware of the crowd that had gathered that morning. Only a few were willing to vote against an issue that had generated such an impassioned response, especially in an election year. By votes of sixty-four to three, both of Colfax's initiatives passed the Senate. The governor signed them into law the next day with great fanfare. The *Wall Street Journal* ran an editorial entitled "Presidential Timber," praising Colfax's bold, uncompromising leadership. The *New York Times* declared him "America's boldest governor" and "a legitimate contender."

* *

"The exit polls reflect a stronger turnout than expected, Brian," said veteran political reporter Foster Logan via satellite feed to the network anchor, Brian Dupont, back in the New York studio. "And our preliminary numbers show that both Stanley Cross and Reginald Greene are doing better than expected."

"This is quite a surprise, isn't it, Foster?"

"It is, Brian. After the devastating losses both candidates suffered in the March 7 primaries, most experts—and I will include myself in this category—assumed they were finished."

"What are the consequences if one or both wins the Colorado primary?" asked Dupont, genuinely intrigued at the prospect of an upset victory.

"Unlike their victories in South Dakota, these victories would be serious setbacks for the front runners. It would mean that both Governor Prescott and the vice president will have to continue to campaign all the way up to their conventions. They can't take victory for granted. It also means that they will have to continue spending money on beating back opponents from within their own parties."

"If either Cross or Greene wins, will either have a legitimate chance at securing their party's nomination?" asked Dupont.

"Realistically, no. But then, realistically, neither was expected to register on the radar screen here in Colorado. I think Byrne's and Prescott's campaigns were caught asleep at the switch," said Logan.

"If they both win, they'll be able to call for a greater role at their party's conventions. What does that mean for the Republicans and Democrats?"

"It means that Greene will make sure a plank on universal health care is included in the Democrat's platform. And if Cross wins, the Christian conservatives will have increased clout over the Republican platform?"

"Interesting. Who wins and who loses under this scenario?" asked Dupont.

"Obviously, the uninsured and the religious right win. One unexpected beneficiary will be Governor Colfax. If Republicans portray themselves as too conservative and if Democrats appeared to want bigger government, many centrists will gravitate toward Colfax. The scenario is very similar to how Colfax was elected governor."

"Couldn't the situation be exacerbated if the eventual nominees must buy-off these groups with their vice presidential candidates?"

"Absolutely, Brian. In fact, I'm sure Governor Colfax is back in Minnesota silently cheering Greene and Cross on to victory."

"Given his victories in the Minnesota legislature today, it could be quite a week for the maverick governor," said Dupont, concluding the interview.

* *

The large, plain brown envelope was inside the screen door and leaning up against the main, wooden door. It was addressed to the occupant of the third-floor apartment, Lee Murphy. Manning casually looked at the printed label and then looked around to see if anybody was watching—or if the deliverer was still in the vicinity. Seeing no one, the sniper entered the apartment, flipped on the kitchen light and tossed the envelope on the table. Manning used a dull steak knife to open the package, which was sealed with heavy-duty cellophane tape. Inside were two sheets. One was a set of instructions. The other was a map.

The first sheet was very similar to the one that Manning had received in Colorado Springs. It was a detailed explanation of how the sniper was supposed to prepare for the next job. It listed the type of gun and bullets to be used, the time of day practice was to occur, and the distance and the conditions under which the shot was to be fired. As in Colorado, Manning was to split the time practicing between night and day.

The sniper reread the information. The specifics were intriguing. The breakdown told Manning that the shot would probably come during the day. But it was the type of gun and the last requirement that really caught Manning's attention. The gun to be used was a Barrett .50 caliber and the practice distance was to be conducted from 1,000 to 2,500 yards. If Colfax was the target, thought Manning, these distances at least provided an outside chance of escape. The downside was that the distance also decreased the odds of a successful shot.

The second sheet contained a detailed set of directions and a map to a remote location in northern Minnesota, fifty miles south of the Canadian border. The directions indicated that at the end of the five-hour drive there was an isolated cabin stocked with ammunition and the Barrett .50. Taped to the backside of the sheet were two keys, one to the front door and the second to a storage cabinet inside the cabin. The note went on to explain that the nearest person to the cabin was twenty-five miles away, and thus there was no danger of any practice rounds being heard. Manning was also told to bring reading material because there was no radio or television at the cabin.

It had been over two months since Manning had killed Seselj, and the former Marine was itching to pull the trigger again. After a restless night, the sniper loaded up the 1987 Honda Accord in the cool darkness of an April morning and departed for the small spot on the map.

The trip took closer to six hours after a few coffee breaks, lunch and a series of wrong turns on the final few miles along the back roads. At a little after one o'clock, Manning studied the directions on the map again and turned right at the T in the dirt road and followed it for another half mile. There, just as the directions indicated, was a patch of larger birch trees off to the left of the road. Behind the trees was a small log cabin. Manning followed the trail, now covered almost entirely in vegetation, back to the cabin.

Manning put the key into the door and twisted it. The first thing the former Marine noticed was the smell of cleaning fluids. The odor told the sniper that someone had recently been in the cabin. Manning wondered if it was Baptista. The sniper couldn't picture Baptista cleaning.

The only light into the cabin came from the door behind Manning. There were no windows. Manning thought the cabin resembled a slightly larger version of the cabin that the Unabomber had called home.

Straight back from the front door was a large metal locker. Manning used the second key to open the locker. Inside were the ammunition and the rifle. The Barrett .50 was lighter than Manning expected, but the sniper gently took it out of its large case and assembled it on the floor of the cabin. Stroking the well-designed rifle, Manning admired its craftsmanship.

Despite seven years in the Marines, Manning had never had the opportunity to fire the premier long-distance sniper rifle. Manning still remembered reading the message from the secretary of the Navy prohibiting certain soldiers from engaging the Iraqis. The message was not issued directly to Lee Manning. It only felt that way to the sniper. The Persian Gulf War was the perfect opportunity to employ someone of Manning's skills, but the opportunity had not arisen—for political reasons. "Fuckin' politicians," thought Manning. "What difference did it make at whose hands an Iraqi died? Death was death. Who really cared from where or from whom the final blow came? The important thing is that it was delivered with maximum efficiency." Secretary of the Navy Robert T. Colfax had had a different opinion.

✳   ✳

Shortly after 10:00 P.M., the ABC affiliate in Denver flashed Stanley Cross' picture across the screen with a label reading "Projected Winner." The affiliate then cut away to a crowded hotel ballroom at the Broadmoor Hotel in Colorado Springs. Enthusiastic Cross supporters surrounded the local reporter assigned to cover the campaign, and he was having a hard time hearing his producer. He reported that the candidate was going to be on the floor of the ballroom any minute, where he was expected to declare victory. In the meantime, the reporter kept himself busy by interviewing a passionless young Cross supporter who had a hard time articulating why his candidate would make a good president.

Stanley Cross entered the ballroom from a side door. At only five feet, eight inches, he was difficult to spot in a crowd, but as he stepped up to the podium, a net full of red, white and blue balloons was released from the ceiling and all eyes turned toward him.

Cross thanked his supporters and quickly launched into his remarks. "The political pundits of the liberal, elite, Eastern establishment had declared my candidacy dead. But they were wrong," he shouted to the obvious approval of the crowd. "They are also wrong about my ability to become president. We will prove them wrong."

Each sentence was punctuated with wild clapping and cheering.

"The media might not want to hear it, but the people of Colorado spoke loud and clear today. A silent majority of Americans are beginning to wake up to the moral crisis that is confronting this country," said Cross, who had, over the course of the last four years, begun to take more socially conservative positions in a thinly veiled attempt to court the religious right.

"It is time to say yes to God and no to abortion," screamed Cross, pounding the podium. "It is time to say yes to parents and no to the homosexual agenda that the Hollywood liberals are stuffing down our throats. It is time to say yes to returning discipline to our schools and no to the fluffy multicultural psychobabble that bureaucrats in Washington are forcing our children to ingest. . . ."

For nearly twenty minutes, Cross spewed rhetorical red meat to his ravenous crowd of supporters. The $50,000 he paid for a professional speaking coach and the $150,000 he shelled out for a famous conservative speechwriter were beginning to show some payback. Unlike in 1996, he actually sounded like he believed what he was saying.

Across town in a small but equally boisterous room, Congressman Reginald Greene was making a victory speech similar in enthusiasm but different in content. He praised the hard-working blue-collar workers who got out and voted for him. He invoked the names of past great Democrats—Roosevelt, Truman, Kennedy, Johnson, and even Jimmy Carter. He did not mention the current president. He also acknowledged the large role Latino voters played in his upset victory.

* *

The daily practice sessions took almost twice as long as the ones in Colorado. After every shot, whether it was taken from 1,000 or 2,000 yards, Manning would jog the distance to the target and record the bullet's exact location on the target. The

216

sniper also diligently recorded the precise conditions under which the shot was fired—including the time of day, temperature, humidity, barometric pressure, and wind condition.

It took Manning almost three days to zero the rifle. But when the job was complete, the sniper was confident that a kill could be achieved even at the maximum range of 2,500 yards. If Colfax were the target, thought Manning, a mile and a half head start against the Secret Service would be an essential component of any escape plan.

On the sixth day of practice, Manning began to use different size targets. Unlike Colorado, where eggs and small balloons were the targets of choice, Manning used larger Styrofoam mannequin heads. Slightly larger helium balloons were also used to simulate the sudden movement of a human head. With nothing to do except practice, eat, read and sleep, Manning practiced twice a day, once in the daytime and once again in the evening. The sniper never fired more than five rounds in any practice session. To fire any more would allow sloppy, undisciplined, shooting techniques an opportunity to become habit. Manning didn't want to do anything to reduce the odds of a successful kill.

* *

Pete Sawyer walked into the governor's office and knew instantly that he wouldn't be able to talk Colfax out of giving the speech he intended to give. The candidate did not get up from behind his desk.

Sawyer took a seat across from Colfax and stared at the two posters directly behind him. One was a beautiful color photo of an American bald eagle soaring high above a crystal-blue lake. On the print were the words: "Leaders are like eagles. They don't flock, they soar alone." To the left of the photo was a black-and-white photo of an ancient oak tree tilting heavily to one side on an otherwise barren prairie. Sawyer felt Colfax resembled the oak tree at this moment—tilting against the wind, not giving an inch. Still, Sawyer, as his campaign manager, knew he had a responsibility to try.

"Governor, if you give this speech, you'll be handing votes to Prescott."

"Bullshit."

"With all due respect, Governor, I disagree. The gun control lobby is going to go ballistic."

"Let the bastards go ballistic."

"Governor, many of these gun advocates are independents."

"Good, then they'll understand we won't see eye-to-eye on every issue."

"But this isn't just another issue for them."

"Nor is it for me," replied Colfax, staring intently at his campaign manager.

"I know, Governor—that's not what I was implying."

"Pete, this is the right thing to do. Even if I hadn't seen nine of my own men ripped apart by gunfire, I'd still believe in this issue. I mean for Christ's sake, 44,000 Americans were killed with firearms last year. Just imagine if a plane carrying 100 people crashed everyday. As a nation, we would be outraged, absolutely outraged. People would be calling upon their political leaders to do something. Because the same number of people are slaughtered with guns every day, that somehow makes a difference?"

Sawyer knew Colfax was passionate about the issue.

"Well, it doesn't. And unlike Prescott, I'm not going to avoid the issue. And unlike Byrne, I'm not going to propose some lame-ass half-measure that won't do a goddamn thing to stop the killing. I mean, I'm all for gun safety courses, but as a stand-alone measure, they won't do a thing. It's a cop out and Byrne knows it."

"You're right. I guess your proposal might win over some Byrne supporters."

Colfax ignored his remark. "You know, I'm so sick and tired of the 'guns don't kill people, people kill people' bullshit," said Colfax. "If that's the case, why did Great Britain, which is similar to us in almost every way, have only thirty-three killings last year. Thirty-three, Pete! More Americans are killed in eight hours in this country than were killed in all of Great Britain last year. Why? I'll tell you why—because they don't have the unlimited right to buy and sell guns.

"Well, I'm not going to wait for the next mass murder at some school to address this issue. I'm going to do it now. I'm telling you, I'm going to propose a ban on the manufacture, import and sale of handguns and assault-style rifles, and I'm also going to propose that we license all guns—including those in circulation. If we can license cars, we sure as hell ought to be able to license guns. This nonsense has to end."

Sawyer began to say something, but Colfax stopped him, "Was there anything else you wanted to say about my speech?" Sawyer remained silent. "Good. I have state business I have to conduct."

Sawyer knew he was dismissed.

✳   ✳

Sean McGowan, Luke Parish, and three other Secret Service agents were only halfway through their daily debriefing report, and the tension was already palatable.

"Sean, we're understaffed," pleaded Parish. "We've got to let Washington know. If we don't get more help, we can't guarantee the governor's safety."

"Luke is right, Sean," said Todd Lehman, a short, stocky, forty-two-year-old agent who desperately wanted to work on the presidential detail someday and resented that McGowan, eight years his junior, had already done that and was now his supervisor.

"I've spoken with the Washington office, and they're well aware of our situation," said McGowan calmly. "Everyone is being stretched thin. In case you have forgotten, the pope is planning on visiting Miami next week and sixty agents have been called in to assist with the security arrangement."

"Sixty? You're shittin' me," said Parish. "We're in the middle of the busiest presidential campaign in twenty years and the Secret Service has to send sixty agents to protect the pope? Something is going to break, Sean."

"We'll have to make do," replied McGowan in a tone that did not completely mask his annoyance.

"How?" asked Lehman. "You and Parish are covering Colfax's daily movements. I'm covering the campaign headquarters and the growing number of volunteers flocking to his office. Brix is covering the Governor's mansion, and Lefebvre is responsible for protecting the Capitol. That doesn't leave anyone to plan for future travel."

"Lehman's right, Sean," replied Parish. "Colfax hasn't been campaigning much lately, but now that the legislative session is over, he's going to start up again. His campaign manager just provided me a tentative itinerary. He's scheduled to give a speech in Cape Girardeau, Missouri, on Wednesday, travel to Austin, Texas, on Thursday morning, Phoenix in the afternoon, and then Los Angeles on Friday morning, San Francisco for lunch and Silicon Valley in the evening."

"It's not going to be easy. We'll have to improvise and play a lot of leapfrog," answered McGowan. "Parish and I will continue to travel with the governor. We'll also take over your responsibilities at the campaign headquarters," he said, looking at Lehman.

"When?"

"Beginning on Monday. That'll free you to go to Cape Girardeau on Monday to do advance planning for Wednesday's appearance. Joe, you will leave for Austin on Tuesday," he said to Agent Lefebvre. "And Todd, after you're done with Cape Girardeau, you will go to Phoenix. Joe, after Austin, you'll go to L.A. From Phoenix, Todd, you'll go to Silicon Valley. I'll arrange with the local field office to assist us with Colfax's security in San Francisco." Every agent stared at McGowan. He knew they all despised the presidential campaign season. But he also knew that every agent in the room was a consummate professional and would rise to the occasion.

CHAPTER TWENTY-TWO

The small King Air plane lifted off from St. Paul's Holman Field just as the sun was rising. Colfax, Pete Sawyer, Sean McGowan, Luke Parish, and the pilot were on board. Colfax was seated near the rear of the plane, sipping from a large cup of coffee. He began the flight by first reading the *Wall Street Journal*, a ritual he had developed shortly after he left the Navy to start his own business. Colfax also had copies of the *New York Times* and the *Minneapolis Star Tribune*. On the bottom of the stack of newspapers was his reading file, which consisted of two briefing papers—one on Cape Girardeau, Missouri, and another outlining the significance of Taxpayer Freedom Day.

Pete Sawyer had copies of the *St. Paul Pioneer Press*, the *Los Angeles Times*, and day-old copies of the *Austin American Statesman* and the *Arizona Republic*. Like Colfax, he also had a stack of briefing papers—most of which were articles that he felt either he or Colfax should read sometime during the flight.

Sean McGowan also brought reading material. He had a thin, professional briefing book that outlined in excruciating detail whom the candidate was to meet in Cape Girardeau and what route they were to take to Colfax's campaign event. The book also contained detailed maps highlighting alternative routes, the nearest hospitals, secondary airports and the most vulnerable points—from an assassin's perspective—along the route. Every leg of Colfax's trip was documented down to the exact second. McGowan committed every piece of information to memory. After he finished digesting his briefing book, he began working over possible contingencies in his mind.

From where Sawyer was sitting, in the seat directly across the aisle from the Secret Service agent, it appeared as though McGowan had finally taken a break from his reading. He used the opportunity to strike up a conversation.

"Taking a little break?" asked Sawyer.

"Excuse me?" said McGowan who was trying to visualize where an assassin or a sniper would hide if he knew Colfax was arriving at the airport. Colfax's arrival time was confidential. The fact that he would be in Cape Girardeau was not.

"Admiring the sunrise?" repeated Sawyer.

"Yes," lied McGowan.

"How many campaigns have you worked on?" asked Sawyer.

"This is my fourth," replied McGowan.

"Really? You look kind of young to have already worked that many."

"Thanks. I don't feel young."

"Do you still enjoy them?" asked Sawyer.

"I don't know if a Secret Service agent ever enjoys a campaign," said McGowan, knowing full well that no agent did.

"Why did you become a Secret Service agent? You don't mind me asking, do you?"

"No. I guess I joined because I felt it was an honorable calling. I remember sitting in my high school pre-calculus class in March of 1981 when the principal of the school came over the intercom and announced that President Reagan had been shot. It made me really angry—not in a political sense, I'm apolitical—but in a patriotic sense. Shortly after, there was an attempt on the pope's life. I remember watching the footage of both assassination attempts—I was impressed with the actions of the president's and the pope's security teams. I thought it was something that I would enjoy."

"Do you really think you could take a bullet for someone else?"

"Absolutely," McGowan said without a moment of a hesitation. "But my primary job is not to take a bullet for someone. My job is to stop that bullet from being fired in the first place."

"I don't know how you guys do it. I mean, I don't think I could ever do what you do."

"You might be surprised," said McGowan.

"What's the most important characteristic—I mean, for a Secret Service agent?" asked Sawyer. "Courage? Quickness? Intelligence?"

"Maybe stupidity," said McGowan in a self-effacing manner. "It's definitely not courage. If you think that all Secret Service agents come prepared to take a bullet for the president, you're mistaken. That aspect of the job is learned. The only to way to overcome the human instinct to protect oneself is to practice not to do it. And practice we do—constantly. To answer your question, though, I think the most important characteristic—the characteristic that is most common to all Secret Service agents—is that we have heightened senses of observation and awareness."

"Interesting," said Sawyer, not fully understanding McGowan's response. "Like what?"

"Let me give you a quick test of your observation skills," said McGowan.

"Okay."

"Which way does Abraham Lincoln's head face on a penny when you're holding it?" Sawyer paused to think.

"Quickly," said McGowan, forcing Sawyer to answer.

"I don't know—ah—left, I guess."

"Does a can of Coke say 'Coke' on it or 'Coca-Cola'?"

Sawyer was stumped but wagered a guess. "Coke?"

"In which hand does the Statute of Liberty hold her torch?"

"Right?"

"How many tines are there on a standard fork?"

"Five?"

"What government building is on the back of a five dollar bill?"

"The Capitol?"

"Thank God you're not protecting me, Pete," said Colfax from the rear of the plane where he had been listening to the conversation. "You only got one right. I believe Lincoln's head faces right, a Coke can reads 'Coca-Cola,' Lady Liberty holds the torch in her right hand, a fork has four tines, and the treasury building is on a five-dollar bill."

"I'm impressed, sir. You're fully qualified to protect yourself," joked McGowan.

"I think I'll take you. I had to think about some of those questions for a second," said Colfax returning to his papers.

＊　＊

Seven hundred miles north of Cape Girardeau, just about the time Colfax's plane left Holman Field in St. Paul, Father Otto Wilhoit was beginning his morning ritual. A ritual that had not varied in thirty-five years—ten minutes of stretching, followed by a five-mile run, then fifteen minutes of calisthenics, a quick, cold shower, prayer, and finally breakfast.

The morning of May 9 began as thousands of days before had for Father Wilhoit—in solitude. It quickly changed. The seventy-two-year-old priest had not finished stretching when his daily ritual was interrupted.

222

"Excuse me," said the gray-haired man to the priest, who was so intent on loosening his hamstrings that he had not noticed the runner approach from the direction of the college campus. "I was wondering if you know a nice four- or five-mile circuit that I might run here on campus?" The gentlemen explained that he was doing some research at the university. He wanted to explore the campus—and get his daily run in—at the same time.

"You startled me," said Father Wilhoit, "I don't often see many other people about this time of morning."

"I'm sorry."

"Quite all right. I'm very familiar with the campus. Might I first ask at what pace you run?"

"Anywhere from seven-and-a-half minutes—on a good day—to nine minutes," replied Raphael Baptista. He knew exactly at what pace Father Wilhoit ran.

"Well, if you'd be comfortable at running toward the slower end of your pace, I'd be happy to personally show you a nice five-mile loop."

"That would be wonderful. I don't want to inconvenience you," said Baptista, sounding genuinely sincere.

"Absolutely not. I'd welcome the company. I just need a minute to finish my warm-ups." Baptista used the opportunity to introduce himself.

"I'm Joel Davis—Dr. Joel Davis," said Baptista, extending his hand to shake the priest's.

"Otto," replied the priest, "Father Otto Wilhoit."

With their stretching complete and the first rays of the early spring morning just beginning to light up the eastern sky, the pair set off down the blacktop road that wound around the prep school campus.

"What type of research brings you to our university?" asked Otto to his new running partner. "Your accent tells me that you are not a native Minnesotan."

"No, I'm not," laughed Baptista. "I am from Virginia—by way of New York."

"That explains the accent."

"I'm a professor at the University of Richmond. I'm researching the role of the Catholic Church during times of war and your Alcuin Library and center for ecumenical research are world-renowned."

"Couldn't you have conducted most of your research via the Internet?"

"Not really. Many of the documents I'm interested in haven't been placed online. Plus, I'm from the old school—if I'm not doing research in a musty old library, it just doesn't feel like research."

Father Otto laughed and took an instant liking to his running partner.

"Furthermore, I have reached a point in my life where I can afford to travel. I've never been to Minnesota, and thought this would be a good opportunity."

"What do you teach?" asked Otto.

"History. I did my original dissertation on the role that the churches played in the Civil War. Since then, I have specialized in studying and writing about the roles that various religious institutions have played in war."

"Fascinating. I grew up in this area, which was—and still is though to a lesser extent—heavily populated with German Catholics. There were always many in the community who were very critical of the church not speaking out more vociferously against the German government before both the First and the Second World Wars."

The two continued to talk.

Eventually, the pair turned north and completed a three-mile circuit that reconnected with the campus, via a giant footbridge that spanned the interstate. Instead of running straight back down the road that would have lead them to where they had started almost a half hour earlier, the two headed into the woods and onto a solid, dirt path.

The path continued toward the shore of Lake Sagatagan, where it narrowed so much that the two were no longer able to run side-by-side. Their conversation came to a graceful conclusion as Wilhoit took the lead. The path hugged the lake for almost a mile. A light fog, one that would quickly dissipate when the first solid rays of sun hit it, hung over the lake, and a pair of mallards silently glided onto the almost perfectly still waters. Baptista, who was now behind Father Wilhoit, was oblivious to the natural beauty of the scene. Instead, he was scanning his surroundings to determine how isolated the location was. He would revisit the site later in the day.

After about a mile, the prep school came into view, and the pair passed a statue of the Indian explorer Sacagewa and glided past the base of the Abbey. Baptista followed the old monk around the monastery, and together they made the mile run back up the west side of the campus before ending up back at the school.

"I really enjoyed our run, Father," said Baptista, who was not at all winded by the five-mile run.

"So did I," said Otto, wiping his brow.

"I'm hoping to have my research completed by tomorrow afternoon. Would you mind if I joined you again tomorrow morning?"

"It would be my pleasure," replied Otto. "It would give me an opportunity to learn more about your research."

"Great. I'll plan on seeing you tomorrow morning. Have a great day," said Baptista with his most earnest smile.

"Thank you. The same to you, Joel."

* *

It had taken Anne Strong three days to get through to Jacob Mance. The principal partner in the firm of Lawrence, Mance & Scott only returned her call when his assistant said that Ms. Strong wanted to confirm Mance's involvement in the "Gibraltar Conspiracy."

Mance stared at the pink message slip. At first, his heartbeat quickened and he grew faint. He quickly recovered and contemplated calling Murdock but decided against it. Mance came to the conclusion that the *Washington Herald* reporter was bluffing. He collected his thoughts, scribbled some notes down on a legal pad and dialed Strong's number.

"Strong," said the reporter, picking up the phone on the first ring.

Mance could hear all the noise of the newsroom in the background and wondered how reporters ever concentrated. Maybe they didn't, he thought to himself. "This is Jacob Mance. I'm returning your call. Did I catch you at a bad time?" Mance tried to sound nonchalant.

"No, no," responded Strong, scrambling to find her notes on her conversation with Freeberg. "Thank you for returning my call."

"I'm sorry it took me so long to get back to you. My assistant said you have been trying for a few days. I've been busy up on the Hill," lied Mance.

"I understand," said Strong, who knew Mance was lying and figured he was only calling because of her reference to the Gibraltar Conspiracy. "I'd like to ask you a few questions about the Coalition for a Prosperous New Millennium. The Federal Election Commission has you listed as the treasurer for that organization. Is that correct?"

"Is this conversation for the record?" asked Mance.

"It is," replied Strong, who was surprised by Mance's question. "Would you prefer that it not be?"

"No. I just wanted to know."

"The coalition has raised over fourteen million dollars to date. What can you tell me about it?"

"The coalition is a group of diverse organizations and individuals dedicated to educating the public about the positions and policies of presidential candidates," replied Mance. "We are an issue advocacy organization—although we cover a wide variety of issues. In some cases, we take no position on the issue. We just want to make sure the public knows where candidates stand on various issues."

"Who has contributed to the coalition?" said Strong, trying the direct approach.

"I have been requested by the contributors to keep the names of the organizations and individuals private."

"Why? If the coalition is simply trying to educate the public, what do they have to be concerned with?"

"Our contributors are proud of their efforts," said Mance, stressing the word proud. "They wish to remain anonymous because they want the efforts of the group to be neutral. They do not want themselves or their organizations to become the focus of attention. They truly see themselves as serving a useful public service. I'm sure you can understand that."

"But isn't their anonymity itself becoming a focus of attention?"

"I don't follow you," answered Mance, who knew exactly to what Strong was referring. "Although, as you probably know, we are under no legal obligation—being an issue advocacy organization—to disclose our contributors."

"The *Moriarty Minute* has recently reported that the coalition is just a front for an anti-Colfax movement."

"I'm familiar with the *Moriarty Minute*, and I'm unwilling to dignify her scandalous report with a comment. But as counsel for the coalition, I will state, for the record, that that accusation is absolutely false." Mance paused and then added, "Off the record, I will tell you this: if the *Moriarty Minute* weren't so sleazy, I would sue the author for libel. But frankly, the report—and its author—don't even merit my time. Plus, a lawsuit would be counterproductive because it would just give her worthless rag free publicity—which is what I'm sure she's hoping for. I have nothing else to say about the report."

"Without providing names, can you give any hint of the types of people who would contribute fourteen million dollars to such a cause?"

"Certainly. Our contributors are male and female, Republican, Democrat, and independent. There is no compelling interest other than public education," said Mance with false sincerity.

"Why has Governor Colfax borne the brunt of the coalition's ads?"

"He hasn't. Our organization has profiled Governor Colfax, Congressman Greene, and Mr. Cross."

"But Governor Colfax is receiving a disproportionate amount of the attention."

"Perhaps so. But unlike Greene, or Cross, no one else is campaigning against Mr. Colfax."

"Interesting," replied Strong as though she was satisfied with the answer. "Does the organization, in the spirit of nonpartisanship, intend to highlight the positions of Governor Prescott or Vice President Byrne?"

"Our members have discussed this matter in great length but have chosen, for the time being, not to. Ms. Moriarty's conspiracy theory not withstanding, they have reached this decision because they feel Prescott and Byrne will likely be the nominees of their respective parties and thus will do a good job of educating the public about the various differences between themselves. Should they fail to do that, I don't think our members will hesitate to help educate the public."

For the next few minutes, Strong probed around the edges of the coalition. When she asked about Murdock's role, Mance replied there was none. She asked about the fundraising goal of the group, but Mance said only, "No comment."

Just as Mance was about to excuse himself from the conservation, Strong happened upon a random note in her book—one she had scribbled down on Sunday morning after she read about it in the paper. It was a long shot, but then so was her message about the "Gibraltar Conspiracy."

"What was J. Preston Briggs' role in the coalition, Mr. Mance?" There was a temporary silence on the line. "Mr. Mance?"

"Yes. I'm sorry," said Mance, quickly recovering. "Preston was a close friend of mine. I am still a little shaken by his suicide. I'm sorry, what was your question?"

"What was Mr. Briggs' role in the coalition?"

"He wasn't involved."

"His suicide wasn't work-related?"

"Ms. Strong, I have answered your questions with great patience. Preston had a number of issues he was dealing with—some may have been related to his work. He was not, however, involved in any way with the coalition. If you have no further questions of substance," said Mance curtly, "I have a lot of work to do."

Strong politely thanked Mance, hung up and turned off her tape recorder. She pondered Mance's reaction to her question about Briggs. Was he caught off guard by the question, or was he really a friend of Briggs and just temporarily taken aback by the mention of his dead partner's name? Something felt odd about Mance's reaction. She pulled up the article about Briggs' death on her computer and printed out a copy. She read the article twice. Something was gnawing at her, but she couldn't put her finger on it. Finally, on the fourth reading, it came to her. Briggs had graduated from the University of Virginia Law School in 1984—the same year as David Pollard.

* *

The commercial didn't pull any punches. It was graphic and hard-hitting and aired less than twenty-fours after Colfax's gun control speech. The thirty-second piece showed Adolph Hitler thrusting his right arm up in a salute. It then cut to a picture of Nazi soldiers goosestepping through the pre-war streets of Berlin. This was followed by a clip of Joseph Stalin and other aging Politburo chieftains presiding over a Soviet May Day parade, replete with scores of tanks and military trucks loaded with ominous-looking rocket launchers. The voice-over announced: "Adolph Hitler and Joseph Stalin prohibited their citizens from owning guns. Robert Colfax wants to do the same thing. Please call Governor Colfax and tell him to read the Second Amendment. Our forefathers had it right." The picture then returned to the clip of the Soviet Politburo members and Colfax's face was morphed onto that of the man standing next to Joseph Stalin. At the bottom of the screen, the fact that the ad was paid for and prepared by the Coalition for a Prosperous New Millennium was plain to see.

Brent LaFond, the executive director of Second Amendment Advocates, a pro-gun, Washington-based lobbying organization, had specified that in return for a two-million-dollar contribution to the coalition, Mance and the coalition take responsibility for the piece. Because it ran only in the more conservative rural districts across the country, Mance agreed to the request.

* *

The Arena Room of Cape Girardeau's Show Me Center had reached maximum capacity ten minutes after the doors opened. The Taxpayer Freedom Day Rally had been growing in participants each year since Diane Kilgore had begun the annual rally in 1995 to recognize the day to which average Missourians must work to fulfill their tax obligations to the local, state and federal governments. In 1995, the date had been April 30. Five years later, it was May 10. Kilgore, a staunch, lifelong Republican had signed on to Colfax's campaign the day he announced for president in October. Kilgore was a huge fan of a national sales tax, and Colfax was the only candidate advocating the idea. In late January, Kilgore sent a letter to Pete Sawyer, inviting Colfax to be the keynote speaker at the annual rally. Much to Kilgore's surprise and delight, Colfax personally scribbled a note back to her, accepting her invitation. At the time, Colfax had told Sawyer that if he was to win, he had to reach out to his supporters in ways that the other candidates would never consider. Kilgore returned the favor by personally committing to gathering a crowd that would make Colfax's trip to Cape Girardeau worth the effort.

Colfax arrived at the Civic Center right on schedule. Once the candidate's car had pulled up to the rear of the building, McGowan efficiently escorted Colfax into a holding room behind the main stage in the auditorium. Sawyer introduced Kilgore to Colfax.

"It's a pleasure to meet you, Governor," said Kilgore. "It's an honor to have you here in Cape Girardeau. I can't tell you how surprised—and pleased—I was when I received your gracious note accepting my invitation. I thought my husband was playing a practical joke on me," gushed Kilgore, who would have continued to talk had Colfax not interrupted.

"The pleasure's all mine, Diane. I appreciate the efforts that you have made in organizing this event," said Colfax, drawing on information he had read in Sawyer's briefing paper. "How's this year's crowd?"

"Our largest ever—almost 1,000. You're becoming quite popular, Governor."

"Thank you. The turnout, however, is a result of your efforts. Tax reform won't happen in a vacuum. It takes citizens like you educating the people and demanding change."

The two continued to talk for a few minutes until Agent McGowan received word via his radio earpiece that the auditorium was secure and it was safe for Colfax to enter.

Colfax followed Kilgore up to the stage and was delighted by the boisterous response from the crowd. Kilgore tentatively approached the microphone, and her mind went blank when she saw the C-SPAN camera. Forgetting her well-prepared remarks—she was going to tout Colfax's tax-cutting accomplishments in both Congress and as governor—she instead simply said, "It is with great pleasure that I introduce to you Governor Robert Colfax!" She was turning away from the podium when she snapped back and added, "The next president of the United States!"

Colfax sprung to the podium. "Thank you, Diane. I always appreciate quick introductions. I also know that most audiences appreciate quick speeches. So in the spirit of the brevity that you so eloquently demonstrated in your introduction, Diane, I simply say this: when elected president, I will replace the current convoluted special interest-laden income tax system with a simple, straightforward national sales tax. Thank you!" said Colfax, gesturing as though he were finished speaking. He then paused and smiled. "You're not going to get off that easy."

The crowd responded with a laugh.

Colfax had their attention. "I flew down to your fine city today because I wanted to recognize the efforts of Diane Kilgore—and talk to you about the benefits of a national sales tax. Tax reform is this country isn't going to happen until of all us—not just people like Diane and myself—but you," said Colfax, sweeping his arm across the entire auditorium, "get involved."

"Five years ago, after spending thirty-seven hours trying to figure out her state and federal tax forms, Diane said enough is enough: the tax system in this country is broken and someone has to do something about it. Seeing no one else tackling the problem and knowing merely complaining wouldn't change a thing, Diane decided to do it herself. First, she figured out that she had to work until April 30 just to pay all her taxes for the year. This year, she will have to work until today—May 13, 135 days—just to pay all of her taxes. It just didn't seem right to Diane, and it's not. But Diane didn't stop there. She also began asking herself a lot of other questions. She asked: Why do I have to spend thirty-seven hours figuring out my taxes? She asked: Why does the IRS have 569 different tax forms and 1,800 pages of rules and regulations? Why does the government tax me when I earn my money? And when I save my money? And when I spend my money? And when I invest my money? And why, after all of this, does the government tax my family one last time—after I'm dead?

"Diane said to herself that there has to be a simpler way. There is, my friends," said Colfax pausing again. "It is called a consumption-based tax.

"A consumption-based tax, like the national sales tax, is simple. It is fair and it encourages investment. Furthermore, by taxing people when they buy something, everyone must pay taxes—including the drug dealers and the wealthy tax cheats—who presently avoid paying any taxes.

"With a consumption-based tax, we can get rid of the entire tax code—which is really nothing more than a 44,000-page document filled with special tax breaks and loopholes for powerful special interest groups and wealthy Americans.

"Let's scrap the whole deal!" said Colfax to the appreciative crowd. "As president, I will. Vice President Byrne is calling for a new bipartisan commission on tax reform, and Governor Prescott is advocating a comprehensive review of the entire tax code." Colfax's voice dripped with sarcasm. "We don't need another commission, and we don't need a line-by-line review. We need leadership," he said to the crowd's obvious approval. "Leadership that is willing to say no to special interests and yes to a simpler and more fair tax system. I will provide that leadership, and I'm asking for your support this November. Together, we can change government and restore power to you."

Energized by the speech, Diane Kilgore grabbed the microphone and, shedding any nervousness that held her back earlier, exhorted the crowd to join Colfax's campaign. She also had the presence of mind to remind the C-SPAN viewers to support Colfax and call his toll-free number or visit his web site for more information. Hundreds of viewers followed Kilgore's instructions. Many contributed money via the Internet, others signed on as e-precinct captains, and almost everyone who logged on signed up to receive the Colfax campaign's weekly e-mail update.

* *

A thousand miles away, Jacob Mance watched the speech on C-SPAN. Afterwards, he began placing calls to a slew of tax lobbyists who made their bread and butter by complicating the tax code every year with new tax breaks and loopholes on behalf of their wealthy clients. It was the coalition's most successful solicitation to date. The four million dollars raised even surpassed the amount the trial attorneys contributed to help defeat Robert Colfax.

* *

Anne Strong read her story one last time and cringed. It was a piece of shit, she thought. Entitled "Unseen Money, Unseen Influence," it documented in great detail the loopholes in the campaign finance system, but Strong had not been able to give the story a "face." She couldn't make it come alive in a way that the readers would understand. Her efforts to use the Coalition for a Prosperous New Millennium as the "face" went absolutely nowhere. By law, the coalition was not required to disclose its members, and Jacob Mance and his team of lawyers threatened the *Washington Herald* with a massive lawsuit if the story so much as even hinted at its membership.

So she wasn't surprised when the story received little attention within the Beltway and even less outside. The small portion of the American populace that was following the election was absorbed in a shallow conversation over whether C. Elliott Prescott's penchant for winking at people, especially women, was part of his charm or was patronizing and degrading. *USA Today* was so enamored of the story that it commissioned a poll. By a margin of fifty-two to forty-eight percent, the American population liked the Pennsylvania governor's habit.

* *

To Sean McGowan's annoyance, Pete Sawyer resumed their earlier conversation on the flight to Austin. "So give me an example of when your observation skills came in handy."

"I can't do that," responded McGowan, who really wanted to review the security briefing book for Colfax's trip to the capital of Texas. "The Secret Service can't afford to reveal that kind of information—it could potentially be used by someone to harm a person we're trying to protect."

"Can you give me a hypothetical example?"

Hoping that a short answer would mollify the inquisitive campaign manager, McGowan answered. "Well, let's see," began McGowan, thinking about it for a moment. "The Secret Service has a list of known threats to the president. It's called the 'Hot List' and it contains about 400 people. Every Secret Service agent has to be able to recognize every one of those faces."

"Is that what you most fear, then, one of those faces popping up somewhere?"

McGowan again thought about his response. "No, just the opposite, in fact," he said. "I wish our job were that easy. What most agents fear, including myself, is one well-trained assassin who is motived by unknown reasons. That person can strike almost anywhere, at anytime, and there is little the Secret Service can do to antici-pate the danger." McGowan did not share his other fear with Sawyer—the fear of being blinded to the obvious.

CHAPTER TWENTY-THREE

The alarm went off at 4:50 A.M. Robert Colfax and his wife lifted themselves from bed as they had done almost their entire adult lives. Both were early risers—a habit instilled by their rural upbringings.

Linda Colfax had, until recently, always done her own thing in the morning. But with the onset of the campaign, she vowed to find time with her husband wherever she could. The best way to do that, she figured, was to run with him occasionally. On many days, it was the only time the couple had an opportunity to talk about their marriage, their children and, if necessary, the campaign.

By five o'clock, the two were being escorted by Sean McGowan and Luke Parish to an isolated stretch of Town Lake, which made a five-mile loop just south of downtown Austin. The route had already been searched and secured an hour earlier by a local Secret Service team. Three local police had strategically placed themselves along the route and continued to guard it.

McGowan ran about five feet behind the couple and Parish a few feet in front. Both agents were close enough to hear the couple, but neither paid any attention. Beneath their loose-fitting running clothes, each agent sported an extensive amount of communications gear and a gun.

"How is Catherine doing in pre-calc?" Colfax asked his wife, who was an excellent runner, as they settled into a comfortable pace.

"Not good. She received a C on her last exam. I spoke with her teacher, and he indicated that the problem isn't her aptitude, it's her attitude. She refuses to fully apply herself."

Colfax was silent for a moment. He knew he had to find more time for his daughters. "Have you spoken with her?"

"Yes. But daughters don't always appreciate their mother's comments when they're sixteen years old."

"Do they ever?" joked Colfax, as the pair continued to glide effortlessly along the bank of the river.

"Not until they have kids of their own. That's how I was," replied Linda, smiling back at her husband.

"I'll talk with her when I get back. Do you think the problem is serious?"

"No. But I think we'd be wise to nip it in the bud."

"Do we know if her new boyfriend is in the same class? Maybe she's just having a hard time understanding where high school calculus fits into the grand scheme of things. After all, she is a teenager."

"That reminds me," said Linda, "Catherine has been invited to the prom."

"Is an updated and modernized version of the birds and bees in order?"

"Oh, she understands that part. A little lecture on responsibility, however, is appropriate."

"I can't believe how fast she's growing up. I know you're right, but it just seems way too soon to be talking about these things. Growing up, I know neither of my parents ever mentioned sex to me."

"They just left it to the priests at St. John's to do that?"

"Yup. I guess that explains a lot, doesn't it," chuckled Colfax.

"I never understood the logic of having Catholic priests teaching sex education. It makes about as much sense as having an illiterate teach reading."

"Are you implying I'm a sexual illiterate?" laughed Colfax.

"There have been times," responded Linda with a wink. "I'll talk with Catherine when we get back. I just thought you'd want to know that the discussion is coming up. If you notice a little chill in the air between Catherine and myself in the next few weeks, this might explain it."

"We'd better talk about drinking and drugs as well. I'll take the lead in that department. If I can work it into our talk, I'll also reinforce your conversation. How's Colleen doing?"

"She's doing well. The commercials that the coalition has been running against you have disturbed her, but I think I was able to sooth her anxieties."

"Which ones?" asked Colfax.

"I think the one that most disturbed her was the one that distorted your position on legal reform."

"The one showing the elderly woman softly weeping?"

"That's the one."

"That commercial was complete bullshit."

"Of course, it was."

"A person would still be able to sue anyone they please under my bill. All my bill says is that if you file a frivolous lawsuit—and it is found to be frivolous—you have to pay the defendant's costs. There would be no reason for Grandma to weep as long as she had a good, strong case. I'm just trying to bring a little bit of common sense back to justice system. I've never understood how a company or person can be found to be partially liable for something but be required to pay the full amount of the damages."

"I know," said Linda, "you're preaching to the choir."

"But you know what really angers me? It's not that the coalition is running these ads against me. Or even that they are distorting my position. What really angers me is that the public has no idea who is behind the ads. Hell, I don't even know for sure who is behind the ads. . . .

"The answer is complete disclosure. The only way to reform this crappy system is to require everyone and every organization that contributes to a campaign, a political action committee, or an independent campaign organization to reveal who they are and how much they have given. If that information is available, the public could figure out the hidden agendas of all these independent expenditure groups like the Coalition for a Prosperous New Millennium."

Linda Colfax was used to her husband going off on passionate diatribes about public policy issues.

"I'm sorry," said Colfax, a little embarrassed. "We were talking about Colleen. So, she's relatively sure that her father has no intentions of denying grandma her day in court?"

"I think so. But you'll have to ask her yourself."

"I'd love to. But we have to fly from here to Phoenix and then to California. We won't get back home until late Sunday night."

"You might get an opportunity to ask her tomorrow night. I'm flying them out to meet us in San Francisco. They leave right after class on Friday. Annette is driving them to the airport."

"That's the best news I've heard in days. Did you arrange for that?"

"Yes and no. I told Pete that I thought you needed a boost and he agreed. He worked with Annette to make it happen."

"I ride Pete and Annette pretty hard, but they're great. I'm lucky to have surrounded myself with such good people," said Colfax. "Starting with my wife, of course."

"Nice catch," she replied. "Remember to ask Colleen about softball. She really wants you to attend one of her games before the season is over." The couple continued to talk as they ran a few more miles until Colfax suddenly slowed down and stopped.

Instantly, McGowan was on his radio, "Gibraltar is stopping."

"Are you okay honey?"

"I don't know," replied Colfax, trying to get a hold of his feelings. "I just had a feeling that something has happened."

"Oh, God," gasped Linda, who had never known her husband to have anything approaching a premonition in his life, "please don't let it be the girls."

"It's not the girls," said Colfax with certainty. "It's probably nothing." It was 5:47 A.M. Colfax grasped Linda's hand, gave her a forced smile and started running again.

* *

Baptista was already waiting outside the prep school when Father Otto stepped in the cool, fresh spring air. A light dew was resting on the grass, and a gentle breeze swayed the large pine trees that encircled the old school.

"Top of the morning," barked Father Otto in welcome to his new friend. "It looks like it's going to be a great day!"

"That it does, Padre. Still, it's a little cold for my taste."

"Ah, yes—you're a Virginia boy. You'll warm up soon enough. I was thinking that I'd like to pick up the pace a little this morning."

"How fast were you thinking?"

"You said yesterday that you could comfortably run at a seven-minute pace?"

"Seven and a half. But I think I could handle seven."

"Great! Let's do it. You might want to leave your jacket in your car."

"It's still a little chilly. Anyway, I could use a good sweat," lied Baptista.

The pair stretched together for a few minutes before beginning their run. They started at a slow pace until they reached the bottom of the hill upon which the school sat. The entire time Father Otto queried his new friend about his research. He was pleased that the professor had found the resources at the university worth the effort of traveling to Minnesota. As the pace quickened, the conversation ceased as Wilhoit's breathing became slightly more labored.

"Would you like to slow down a little, Padre?"

"No," gasped Wilhoit, "I'm fine. I need to push my lungs a little bit. I was pretty lazy the last few winter months."

The two continued over the rolling hills for a few minutes and crossed over the bridge spanning the interstate, which connected the public road back to the private campus road. As they did, Arnold Krebsbach, a cook at the university refectory, passed them on his bike. Krebsbach lived in St. Joseph, a small town three miles from the university, and had chosen to bike to work because of the mild weather. The sun was just beginning to turn the sky from dark to mild blue. Krebsbach instantly recognized Father Wilhoit's distinctive running gait from about fifteen yards.

"Good morning, Father," shouted Krebsbach, slowing down. He did not recognize the other runner.

"Good morning," wheezed Wilhoit. "Is that you, Arnold?" said the priest, squinting his eyes in the direction of the young man he had baptized twenty years earlier and whom he saw almost every Sunday at Mass.

"It is."

"Good to see you exercising," he cried out to the slightly overweight Krebsbach, who continued peddling away into the early morning light.

"You might want to slow down, Father. You don't sound so good."

Neither Father Wilhoit nor Krebsbach noticed that Baptista kept his face down and shielded from Krebsbach.

Like the day before, the runners turned up the road to the baseball field and onto the dirt path that ringed the shoreline of the lake. The cooler air off the lake reinvigorated Wilhoit, and as he had the day before, he stepped in front of Baptista. The two ran single file on the well-shaded path.

Wilhoit never heard Baptista unzip his Gore-Tex windbreaker. As the seventy-two-year-old priest pushed ahead, Baptista silently lifted a device from inside his jacket where it was attached in a specially designed holster.

Baptista eased the injectionless syringe into his left hand and continued to run while familiarizing himself with Wilhoit's fluid motions. Baptista made up the few remaining yards between him and the priest, and then, when they reached the most isolated part of the run, the trained killer deftly placed the device, filled with prostaglandin, near the priest's heart. In large doses, the drug causes coronary arteries to constrict severely, bringing on a sudden, massive heart attack, a propensity for which Baptista knew ran in Wilhoit's family.

The priest felt the sting and his vision began to blur. His last thought before he expired from this earth was that he was happy that his new friend was nearby in case he needed emergency assistance.

The time was 5:47 A.M. Father Otto was dead, and his new friend continued to run. He was not going to get help.

* *

The school auditorium was already warm, and the prospect of it getting hotter was increasing with each additional person who squeezed into the packed room. Governor Colfax's position on immigration was widely anticipated by the largely Mexican-American audience. Many had driven for hours to attend the speech in Austin. The lines outside the auditorium grew longer with each passing minute.

Agent McGowan was stationed outside the main door, the only entrance people were being allowed to use. He could feel the warm air spilling out on the back of his neck. He could also sense the frustration of those people who were still waiting in line. Many were growing anxious, afraid they would miss Colfax's speech, which was scheduled to begin promptly at noon.

Carmen Jimenez was wearing polyester pants, a short-sleeve shirt, and a wide tie that didn't quite reach his belly button. McGowan couldn't determine if he was a manual laborer wearing his Sunday best or a laborer who had risen to middle management. Regardless, the agent quickly determined that Jimenez could not be hiding any weapons under his tight clothes, so he continued past him, looking for potential problems in the throng of people waiting to hear Robert Colfax.

"I bet you wouldn't be searching us if we were a group of wealthy, white snobs from Dallas," said Jimenez to McGowan.

"Yes sir, we would," said McGowan softly, never losing his focus on the crowd.

"That's bullshit," said Jimenez in a loud, thickly accented voice. "It's the same everywhere. As soon as you people see a large group of Mexican-Americans gathering, you begin to get nervous."

"That's not true, sir," responded McGowan diplomatically, still scanning the crowd. "The standards for all candidate events are precisely the same."

Jimenez was about to say something when McGowan, recognizing that he had a chance to soothe the middle-age man's growing anger, asked him his name.

"Carmen Jimenez. Carmen Hector Jimenez."

"Where are you from, Mr. Jimenez?"

Thinking his citizenship was being questioned, Jimenez spat out, "El Paso."

"That means you must have driven at least ten hours," said McGowan, taking off his sunglasses and looking Jimenez squarely in the eyes.

"Damn straight," replied Jimenez, who was surprised to see the large Secret Service agent smile back at him.

"I understand that you must be frustrated at having driven all this way only to find that you must now stand in line for another half hour. I can only ask for your continued patience, and I can assure you that the lines have nothing to do with the ethnic makeup of the crowd—and everything to do with the size of the crowd. We honestly didn't expect this large of a turnout."

Jimenez smiled back at McGowan and apologized for his earlier outburst. A potential problem had been easily averted. McGowan put his sunglasses back on and continued to monitor the crowd.

Inside the auditorium, Colfax sat on a podium with his wife and the mayor of Laredo. The three patiently waited as people continued to stream into the building. Almost a half-hour after the scheduled beginning, Linda Colfax, who had been a high school Spanish teacher in San Diego before she had met and married Lieutenant Robert Colfax, strode to the microphone.

In fluent Spanish, she introduced her husband as a loving father, a wonderful husband and a devoted public servant who would strive to represent all Americans, regardless of race or ethnicity, when he became president. Many of the men in the crowd were immediately infatuated with the tall, dark-haired woman with the emerald green eyes. Colfax was a lucky man to have such lovely woman love him, thought Carmen Jimenez, who already liked Colfax before he even heard him speak. Anyone with such a beautiful wife and kind security agents must be a good guy, reasoned Jimenez, who did not understand that Secret Service agents were politically neutral.

When his wife finished her introduction, Colfax walked up to the stage, lightly kissed her on the cheek and told the audience in Spanish that he was the luckiest man in the world and that when he became president, his wife would make the best First Lady in the history of the country. The audience responded with whistles and loud cheering.

For the next fifteen minutes, Colfax provided the crowd with a stirring defense of a more open immigration policy. It was time, he told the audience, for America to return to its former glory and once again become a beacon for freedom-loving people all over the world. Colfax did not elaborate on how his experience of trying to assist the families of many of his South Vietnamese Army colleagues immigrate to the United States, in the wake of the fall of Saigon, shaped his position on the issue.

"It is worthy responsibility—not a burden—for this country to welcome immigrants," said Colfax. "It is my sincere belief that immigrants provide more to this country—in terms of individual value, work ethic, new ideas, understanding of freedom—than they receive in return. As president, I will work tirelessly to allow more of your brothers, sisters, cousins, and parents into this country. And to those who oppose me, I will remind them that their forefathers—whether they were Irish or Italian, Jewish or Jamaican, Croatian or Korean, or Venezuelan or Vietnamese—

were once immigrants as well. If this country was good enough for their family, it is good enough for others."

Colfax then thanked the audience in Spanish and introduced the mayor, who spoke for a few minutes about issues specific to the Mexican-American audience. After he had received an enthusiastic approval from the audience for each of his initiatives, the mayor surprised the audience by stating that Governor Colfax supported the same positions. For this reason, he said, he was proud to become the first Hispanic elected official in the country to publicly endorse Robert Colfax in his quest to become the president of the United States.

* *

Only three people had Pete Sawyer's private pager number and two of them were already with him. When the pager went off, he immediately knew it was Annette Christianson. Sawyer's first thought was that a crisis had erupted in Minnesota. He immediately pulled out his pocket-sized cell phone and dialed the ten digits to her office phone.

"What's up, Annette?"

"Is the governor with you?" asked Christianson.

"Of course, he is. What's wrong?"

"Is he standing there with you?"

"No. He's in the next room speaking to a select group of Latino elected officials. His speech was fantastic. They love him down here."

"Great," said the chief of staff with a little enthusiasm. "We're already getting calls from people who saw his speech on C-SPAN. The calls are at least five-to-one against him . . . more immigration isn't a very popular issue."

"I know—I've seen the poll numbers. But you know how he feels about polls. And you know how he feels about this issue. I think he feels personally responsible for some of the South Vietnamese families who were left behind and suffered under the communist regime."

Interrupting Sawyer, Christianson said, "I've got some bad news."

"Worse than the ratio of calls?"

"Much worse."

"What is it?" asked Sawyer, who was sure by the tone in Christianson's voice that he didn't really want to hear it.

"Father Otto died this morning."

"Oh, Christ—that's going to break the governor's heart."

"I know. I've heard him say on a few occasions that he owes everything he has achieved to him."

"He's told me the same thing. I'm glad he had a chance to see him over Easter. How did he die?"

"Heart attack. He was running this morning and his heart just gave out."

"Thanks, Annette. I think I'll let Linda know first. She's probably the best one to break the news to him."

"I agree. Let me know how he's doing when you get to Phoenix."

* *

Lee Manning returned from another fours days of target practice in the northern woods of Minnesota and found a familiar looking envelope between the screen door and the back door of the third-floor apartment. Inside was a single sheet of white paper. Handwritten in block letters was a simple message instructing Manning to be at Key's Cafe on Robert Street at 7:00 A.M. The sniper sensed the moment of reckoning was rapidly approaching. The timing couldn't be better, thought Manning. Not a single shot in the last three days had missed the target by more than five inches—and that was from as far away as 2,500 yards.

Manning left the apartment fifteen minutes early because the streets of St. Paul still confused the former Marine. Manning easily located the diner and was surprised to see Baptista already there, drinking a cup of coffee.

"Good morning, Sergeant," said Baptista, with no inflection in his voice.

"Good morning."

"How was your trip up north?"

"Outstanding," replied Manning with great confidence.

"Tell me about it," said Baptista, looking around the diner to see that no one was within earshot.

"It couldn't have been better. The rifle you provided is top line. And the bullets slice through the air like an F-18 fighter at supersonic speed."

"How confident are you of hitting a relatively stationary target at 2,500 yards?" asked Baptista with his customary directness. Manning looked back at the man across from the table for a few seconds.

"Depends. What do you mean by relatively stationary?"

"Good question. I mean, the target will probably not be moving, but that can't be completely guaranteed."

"If that's the case, I feel very confident. I've been consistently plugging shots at a mile and a half."

241

"How were the conditions? Did you split your practice time as requested?"

"I did. The weather was a problem, though."

"How so?" asked Baptista, who was surprised by the comment. "The weather has been almost perfect lately."

"It has," said the sniper. "That was the problem—it's been too nice. The temperature was warmer than average and the winds were minimal. If the weather stays this way until I get my shot off, we'll be fine. If it turns windy or cold, the odds of successful shot will decrease dramatically."

"I understand. Here is a five-day weather forecast from the National Meteorological Center," said Baptista, sliding a detailed weather report across the table to Manning. "If the weather forecast for Tuesday holds, how would you assess your odds of success?" Manning flipped through the report to the forecast for Tuesday, May 16. It took the sniper two minutes to read the report and render an assessment.

"If the wind stays out of the southwest and gusts at no more than five to seven miles an hour, I'd say the odds are sixty to sixty-five percent in our favor. I'd like to promise more, but a lot can happen to a piece of hot lead over the course of 2,500 yards."

"Of course. My employer understands the difficulty of the task we have assigned you," said Baptista with a straight face. "Would you care to know what the assignment is?"

"Yes."

"I think you have probably already figured it out, haven't you? Why don't you tell me who you think it is."

"Governor Colfax," said Manning softly.

"And you're comfortable with the target?"

"Yes. I haven't cared for the son of a bitch since he was secretary of the Navy. If you ask me, he's a first-rate asshole who had no idea how to use Marine Corps assets in time of war. And his position on women in combat is ass-backwards."

"My employer agrees," lied Baptista. "They also thought you might be interested in some of his latest positions." Baptista slid Manning a copy of the *New York Times*. "Read what he said yesterday in Texas."

Manning read the account of Colfax's immigration speech and grew visibly disgusted. It was just the type of reaction that the agency's psychologists determined Manning would have.

"That bastard wants to open the doors to this country to anybody? That's fucked up. We've got enough foreign trash right now! It would be my distinct pleasure to pull the trigger."

"Good."

"But before I do, I'll need more than just a rifle and bullets from you," said Manning.

"You were reading my mind, Sergeant. My employer is very interested in insuring your successful escape. Enclosed in the packet is a detailed explanation of the Secret Service protection plan. They rely on something called the concentric circle theory. The easiest way to think of it is this: the first ring is human instinct, the second relies on raw muscle—a lot of agents and police, and the third is technology laden." Baptista could sense Manning's apprehension. "You are right to be concerned, Sergeant. It is an impressive strategy—usually. The good news is that the Secret Service is stretched so thin right now that they can't effectively employ the second and third rings for Colfax."

"I'll still need a comprehensive escape plan."

"Of course. I am just finishing the final touches. You'll have the plan soon. Do you feel comfortable with what I've outlined so far?"

"So far—."

"So you think it can be done?"

"I have always felt with the proper training, equipment, and initiative any goal can be accomplished."

CHAPTER TWENTY-FOUR

B
rother Linus answered the phone at the Abbey information center with his customary courtesy. He had no reason not to believe the caller was exactly who he said he was—just has he had no reason not to believe the two dozen other calls he received afterwards. Father Otto was a popular figure at St. John's Prep, and he had influenced hundreds of young men and women during his forty-five years at the school.

"Good morning, Brother Linus," said Baptista solemnly to the thirty-three-year-old Benedictine monk. "This is Vincent Smith. I was a former student of Father Otto's, and I just learned of his death. I am so sorry. It must be a sad day at the monastery."

"It is," said the monk sincerely.

"Do you know when the funeral is?" asked Baptista. "I live in North Dakota and would like to attend."

"It's scheduled for noon on Tuesday."

"Will the burial follow immediately afterward?" asked Baptista.

"I would assume so," replied Linus.

"The reason I ask," volunteered Baptista, "is because I'm a farmer. I would like to pay my final respects, but I have to get back to the farm by sunset."

"Yes, it will," answered Linus, more confidently. "It will begin about fifteen minutes after the service. This will be the fourth funeral here this year, and they all follow the same procedure."

"Really?"

"Yes. It is a sad fact of life, but Father Otto is the fourth brother we have lost this year. Otto was relatively young, but the advancing age of our ranks has made death an all too frequent visitor at the Abbey. The bells will be tolling again—"

"Excuse me?" said Baptista, not understanding Linus' last comment. "The bells will be ringing?"

"Oh, I'm sorry . . . maybe they didn't toll the bells when you were here. Whenever a brother dies, the bells in the tower toll, the number corresponding to the brother's age."

"So, Father Otto will receive . . ."

"Seventy-two."

"And the bells will toll immediately after the mass?"

"No, the burial."

"I see. How long will the burial service take?"

"Approximately half an hour. The entire service should be over before two. Will that leave you enough time to get back to your farm?"

"Yes, it should," said Baptista. "I hate to bother you, but could I ask one more question? I read that he died of a heart attack. When I went to the prep school, Otto was always in such great shape."

"He did. He died on one of his early morning runs. Right on the shore of Lake Sag. Apparently, heart disease ran in his family."

Baptista cracked a smile. He knew that the cause of death he had chosen for Otto insured that the priest's demise would not draw any suspicion.

"Well, that certainly sounds like Otto. Nothing was going to get in the way of his daily workout."

"It sounds like you knew him fairly well, Vincent."

"Just one of the thousands . . . thank you for your time, Brother Linus. You and the Abbey are in my prayers."

The Secret Service would later determine that no calls to the Abbey information line were placed from North Dakota on Saturday, May 13. In fact, every call except one, which was traced to a pay phone at a convenience store in Monticello, Minnesota, could be linked to a specific caller. The unidentified call was placed from 8:32 to 8:34 A.M., almost an hour after Baptista left Manning in the diner.

✳ ✳

By 9:30 A.M., less than an hour after the call, Baptista was back on the campus of St. John's. He drove straight to the Abbey cemetery. Baptista casually strolled through the field of simple, fading granite tombstones as though he were looking for a particular grave. As he did, he read with little interest the names of the monks who died over the last hundred years. Many were names that Baptista had never heard before, names like Anselm, Placid, Bede, Fidelis, and Romualdus.

Eventually, Jeffery Payne's top assistant came to the freshest burial plot, a plot that had been dug only the day before for Father Otto. From the plot, Baptista surveyed the entire field of vision around the grave. When he had visited the cemetery weeks earlier—before he had given Manning specific practice instructions—he had assumed the plot would be in the vicinity of where he was now standing. The original hiding spot that he had laid out for Manning would still suffice. It was 2,367 yards from the plot and well concealed. From the cemetary, it was almost invisible.

Just before he left the scene, Baptista placed a small American flag on the grave of a long-dead Benedictine monk named Othmar. From a distance of 200 yards, Father Jerome Bechtold, who was eighty-seven-years old and had failing eyesight, could not see who was visiting the grave site or what he was placing on the graves, but he was happy that someone was paying his respects. He didn't see many people visit the cemetery anymore.

* *

Carmen Jimenez patiently waited outside Angie's restaurant for an hour and a half, hoping to shake Colfax's hand. He had long since convinced the local Secret Service agent that he was an avid Colfax supporter and all he wanted to do was introduce himself to the man he felt would be the next president of the United States.

Shortly before the lunch with Latino dignitaries was to break up, Pete Sawyer excused himself and tried to gather his thoughts before telling Linda Colfax the bad news about Father Otto.

He stepped outside the front door of the hotel to catch a breath of much needed fresh air.

Suddenly from almost nowhere, Carmen Jimenez appeared and asked Sawyer if he was affiliated with the Colfax campaign.

"I am," said Sawyer, who quickly looked over Jimenez. Sawyer had long grown accustomed to answering all types of questions from complete strangers and had developed a fairly accurate sixth sense for separating out the nuts and single-issue fanatics. Jimenez passed Sawyer's screening.

"I just heard Mr. Colfax speak this morning, and I was very impressed," said Jimenez.

"I'm glad," replied Sawyer. "I hope we can count on your support this November."

"Absolutely . . . but I would like to get involved in the campaign today," replied Jimenez.

"I would be happy to put you in contact with our Texas volunteer coordinator. Her name is Gloria Salinas," said Sawyer, scribbling her number down on the back of his own business card. "You can reach her at this number," he said, handing Jimenez the card.

"Great. I really appreciate this," said Jimenez as he accepted the card. "I have a software development firm in El Paso, and I'd like to help your campaign recreate Mr. Colfax's web site in Spanish."

"Seriously?" asked Sawyer, suddenly more interested in the stranger standing before him. He was a strong believer in fate. "The governor and I were just talking about doing that this morning. As you could tell from his speech this morning, he has a message that will resonate with the Mexican-Americans. He wants to get the message out and the Internet is the most cost-effective way for us to do it. Unfortunately, we don't have a lot of money. . . ."

"I'm not interested in money. I just want to help Governor Colfax. I visited your web site before I drove from El Paso. I think it's excellent. It would be even better if there were a Spanish version," said Jimenez, smiling at Sawyer, "and I can do it."

"That's fantastic. Let me put you in touch with another person. His name is Josh Parker and he is our Internet coordinator at our headquarters in Minneapolis." Sawyer wrote down Parker's e-mail address. "You can reach him here."

"I'll contact him as soon as I get back to El Paso," said Jimenez.

"Tell him that I told you to contact him. That will get you a faster response."

Just as Sawyer and Jimenez were shaking hands, McGowan, who had been scanning an arc of 180 degrees from his position at the front of the hotel doors, brought his right wrist near his mouth and ordered Colfax's limousine, codenamed Secretariat after the 1973 Triple Crown Winner, brought around front. On cue, Agent Parish pulled up in front of the hotel, and the passenger doors swung open. Colfax and his wife were three feet from the car when Sawyer called out to his boss.

"Governor," he shouted as Colfax, his wife, and McGowan all turned in his direction. "I have someone I want you to meet." McGowan immediately recognized Jimenez and moved to place his body in between Colfax and the approaching man. He didn't think Jimenez posed a threat but he wasn't about to take any chances. McGowan drifted to the side after confirming visually that Jimenez had no weapons and allowed the campaign manager to introduce Jimenez to Colfax.

"Governor," said Sawyer, "this is Carmen Jimenez, and he'd like to help you develop a Spanish version of your campaign web site."

Colfax looked at Sawyer and lifted an eyebrow, "We were just talking about this very thing this morning. Your timing is perfect, Mr. Jimenez," said Colfax, gripping the thick hands of the former field hand, who had put himself through a computer programming course at a local community college and was now a successful businessman.

"It's a pleasure, Mr. Colfax, I mean Mr. Governor, I mean . . ." replied Jimenez, in a surprisingly shy voice.

"You can call me, Bob," said Colfax, which immediately put Jimenez at ease.

"Unfortunately, I have to go. I have another campaign event in Phoenix. But I tell you what, why don't we have Pete take a picture of the two of us with our digital camera, and you can post the photo on the web site once you get it up and running." Both men were grinning widely when the picture was snapped.

On a whim, Colfax then called out to Linda and asked that she join them for a second photo. Jimenez was elated. As the three waited for Sawyer to take the photo, Colfax explained Jimenez's offer. Linda offered to film a short video in Spanish that could be included on the web site.

"I'll send you the photo," said Sawyer, who had Jimenez's business card. "And we'll be in contact about the video."

*　*

Luke Parish eased the limousine away from the hotel the instant the car door shut. A Texas Highway Patrol motorcycle escort led the way and two more unmarked police cars followed as the small motorcade headed to the Austin airport, where a charter jet was waiting to fly Colfax to Phoenix.

"How'd you meet Mr. Jimenez?" asked Linda Colfax.

"Fate," replied Sawyer.

"Well, it certainly appears we have a friend somewhere," added Colfax. He then watched as the smile vanished from his campaign manager's face. "Is something wrong, Pete?"

"Yes," replied Sawyer, stoically.

"What is it?" asked the Colfax.

"You do have a friend somewhere . . . now." Sawyer regretted not first telling Linda about Wilhoit's death.

"What? What are you talking about, Pete?"

"Annette called me about half an hour ago . . ." A long pause followed.

"What is it, Pete?"

"Father Otto died of a massive heart attack early this morning."

Colfax's solid shoulders slumped and he slid back into the seat as though all the energy had been sucked from his body. He turned his head to the window.

"Bob, I'm so sorry," said his wife, gently lacing her fingers through his.

"I can't believe it," said Colfax, softly. The nondescript stores in a nondescript strip mall blurred across his vision. He was silent for a long time. "Father Otto meant as much to me as my own father."

"Do you want to return to Minnesota, Bob?" asked his wife. Colfax contemplated the question for a moment. He certainly didn't feel like campaigning.

"No," he said finally, "let's go on with the trip . . . there's nothing I can do. Did Annette have any details on the funeral?"

Sawyer shook his head.

"My guess is that it will be Tuesday or Wednesday." He then turned to Sawyer who was next to McGowan on the seat across from him and said, "You'll have to excuse us."

Colfax then placed his left hand on top of Linda's so that the pair now had their hands layered and began saying a prayer. "Dear Father in heaven," began Colfax, "welcome Your humble servant Otto into Your presence and may he bask in Your eternal grace. Many benefited from his wisdom, patience, and kindness. And many more from the faith that he had in You. I thank You for sharing Your humble servant with me—during my early years and through to this very day—and I pray that You and Otto continue to look out over all of us whom he touched during his short presence on earth. In the days, weeks, and years ahead, my family and I ask that You continue to guide us. We ask this through Christ our Lord. Amen."

Colfax then added a short prayer Wilhoit frequently quoted: "None of us lives for oneself, and no one dies for oneself. For if we live, we live for the Lord, and if we die, we die for the Lord; so then, whether we live or die, we are the Lord's. Amen."

When Colfax looked up, he saw Sawyer's head bowed in prayer and tears streaking down his wife's cheeks. He also caught McGowan's eyes for a brief moment and knew that he understood his pain. In return, McGowan saw a single tear spring from Colfax's right eye and run down his cheek. Colfax made no attempt to wipe it away.

For the next several minutes, Colfax kept his eyes closed and his hands pressed together as in prayer. His index fingers rested just on top of the bridge of his nose and his thumbs under his chin. He stayed that way until Parish steered the limousine into the private holding area for charter jets. The jet's engines were running as it waited to take its five passengers to Phoenix.

Somewhere over western Texas, Colfax asked Sawyer to confirm the day of the funeral and free up his calendar for the day. Sawyer had already made the arrangements.

"I will be going to St. John's that day."

* *

Carmen Jimenez received the photos much sooner than he expected. Sawyer downloaded the digital photos and requested that Parker forward them to Jimenez. They were waiting in Jimenez's e-mail when he arrived back home in El Paso that evening. Before sunrise the next day, Jimenez had forwarded the photos to about 200 friends and acquaintances. The following day, Parker and Sawyer approved Jimenez's Spanish version of the Colfax web site. All told, it was operational only forty-eight hours after Jimenez had met Colfax. Within the first week, it had received over 10,000 visits. Linda Colfax's video came the following week and continued to draw viewers.

* *

The cool spring air created a thick fog over the Mississippi River. Lee Manning had come to enjoy running the scenic eight-mile loop along the river between the Ford and the Marshall Avenue bridges. At five in the morning, the former high school miler would often be the only person near the fog-cloaked Mississippi, with the occasional exception of a lone rower navigating his scull on the calm waters.

But when Manning returned, there was a packet inside the door. Instinctively, the sniper looked around. No one was in sight. Baptista's ability to monitor Manning's comings and goings unnerved the sniper. The ability to see without being seen was the essence of sniping, and Manning did not enjoy being secretly observed.

Once inside, Manning tossed off the sweat-drenched, faded green Marine Corps T-shirt, opened the refrigerator and took a long swig of orange juice straight from the container. Sitting at the small table, covered by a cheap red-and-white checked tablecloth, Manning opened the plain white envelope and pulled out three neatly folded white sheets. A Post-it note attached to the top sheet said the previously scheduled morning meeting would not be necessary.

The first sheet described the target, the location, and the time of the assassination: "The Mass begins at noon, Tuesday, May 16. The burial is scheduled to start at 1:15. Colfax will be in attendance. The Secret Service, in an attempt to keep the event low-profile, is not expected to assign any additional agents. Based on past experience, Colfax will be covered by three agents. The chance that surveillance dogs will comb the area over a mile and a half away from the church and cemetery is remote. Even if they do, the sniper hide is well covered with at least a foot of earth. You should still take precautionary measures. The foodstuffs, which await you in the hide, will yield little odor. Plastic bags are provided for your refuse." The first sheet concluded with an order to Manning to commit the entire contents of the envelope to memory and to properly dispose of the material.

The second sheet contained a detailed black-and-white map of the campus of St. John's. Lake Sagatagan covered the better part of the map. To the north and west of the lake lay the main campus of the university, along with the church, the monastery and the cemetery. All were properly identified. Almost indistinguishable on the map was a small red dot on the south side of the lake. It designated the location of the hide. Farther to the south of the hide, almost on the periphery of the map, was a county road. Running parallel to the road was a pair of railroad tracks.

The third page outlined a very elaborate and specific escape plan. The sniper hide was precisely 2,367 yards from where the target was expected to be standing at noon. The hide included two days' worth of supplies, including sunflower seeds, beef jerky, bananas, a box of Fig Newtons, four high-energy bars, three peanut butter sandwiches, and four liters of water. Also in the hide were a set of small plastic bags and one large garbage bag. Manning was told the specific use of each bag.

Eventually, Manning got to the most valuable part of the letter—the specifics of the escape plan. Manning read the plan several times. Each time, it seemed more feasible.

"At approximately 1:30 P.M., the large bells will begin tolling in memory of Father Otto Wilhoit. They can be expected to ring for nine minutes—exactly seventy-two times. A shot from over a mile and a half will not be easily heard over the sound of the bells if it is timed properly. Between 1:39 P.M. and 1:44 P.M., a 110-car freight train heading east from Fargo to Chicago will pass within a quarter mile of the hide. It will slow to ten miles an hour—slow enough to let you jump on board. The last three cars will be empty. It will take nineteen minutes to reach the city of St. Cloud. You are to get off the train just after it passes over the Mississippi River bridge. Down on the embankment of the river, a change of clothes will be awaiting you. After sunset, you are to recross the bridge. Halfway over the bridge, dispose of the rifle. On the other side of the bridge, a quarter mile on your right, will be two old garages. In between the two buildings will be a motorcycle. Attached is a map. The highlighted backroads, which are unlikely to be patrolled by law enforcement officials, will return you safely to St. Paul."

The plan was not foolproof, but Manning was comfortable with its contents. Three million dollars was a lot of money and worth the risk. Plus, thought Manning, Colfax was a target worth taking a risk for. "The son of a bitch," thought Manning, "fucked me over in the Persian Gulf and would be a disaster as president."

CHAPTER TWENTY-FIVE

Bernie Snyder was fifty-seven years old and had snow-white hair and a massive barrel chest. He was also second in command of America's most powerful labor union. He had been a member of the Federated Workers of America since he was a young electrician apprentice. He never graduated from high school.

If Snyder felt any discomfort at being in the opulent offices of Lawrence, Mance & Scott, he didn't show it. Snyder had been staring down powerful people since he was thirteen years old and had organized the altar boys at St. Agnes' in Bayonne, New Jersey, to demand a small payment for serving special occasions.

The growing stature of the Federated Workers of America in recent years was largely attributed to Snyder's take-no-prisoners attitude. During his four years as secretary-treasurer, the union had added 250,000 members and increased its campaign contributions by twenty-five million dollars. Political experts calculated that the FWA had made the difference in eleven congressional races and two Senate races in 1998. Washington insiders now cautioned their clients that to vote against labor was to face possible political defeat in the fall. Only politicians from safe Republican districts were free of the bruising impact of the union's raw political muscle.

Jacob Mance and Bernie Snyder did not like each other, and neither attempted to hide their mutual contempt. They did, however, respect the distinctive talents each brought to a political fight.

"Thank you for coming, Bernie," said Mance, greeting Snyder by the receptionist's desk. The receptionist was surprised that Mance knew the man. It wasn't often that Mance would talk with—let alone invite into his office—a man wearing an old tattered windbreaker.

The union boss knew how to dress to impress the Washington establishment. He had a few $2,000 suits but, more often than not, he chose to wear the clothes of a tradesman. He felt the shock of his appearance was often enough to give him a distinct advantage in negotiations by reminding people that he was representing over a million working stiffs who were ready to squeeze blood from any corporation or politician who chose to go against their wishes. Jacob Mance was not easily intimidated. In fact, he smiled when he saw Snyder's appearance. "Would you like a cup of coffee?"

"I take it black," said Snyder, who figured, correctly, that the law office probably had a dozen different types of coffee to choose from and added, "I can't stand any of those fancy Amaretto coffees." Mance nodded his head at the receptionist, who then asked if he would like cream or sugar. Snyder answered with a simple no as he followed Mance into his private office. Snyder didn't look around. He was not impressed with the size, space, view, furniture, wet bar, or diplomas and photos that hung on the wall.

"Let's not waste each other's time, Mance. Why the fuck am I here?"

"I've always appreciated your candor," said Mance, picking up a remote control device and turning on a video player. He turned so he could watch the projection on the screen behind him. The video was a copy of Colfax's speech to the Mexican-American League in Austin, Texas. Mance turned the video off right after Colfax told the audience that it was his intention to increase immigration by a million people over the next four years.

Mance turned back to Snyder and stared at him. Snyder's face showed no reaction as he said only, "So?"

Mance knew that Snyder would be suspicious of anything that he was behind, so he chose to start slowly. "Bernie, I know you and I have historically worked against one another. And I suspect that we'll do so again—maybe even this year. But right now, I think we have a mutual interest in seeing that Governor Colfax does not become president."

Snyder remained silent.

"I know you are opposed to Colfax's position on immigration," continued Mance. "I also know that his position on education goes against the interests of your brethren in the educational community. And I know for a fact that his position on Social Security reform is in direct contradiction with your union's position."

"So? We're also opposed to most of the crap that Prescott is spouting."

"I understand. I just think that at this time, Colfax poses a larger threat to you and your members."

Snyder gave a Mance a quizzical look. "His positions are suicide. Colfax doesn't concern me in the least."

"Have you heard his position on campaign finance reform? If you haven't, you should."

Snyder remained stone-faced.

Mance continued. "If Colfax has his way, your union will no longer be able to automatically deduct money from your member's paychecks." Mance got up from his seat and put in another videotape. On the screen came Colfax speaking before a large group of reformers, third-party activists and libertarians in downtown Phoenix.

"The unions don't ask their members for permission to take money out of their paychecks—they just do it. They take the money and use it against politicians the union leaders don't like. They couldn't care less about what their members want. Why does someone like Bernie Snyder think it is okay to use his union's money against candidates whom many of his own members support?"

Mance extracted that tape and put a third tape into the machine. Snyder saw only a portion of Colfax's speech to a group of entrepreneurs in San Francisco advocating a more open trade policy—a position Mance knew Snyder hated because he feared it would lead to the loss of union jobs. What Snyder didn't see was Colfax committing himself and his administration to retraining any worker who lost his or her job to foreign competition. The clip went on to show a young entrepreneur standing up before the group and declaring her support for Colfax. Pulling out her checkbook, she announced that she and her husband were contributing $2,000 and urged others in the audience to do the same. Twenty-three others followed the young entrepreneur's example.

"I'm beginning to see your point," said Snyder. "I still don't think he has a chance but . . . what are you asking?"

"I would like you to commit $500,000 to the Coalition for a Prosperous New Millennium today. And pledge another $500,000 by Labor Day if Colfax is still a factor in the presidential campaign."

Snyder didn't blink at the request. He had heard privately about the coalition. "Do you have any reason to believe that he will not be a factor?"

Mance used the opening to sketch the details of the coalition's campaign against Colfax.

Snyder had heard enough. He was impressed with Mance's plan, and he was familiar with the work Mance's firm did. Snyder also didn't want to directly attack Colfax too early for fear of driving independent voters away from his preferred candidate, Martin Byrne, to Elliott Prescott. "I'll commit to one million dollars." Staring at Mance, he added, "You'd better not be fucking with me. I want every penny of my contribution to be used against Colfax."

"You have my word."

* *

The flight from San Francisco had taken over four hours, and Sean McGowan hadn't gotten back to his uptown apartment until almost 2:30 in the morning. He chose to skip his morning run and instead get some sleep. Still, he was in the office by seven. The first thing he did was call the Washington office.

"Good morning, Sean. What can I do for you?" said his boss, Dirk Osborne.

"I need some help. Colfax is kicking his campaign into high gear, and my staff is being stretched thin. In the last four days, we have been to Missouri, Texas, Arizona, and California. Tomorrow, we have a funeral here in Minnesota, but after that he is campaigning in Maine, Connecticut, Pennsylvania, Ohio, and Michigan."

"I know it's tough, Sean. You're not the only one who is being asked to do the impossible."

"Goddammit!" said McGowan, uncharacteristically. "We're going to lose someone if we don't get more support. How the hell does Congress expect us to protect the president, the vice president, and a handful of other candidates, plus maintain all our other responsibilities on a flat budget?"

"Easy, Sean, easy."

"I have to protect Colfax with three agents tomorrow. Tell me what's so easy about that?"

"It's not," replied Osborne, who understood the stress McGowan was feeling. "How much support are you receiving from the local police units?"

"It's not the numerical support, sir. It's the quality. The lead agent in central Minnesota is a twenty-seven-year-old detective who is still wet behind the ears. I asked him what detection equipment my agents could count on, and he said he'd have to check with the local National Guard unit. The National Guard! How can I be expected to ensure Colfax's safety with National Guard assets?"

"Are you telling me you need additional agents? If you are, tell me how many you need, and I'll fly them out this morning. How many do you need?" said Osborne, pushing McGowan to determine whether he was expressing the frustration of an overworked agent—a common enough situation—or if he really had a problem.

"Truthfully?"

"Truthfully."

"I need at least one extra agent."

"You've got it. I'll send Robertson out to Minneapolis this morning. But that's the best I can do. Our analysis indicates that Greene requires extra protection because he's going to Alabama. And Cross is going to New York City to speak at an anti-gay rally, so he needs extra protection as well. Both are walking into the lion's den." McGowan knew the Secret Service's analysis relied heavily on a sophisticated computer modeling program that estimated the threat level to a candidate based on a variety of factors and allocated Secret Service resources accordingly. But McGowan also knew that his boss still gave credence to a field agent's gut call.

"I appreciate the help. It sounds like Durbin and Tompkins could use some help to," said McGowan, referring to his counterparts, the lead agents for Greene and Cross. "How much longer do you think Greene and Cross will be in the race?"

"It looks like they're in it through the conventions," replied Osborne.

"Shit. My guy is starting to pick up some pretty big crowds. I'll need more help before then."

"I understand, Sean. I'll speak with Walters this morning," said Osborne, referring to the director of the Secret Service. "I think he's already aware of the situation out in the field. In fact, I know he brought the matter up with the new assistant secretary yesterday."

"Good. Who is the new assistant?" asked McGowan.

"His name is Wells, George Wells."

"Never heard of him. Does he come from the law enforcement community?"

"No. He's a politico. Some friend of the president."

"Great . . . just what we need."

What neither knew was that Wells was also an old friend of the deputy director of the CIA, Jeffery Payne.

* *

Lee Manning purchased a one-way ticket, in cash, to St. Joseph at the Minneapolis Greyhound bus depot shortly after midnight Saturday night. The disinterested clerk never once looked up at Manning. She simply punched some keys on her aging computer and handed Manning the ticket.

At 1:30 A.M., the bus pulled into the station. A handful of people disembarked and three people, including Manning, climbed abroad the nearly empty bus. The two other new passengers immediately fell asleep. Only Manning stayed awake as the bus moved from Elk River to Monticello to St. Cloud and eventually to St. Joseph.

A little after four in the morning, Manning jumped off the bus in front of a deserted grocery store. The town was utterly silent. The street lamps weren't even turned on.

Manning, with a light green Army duffel bag over one shoulder and a long, black sleek case in the other hand, began walking down the empty streets toward the interstate. Once at the interstate, the sniper crossed under a bridge and started down a seldom-used county road. Every few hundred yards, Manning would see an isolated farmhouse. Baptista's note indicated that the path to the sniper hide would begin about a quarter mile past the fifth house on the right. Manning counted each house.

Just past the fifth house, Manning saw the white cloth tied around the trunk of an elm sapling. From the road, Manning took two burlap sacks out the duffel bag, placed them over both shoes, and then tied their tops tight with a piece of twine. Next, Manning untied the cloth from around the tree and stuffed it in the duffel bag.

Silently, the sniper moved into the woods, leaving small traces of cayenne pepper occasionally to throw off any dogs searching the area. No imprints were left, and no branches or twigs were broken. In broad daylight, even a trained hunter would not have been able to tell that a human had crossed over the area.

The hide was exactly where Baptista had said it would be—which was a good thing because, even ten feet away, it could not be detected. Whoever constructed the hide was a professional. Manning had read about igloo hides in professional journals but had never used one.

Manning gently lifted the thick, concave, thatch roof and slid into the earthen hole beneath it. The pit was six feet deep, four feet wide and seven feet long. The moist black soil smelled rich and earthy.

Manning set the duffel bag in one corner and the rifle kit in the other. The sniper then stared out the three-inch crack in the earthen igloo and looked across Lake Sagatagan, which was only thirty yards from the hide. The sun was just beginning to rise. Manning could make out the cemetery across the lake but no details without a riflescope.

By 8 A.M., Manning had assembled the rifle and was staring through the scope at the cemetery. Fifteen feet from the hide, a large branch of a pine tree had been pulled to one side to leave an unobstructed the view of the cemetery. A human eye would never detect the ultrathin filament holding the branch back.

For the next few hours, Manning meticulously documented every gravestone and marker and wrote down the precise distance from the hide to the grave. Manning easily detected the plot for Father Otto—it was the one with a bright white tarp over it. Manning presumed that Colfax would be somewhere within a sixty-foot perimeter of the grave. But just in case, the sniper marked off every possible landmark.

Manning smiled again at Baptista's attention to detail. On a small tree across the lake, about 200 yards to the west and 500 yards south of the cemetery, was a thin white cloth. Every time the wind blew, the cloth fluttered appropriately. Based on its degree of stiffness, Manning could gauge the strength of the wind—a necessary ingredient for a successful shot from 2,500 yards. Farther afield, at the base of the grave of Brother Othmar, was a small American flag, which also fluttered in the breeze. The sniper had two independent means to gauge the wind.

Manning smiled because both flags moved only rarely in the light wind from the west. Baptista's weather report was correct. Manning hoped it was correct again on Monday and, more important, Tuesday.

A little before noon, Manning took a Gore-Tex suit out of the duffel bag along with a thin straw mat. The sniper put on the Gore-Tex suit, laid the mat down and closed the eye slit of the hide. Six hours of sleep came easily in the perfectly dark igloo.

* *

Manning woke feeling well rested. Looking at the luminous face of the digital watch, the sniper was surprised to find that it was late afternoon. Difficult as it was in the confined space, Manning did some basic stretches to get the blood circulating again. A light meal was next—a peanut butter sandwich, some beef jerky, an energy bar and a liter of water. Before the sun set, Manning conducted some visual exercises from the hide and tried to work through a variety of possible different scenarios. All the while, the sniper methodically popped sunflower seeds, sucked the salt from each, cracked the shell and consumed the nut meat. Each empty shell was meticulously spit into a sealable plastic bag.

Manning spent the last few minutes of daylight dissembling the rifle. From start to finish, it took seventy-three seconds. Dissatisfied, Manning reassembled and disassembled the rifle again. This time, the former Marine did it in sixty-two seconds.

A half-hour after dark, the sniper left the hide for the first time since arriving. Strapping on the burlap sacks again, Manning slowly headed toward the lake. It took five minutes to cover the thirty yards to the shore. The sniper was careful to leave no signs. At the shore, Manning backed up to the lake, quietly pulled down the Gore-Tex pants and urinated and defecated into the water. Without the benefit of toilet paper or even leaves, Manning wiped clean the remaining excrement and washed both hands in the cold water. Manning had never been fond of this aspect of sniping—but a sniper who didn't want to be found could leave no traces. And Manning knew that if any organization could find a trace of anything, it was the Secret Service.

With the burlap sacks still on, Manning painstakingly moved in the direction of the railroad tracks that Baptista had highlighted on the map. The distance from the hide to railroad was less than a quarter of a mile. But because Manning was careful not to leave tracks or any sign of movement, the trip took over an hour. After almost every step, Manning took notes. After the shot, the same trip would have to be made in a fraction of the time. The trick was to move fast and still not leave any sign of movement. Manning knew it was possible, but the additional burden of carrying a trash sack and a rifle case was going to complicate matters. Manning would repeat the procedure Monday night.

Before the sniper could return to the hide, one last piece of business had to be completed. A false trail had to be prepared. If the shot was successful, it would be a matter of hours—possibly less—before law enforcement officials would locate the hide. A diversion was a necessary component of a successful escape. Manning replicated the process of going to the railroad tracks, only this time moving away from the hide and back toward the road. The purpose was to make the pursuers believe that the road—and not the railroad—had been the path of escape.

Manning returned to the hide just as the sun rose on Monday, May 15. The temperature had dropped a little overnight, but the wind was still light. Baptista's weather forecasting appeared to be holding up. Manning ate a banana, another energy bar and drank some water before catching a quick nap. The sniper was asleep when the first Secret Service agent arrived at the cemetery and began surveying the scene.

* *

Sergeant Gregg Brown was a seventeen-year veteran of the Minnesota National Guard and had been its canine specialist for the last ten years. He was widely recognized as one of the best canine specialists in the Midwest. The call from the Secret Service had not surprised him—he had worked for the agency on a number of occasions. As had his dog, Rusty, a ten-year-old German shepherd.

The pair started out on their assignment on Monday afternoon. It took them close to four hours to walk the perimeter of the campus. Toward the end of the walk, Rusty pulled on the leash and stopped.

"Do you smell something, boy?" said the veteran cop to the dog. "Do you smell something?" The dog looked up at its master and continued walking. Sergeant Brown thought nothing of the incident and did not mention it in his two-page report to Secret Service Agent Sean McGowan. Forensic experts would later detect cayenne pepper in the place where Rusty had stopped.

* *

The makeshift Secret Service command center was located inside the Great Hall, a turn-of-the-century brick building that had once been the center of the university. Today, the building housed mainly administrative offices.

Sean McGowan arrived at St. John's fifteen hours before Colfax was expected. The candidate's travel itinerary had not been made public at the request of the Secret Service. He was concerned that public knowledge of Colfax's trip would compromise his team's limited capabilities. Colfax quickly acceded to the request. The funeral was a private matter, and he wanted to keep it that way. A series of disturbing Internet threats had also heightened McGowan's anxiety.

When McGowan arrived at the command center, Parish and Robertson, the young agent who had arrived from Washington, D.C., the day before, were already in the room along with Doug Turk, a thirty-one-year-old cop from St. Cloud who had recently been trained in security matters and was the department's lone Special Response Unit officer. Also in the room was Lance Wenner, the sheriff of Stearns County.

"Good evening, gentlemen," said McGowan, firmly. "Time is of the essence. Gibraltar is expected to arrive at 1145 tomorrow. I would like to go over a quick review of the security arrangements already made and assign additional responsibilities to fill whatever gaps we might have. Later this evening, I expect all of you to familiarize yourselves with the contents of this book," he said, holding up a copy of the 110-page briefing book labeled "confidential."

Luke Parish, the lead advance agent, then briefed the group on the primary and alternate arrival and departure routes. He presented an aerial photo of the campus, designated all potential trouble spots and outlined the security precautions that had been taken. He described the security checks that had been conducted on every priest at the monastery, as well as every student and worker at the university.

"Only one priest, Father Michael Friedl, is considered problematic. He is a fairly vocal anti-abortion leader, but our intelligence suggests that he is not considered a threat. As a precaution, however, we have assigned him a seat in the church far away from Gibraltar—where he can be easily observed. Our review of the student population revealed only one possible threat. His name is Landon Clarke, a freshman physics major. He is a certified genius and was once arrested, when he was in high school, for building a sophisticated bomb. We have already visited him, and our search of his dorm room revealed nothing."

"Please familiarize yourselves with the photos of both Friedl and Clarke," said McGowan to the entire group. "If you see either of them in the vicinity of Colfax, alert the entire radio network immediately."

Parish also explained all the security precautions that were being established inside the church. "Everybody attending the funeral tomorrow will be channeled through one of two doors. Each door has been lined with discrete metal and chemical detectors. The church has also been thoroughly searched and will be continuously guarded until after Gibraltar departs. As we speak, Agent Brix is inside the church. Following the funeral service, it is expected that Gibraltar will attend the burial. The route is highlighted on page seventy-one of your briefing book. He is estimated to depart the church at 1300 and will be driven to the cemetery—which is also shown on the map. We must also be prepared that Gibraltar will want to walk to the cemetery. We have requested that he not expose himself in that manner, but because the distance is a little over a quarter of a mile, we should be prepared for the possibility. The cemetery itself has been searched. I personally spent the better part of the day securing all possible lines of fire from the two buildings that provide a direct line of sight to the cemetery, and we had bomb experts with two German shepherds from the National Guard search the cemetery and the surrounding area. The area was also electronically swept earlier today. Nothing was found—but the local National Guard crew will resweep the entire area tomorrow to make sure that nothing developed overnight. Their shepherds will also rework the area.

"Are there any questions?" asked McGowan. "I expect each and every one of you to understand the contents of this briefing book. It is vitally important that you memorize the routes, the danger points, and the faces of threats. Above all, keep your eyes open, use common sense, and expect the unexpected."

CHAPTER TWENTY-SIX

L ee Manning fell asleep around 1:00 A.M., Tuesday morning while mentally reviewing the 578 steps to the railroad track. Three hours later, the sniper's watch beeped. During the night, the temperature had dropped seven degrees, and the wind had picked up slightly.

It was completely dark in the deep hole, but Manning knew where everything was in the small, cramped space and immediately reached for the water bottle. The sniper ate the remaining sandwich and banana and finished off the last liter of water. Next, Manning retrieved a pair of running shoes from the duffel bag that were a size and a half too large. They belonged to Rudy Bradford.

Manning carefully laced up both shoes, making sure to push as far as possible to the front of the toe box. In the predawn silence of May 16, the sniper sprinted along the path that had been used to enter the hide. This time, all caution was abandoned. Branches were broken, twigs snapped and tracks were left. If anyone had been within a few hundred yards of the sniper, the movement would have been audible. Nobody was.

The purpose of the sprint was to create an impression that whoever was in the hide had hastily made their getaway in the general direction of the county road—a direction opposite of Manning's real escape route. With each step taken, Manning was sure to strike the ground toe first and hard enough to leave an impression.

It took Manning just less than 120 seconds to make it to the road. Once there, the sniper looked around to make sure no one was nearby. Sitting down on the hard asphalt, Manning unlaced the running shoes, placed them in a plastic bag and replaced the shoes with burlap sacks. Then moving down the road another hundred yards, the sniper slowly reentered the woods and started back toward the igloo hide.

From the relative comfort of the igloo hide, where the temperature remained a stable sixty-three degrees, Manning was unaware that outside the temperature continued to drop. Between the hours of 4:00 and 8:00 A.M. the temperature dropped another five degrees.

* *

Father Francis, like many older monks, was an early riser. He was also an avid walker. For years, he enjoyed the serenity of the morning. He particularly enjoyed walking the western shore of Lake Sagatagan in the spring of the year. The cool air lifted his spirits, as he recalled how his friend, Otto, had also loved this time of day.

As he walked along the road, deep in thought and prayer, Francis looked up to see a white rag fluttering from a tree. He would not have noticed it if a gust of wind had not caused its end to stiffen and stick out from the middle of the tree.

Thinking that it was nothing more than a relic of some prep school biology experiment, Father Francis removed the rag. Twenty-three hundred yards away, Lee Manning was leaning up against the dirt wall in the dimly lit hide, cleaning the rifle one last time before the shot.

* *

"Gibraltar is estimated to arrive at 11:45," McGowan told the assembled group of four Secret Service agents and eight local law enforcement officers. "Let's run through the checklist one last time, starting with internal security. Agent Parish?"

"The church is secured. Agents Robertson and Brix spent the night in the church, and it was cleared again by the bomb detection squad thirty minutes ago. Robertson is still there. All attendees have been cleared."

"What about Friedl and Clarke?" asked McGowan.

"Friedl is not expected to attend the funeral, and Clarke is scheduled to be in class during the funeral. We will know where both are at all times."

"Good. What's the status of the buildings around the church and the cemetery?"

"Every building with a direct line of fire to the church or cemetery has been completely secured. All windows and other openings have been secured, and access will continue to be denied until after Colfax has departed."

"Good," said McGowan. "The limousine will stop directly under the bell tower, and Colfax will immediately be escorted inside the church and down to the basement chapel by Father Tom Burnett—a mutual friend of Colfax and the deceased. It will take eight seconds for Colfax to leave the limousine and enter the church. Each agent is responsible for covering his or her arc of view," said McGowan. Wasting no time, he continued, "External security. Agent Brix?"

"The main campus has been searched by the National Guard canine specialists and their dogs, and no usual activity was detected. We also flew over the campus yesterday and swept the area using electronic and chemical detection equipment. We repeated the process this morning. No problems have been detected as yet."

"How wide of an area did the specialists cover?" asked McGowan.

"The entire campus plus all roads and access points within a mile radius of the church or the cemetery."

"Were you comfortable with their expertise?"

"Yes. I have worked with the Sergeant Brown before and have found him to be very competent. And as for the dogs, well, they're no Belgian Malinois, but they're good." The Secret Service had long preferred using Belgian Malinois because of their superior detection skills.

"What about contingency plans?" said McGowan.

"The nearest hospital is St. Cloud General. It's twelve miles away and has an excellent staff ranging from cardiologists to neurosurgeons. It can be reached in nine minutes in an emergency. The airport is nine miles away and can be reached in seven minutes. Alternative routes have been developed and are on page sixty-seven of the book. Parish has been briefed on the alternative routes, and all routes have been reviewed for vulnerabilities."

"What about air traffic?"

"We'll have our radar system up and operational in advance of Gibraltar's arrival. I'm confident that no aircraft can breech a five-mile radius without our knowing it."

"Have we addressed all other access issues?"

"Yes. We have chosen to place one undercover highway patrolman at the I-94 exit ramp to the campus and another two at the north and south ends of the County Road 53 exit," replied Brix. "Those are the only ways to access the campus. Per your earlier instructions, we have decided not to stop vehicles at the exits. Secondary access points have been established farther down each road. Only at that point will the vehicles and their drivers be stopped and searched."

"Good. No need to unnecessarily arouse suspicions."

"There is also expected to be some train traffic on the Santa Fe line about two miles west of campus—it runs parallel to campus—but because of its distance, we will not be disrupting its normal service."

"Do any of the trains impede any of the routes to either the airport or the hospital?" asked McGowan.

"No. All paths to the airport and the hospital are clear. The rail line never cross-es any of our main or alternate routes. I should add," said Brix, "that there are two trains scheduled to pass by between 1300 and 1430—one headed west and the other headed east."

"And all the trains are regularly scheduled traffic?"

"Yes. The rail manifest for today has been set since last week."

* *

Shortly before the service was to begin, eighty-four monks in traditional Benedictine robes entered the church through the rear passageway that connected to the monastery to the church. The last in line hesitated slightly at the security detector. Under the robe was the face of Agent Robertson. His role was to watch the crowd for possible threats coming from the audience.

Everyone else entered the church through the large wooden doors in the front of the structure. Few people were aware that they were walking through a security detector. Even fewer noticed that no one was allowed to enter the church through the side doors, and no one noticed the sharpshooter on a catwalk seventy feet above the main aisle of the church.

The monks lined the pews that surrounded the altar. Hundreds of other people whom Father Otto Wilhoit had touched in his life—students, parents, and parish-ioners—filled the remainder of the huge, concrete church.

At precisely 11:45, Governor Colfax, along with his wife and two daughters, pulled up in front of the church. McGowan, who had met Colfax at the airport, was on the jump seat next to the family. A quick radio conversation informed McGowan that the area was secure. With approval from Brix, who was standing outside the door of the church, McGowan swung open the door of the limousine and escorted the family into the baptismal area at the entrance to the sanctuary, where Father Tom Burnett greeted them.

Colfax and Burnett hugged and exchanged a few words. Linda Colfax also embraced the old family friend and introduced her daughters to the priest. The five, with Agent McGowan right behind them, walked down the granite stairs into the smaller private chapel. Immediately behind them, locked in a vault, lay the relics of a long forgotten saint, Saint Bede.

"How are you doing, Robert?" asked Burnett tenderly. He knew how much Otto meant to Colfax.

"Truth be told," said Colfax, "it's been harder on me than I expected. I felt like Otto would always be around. Do you know what I mean?"

"I do," said Burnett, placing a hand on Colfax's shoulder. "Many of us here felt the same way."

"It's funny. I think I'm mad at him for dying right now. Isn't that selfish?"

"It's a more common emotion than you might think."

"I miss him—"

"I know—we all do," said Burnett. "The pain will ease . . . with time."

"I know," said Colfax, drawing his wife closer to him and grabbing the hand of his youngest daughter, Colleen.

"The service is about to begin. I have been asked to escort you to your seats," said Burnett, leading them to the back of the private chapel and up a secluded stairwell. "Will we get a chance to catch up after the service, or do you have to return to the campaign trail?"

"Unfortunately, I have to fly to Baltimore this evening."

"Well, in that case, I had better say goodbye now," said Father Burnett, embracing Colfax tightly. "Otto was always very proud of you, Robert," whispered Burnett. "His spirit is with you. God bless you and your family." Burnett had forgotten about a letter that Wilhoit had written to Colfax before his death but which was never posted. The brother who had cleaned out Wilhoit's room the day after his death came across it and passed it to Burnett, who meant to give it to Colfax.

Father Burnett, Agent McGowan, and Colfax's family waited behind the closed door as Colfax tried to regain his composure. He had begun to cry when Father Burnett had told him that Otto had been proud of him. Otto himself had told Colfax the same thing many times throughout the years, but this was the first time he had ever truly felt it. It was as though he felt Otto's presence.

Linda Colfax wiped a tear off her husband's cheek, and their two daughters, witnessing their father cry for the first time in their lives, drew nearer to him.

Seeing that Colfax had composed himself, Agent McGowan gently pushed the door open, and the family and the priest walked down to the reserved seats in the front row. Only those in the first few rows noticed Colfax's entrance.

*   *

A mile and a half away, almost due south of the church, in a small earthen pit covered by a foot of solid dirt, Lee Manning finished the ritual of cleaning the rifle.

Gently, Manning eased the stem of the rifle out the slot so that no more than four inches stuck out. Manning then slid the rifle back into the igloo and placed a piece of fine camouflage cloth over the stem. It would have been difficult to see the barrel at ten yards; at 2,400 yards, it was impossible.

Only after Manning put the rifle out the second time did the former Marine notice that the white rag on the tree had disappeared. Quickly, Manning scanned the area looking for the rag. It was nowhere in sight. Manning's mind raced. How tightly had Baptista tied the cloth? Did it blow off? Did someone take it off? Did whoever take it off know the purpose of the cloth? If it was a Secret Service agent, were they looking for the hide? Manning worked through the possibilities while frantically searching for the cloth. The sniper then remembered the flag on Othmar's grave. A quick look revealed it was still there. Manning breathed a sigh of relief.

The shot would only be marginally affected, thought Manning. The wind speed at the shore of the lake might differ from that at the cemetery, altering the projection of the bullet ever so slightly, but the relatively light wind made that unlikely.

Manning stared at the digital watch and listened for any sounds outside the hide. There were none. The watch read 12:11.

* *

Father Burnett had called Colfax a day after Otto's death and asked if he wanted to give the eulogy. Colfax considered it but decided that because Wilhoit had touched so many people's lives, it was more appropriate that a fellow Benedictine give the eulogy. Besides, he didn't think he could make it through without breaking down. Colfax remembered the first time the priest had comforted him when he was a lonely, homesick boy. He also remembered how the priest had helped him remain at the prep school after his father's bankruptcy and suicide, and his family could no longer afford the tuition.

As he listened to Father Abbott tell story after story of the heart and spirit of Father Otto Martin Wilhoit, Colfax was glad he had chosen not to give the eulogy. He had never heard many of the stories. He learned of the poor black boy Wilhoit mentored in the 1950s when he was working at the monastery in the Bahamas—a boy who grew up to become an accomplished doctor and a founder of seven AIDS clinics in the Caribbean. He learned of a CEO who bequeathed a million dollars to the prep school simply because Wilhoit had taken time to help him with trigonometry. Colfax smiled. It didn't surprise him that the man who had shaped his own life had kept all his kind deeds to himself. It was his way. There were hundreds of other such stories. His own was just one of them.

* *

The funeral ended promptly at one o'clock. Everyone, except the monks, the Colfax family, and Agent McGowan, departed through the front doors of the church.

A very light breeze greeted the attendees. No one noticed that the temperature had dropped another two degrees.

The cemetery was not far from the church—200 yards due south. The most direct path to it, however, was through the monastery, thus accessible only to the monks. Lay persons had to take a very circuitous route to the cemetery on a public road that wrapped around the northwest side of campus, past a number of modern college dorms on one side and a patch of thick trees on the other.

As the mourners made their way to the picturesque plot of land on the western side of Lake Sagatagan, six younger monks wheeled the casket carrying the body of Father Otto out of the church and through the monastery that Wilhoit had called home for the last fifty-two years of his life. By this time, the first of the mourners were arriving at the cemetery. Those who came by car parked along the road on the western side of the lake and walked up the path that sliced the cemetery in half to the plot where Wilhoit would be laid to rest. The only car allowed to park in the cemetery was Colfax's limousine.

Ten minutes after one o'clock, Father Abbott, the head of the Abbey, led a procession of monks in their solemn walk to the cemetery. In two lines, with their heads bowed, the monks prayed the psalms as they slowly made their way out of the building and down the path by the lake to the cemetery. Colfax and his family, with Agent McGowan, followed behind the last monk.

Like the monks, the Colfaxes bowed their heads in prayer. Agent McGowan did not. Two thousand yards away, on the opposite side of Lake Sagatagan from a six-foot deep hole, Lee Manning picked up the funeral procession through a pair of Zeiss binoculars.

So powerful were the binoculars that when Robert Colfax came into sight, the scar above his left eyebrow, a remnant from a childhood biking accident, was as visible as one's reflection in a mirror. Manning, now holding the rifle, easily placed the cross hairs on Colfax's head. All the sniper needed was for the tolling of the bells to start.

CHAPTER TWENTY-SEVEN

Manning's Marine Corps gunnery sergeant had always said it took a different kind of courage to be alone and act alone. Until now, Manning had not fully understood what the old Marine was talking about. In North Carolina, outside the school, the sniper had felt nothing. The same thing in Kosovo. Now, for the first time, the statement made sense. Manning estimated the odds of a successful shot to be about seventy percent. Escaping would be even more difficult. Knowing that the Secret Service would engage in a vigorous pursuit, Manning figured there was less than a fifty-percent chance of collecting the three million dollars. Under normal circumstances, Manning reasoned, it would not be worth the risk. But Colfax was no ordinary target.

Manning quickly swept the thought away. The sniper knew that anything less than perfect concentration could lead to a miss.

The sniper peered through the scope again and lined up the crosshairs on Colfax's head. The quality of the target was immaculate. The handsome crinkles on the sides of Colfax's eyes were clearly distinguishable. The officiating priest, Father Abbott, had begun his remarks. Everyone was focusing on him—except for Agent McGowan, who was now two feet behind Colfax and continuously scanning the horizon. Manning also noticed that one monk did not appear to be paying particularly close attention to the priest.

After weeks of practicing, analyzing, reanalyzing and rehearsing the shot, Manning knew the moment was getting close and contorted into a rock-solid position. The sniper drew away from the scope and surveyed the scene. The bushes in front of the hide were not moving, there was barely a ripple across the lake, and the light clouds that drifted above the cemetery and over the lake suggested the wind was minimal. The tops of the large pines in the cemetery swayed just enough to give Manning pause.

As a life-long hunter and a sniper, Manning was an expert at gauging the wind speed and direction by eyeballing such things as the sway of treetops, the chop on a lake and the speed of cloud movements.

"Be patient, be patient," thought Manning, "wait for a complete lull." There was only going to be one shot. It had to be perfect. Manning wished that Baptista had provided more information on the expected length of a Catholic burial service.

Then, about fifteen minutes after the monks had arrived at the grave plot, the Abbott began to sprinkle water on the casket of Father Otto. He made the sign of the cross and everyone in the audience, except McGowan, did the same. The priest then moved closer to the casket, and, through the lens, Manning watched the casket being slowly lowered into the earth. Finally, the priest reached down to a pile of rich, black soil and tossed a handful onto the grave. Another prayer ensued, and everyone bowed their head.

This time, it was unmistakable. The same monk who had earlier appeared to not be paying attention did not lower his head in prayer. He continued to scan the audience.

"He's Secret Service," thought Manning. But before the sniper could contemplate the odds that the agent might be able to see the compressed flash of the rifle, the bells began to toll. The loud gong reverberated over the campus and across the lake. One for every year of Wilhoit's life. Ten seconds separated every new knell.

Gong . . . gong . . . gong . . .

The crowd of mourners began to slowly break up. Some people hugged, others talked quietly among themselves, a few monks circled the grave and appeared to be saying additional prayers for Father Otto. But most began moving back in the direction of campus, toward the sound of the bells. Only one person came to greet Colfax. He stood directly between Colfax and the path that Manning's bullet would have to pass.

"Move, motherfucker," whispered Manning silently. "Move."

Gong . . . gong . . . gong . . .

"Pat, how are you?" said Colfax to his old classmate Pat Turk, who he then introduced to his wife and children.

"I've been better. How about you? I didn't know if you'd be able to make it— with your campaign and all."

"Like you," said Colfax looking squarely into Turk's eyes, "I've been better. I just can't believe he's gone,"

"Me either. But I'm sure grateful for all the time that he spent with us. The man shaped my whole life. I'd probably be tending bar in north Minneapolis if he hadn't seen something in me and decided that I warranted a scholarship. I thank God every day for Otto's ability to see my potential—even when I didn't see it myself."

"I know," said Colfax, as the pair continued to talk to the obvious annoyance of Agent McGowan. After a minute, Turk picked up on McGowan's body signals and concluded the conversation.

Gong . . . gong . . . gong . . .

"Well, I know you've got to be busy, Bob. I wish you the best of luck in the campaign—you've got my vote. It was nice to see you again, Linda, and it was a pleasure to meet both of you," said Turk to Colfax's two daughters, shaking their hands. As Turk walked away, Colfax became fully exposed.

The cemetery was almost empty. Besides the Colfax family, only Father Francis and the Secret Service agent dressed as a monk remained in the cemetery. Father Francis continued to pray at the open grave. Everyone else, including Father Burnett, had headed back to the Great Hall for a reception.

A mile and a half away, Manning placed the crosshairs on Colfax's head. The timing looked perfect. The lake and the treetops were still, the clouds were barely drifting and the small American flag at the base of the gravestone of Othmar lay limp.

All the sniper had to do was time the shot with the tolling. The knells were coming in precise increments of ten seconds.

Gong . . . counting backward, Manning waited for the next knell. Nine, eight, seven. . . . At the same time, Father Burnett, remembering the letter in his pocket, turned back toward Colfax.

The sniper took one last breath and waited for the body to come its natural respiratory pause. Six, five, four—.

"Robert," Burnett cried out.

With a touch ever so slight, Manning applied pressure to the rifle trigger and waited.

"I have something for you," said Burnett, flashing the letter at Colfax.

Three, two, one . . . Colfax leaned toward Burnett, who was holding out the letter.

Gong! Manning pulled tight on the firing pin. The rifle violently expelled its lethal content. At precisely the same time, a soft, almost imperceptible breeze pushed its way in a southwesterly direction across Lake Sagatagan.

Less than a second later, Robert Colfax, clutching the letter, heard the distinctive whistle as the bullet sailed past the back of his head by less than an inch.

* *

Sean McGowan heard the same sound and instinctively yelled, "Gun!" Everyone froze, except the Secret Service agents who seemed to defy reality with their speed. McGowan, simultaneously with sounding the warning, threw his body into Colfax's and forcefully thrusting his knee into the back of Colfax's legs. Colfax crumbled— and McGowan had succeeded in reducing by half the amount of Colfax's body that would be exposed to a second shot.

McGowan then pushed Colfax to the dry ground and lay spread-eagled on top of him—effectively eliminating Colfax as a target. At the same time, Luke Parish, who was behind the wheel of the limousine, thrust the massive vehicle into reverse and in less than two seconds covered the fifteen yards that separated the Colfax family from the car. By moving the car so quickly, Parish unwittingly severed the line of fire between Colfax and Manning.

As McGowan lay on top of Colfax and Parish maneuvered the limousine, Agent Robertson jumped in front of Linda Colfax and the girls. He threw open his black monk's robe in an attempt to cut off the widest possible angle from the sniper. He didn't hear the shot, and he didn't know from what direction it came, but he assumed that it came from the college dorm that lay about 400 yards to the northeast of the cemetery. A thorough review would later show that if Linda Colfax or her daughters had been the target—or an acceptable alternative—his efforts, while technically correct, would have been in vain because he was covering the wrong line of fire.

As the limousine screeched to a stop a few feet from McGowan and Colfax, Robertson lowered his robe, reached for the handle and yanked the armored steel door open. He quickly moved to his left and with no tact whatsoever reached down, grabbed Colfax and pulled him next to his large body. McGowan picked himself up at the same time, and together, he and Robertson created a human shield around Colfax and pushed him into the safety of the idling vehicle.

Next, Robertson turned and grabbed Linda Colfax and shoved her onto McGowan and Colfax. His final action was to extend his two arms and, with a wide sweeping motion, nestled both daughters into his chest and dived into the limousine.

"Go," yelled McGowan, reaching up to close the door behind Robertson. Parish hit the gas and the force of the car slammed the door shut before McGowan had a chance to close it. In a matter of seconds, Parish cleared the cemetery and turned right on the road that circled the lake. It had taken only seventeen seconds from the time McGowan heard the shot to when the limousine was off the grounds of the cemetery.

McGowan immediately turned his attention back to Colfax and conducted a quick search of his body for any wounds. He found none.

"Are you all right, sir?" he asked Colfax.

"I think so," said Colfax, who was more concerned about his wife and daughters, who lay paralyzed by fear on the floor of the accelerating limousine.

"What about everybody else?"

No one said anything. The speed of the entire event had stunned everybody. And because only Colfax and McGowan had heard the shot, no one really knew what had happened.

"They're fine," replied Robertson.

"Parish," McGowan barked into the radio, "take the secondary route to the airport." Parish breathed a sigh of relief—a visit to St. Cloud General Hospital would be unnecessary.

"Gibraltar is safe," McGowan said into radio. "Repeat, Gibraltar is safe and heading for home."

* *

Manning knew instantly that the shot missed. If it had been successful, Colfax's head would have exploded in a mass of blood, gray matter and skull fragments. Instead, Manning watched in stunned amazement as the Secret Service agent nearest to Colfax immediately closed the distance between himself and the target and threw the candidate to the ground. Before Manning could even begin to contemplate—let alone calculate—another shot, the limousine eliminated that possibility.

Remembering the old Marine Corps sniper slogan, "He who runs away lives to shoot another day," Manning opted against a second shot and rapidly dissembled the rifle. It took only forty-one seconds.

In the time it took the Secret Service to protect, collect and remove Colfax and his family from harm's way and place a quarter of a mile between the site of the shot and the target, Manning had taken the rifle apart and stored it securely in its container. Using the straps on the outside of the container, the sniper put it on like a knapsack. With the burlap sacks tied firmly around both feet and the rifle in one hand and a small plastic bag containing the water bottles, expelled sunflower seeds shells and discarded wrappers in the other, Manning lifted the lid of the igloo and sprinted toward the railroad tracks. All the mental practice paid off as Manning deftly avoided branches and tried to step on ground that wouldn't even leave a hint of a human foot impression. It took the sniper less than two minutes to reach the tracks.

273

* *

As Parish steered the limousine smoothly around the lake road at eighty-five miles an hour, McGowan called into the command center back at the university, which was already a flurry of activity. The word "gun" had triggered a set of actions that were already known in Washington.

"Gibraltar is healthy," reported McGowan matter-of-factly to the agent-in-charge, Julie Brix.

"What about the others?"

"They're fine."

"Good. The plane is taxiing as we speak. It looks like you're four minutes out," replied Brix, scanning the computer terminal tracking the limousine's progress. "We've got local law enforcement securing the airport. What else can you tell me?"

"Not much," said McGowan, "I heard the distinctive whistle of a bullet and then went into reactive mode."

"Did you hear a second shot?"

"No."

"Are you sure?"

"Positive."

"Do you know what direction the shot was fired from?"

"No. The bells were ringing. If I had to guess, I'd say from the north."

"From the dorm?"

"It's possible."

"We've got someone in the building, but they're reporting that no one has been allowed in since it was secured this morning. We're sending two more people to check it out just in case."

"I'm positive it was a shot," said McGowan.

"We'll let you know what we find," said Brix. "You just get Gibraltar safely out to the airport and into the air. We're calling in reinforcements to comb the campus. I'll let you know what we find."

"Thanks," said McGowan, who instinctively peered out the rear window to see if they were being followed.

As soon as McGowan hung up, Brix directed the local police still on the scene to concentrate on the dorms and woods on the west side of campus. She also ordered the two entrance points to the campus closed to all outgoing traffic. A quick review of the map dictated that the county roads near the campus should also be secured as quickly as possible. She then ordered a net to be set up over a ten-mile radius of the campus and for all people and cars to be stopped and searched.

As Brix continued to bark orders, less than two miles away a freight train began making its way past the periphery of the campus. Brix did not issue any specific instructions to insure that the train be stopped.

John Dalton, a railroad engineer for thirty-five years, had made the Fargo-St. Paul-Chicago run hundreds of time. When he received the "slow order" from the track foreman requesting the train slow to ten-miles an hour for a section of track just north of County Road 53, Dalton didn't think anything of it. Slow orders were pretty common. The foreman had indicated that there was probably no problem and that the "slow order" was the result of the more cautious management style of the railroad's new owner, Holten, Inc.

By the time Colfax was halfway to the airport and Manning was waiting patiently in dense pocket of brushes for the train to lumber by, the first Highway Patrol officer was arriving to block the northern exit of the campus. It would take another five minutes before the thinly stretched patrol could get a second car to the southern exit. It would be over a half-hour before they could get a helicopter on the scene. The lone State Patrol helicopter dedicated to central Minnesota—and the one slated to help orchestrate the containment strategy—had an hour earlier been dispatched sixty miles north to the town of Brainerd to evacuate a young boy who had capsized in his father's sailboat and was hypothermic. By the time the helicopter pilot received word that he was to proceed to St. John's, he had just landed to pick up the boy. The detour to St. Cloud would delay the helicopter's arrival over St. John's by thirty-two minutes. It would take the same amount of time for two additional helicopters from the Twin Cities to arrive on the scene.

As the sniper waited in the bushes for the train to arrive, each second felt like an eternity. But within three minutes, Lee Manning heard the train charging down the tracks. It took less than a minute for the first car to pass the bushes. The sniper pressed the stopwatch function on the digital watch and began visualizing jumping on the moving train.

Manning quickly scanned the train and confirmed that it was a long one. Baptista had told the sniper that the train would be over a mile long, meaning it would be virtually impossible for the train's engineer to see anyone jumping on board.

275

Manning, feeling slightly more relaxed with the train in sight, patiently studied each car. Baptista had indicated that three cars toward the end of the train would be completely empty. The empty cars would be numbers 123, 345 and 789. Baptista, in his instructions, noted that only car numbers that were sequential in order would be empty.

It took a full minute for the first empty car—number 123—to pass by. The sniper contemplated trying to match the pace of the train to jump in between cars 122 and 123 but opted to mentally practice the procedure one more time.

By the time car 345 came into view, Manning was comfortable with the speed and confident that jumping onto the slow-moving train would prove to be no more difficult than completing one of the obstacle courses at Camp Lejuene.

As the car approached, Manning began counting the amount of time that elapsed between cars. As soon as car 345 came into view, the sniper bolted from the bushes at a forty-five-degree angle. By the time Manning had reached the tracks, the car in front of car 345 had pulled out of reach. The small crushed rock that lay on both sides of the railroad track allowed Manning to get good traction on the ground, but the burlap sacks made it difficult to match exactly the pace of the train. Manning was running at about an eight-mile-an-hour clip, and the train was still moving at ten miles an hour, so for a full ten seconds, the sniper ran parallel with the train until it eventually gave way to the slight two-foot opening. Manning tossed the plastic bag onto the platform and grabbed the railing handle. The motion of the train hoisted the sniper aboard.

* *

Linda Colfax didn't know what was more frightening—what had just happened at the cemetery or the drive to the airport. Agent Parish had now taken the limousine up to over a hundred miles an hour. The trees outside were nothing more than a blur. Inside the car was complete chaos. McGowan was barking commands into a radio, both girls were crying, and Colfax was utterly silent. Moments earlier, he had mindlessly placed the letter from Wilhoit, which he had clutched in his hand, into his breast pocket.

He just sat with his arms draped over his two daughters, comforting them, and stared back at his wife. What Linda didn't know was that besides McGowan, her husband was the only other person who could confirm that he was definitely the target of an assassin's bullet. Thirty years earlier on the Mekong Delta, when he was a lieutenant j.g. in the Navy, Colfax had been engaged in a deadly fire fight with the Viet Cong. He vividly remembered the sound of bullets as they whizzed by his body. It was a sound he could never forget.

Not one to lay back, Linda Colfax demanded answers—if for no other reason than she felt the need to do something, to have some control over the situation. "Agent McGowan," she yelled, "where the hell are we going?"

McGowan looked at her but continued to talk into his radio. "Gibraltar is safe. We are currently enroute to the airport. We'll not approach until the integrity of the airport has been confirmed. Make sure the plane is ready to go. I want Gibraltar off the ground less than thirty seconds after we arrive."

"Goddammit! What just happened and where are we going?" persisted Linda Colfax.

"Mrs. Colfax," said McGowan coolly after he finished his radio conversation with the governor's state security team, which was waiting at the airport, "we have reason to believe your husband was the target of an assassination attempt. Once that happens, I'm in charge. And I will remain in charge until I have been relieved of my responsibilities. I'll debrief you when our safety is ensured."

Linda began to protest, but McGowan's sharp look and a gentle tug on her shoulder from her husband stopped her.

"It's okay," said Colfax calmly, "Everything's going to be fine." He then lifted his right arm off of Catherine's shoulder and extended his hand out to his wife.

The Colfax family silently prayed. Colfax thanked God that his wife and daughters were not harmed. He contemplated asking God for the courage to continue with the campaign but didn't—he knew that nothing was going to deter him. He did ask for forgiveness for putting his family through this ordeal. He would need it. He knew that today's shot would probably not be the last.

* *

Once on board the train it took Manning only a second to scale the thin metal ladder to the top of car 345, lift up the sturdy tarp cover, which was held in place by a series of bungy cords, and descend into the empty interior. Normally, the loud rattling noise would have made it difficult to think, but Manning couldn't help but think about what caused the shot to drift. Manning speculated that it had to be the wind. Every other factor, right down to the exact weight of the bullet, had been taken into consideration. The sniper would replay the shot over and over again for the next five months.

CHAPTER TWENTY-EIGHT

M anning's Ironman watch ticked off every hundredth of a second, but each full minute still seemed to take an eternity. From the inside of the car, it felt as if the train were inching forward. Manning knew it was only a matter of time before the Secret Service uncovered the hide. The sniper just hoped they wouldn't find it in the next twenty minutes.

When the watch signaled eighteen minutes had passed, Manning got off the steel floor of the vibrating car and secured the rifle. Grabbing the clear plastic bag containing the refuse of two days in the hide, the assassin climbed up the ladder, cautiously lifted the tarp and peered at the landscape. The farmland had given way to more trees, and the train was passing by some small, run-down houses on the outskirts of St. Cloud. Baptista had told Manning that the train would reach the bridge over the Mississippi nineteen minutes after the sniper boarded.

When the train was half way across the bridge, Manning stood fully exposed on the narrow platform between cars. As soon as the cars reached the other side of the river, the sniper jumped off the train with the rifle and the garbage bag and scrambled down to the river embankment. The change of clothes was exactly where Baptista said it would be. The sniper did not notice a second bag a hundred yards away. The bag contained a few of Rudy Bradford's belongings.

* *

The limousine skidded to a halt directly in front of the stair dolly. Agent Parish dashed around and, after confirming it was clear, pulled open the door. Led by Agent McGowan, Colfax, his daughters and his wife were escorted up the stairs and onto the plane.

Luke Parish followed behind and slammed the door shut from the outside. McGowan sealed it from inside. Instantly, the plane lurched forward—leaving Parish standing alone on top of the stair dolly. The whole operation took eleven seconds. Within a half minute of the limousine's arrival on the tarmac, the plane was airborne and heading back to St. Paul.

"Is everybody okay?" asked McGowan, looking past Colfax, toward the candidate's wife and two girls, who had begun to calm down. Everyone nodded in the affirmative.

"Good. We have reason to believe your husband—and your dad," said McGowan, looking at the daughters, "was the target of an assassin." Catherine, Colfax's oldest daughter, began to sob upon hearing the word "assassin." Colfax put his arms around her shoulders and drew her close. McGowan continued. "Law enforcement officials are searching the dorms and wooded areas surrounding the campus. They haven't found anyone—or anything—yet."

"I didn't hear anything," said Linda. "Are you sure it was a shot?"

"I'm almost positive, Mrs. Colfax," responded McGowan.

"It was," said Colfax softly, as the reality of what had happened began to hit him. McGowan turned and looked at him. Returning his look, Colfax said, "I've heard the sound before—when I was in Vietnam." McGowan knew that Colfax earned a Purple Heart in Vietnam, but because the governor never mentioned it in his speeches and refused to highlight it in his campaign literature or commercials, the agent didn't think to ask Colfax for confirmation.

"Unfortunately, I don't know anything more at this time—other than that you're all safe. We'll be met in St. Paul by additional security forces and be escorted directly to the governor's mansion. You'll be provided information as it becomes available."

"Was anybody hurt?" asked Linda Colfax.

"No," said McGowan, adding, "according to preliminary reports."

"Thank you, Agent McGowan," said Colfax.

"You'll have to excuse me," said McGowan, barely acknowledging Colfax. McGowan viewed the fact that an assassin was able to fire a shot at his candidate as a personal failure. "I have to radio the command center." McGowan silently motioned for Colfax to follow him to the back of the plane. There, McGowan continued, "The Secret Service can make available counseling resources for you and your family. Would you like me to make any arrangements?"

"Thank you—that won't be necessary. I know Linda will be fine, and she and I will work through this with the girls."

"Please let me know if there is anything we can do."

"I appreciate that, but you and your team's actions have been more than sufficient." Colfax paused before asking, "Did you hear a second shot?"

"No. Did you?"

"I don't think so—but if there was one, I probably wouldn't have been able to hear it anyway. Your chop block had me to the ground so fast that my head is still ringing," said Colfax, smiling.

"I'm sorry about that. You'll probably be a little sore tomorrow."

"Tomorrow? Hell, I'm sore right now," said Colfax, rubbing his wrist, which had begun to swell from his attempt to break the fall.

"We need to get some ice on that immediately," said McGowan, taking Colfax's wrist and gently pressing around it to detect any fractures or breaks. He felt none.

"How much do you think the bullet missed by?" asked Colfax. McGowan was surprised by the calm manner in which the candidate asked the question.

"I think it passed between the two of us."

"And how much space separated us at the time?"

"About twelve inches."

"Sweet Jesus—maybe my old friend was in Heaven watching over us."

McGowan, like Colfax, was Catholic; unlike Colfax, McGowan had given up on the religion after his brother was paralyzed.

Colfax suddenly remembered the letter that Burnett had given him just before the shot and reached into his pocket. Opening the letter, he immediately recognized Wilhoit's immaculate penmanship.

> Dear Robert,
>
> I hope and pray that this letter finds you in good and healthy spirits. I know you are busy campaigning, so I shall keep this note short. I was reading the Bible this morning and came across this quote. It is one of my favorites and I immediately thought of you. It is from Jeremiah, 29:11.
>
> "For I know well the plans I have in mind for you says the Lord, plans for your well-being. Plans to give you a future full of hope."
>
> Robert, you are now in a position to help a great number of people—to give others a future full of hope. I know you will do everything in your power to live up to these words.
>
> You and your family are in my thoughts and prayers everyday.
>
> God bless,
>
> Otto

"Is everything all right, sir?" said McGowan as the tears streaked down Colfax's face.

Colfax had forgotten McGowan was even standing next to him. Turning back toward the agent, he said, "Do you believe in divine intervention?"

McGowan gave the candidate a quizzical look.

Colfax handed him the letter. "If I would not have reached for this letter when I did, I'm not sure if I ever would have."

McGowan read the letter and felt a chill go down his spine.

* *

Myrna Nilan was an enthusiastic bird watcher. The hobby not only occupied her free time, she also enjoyed it during the slower moments during her catering job at the St. Cloud Civic Center. As she sat staring out over the river, enjoying the cool breeze, Nilan noticed an eagle approaching from the north. Peering through the small binoculars she kept in her purse, Nilan followed the eagle's progress as it passed over the speeding train that was crossing the Mississippi. She did not see Manning jump from the train.

"Break's over, Myrna," said her manager, sticking his head out the balcony door. "The group in Conference Room A needs a pot of decaf."

Nilan was just setting her binoculars down when her eye caught a slight movement on the river embankment. She focused on the area. To her surprise, she saw a person dressed in camouflage. Nilan strained to see more, but even the person's face was camouflaged. She did make out that the person was wearing a backpack and appeared to have a dark bag of some sort.

"Myrna, they need the coffee right now," said her manager loudly. Always a nervous woman who liked to please, Nilan set down her binoculars and returned to work. It would be more than twelve hours before Nilan reported what she saw, and it would take almost six months for the Secret Service to figure out what she had really seen.

* *

Sean McGowan arrived back at the governor's mansion at a little after four o'clock in the afternoon—barely an hour after the assassination attempt—and headed directly to the command center on the ground floor. He was instantly in three-way communication with Washington and the command center at St. John's.

"Gibraltar is secure and resting at the Ice Castle," said McGowan, using the codename for the governor's mansion. "What else have you found?"

"Nothing," replied Agent Brix, who had returned from the scene and was still working feverishly to determine if there had even been a shot. "We've rechecked every dorm and building on campus with no results. We are using every available resource in the area, and we're expanding our search out from the site of the target."

281

"Have you found the bullet?" asked the Max Walters, the director of the Secret Service from his office in Washington, D.C.

"No. But then we don't have available the most sophisticated detectors. Can you rush some up here?"

"I'll take care of that," said Walters. "The FBI's got some equipment, I'm sure. You'll have it ASAP."

"What's the status of the perimeter?" asked McGowan.

"The entire campus is secure," responded Brix. "All cars, persons and their possessions are being checked as they leave campus. We're also putting together a search team to comb every inch of the campus. As we speak, three helicopters are overhead with infrared and metal detectors. They haven't found anything yet."

"How large of an area are they covering, Agent Brix?" asked McGowan.

"We're presently working a twenty-five-square-mile radius. That's up from a ten-mile radius an hour ago. We're moving up to a 100-mile radius."

"I am not sure a hundred miles is going to do it," replied McGowan. "Have you secured the eastern side of the campus?"

"It falls within the twenty-five-square-mile radius."

"I know it does, goddammit," said McGowan, losing his temper with the junior agent. "What I meant is, have you secured all the ingress and egress points along the eastern side of the campus?"

"Yes, we have," responded Brix in a defensive tone.

"When?" asked McGowan.

"Within the last twenty minutes."

"So they were unsecured for forty minutes?"

Agent Brix snapped back, "You said the shot came from the west! That was our first priority. We secured the western perimeter first."

"I said I thought the shot came from the west. I didn't tell you—for a fact—that it came from that direction. Nor did I tell you not to secure the eastern flank!"

"Goddammit, I'm the only Secret Service agent here. I'm relying on local law enforcement—and I had to prioritize my resources," said Brix.

"Hold on," said Walters sternly, imposing some order on the conversation. "Nobody is blaming anyone for anything. Agent Brix, you did the right thing by concentrating on the dorms. I think what Agent McGowan is trying to say is that if the assassin did operate from the western perimeter, he—or they—have had an hour head start—even a hundred-square-mile-radius search may now be irrelevant."

"What do you suggest?" asked Brix.

"Let's keep up the air search. But I'll try to get you as many additional resources as possible to search the area," said the director. "I want you to report back as soon as you find the bullet or the sniper's location. In the meantime, I'll get you the equipment you need."

"I need it fast. We've got about four more hours of daylight."

* *

The sun was just beginning to dip toward the horizon when Ted Cochrane, a twenty-two-year-old cop from St. Cloud called in to help with the search, stumbled upon a broken branch and some footprints. He immediately radioed the command center. In minutes, the entire surrounding area had been cordoned off. Within a half an hour, casts of the shoe print were packed off to the FBI's lab in Quantico, Virginia. Experts in forensic analysis were already on their way to St. John's to help with the investigation.

* *

About the same time the experts were tracing Manning's diversionary tracks back to the hide, the sniper was crossing back over the Fourth Street Bridge. Halfway across, Manning—facing north, away from the bridge—heaved the rifle into the Mississippi River below. It settled neatly on the silty bottom.

Manning continued across the bridge and located the motorcycle wedged between the two dilapidated garages. The key was under the rear tire.

Three hours later, using only back roads, Manning was back in St. Paul.

* *

Four hours after the footprints were first discovered, the FBI experts determined that there was no way they could have been left by the escaping sniper; the impressions suggested that they were at least twelve hours old, possibly more. If they were left by the sniper, and the experts believed they were, they were meant as a diversion. The good news was that they did lead to the igloo hide. Using the hide as the location of the shot, the FBI was able to find the bullet an hour later.

* *

The discovery of the hide confirmed beyond a doubt that there had been an attempt to assassinate Robert Colfax. CNN was the first to confirm the story and began leading its half-hour news with it, starting at 8:00 P.M. By 8:15, the networks were interrupting their regularly scheduled broadcasts. By nine o'clock, the major networks had live reports from their local affiliates in Minneapolis and St. Paul.

The following morning, *Today* and *Good Morning American* devoted half-hour segments to the story. Myrna Nilan listened to Katie Couric recount the story and couldn't believe her ears. She turned on Minnesota Public Radio for more information after the NBC anchor moved to another story.

* *

In room 108 of the State Office Building at precisely 8:00 A.M., Pete Sawyer and Michael Nathan, the spokesman for the Secret Service, squeezed past dozens of reporters and took their place in front of the bright lights. Each read short, carefully scripted statements that were covered live on national television. Pete Sawyer was the first to take questions.

"Anne Strong, *Washington Herald*," said Strong forcefully, edging out the local reporters for the first question. "What can you tell us about the condition of the governor—both physically and mentally?"

"The governor and his family are fine—both physically and mentally." Sawyer scanned the crowd, ready to answer the next question.

"And what is the current status of the search? Do you have any clues about motives of the assassin?" Sawyer looked at Nathan as if to say, "This is your question."

"The Secret Service, in cooperation with the FBI, the Minnesota State Patrol and the Stearns County Sheriff's Office, are still in the process of gathering all the information. At this time, it would be inappropriate to speculate on who the assassin or assassins might be and what their motive is."

"John Sykora, Minnesota Public Radio. You said 'assassins.' Do you have reason to believe more than one person was involved in the attempt?"

"No. But we're not ruling anything out," said Nathan.

"Where are you concentrating your search, and is there anything the public can do to help?" pressed Sykora.

"On the chance that the assassin is monitoring the news, I would prefer not to disclose the area or areas that we are searching. With regard to your second question, if anyone was in the vicinity of St. John's yesterday and saw anyone or anything, we would appreciate hearing from them."

"Martha Brown, *New York Times*. Can you provide any information on motives? Governor Colfax has taken a number of controversial stands. Is it possible that the attack is related to his position on abortion, which is at odds with that of the Catholic Church?"

"We aren't ruling anything in or out at this time," answered Nathan.

"What about his position on immigration?" pressed Brown.

"We're not ruling anything out," said Nathan, pointing his finger in the direction of the next questioner.

"Is the governor going to continue campaigning?"

"Yes. Governor Colfax and his family will not be deterred by this cowardly attack," said Sawyer. "He intends to resume his campaign immediately."

"Where is the governor now?"

"The governor and his family are at a private location. He will be making a public statement later this afternoon."

Anne Strong shot up again and blurted out over the dozen other questions that were being asked simultaneously, "How did the assassin escape? Specifically, how did the Secret Service allow this to happen, and what are you doing to prevent this from happening in the future?"

Michael Nathan knew the second question was coming. It still didn't make it any more palatable. "In response to your first question, we believe the assailant—or assailants—left on foot and then used a car, bike, or train to escape. It is possible that more than one—or all three—were used in combination."

A hundred miles away, in the comfort of her small apartment, Nilan heard the word "train."

"How did the Secret Service let this happen?" asked Strong, reminding Nathan that he still had one more question to answer.

"The Secret Service succeeded in its ultimate mission—protecting Governor Colfax and his family. However, we are assessing the assault, and a report will be made available to Congress after the investigation is complete. In response to your last question, all relevant lessons learned from this investigation will be incorporated into the operating procedures of future Secret Service activities."

Sawyer then looked at his watch and declared, "Last question."

John Sykora, using a page out of Anne Strong's book, jumped up and asked, "Is there any credence to the so-called Gibraltar Conspiracy?"

Sawyer and Nathan looked at one another for a second, trying to determine who would answer the question. Both were familiar with the phrase. Eventually, Nathan answered, "We have no reason to believe at this time that the assassination attempt was part of a larger conspiracy. But, as I said earlier, we are not ruling anything out."

"Thank you," said Sawyer as he and Nathan squeezed past the throng of reporters still shouting questions and pressing microphones in their faces.

CHAPTER TWENTY-NINE

S ean McGowan was temporarily put in charge of the assassination investigation for two reasons: he was the most experienced Secret Service agent in the Minneapolis-St. Paul region, and he needed something to do. He had been taken off Colfax's protective detail until after he could be debriefed on the assassination attempt.

McGowan called his first meeting for 9:00 A.M., the day after the shooting. Around the large conference table sat two officials from the Federal Bureau of Investigation, two new Secret Service agents, a high-ranking official from the Minnesota State Patrol, the adjutant general of the Minnesota National Guard, and the sheriff of Stearns County.

"So far," McGowan started, "we know two things. One, the footprints that were found late last night were meant to deceive us. Second, early this morning, we found the bullet. It was a custom-made 750-grain, depleted uranium bullet. Whoever was gunning for the governor was not messing around. They were well prepared, and we have reason to believe that Father Otto Wilhoit's death may have been part of the plot."

"By killing Wilhoit—and assuming that Colfax would attend the funeral—the assassin would have had the benefit of knowing almost exactly where Colfax would be at a certain date and time," said Lance Wenner, the Stearns County sheriff.

"Precisely. The assassin created the two elements that any successful sniper needs—knowledge of when and where the target would appear," replied McGowan.

"Are the results of Wilhoit's autopsy available?" inquired Frank Bell, the senior FBI agent at the table.

"Soon—his body has been retrieved and the bureau's top coroner is conducting it as we speak. We should have an answer within the hour."

"Have any other tracks been found?" asked Bell, looking directly at McGowan. He was not happy that McGowan had been given the role of lead investigator. He was even less pleased that he had to defer to a Secret Service agent twenty years his junior.

"No."

"So we still don't know what direction the assassin fled after firing the shot?"

"That's correct."

"And by now, all the National Guard troops have made a fucking mess out of the area up there," said Bell.

"Look, Mr. Bell," said Adjutant General Dusty Larson, "we were asked to help search the area for an armed assailant. We're weren't given orders not to break any branches or to leave the ground undisturbed. We did our job as we were ordered to do it!"

"Hold on, General. No one is accusing your troops of any wrongdoing. Your men have done a good job, on short notice, under stressful conditions," said McGowan, trying to calm the nerves in the room. "Based on our preliminary interviews, we speculate that the assailant either had a car hidden along County Road 53—along the eastern side of campus. Or he escaped on one of the trains."

"How long did it take for you to shut down the roads around campus?" asked Bell.

"Forty minutes," replied McGowan, knowing that Bell was going to use the answer to embarrass the Secret Service. Bell did exactly that.

"Forty minutes! Jesus H. Christ, you mean that it's possible that he was halfway to Minneapolis, Duluth or Fargo before you even shut down the roads? The guy could have easily covered fifty miles without arousing any suspicion."

"You're right, Frank."

"You're goddamn right I'm right. What the fuck were you guys doing?"

"Listen, detective," said McGowan, fighting to keep his composure. "It's the job of the Secret Service to protect those we are charged with protecting. Our primary responsibility is to ensure the safety of our principals. That is exactly what we did in this case. In a perfect world, with unlimited resources, we could have done everything you suggested. We did not. Now, our mission is to find the person or persons responsible for this attack. If you are unwilling to provide constructive criticism, I will ask that you be removed from the case. Have I made myself clear?"

Bell stared hard at the agent before spitting out a yes.

"Good! Then I suggest we get back to the business at hand." Continuing, McGowan said, "The Secret Service psychologist has put together a preliminary analysis of a possible assassin. We believe the person in his or her late twenties, former military, politically conservative views, possibly racist and may have a real or perceived grudge with Colfax."

"Any height or weight description?" asked Roy Marker.

"We believe the assailant probably weighs between 120 and 145 pounds. We believe the shoe prints that we found cannot be trusted to provide any useful information—they were fakes. But, based on the depth of the impression, the FBI believe the person weighs somewhere in that range."

"Has a general description gone out on the wires?" asked Bell.

"Yes, but it's not really much of a description. The airport and the bus and train stations have all been provided the general description. We have also notified the state patrols in Wisconsin, Iowa, and the Dakotas."

For the next half an hour, McGowan gave everyone at the table very specific instructions. The two Secret Service agents were to follow up on the leads at the university and interview everyone who might have information about the attack. The FBI team was to take the lead in testing the area around the hide for clues. Anything found there—hair samples, feces samples, food remnants—was to be analyzed. The National Guard troops were instructed to continue their search but to keep their eyes open for signs of human activity—specifically, broken branches and footprints.

McGowan concluded the meeting by directing Peter Tingley and Dan Piche, the two Secret Service agents, to re-interview the engineers of the two trains and lead a thorough search of each train.

* *

Myrna Nilan picked up the phone and dialed 411 after Minnesota Public Radio ended its live coverage of the new conference. An automated voice asked Nilan for the city she wanted to call.

"St. Paul," she replied.

"Name?" asked the automated voice.

"The Secret Service." There was a lengthy pause and then a human answered and said, "Here is your number."

Nilan scribbled it down and dialed.

"Secret Service," answered the receptionist.

"Hello. I was just listening to MPR, and I think I saw something that might be related to yesterday's attack on Governor Colfax."

"One moment, ma'am." It was about the tenth call the receptionist had handled in the last few minutes. She transferred it to Dan Piche.

"This is Agent Piche. I understand that you might have some information."

"Yes. Yesterday afternoon, I was working at the St. Cloud Civic Center, and I was taking a break on a balcony overlooking the Mississippi when I noticed a bald eagle. I followed it for a while, until I saw something on the edge of the river. When I looked closer, it was a person in camouflage."

"Where precisely did you see this person? Was he directly across from you?"

"No. He was further down. Under the Fourth Street train bridge."

"And how far was that from where you were?"

"I don't know. Maybe 200 yards."

"And you could see that far?" asked Piche skeptically.

"Oh, I'm sorry. I had a pair of binoculars."

"A pair of binoculars?" Piche was becoming convinced the caller was just another in a long line of nuts and crackpots.

"I'm a bird watcher. I'm telling you, I saw someone," replied Nilan, definitively. "He was wearing camouflage, and he appeared to be holding a bag of some sort. There was also something attached to his back."

"What's your name again, ma'am?"

"Myrna. Myrna Nilan."

"Is there anything else you can tell me?"

"No, sir. I was on break and had to get back to work."

"Well, thank you. May I have your number, in case we have to contact you again." Nilan gave Piche her number.

"I'm sorry I didn't call sooner. I thought it strange when I saw the person. But I didn't hear about what had happened to Governor Colfax until this morning."

An hour after Nilan's call, the Secret Service had located the clothes that Raphael Baptista had planted on the shore of the Mississippi. He had not expected the Secret Service to find the clothes so quickly. But it worked to his advantage. It was better to have an identified source lead the Secret Service to the clothes than an anonymous caller.

* *

The anonymous call came later the same morning. Baptista made it from a pay phone next to a fast-food restaurant on the outskirts of St. Cloud. He was on the phone for no more than five seconds.

The answering machine, which the Secret Service quickly setup after being deluged with calls, asked each caller to clearly state their name and telephone number and to leave a detailed message. The recording informed the caller that the Secret Service would return all calls. Baptista smiled. Talking to a machine gave him a convenient reason for not leaving either a name or telephone number.

"Hello," said Baptista, using a false voice. "I was walking on the Fourth Street Bridge last night about 7:30, and I saw someone throw what looked like a piece of metal into the river. I don't know if it's related to yesterday's shooting, but I suggest you search the river under the bridge."

Under normal circumstances, it would have taken the Secret Service a few days to confirm and follow up on the lead, but with the discovery of clothes, as a result of Myrna Nilan lead, they dredged up the Barrett .50 caliber less than twenty-four hours after it had been thrown into the murky river.

Within two hours of its recovery, the rifle was traced back to Fort Bragg. An hour after that, Russ Walker, the Army sergeant who originally sold Bradford the weapon, was telling the Secret Service he had no idea where Bradford was, why he wanted the gun, or how he intended to use it. Walker said he sold the gun because he needed the money. He pleaded that he wasn't involved with Bradford, and he had no idea where the gun dealer was. In fact, he said, he hadn't seen Bradford since he sold him the gun. Walker swore he did not supply any bullets to Bradford.

By 3:00 P.M., the Secret Service had a search warrant for Bradford's trailer home. Shortly thereafter, the articles on Governor Colfax were found in the trailer and faxed to psychologists at the Secret Service's headquarters. By 8:00 P.M., the lead psychologist had drafted a preliminary report saying that Rudolph Emerson Bradford had the personality traits of a person likely to attempt an assassination of a political leader with Colfax's beliefs.

The following morning, the Secret Service, in cooperation with the FBI, commenced a long and arduous search for Rudolph Bradford.

＊　＊

Win Murdock had already finished his caesar salad and a cup of French onion soup by the time the maître d' escorted Jeffery Payne into the private dining room in the back of the Congressional Country Club. As soon as the maître d' was out of the room, Payne whispered, "He missed."

"I know it, goddamnit!" said Murdock more loudly than usual. "What the fuck happened?"

Payne did not look Murdock directly in the eyes. "We knew going in that the odds of success were less than fifty percent."

290

"I know the goddamn odds—and I'm paying your professional assassin three million dollars to produce results. I don't like to pay for the fifty percent that fails. The remainder will be paid only if Colfax is terminated."

"Of course," replied Payne, trying to appease Murdock and, if possible, get him to lower his voice a little. "I understand."

"I'm not sure you do," Murdock said with a coolness in his voice that Payne had not heard before—and was sure he didn't want to hear again. "If Colfax becomes president, he'll shake up this town in a way that leaves you and me on the outside looking in. I stand to lose at least a billion dollars each year that asshole is in office. More if his environmental plans force me to upgrade our oil refineries. I'm talking billions—not millions. And you can kiss your dream of becoming director of the CIA goodbye. If Colfax has his way, there won't even be a CIA."

"I understand, Win. It's just that the Secret Service is going to tighten up their protection even more. I'm not sure if we can even get close again."

"Just shut up for a minute," Murdock said to Payne, who was visibly annoyed at being addressed like a private in the Army, "I have to think."

Payne said nothing until the maître d' came to ask for his order five minutes later.

Ten minutes after that, the maître d' was back with Murdock's usual entree and Payne's grilled chicken caesar salad. Murdock still had not said a word. Finally, after taking a few bites of his food, he spoke.

"I think I've got a new contingency plan. It's not without risk, however. But if the coalition's continuing ad campaign against Colfax is unsuccessful, we might even be better situated if he somehow wins. He will still have to die—we just have to be prepared to do it before he actually takes office in January 2001."

"What?" said Payne, thinking Murdock had lost his grip on reality. "That presupposes that Colfax selects a vice president who is supportive of our interests."

"Exactly, Jeffery, exactly. And that is why I have to work on grooming a candidate who would be acceptable for Colfax and amenable to our interests."

"Do you have anybody in mind?"

"As a matter of fact, I do."

"And who would that be?"

"Elizabeth Vandiver."

"Vandiver?" said Payne, studying Murdock's face and contemplating the name. As he did, he slowly began to smile. "She's a female—which gives Colfax the gender balance that every man running for president needs—and she has impeccable bipartisan credentials. Vandiver would fit Colfax like a glove."

"She also has the benefit of being rejected by Governor Prescott as his running mate. In the eyes of the pro-choice, feminist crowd, she is the political martyr du jour," added Murdock.

"That's right. The conservatives forced Prescott to renounce her as a possible running mate. The question is, will she do it?"

Murdock just smiled. "Oh, she'll do it. The real question is whether Colfax will fall for the bait and ask her to be his running mate."

"Care to share your plan with me?"

"In due time, Jeffery, in due time. In the meantime, I want the coalition to continue with the character assassination of Mr. Colfax. But if your assassin avoids the manhunt being waged, the remaining money can be collected by eliminating Colfax on November 8. I know exactly where he'll be on the Wednesday morning after the election, if he wins."

"Jesus, Win, you're playing with fire. Vandiver will help Colfax in the polls. I hope you know what you're doing."

"I do."

"What can I pass on to my contact?"

"Tell him that the assassin should return to St. Paul as soon as things cool down—and stay there. In the meantime, you can return to Langley and your regular responsibilities."

With a wave of his hand, Murdock beckoned the maître d', ordered a cup of coffee and signed the bill to his account at the restaurant. "Thank you, Sam. As always, your service was impeccable. Add an additional ten percent to your normal gratuity. I'm in a good mood."

Sam Matheny bowed ever so slightly, thanked Murdock for his generosity and left the room.

* *

Catherine Colfax was staring out the second-story window of her family's summer cottage on Madeleine Island, listening to Ricky Martin on her Walkman. She did not hear her father knock. Her sister, Colleen, who was writing in her journal, did.

"Hi, Dad," said Colleen nonchalantly, as though her father had just come home from a hard day's work—rather than having dodged an assassin's bullet.

"Hey, Pumpkin," replied Colfax, lightly kissing the top of his daughter's head. "How's Cath?" he asked, signaling toward his oldest daughter, who was oblivious to his entrance. Colleen just shrugged her shoulders.

"How long as she been listening to music?"

"I don't know—an hour or two."

"What have you been doing?"

"Writing in my diary."

Colfax could only imagine what a ten-year-old would write about a possible assassination attempt on her father. He hoped it wouldn't affect her too severely.

"I'd like to talk with Catherine."

"Sure, Dad," replied Colleen, going over to the window and tapping her sister on the shoulder.

Without taking her headphones off, Catherine turned around to look at her father. She then turned back to the window.

"Cathy," pleaded Colleen.

"It's okay, Colleen," said Colfax, laying a hand softly on his younger daughter's shoulder. "Why don't you go help your Mom—she's downstairs."

Colleen gave her father a smile and left the room.

Colfax moved closer to his oldest daughter and kneeled down next to the chair where she was seated with her knees pulled in, tight against her chest. For a minute, he just looked out the window as she did at the blue-gray water of Lake Superior, which extended as far as the eye could see.

It wasn't until he noticed the tears streaming down his daughter's cheeks that he gently lifted the headphones off her ears and placed her hands in his. "It'll be all right, Catherine," he whispered. "We're safe now. No one is going to hurt us."

She tried to say something, but her sobbing became more pronounced, and it was difficult for her to speak between the gasps. Colfax did the only thing he could— he pulled her close and hugged her.

Finally, after about a minute, she was able to articulate what she had been trying to say. "Daddy," she wheezed, "I don't want you to run for president."

"Catherine . . ." he started to say, but his daughter pressed forward with her thoughts.

"—I don't want you to die."

The statement hit Colfax with the force of Mack truck. *How do I explain concepts like duty, commitment and courage to a sixteen-year-old?* he thought.

"Catherine, I'm not going to die."

"What about yesterday? You could've died. It was just luck that the bullet missed."

Colfax knew that his daughter was right and struggled with his response, but he quickly settled on the truth—leaving out the story of Wilhoit's letter.

"You are right, Catherine. I could have died. And you are right to be concerned with my safety. There are probably a lot of people who want to see me dead."

"Then why don't you just drop out? We don't need the money. You could spend more time with Mom and us."

"It's not that simple, Catherine."

"Yes, it is," she pleaded.

"No, it's not," replied Colfax, looking directly into his daughter's green eyes. "Catherine, there will be times in your life when you are faced with great challenges. How you address those challenges will come down to character—what's inside you. In my case, I believe I was meant to be president—I believe strongly that I am the best person to lead this country. And it's very important to me. It also means that I must be willing to make some sacrifices for what I believe. The biggest of which is not being able to spend as much time with you, Colleen, and your mom as I would like. I pray every day that I have made the right decision—and what my heart tells me is that I have a unique opportunity to make the world we live in a better place." Colfax paused to see if Catherine was following. She was. "Unfortunately, that means that our family must also make some sacrifices. I know it might not seem fair to you that you have to make some sacrifices, but the Lord has blessed us with much, Catherine. It is our obligation to serve Him by living up to that potential. I know this probably doesn't make a lot of sense—but some day I hope it will."

"I know you'd be a great president, Dad. And I want you to be president. I just want my dad, too."

"I know, Honey, I know," said Colfax, stroking his daughter's long black hair. "I can't let the actions of some coward derail me from a path that I believe God has asked me to pursue."

"I understand, Dad."

"Everything's going to be okay. The men and women protecting me are the best in the world. And because of yesterday's attack, they're only going to get better."

"They did get us out of the cemetery in a hurry, didn't they?" said Catherine, mopping the tears from her cheeks.

"Did they ever. We were in the limo and at the airport before I even knew what happened," said Colfax, cracking a smile. "They don't even give you a chance to get scared until the whole thing is over."

"Do you ever get scared, Dad?"

"All the time."

"What scares you the most?"

Colfax pondered the question. The truthful answer was that he was most fearful that his family might some day be the target of an attack. He wasn't sure if his daughter was ready yet for that answer, so he gave the next most truthful answer.

"I guess it would be making the wrong decision."

"What do you mean?"

"Well," Colfax said after a long pause, "let me give you an example. As governor, I make decisions almost every day that affect people's lives. Often, I don't have as much information as I would like to make a decision—and that scares me. It scares me even more, however, when I have to make a decision knowing that whatever I decide, someone will win and someone else will lose."

"So what do you do?"

"Usually, I pray and search my soul for the decision that I think will benefit the most people for the longest period of time." His daughter turned back toward the window and stared at the choppy, steel-colored waters.

"I think I understand why you feel you have to run, Dad. And I think you'll be a great president. I'm just afraid."

"I know, I know . . ." said Colfax hugging his daughter.

* *

McGowan knew Russ Ernst was a leading expert in his field, but he was still displeased with the coroner's report.

"It's difficult to prove, Agent McGowan," Ernst said. "I cannot, with any certainty, say that Wilhoit was poisoned. Prostaglandin occurs naturally in the human body. It's not uncommon to find high levels in the victim of a massive heart attack. And while it is true that it could be used to kill someone, there is no visible point of entry on Wilhoit's body. I'm sorry."

* *

After concentrating in and around St. Cloud for the first few days, the primary focus of the search switched to North Carolina, where it was believed that Bradford was using his hunting and survival skills to escape capture in the rugged terrain of the Nantahala National Forest. The transfer of the search allowed McGowan to resume his functions on Colfax's detail.

* *

Since her mother's death nine years ago, Stephanie Freeberg had visited her father every Sunday for dinner. With her new job and the approaching election, the visits had become less frequent. She and her two sisters worried that their father was lonely, so they bought him a computer. Freeberg was surprised by how competent he had become on it.

"How are you enjoying the computer, Dad?"

"It's taken a while but the Internet is fascinating. I'm becoming quite the surfer. Actually, I spend a lot of time in a chat room for amateur gardeners. I had no idea so many of us were out there. I've picked up a number of useful tips. I'm also using it to stay abreast of politics. The amount of information available is overwhelming."

"Really," said Freeberg, who had never known her father to take an active interest in politics.

"Oh, yes. I'm quite a fan of Ellen Moriarty. I read her *Moriarty Minute* religiously."

"You don't say." Freeberg was seeing her father in a new light.

"I saw her on the *McNeil-Lehrer News Hour* a few months ago and have been following her ever since. I have her site bookmarked. I've even seen her at the club a few times."

* *

Dirk Osborne understood where McGowan was coming from. Someone had tried to kill the man he was charged with protecting and he wanted to help bring that person to justice. But Osborne also knew the Secret Service needed agents in the field. They were still stretched dangerously thin, and he needed his best agent on protective duty, not searching for the assassin.

"Sean, this discussion is over. I need you in the field."

"But—"

"No—no buts. The FBI can handle the search."

"The fuck they can. They still haven't been able to locate that anti-abortionist who blew up the clinics in Alabama and Georgia two years ago."

"Look. We know Bradford is our man. We've found his clothes. The shoe prints are his. We located the rifle. The clues in his trailer suggest he was opposed to Colfax's positions on gays in the military, immigration and a host of other issues. Everything fits."

"What about the bullets? Where does a guy like Bradford get depleted uranium, 750-grain bullets with a ballistic coefficient of .93? His friend at Fort Bragg didn't supply them to him, and you can't just pick up something like that at Wal-Mart. The same thing with the specially formulated gunpowder. Someone had to be helping him. And what about Krebsbach?" continued McGowan. "The guy said he saw Wilhoit running with someone the morning he died. Who was it?"

296

"Two things. First, Bradford probably could get specially made bullets. If the guy could get a gun like that, it's not a stretch to assume he could also get the bullets. And two, Krebsbach said it could have been Bradford."

"He also said he couldn't tell for sure."

"Kresbach also said Wilholt was having difficulty breathing—like he could have had a heart attack."

"I don't buy it."

"Look, Sean. This conversation is over, I mean it. The FBI has sixty men looking for Bradford and a number of others looking into the very questions you are posing. We can't even afford one agent—we still have to protect the president, three major presidential candidates and shitload of other special events, including a growing 'Hot List' that now numbers over 500. The fact is, a decision has been made at a higher level than you and me. Wells has officially transferred the investigation over to the FBI."

What neither man knew was that Jeffery Payne had suggested in a side conversation to his old friend, Assistant Secretary of the Treasury George Wells—the man charged with overseeing the Secret Service—that he should transfer the responsibility of the investigation to the FBI. With the presidential campaign season in full swing, Wells happily agreed. On the other end, Win Murdock was using his relationship with the FBI director, Tom Geary, to speed up the transfer.

"Jesus, Dirk, we've been down this road before. Didn't we learn anything from the Kennedy assassination? We turned that investigation over to the FBI, and we still don't know the truth today. If there's a conspiracy, I don't trust them to uncover it."

CHAPTER THIRTY

Vice President Byrne secured the Democratic nomination on June 6, 2000, almost two months later than most experts had predicted, by winning seventy-five of New Jersey's 135 delegates. His less-than-charismatic speaking style, coupled with his less-than-bold policy decisions, left many Democratic activists hungering for a more fiery standard bearer. Reginald Greene, with his passionate calls for universal health care, received over thirty percent of the delegates—in spite of the public teachers unions' active opposition to his plan for school choice for low-income, inner-city children.

In mid-June, Terry Heikes, a long-time Democratic activist and a lukewarm delegate for the vice president, decided she was going to go to Los Angeles, the site of the Democratic National Convention, and create a little trouble. She had been in Chicago in 1968 and felt the Democratic Party of 2000 needed an injection of some 1960s' liberal activism. If no one else was going to do it, she would. In the basement office of her Boston home, she began the "Draft John Gordon" movement.

Heikes began by calling and outlining her strategy to a few fellow Massachusetts delegates who shared her beliefs. She met with a much more positive response than she had imagined. Most of her friends offered the names of others who might be sympathetic to the cause.

Heikes had also made a number of friends over the years at various national conventions. A surprising number of people active in 1968 were still working for change thirty-two years later. Almost everywhere she turned, her idea was warmly received. Especially from Greg Sajbel, a fellow veteran from the 1968 convention who lived in Newport, Rhode Island, where he operated a successful silk-screening and printing business.

"I love it," said Sajbel. "I'm so sick and tired of how lame our conventions have become. I almost decided to stay home this year. But then I thought about the prospect of C. Elliott Prescott becoming president, and I decided to give it one more go. But you know I'm just tired of always being against someone. I want to be for someone. Do you know what I mean?"

Heikes understood completely. "I knew I could count on you."

"Do you think Gordon will be up for the challenge of fighting for the nomination if we can orchestrate a legitimate floor movement in support of his candidacy?" asked Sajbel.

"I think so. I have a friend who was high up in his campaign before he dropped out last December. She says he's been itching to get back in—especially after seeing how well Greene has done."

"How do you think Greene will react? I'm not interested in weakening the vice president only to see Greene get the nomination. I'd love to see an African-American win the nomination. I just think he'd get slaughtered by Prescott in a general election. His position on vouchers would also ruin schools."

"I agree with your first assessment, but I have to admit that I kind of like his willingness to shake things up. The public schools in Boston are hellholes. More money hasn't solved a thing. I'm willing to give his ideas a chance. Why should the poorest children be confined to the worst schools? But look, I don't want to get into a philosophical discussion. We can talk about this issue after a bottle of wine. What I'd like to know is if your company can print up a few 'Draft Gordon' signs?"

"No problem. I can even have them shipped to L.A."

"You're a godsend, Greg. Do you know any other delegates who might be sympathetic to our cause?"

"I think so. Let me do some calling."

"Thanks, Greg. I'm really looking forward to seeing you next month. I think Gordon's got a shot at wresting the nomination from Byrne. Who knows? Maybe we still can change the world," replied Heikes, with a tinge of optimism in her voice.

"We almost did in '68. Why not in 2000? Keep the faith."

* *

Jeremiah Laughlin was a moderately successful businessman who was destined never to become too successful for two reasons. He devoted too much time to politics, and, more important, his archconservative views often offended prospective clients. In the 1992 campaign, Laughlin served as Dick Graham's Georgia coordinator. By the 1996 campaign, he had switched loyalties and was a regional coordinator for Stanley Cross. In 1999, Cross tapped him to be his manager for the 2000 campaign.

299

Although Elliott Prescott, like Vice President Byrne, had his party's nomination in his pocket by June, Laughlin was confident that the race was not over. He had one last ace up his sleeve. Laughlin had secured a prime-time speaking engagement for his candidate on the first night of the Republican National Convention. In return for praising Elliott Prescott and shying away from the issues of homosexuality, abortion, and women in the military, Stanley Cross was given thirty minutes to address the convention—and a national audience. Prescott saw it as throwing a small bone to the far-right wing of his party.

The promise to avoid the controversial issues meant little to Laughlin. It meant even less to Cross. Both men felt that the Republican Party had screwed the conservative wing in 1992 and 1996 by denying their annointed candidate an opportunity to speak at the convention. Cross had eight years of pent-up rage that he intended to unload on the Republican delegates, the national media, and every viewer who would be watching on national television. If his speech didn't ignite a firestorm across the country, he at least intended to go down in a fiery crash.

Laughlin was busily working the phones, contacting his wide network of conservative activists. He was, in his words, "dousing the countryside with gasoline." Cross just had to light the match with his speech.

* *

Anne Strong had been trying to land an interview with Linda Colfax for three weeks. Strong felt it might help her better report on the candidate. Linda Colfax, a fiercely private person, acceded to the *Washington Herald*'s reporter's request after some not so subtle prodding from Sawyer. The scheduled thirty-minute meeting was almost over when Strong started to probe into the psyche of Robert Colfax.

"What makes your husband tick? I mean, what has influenced his thinking? His maverick positions? His willingness to buck the system? Some of his inherent contradictions?"

"I wish I knew," replied Linda, letting out a mock breath of exasperation. "Bob has a very strong set of core beliefs. I think they were shaped by his years at St. John's and by his time in the Navy. St. John's, and in particular Father Otto Wilhoit, instilled in him a desire to serve. The Navy refined his commitment to honor and integrity. His political outlook, which I would define as a belief in limited government, probably comes from his rural upbringing. His parents never expected much, nor did they ask for much from government. His 'inherent contradictions,' as you called them, come from personal experience. His anti-gambling and anti-tobacco positions are directly related to his parents' deaths."

"What about gun control?"

"That's a little more complicated. I should probably let him explain it—but part of it comes from losing nine men in a savage fire fight on the Mekong Delta. The other part, I think, just comes from his belief that our founding fathers got it wrong on the Second Amendment. We would like to see the amendment rewritten in a more limiting form."

"So how would you describe your husband?"

"I call him a warrior priest."

"A what?"

Linda Colfax laughed. "A warrior priest. The warrior aspect comes from his military experience. Bob won't back down from a fight. He doesn't go looking for fights, but he will always stand up for what he thinks is right. He understands Washington, and I know he won't be afraid to mix it up. The priest part comes from St. John's. He has a strong sense of justice. Bob also believes that everyone is good at heart and that people can be motivated to do the right thing.

"The combination can be quite powerful. Over the course of history, a number of reformers have been warriors, and some have been priests. It's rare when the characteristics of both are found in the same person. I truly believe my husband will be a very special president."

* *

Elizabeth Vandiver was not surprised to hear from Win Murdock. He often paid her informal visits when he was in New York City, usually to learn of the latest Machiavellian maneuvers at the United Nations. Vandiver always made time for him on her schedule.

The ambassador was surprised when Murdock wanted to discuss national rather than international politics. The presidential campaign consumed most of their breakfast meeting.

Murdock's job was simplified because it was Vandiver, and not he, who brought up the subject of Robert Colfax.

"I think he's the wild card in this whole thing," said Vandiver. "I don't know if he takes away more votes from Byrne or Prescott. I mean, his liberal positions on gun control and the environment have to siphon votes from the vice president. But his conservative positions on school choice, tax reform, and Social Security bite into some traditional Republican supporters."

"I couldn't agree more, Elizabeth," said Murdock, taking a sip of coffee. "It could get a lot more interesting." Murdock let the phrase linger.

"How so?" said Vandiver, picking up on the secretive tone in Murdock's voice.

"Well, and I hope you take this in the spirit that it is intended because I have long been an avid admirer of yours, but I think you should consider coming out publicly in support of Colfax."

Vandiver was genuinely surprised.

"Now, don't get me wrong, I think it's well known in our circles that Robert Colfax and I have never seen eye to eye. However, from your perspective, I think casting your lot with the governor from Minnesota would be in your best interest."

Vandiver was intrigued. "Go on."

"Well, it's no secret that Prescott left you hanging when he caved into the right wing and announced you weren't even on his short list of vice presidential candidates. I think it was a horrendous mistake, but it can't be undone. And I don't think anyone in Democratic circles trusts you, especially a traditional Democrat like Byrne. He's too loyal to his base. Which means that you're an eminently qualified politician with no home—much like Robert Colfax."

"And it wouldn't hurt you, should Colfax win, that you'd at least have one friend in the administration," replied Vandiver, who knew exactly why Murdock contributed equally to both Democrats and Republicans.

Murdock just shrugged and smiled. "I think of it as a long-term investment. I don't think Colfax is going to win, but I do think the American public will be ready for a female president in either 2004 or 2008. And you, Madam Ambassador, are on the top of the list."

"Thank you, Win. I must say Colfax intrigues me. And, truthfully, I wouldn't mind sticking it to both parties."

Murdock smiled. If he played his cards right, he would not have to coerce her to do it, meaning he could use the video at a later time—in a game with even higher stakes.

The two continued to talk over breakfast and agreed that the best way to handle the situation would be for Vandiver to drop a not-so-subtle hint on a Sunday morning talk show that she was considering supporting Robert Colfax. Win Murdock promised to use his influence, as the major sponsor of the show, to get the moderator to ask some leading questions.

* *

Their lunch meetings had become almost a regularly scheduled event. Jeffery Payne didn't mind. Win Murdock held the key to his future, and he was only too happy to oblige.

"How did your meeting with Ambassador Vandiver go?"

"Better than expected. The contingency plan is almost a lock."

"Can you elaborate?"

"I can't share with you how I will leverage Vandiver. Suffice it to say, she'll do whatever I ask of her."

Payne just smiled. "Can you just outline the general nature of your thinking— of the plan."

"Certainly, Jeffery. The first and most desired outcome is that the coalition take care of Colfax through conventional character assassination and negative advertising. The second plan is, of course, utilizing your asset—who will only be used if Colfax wins outright or if he finishes with the most popular votes but does not receive a majority of the Electoral College votes. If he wins outright, Vandiver will become president when he dies. If, however, he only finishes first but doesn't receive a majority of the Electoral College votes, we can either proceed with the plan, or I can use my trump card on Ambassador Vandiver to discredit and embarrass Colfax. The scandal is of such a nature that it will give the House of Representatives or the Senate a clear reason for denying Colfax an Electoral College victory."

"It sounds as though you have thought this out, Win."

"Trust me, I have."

* *

George Wells had only become assistant secretary of the Treasury four months earlier, but he looked as though he was born for the part. He had chiseled facial features, dark hair that was beginning to gray at the temples and broad, tapered shoulders. Wells had also become very familiar with Sean McGowan, who had been calling him weekly since being removed from the Colfax case.

"Sean, I agree that your theory has merit, and, believe me, it will be pursued. All I'm saying is that it is premature to identify Holten, Inc., and its chairman as suspects in this case."

"Sir," pleaded McGowan, "with all due respect, the train's unusually high number of empty cars is suspicious. It would be irresponsible not to pursue this lead."

"We will pursue the lead, Sean. But we will do it properly. Even if the assassin used the train, that is not proof that Holten or anyone associated with Holten was aware of the plot."

"How do you explain the empty cars?"

"Our rail experts say that the recent merger of the two rail lines—and the organizational confusion it has created—could explain that."

"I don't buy it."

"You don't have to buy it, Agent McGowan," said Wells. "I'm telling you the way things are going to be. Our man is in the woods of North Carolina. He fits the profile—former military, racist, poor, dead parent, sexual inadequacies—the list goes on and on. It is only a matter of time before the FBI finds him."

"How can we be so sure Bradford is even in North Carolina?"

"Listen, Agent McGowan, you no longer have a need to know. Suffice it to say that the FBI has recently received information from a sister organization placing Bradford in North Carolina."

"Which sister organization?"

"If you must know, the CIA. But I don't have to tell you that that's confidential information."

"I understand, sir," said McGowan, who was aware that CIA assets were not to be used in the United States or against U.S. citizens. "Is the information reliable?"

"Of course, it is," replied Wells. He had never thought to question the source.

"Are there other suspects?" asked McGowan.

"Yes, but the clothing found by the river, along with Nilan's testimony, is pretty conclusive."

"What can you tell me about the other suspects?"

"The FBI has completed an initial search for all military and paramilitary snipers in this country and abroad. Based on the profile that their analysts put together, we have a list of thirty-seven additional suspects who meet the criteria of being between the ages twenty-five and forty, are right-handed, have at least four years of military experience, and graduated in the top five percent of their sniper class.

"Of those, we have accounted for thirty-four. Twelve are stationed abroad, eighteen have verifiable alibis, two are women—one is eight months' pregnant. Another is paralyzed from the waist down from a motorcycle accident, and another is a heroin addict who can barely shoot a needle into his arm."

"What about the other three?

"One, Derek Bosseli, a former Green Beret, is apparently hiking somewhere in New Zealand. We have the authorities looking for him. Another, Buford Hansen, is reportedly living in northwestern Idaho with a militia group. And the last one—the next most promising suspect—is Gerald Weber, a recently discharged Marine who was living in Los Angeles. He is apparently on the run. The FBI found a mocked-up poster of the president's head lined up in the crosshairs of a rifle scope in his apartment."

"Do any have a personal reason to want to kill Colfax?"

"No—not that we know of."

CHAPTER THIRTY-ONE

The Los Angeles Convention Center was jammed with Democratic party operatives, political junkies, activists, and elected officials from all over the country. No one, not even the media, was expecting an assault on the vice president's much-expected political coronation. No one except Terry Heikes, Greg Sajbel, and the fifty other members of the "Draft Gordon" brigade.

Working in teams of two, the group hit the convention floor Saturday night, the day before the convention started, and distributed thousands of flyers outlining the rationale for the "Draft Gordon" movement.

Marilyn Patterson, Martin Byrne's high-strung campaign manager, received word of the pamphlets almost immediately and flew into a rage. Wanting a peaceful convention, she ordered a group of campaign volunteers to intercept and destroy as much of the literature as possible. She also intimidated the convention center manager, a mild-mannered wisp of a man, into ceding to her request that the center's security officers be used to help put a halt to Heikes' group.

Larry Black, one of the security guards, thought he was just following orders. He had been told to stop the people who were distributing the yellow "Draft Gordon" flyers. He never expected to have his face plastered on CNN and every other national network by the evening's end.

Black spotted Sajbel at the end of the corridor and walked up to him. "Excuse me, sir, you're not allowed to hand out those flyers."

Sajbel, a veteran of the raucous 1968 Democratic convention in Chicago, had never had much respect for people in uniform. He had even less respect for "rent-a-cops," so he ignored Black and continued to hand out his literature.

"Sir," said Black, moving closer, "you're not authorized to be doing that."

"Doing what?" asked Sajbel, with open contempt.

Black detected Sajbel's sarcasm and instantly took a disliking to him. Black never understood men who wore ponytails, especially older men. "Handing out those," replied Black, pointing at the flyers.

"Are you telling me that I can't hand out political literature at a political convention?"

"I'm just following orders. I'm telling you that you can't hand out that flyer."

"You've got to be fucking kidding me," said Sajbel, in a voice loud enough that he drew the attention of passers-by. Sensing a confrontation, many slowed down to watch the drama unfold.

One of those people in the vicinity was Drew Chase, a free-lance cameraman hired by CNN to help cover the four-day convention. He instinctively turned on his camera, hoisted it on his shoulder and began recording. Black and Sajbel were oblivious to his presence.

"Sir, there is no need to swear," said Black, moving closer to Sajbel.

"Get the fuck away from me unless you and the rinky-dink security firm you work for want to get sued," bellowed Sajbel.

Black, quickly losing patience with the aging hippie in front him, was not happy that a small crowd had begun to gather. "Let's go," he said, grabbing Sajbel's arm.

"Get your goddamn hands off me," yelled Sajbel, slapping Black's hand away. Sensing Black's growing anger, Sajbel decided to take the initiative and use the crowd gathered in front of him to his advantage. "This is a violation of the First Amendment! This man is trying to violate my First Amendment rights!" said Sajbel, pointing a finger directly at Black. "All I'm doing is handing out political literature. Is that a crime?"

"It is when you're campaigning against the sitting vice president of the United States and the guaranteed nominee of this convention," replied Thad Garner, a hyper Byrne campaign volunteer who appeared out of the crowd. He had personally been instructed by Marilyn Patterson to gather up as many flyers as possible "by whatever means necessary." Garner, thinking that he was helping the campaign, sprinted toward Sajbel and stripped the flyers from his hands.

The event might not have been given much air time, except that Garner wore a large white T-shirt with "Byrne Volunteer" emblazoned across the back. Chase captured the whole incident on video. There was more to come.

"Serves you right, faggot," said Black, laughing at Sajbel, who was temporarily stunned by Garner's actions.

"What'd you say?" replied Sajbel, regaining his composure after hearing the term that had been thrown at him countless times during his life. It was a term he never got used to hearing and one he no longer let go unchallenged. "What did you say?" he said again, dropping his voice and turning Black by the arm to face him.

"If you touch me again, I'll sue you for sexual harassment," laughed Black, who was pleased with himself for his rapid and, in his mind, witty comeback. He was sure it would get a good laugh from his buddies at the bar.

"I asked you: what did you call me?" said Sajbel, inching closer to Black.

The CNN cameraman, having captured the fleeing Byrne volunteer moved closer.

"You heard me. I think you like boys," replied Black, shoving Sajbel away.

"You bigot!" said Sajbel, walking back toward Black. He didn't stop until he was an inch from the security guard's face.

Black, who had been in his share of barroom fights, had had enough. He swiftly raised his right arm and let loose a wicked punch that fell flush against the side of Sajbel's face. The punch leveled Sajbel. He was bleeding and confused. Black stood over him.

"Had enough, fag?" said Black. "I'd kick your ass, but you've probably got AIDS." Black had heard stories about people getting the virus by being splattered with blood.

Chase also converged on Sajbel, who was regaining his senses.

On spotting the camera, Sajbel jumped up and took the initiative. "This man is a bigot," said Sajbel calmly. He was looking directly into the camera. "I was simply exercising my rights as prescribed under the Constitution, and I have been both assaulted and robbed. If these are the tactics that the vice president and his supporters condone, then I'm even more committed to John Gordon!"

Greg Sajbel's impassioned statement, made while blood was streaming down his face, made for great television. It also gave the "Draft Gordon" movement more free publicity than its organizers could handle. It also prevented the one thing Byrne's campaign manager had hoped to guarantee by quietly collecting the flyers—a quiet, uneventful convention.

The incident was the spark that the "Draft Gordon" movement needed. By the next morning, sentiment for Gordon sizzled. By noon, the following day, John Gordon was telling the media, "If nominated, I will serve."

✳   ✳

"I don't believe it," exclaimed Pete Sawyer jubilantly. "She really said that she thought Colfax was the most qualified candidate? Get me the tape." The campaign manager hung up the phone and rushed in to see Colfax.

"Elizabeth Vandiver just said on *Meet the Press* that she thought you were the most qualified candidate for president and that if she were to vote today, you'd be her pick."

Colfax took off his reading glasses, set down the editorial page of the *New York Times* and looked at his campaign manager.

"Really?" After some thought, he added, "I always said she was a woman of remarkable foresight and vision." Smiling, he continued, "I was wondering how long it would be before she came to her senses and publicly endorsed me."

"Goddammit, stop being so glib. This is great news. The negative ads that the coalition has started running again have cost us at least eight percent in the polls. This is the first bit of really good news we've had in a month," said Sawyer. "We're presently in danger of not meeting the fifteen percent threshold to get into the debates."

"I'd say surviving an assassination attempt was pretty good news."

"Point well taken," said Sawyer.

"And what about all the small donations that we have been taking in over the Internet?" replied Colfax. "They're paying your salary."

"Another good point," replied Sawyer. "I just think we have to take advantage of this as soon as possible."

"I agree. Get me a transcript of what she said. After I watch the tape, I'll give her a call."

"What are you planning on saying?"

"I intend to thank her and then ask her how she's prepared to help."

"Do you think she's angling for a position in your cabinet?"

"I don't know. If she is, she certainly hasn't hurt her chances. Any politician willing to place money on someone struggling to remain above fifteen percent in the polls has already demonstrated more courage than you could squeeze from a hundred congressmen."

"Maybe she hopes to be your VP?"

"Maybe, Pete, maybe. It's also possible that she is supporting me on principle. After all, she and I see eye to eye on a great many issues."

"True. But, if the media is to be believed, she was crushed when the conservatives derailed her prospects of being Prescott's VP."

"I don't believe that bullshit—the media is not to be believed. She knew her future in Republican politics was over the moment she joined Butler's administration. She knew full well three years ago, when she made her goodwill gesture of bipartisanship, that she had made herself *persona non grata* in conservative circles. I really believe Vandiver is motivated by policy—not ideology."

Sawyer called Parker and asked that he run a copy of the *Meet the Press* interview up to the candidate's office. "While we wait for the tape, I have another question for you," he said. "How do you think we should respond to the incident at the Democratic National Convention last night?"

"What was Byrne's response?" asked Colfax, who had been outraged when he learned of the attempt to stifle the Gordon supporters. He was even more outraged when he saw the clip on CNN.

"The vice president hasn't really . . . he's just distanced himself from the volunteer who took the literature. The kid was asked to leave the campaign last night. And all he's said about the security guard is that he should also be fired."

"What?" said Colfax, incredulously. "You're kidding, right?"

"No, I'm not."

"That's all he's said?"

"Yup."

"Unbelievable. The son of a bitch is probably taking a poll to figure out how he should react," said Colfax, suddenly energized. "I'll tell you how we're going to respond. I'm going to respond from my heart. Schedule a news conference in fifteen minutes. I didn't think it was my place to interfere in internal Democratic politics, but if a man running for president can't stand up against bigotry wherever it raises its ugly head, then that man is not fit to occupy the Oval Office. Or any public office for that matter."

Fifteen minutes later, before a hastily assembled group of reporters, Colfax stood ramrod straight in front of the sea of microphones. Most reporters, already aware of Vandiver's public announcement, were expecting Colfax to capitalize on the good news. Most were surprised when they saw that Colfax was not smiling.

"Thank you for attending this conference on such short notice," Colfax began. "I did not expect to have to make this announcement," he said, pausing. His temporary silence only heightened the drama of the situation. The reporters sensed that Colfax was going somewhere they had not expected and moved to edges of their seats. "Last night, at the Democratic National Convention, Greg Sajbel, a man I do not know, was physically assaulted for one reason—and one reason only: because he is gay. This is wrong. As a candidate for president, I have a moral obligation to condemn hatred and bigotry wherever it soils the American fabric, and I call on every other presidential candidate to condemn this hideous act."

Colfax paused again, and numerous reporters tried to interrupt. He ignored their questions and continued, "During this campaign, I have not gone out of my way to discuss the issue of gay rights because, in my mind, the issue has never been about gay 'rights'—it is an issue of human rights. Every American—regardless of race, creed, color or sexuality—is endowed with certain basic rights. And whenever someone assaults the rights of one citizen, they assault the rights of all. If I have been remiss in not making this point clear, I would like to do so now. And I call on all the other candidates to do the same."

The reporters knew Colfax was challenging Byrne to issue a statement. It took Byrne twenty-four hours to repudiate the attack, and he only did so in a closely worded news release in which he loosely condemned "hate crimes."

That night, a group calling themselves Gay and Lesbian Americans for Colfax opened an unofficial web site. By noon the next day, the webmaster for the Colfax campaign had linked the new site to the campaign's web site. Within the week, the site received over 300,000 hits. Given Colfax's military experience, many were surprised by his willingness to allow gays to serve openly in the military.

* *

The roll call of the states, in which the chairperson from every state announces with great fanfare the number of delegates supporting the various candidates, had taken on the aura of a real drama since the public assault on Greg Sajbel. In the ensuing two and a half days, John Gordon had feverishly worked the phones and convention floor, wooing delegates to cast their ballots for him—or to at least abstain from voting and deny Byrne a victory on the first ballot. The conventional thinking was that if Byrne failed to get the sixty percent needed to secure his nomination and his numbers continued to drop after the third ballot, the momentum would shift from him toward either Reginald Greene or John Gordon.

Gordon picked up a great deal of support from Greene's delegates—many of whom never strongly supported the congressman but liked the vice president even less. The big question was whether Gordon would be able to pick off a handful of Byrne delegates and thus force a second-round ballot. If a second ballot could be forced, something that had not happened since 1972, all bets were off.

An unofficial polling of the state delegations conducted by ABC early Wednesday morning showed Byrne with sixty-seven percent, Greene with eighteen and Gordon with fifteen percent of the delegates. Byrne's press secretary immediately challenged the numbers, accusing ABC of trying to create a political story to increase ratings. The press secretaries for the other candidates began hyping their numbers. Gordon's spokeswoman reiterated again and again, for anyone who would listen, that her candidate was the only one whose numbers were increasing.

By the start of the national evening news, every anchor, all of whom were in Los Angeles to report live from the convention, led with the same story: Martin Byrne was in serious trouble and might be denied a first-ballot victory. Each then followed with live reports from the convention floor in which political pundits assessed the situation and explained the damage such an event would inflict on the vice president. Following these were live interviews with delegates planning on switching allegiances.

Throughout the day and into the evening, the vice president feverishly worked the delegates to shore up his eroding base. His wife, sisters, college-age daughters— even his ninety-two-year-old mother—were sent into state delegation meetings to work on his behalf.

By 7:00 P.M., the Byrne campaign had a hard count that was twenty-seven votes short of the magical number. By 7:30 P.M., Bernie Snyder, the president of the country's largest labor union, knew, in his words, that he "had the vice president by the balls." He was the only person who could deliver the necessary votes—and Byrne knew it, too. What Byrne didn't know was that Snyder had purposely told some of his key loyalists to hold out until he could extract a number of key campaign promises from the vice president.

By 7:45 P.M., Byrne had privately committed to Snyder to appoint key judicial selections, roll back certain provisions of NAFTA, increase the minimum wage and pledge funding for 100,000 new teachers.

At 8:00 P.M., the roll call began as it always does with the state of Alabama. There were no surprises. Byrne received thirty-seven votes and Greene seventeen. Everyone in the Byrne camp breathed a sigh of relief. The next state party chair, an elderly woman with long silver hair and a gravelly, salt-of-the-earth voice, stepped before the mike and proudly announced, "The great state of Alaska, home to three-quarters of America's national forests and home to this country's most beautiful scenery, casts one vote for Congressman Reginald Greene, two votes for Senator John Gordon, and ten delegates for the next president of the United States—Martin Byrne!"

The Byrne supporters, waving placards and banners, erupted in wild cheering at the statement. But everyone in the arena knew that the vice president was supposed to receive all thirteen Alaska delegates. The roll call continued with Arizona and Arkansas. The votes totals were slightly lower than expected, but Byrne was still on pace to receive the nomination. Confidence began to be restored after he picked up the expected numbers in California and Colorado.

The roll call continued without a major surprise until Minnesota's party chair rose. The young, articulate lawyer who aspired to run for the United States Senate in 2002, stepped before the mike, "The great North Star State of Minnesota, home to the Women's National Collegiate Hockey Champions, and home to Hubert H. Humphrey—the man who brought civil rights to the fore of his party in 1948; home to Eugene McCarthy—the man who challenged a sitting president in 1968 over his waging an unjust war in Vietnam; home to Walter Mondale—the man who told the American public the truth about the national budget deficit in 1984—casts sixty-four votes for Martin Byrne and ten for the one man with enough courage and integrity to stand up for the dignity of all American citizens—including gays and lesbians—our governor, Robert T. Colfax!"

The audience was stunned. The vice president was stunned. Bernie Snyder was stunned. Even Colfax himself, watching the convention from two thousand miles away, was speechless. Then slowly, Greg Sajbel and members of the small Rhode Island state delegation, began chanting, "Colfax, Colfax, Colfax!"

The chant did not pick up much support and Byrne supporters quickly drowned it out. But the damage had been done. Byrne was denied a first-ballot victory.

The vice president secured the nomination shortly after midnight on the second ballot, but the price he paid would haunt him. Bernie Snyder was able to extract additional concessions, and Greg Sajbel helped the Byrne campaign get Minnesota's ten delegates back in line in return for a pledge from the vice president to publicly announce his support for additional AIDS funding. Privately, Sajbel vowed to vote for Colfax in the fall general election.

CHAPTER THIRTY-TWO

The red-eye from Minneapolis to New York arrived while it was still dark. Sawyer marveled at the predawn calm of New York City as his taxi made its way to the Waldorf Astoria. Never one to sleep on planes, Sawyer checked into his room, instructed the hotel operators to wake him in two hours, and promptly fell asleep.

Awakened at 7:30, he showered and changed into a fresh suit and a crisp, lightly starched white oxford shirt and ordered continental breakfast for two. Sawyer had been instructed by Colfax to fly to New York City and quietly sound out Elizabeth Vandiver on the possibility of her joining the ticket as his running mate.

The telephone rang precisely at the scheduled time. "Good morning, Madam Ambassador," said Sawyer with more cheer than he actually felt. The rigors of the campaign were beginning to wear on him. "I've ordered a light breakfast. I thought we might be able to cover some things over coffee."

"That would be fine," said Vandiver. "What time did you arrive last night?"

"Actually, I arrived early this morning."

"Even better. Does anyone know you're in New York?"

"No, unless the taxi cab driver or bellhop is a spy for one of the other campaigns."

"It's possible," laughed Vandiver. "I have been living in New York City for two and one-half years now and nothing surprises me in this town anymore. The press has contacts everywhere." Vandiver was telling the truth. She had ended her one-night affair with Colonel DeBretange out of fear that if she continued it, her face would be on the cover of every major paper in the country—beginning with the *New York Post*. "I'll be down in a few minutes."

Sawyer picked up the *New York Times* and began reading the blow-by-blow account of Martin Byrne's second-ballot victory at Democratic National Convention. He just smiled when he came to the article detailing the Minnesota delegation's first-round vote for Colfax. The Minnesota state chair, the article explained, had convinced the ten delegates to cast a protest vote against Byrne for his reluctance to condemn the attack against Greg Sajbel. Many were unwilling to support Gordon or Greene for fear that it would seriously damage Byrne, whom they believed still had the best chance of defeating Prescott in the general election. But they wanted to send the vice president the message that he could not take their vote for granted.

Another article recounted Greene's steep drop-off in vote total and quoted the congressman as attributing his disappointing numbers to the National Teacher's Union, which worked vigorously for his defeat. Like Gordon, he did not appear on stage with Byrne after the vice president won the nomination.

As he was finishing up the articles, Sawyer heard a light knock on the door. He escorted Vandiver into the private office suite, where he offered her a cup of coffee and poured himself another. "I've never cared for these fancy coffee cups," said Sawyer in an awkward effort to engage Vandiver in small talk, "they're too small, too hard to hold, and the coffee gets cold too fast. I much prefer a plain, old-fashioned Styrofoam cup."

Always diplomatic, Vandiver just smiled and said, "The old Styrofoam cups also give you the feel that you're engaged in a campaign. There's nothing like standing outside a steel factory somewhere, shaking hands with one hand and holding a piping hot cup of joe in the other, is there?"

Sawyer immediately liked her. He had known in advance that she was a beautiful woman who carried herself with a very professional demeanor. What he had not expected was a personable politician—he always thought she came across as a little cold.

"I know that you and the Governor spoke for a brief time yesterday," said Sawyer, getting down to business. "And I would like to reiterate our sincere appreciation for your unexpected support."

"It seems, if last night's convention is any indication, you're picking up unexpected support everywhere," said Vandiver.

"Wasn't that something? The vice president must have shit in his pants when the renegade Minnesota delegates went for Colfax," said Sawyer, excitedly. "Sorry, I mean wet his pants."

"No need to apologize. I nearly shit in my pants, too," laughed Vandiver. Sawyer liked her even more.

"Me, too."

"What can I do to help Robert?" asked Vandiver, getting the conversation back on track.

"The governor and I discussed that in some detail last night, and he has a very specific job that he would like you to consider. The governor would like you to consider being his running mate."

If the news startled Vandiver, she didn't show it. Sawyer had a hard time discerning her reaction.

Finally, she responded, "I'm honored."

"But—" said Sawyer, "am I sensing a but?"

"No. I just want to be assured that as vice president, I will be used in a meaningful way. I'm not interested in being VP just to add gender balance to the ticket."

"I can assure you that's not why the governor is asking you to be his vice president. In fact, the governor has suggested that we consider making you secretary of State as well—to take complete advantage of your foreign policy expertise."

"Are you serious?" Vandiver was genuinely surprised. Colfax wasn't just using her for balance.

"The governor has researched this and finds nothing in the Constitution that would prohibit the vice president from serving in another cabinet-level capacity."

"Fascinating. You can tell Robert that I am honored. But before I formally accept, I'd like to speak with him personally."

"Of course. I'll phone him momentarily," replied Sawyer. "It is our hope that we can work out the details quickly and make an announcement this afternoon. Unfortunately, I do have to ask you one further question."

"Please."

"The governor has an immense amount of respect for you—and for all you have accomplished. But we need to know if there is anything in your background that would cause embarrassment to the ticket." Sawyer quickly added, "The governor does not believe in prying into peoples' backgrounds, and it is not his intention to hire a firm to comb through your past history. He is an honorable man and simply asked that the question be posed to you."

"I understand completely," said Vandiver. "As a highly public figure, I've already gone through that ringer. I have nothing to hide."

It never occurred to her that Win Murdock might have copied a key to her apartment months earlier and used it to install a micro-camera in her bedroom.

"Excellent. Let me call Governor Colfax with the good news."

* *

"I have invested over three million dollars on an incompetent," said Murdock, rubbing his temples. "Over the course of his political career, I've probably given him ten million dollars. And for what? So he could barely squeak out a second-ballot victory over a pair of amateurs?"

David Luther knew that when his boss was ranting, the best thing to do was to let him get it out of his system.

"If the Republicans don't keep a tighter reign over their convention, Colfax could have a cakewalk to the presidency."

"Sir, the latest polls show our education ads have damaged Colfax extensively. He has fallen below fifteen percent," said Luther, who made it his business to track the effectiveness of the millions of dollars his boss had raised for the coalition.

"David," replied Murdock, in a tone bordering on condescension, "do you really believe that Colfax won't see a substantial jump in his numbers after the Democrats' pathetic performance in Los Angeles? For Christ's sake, Colfax came out smelling like roses—and the son of a bitch wasn't even there."

"I spoke with Mance this morning, and he's putting together a plan to contain Colfax. He's currently working with the Republicans to coordinate their Focus on the Family night at their convention with the coalition's opening attacks on Colfax's views on homosexuality."

"The plan had better be targeted to conservatives and be below the radar. If the Republicans are too abrasive in Philadelphia or if the coalition's efforts are too public, the media may well come to Colfax's aid."

"We're working through the conservative's network of churches. Colfax won't know what hit him."

"Good," remarked Murdock, finishing off his daily glass of apple juice. "This dovetails nicely with my new thinking. Get Mance on the phone immediately."

Luther left the room and did not return until he had Washington's most expensive lawyer on the portable phone.

"Good morning, Jacob," said Murdock, who knew that Mance was not an early riser and was not happy to have been gotten out of bed before sunrise.

"Good morning, Win," replied Mance, mustering up his most cheerful voice. "To what do I owe this pleasure?"

"There has been a change in plans. A big change."

Mance did not respond.

"I'm writing off Byrne."

Mance let out a silent breath—he wasn't fired.

"The dipshit couldn't even stomp out two pissants like Greene and Gordon. I don't think he can handle Prescott and Colfax."

"What are you suggesting, Win?"

"I'm suggesting that the coalition now focus its resources on both Colfax and Byrne."

There was a long pause on the other end of the line as Mance quickly did the political calculus. Finally, he said, "It'll cause some problems—especially with the unions."

"Fuck the unions! They're the ones that have screwed Byrne by forcing him to cave into their outrageous demands. They've pushed him too far left."

"Win, it's just that—"

"Listen, Jacob, I need either Prescott or Byrne to win enough votes to achieve a majority of votes in the Electoral College. And since Byrne and his team of inept aides have demonstrated that they are not up to the task, I have no choice. I'm placing my chips on Prescott."

"It'll help get the media off my ass about the coalition's decidedly anti-Colfax flavor," replied Mance, who recognized that Murdock had made up his mind.

"Are you getting much heat?"

"Not really, just a little from the *Herald* and some from the Center of Responsive and Ethical Politics."

"Keep me posted."

"I will. I'll also begin targeting Byrne. With your permission, I would like to dedicate only about a quarter of resources to that task. I'll have to smooth out some ruffled feathers with labor and the trial attorneys about why we're focusing on Byrne, but I don't think it'll be too hard. They understand Colfax is a much more serious problem than Prescott."

"Goddamn straight. Prescott won't rock the boat. Tell the unions and the trial attorneys that if they go along with the plan, I'll use my clout with President Prescott to make sure he doesn't follow through on any of his campaign rhetoric. Our problem is Colfax—the guy actually wants to reform politics."

* *

The commercial aired all across the country, but over fifty percent of the air time was purchased in Florida. An elderly man and woman sat across from one another at their kitchen table. In between the two lay a pile of bills. "Our Social Security just doesn't go very far anymore," began the woman.

"And Medicare doesn't cover enough of our prescription drugs," added the man.

"I don't know how we're going to make ends meet. I guess we'll have to skip the trips to visit our grandkids."

"Well, I know one thing," said the man, shaking his head, "I'm going to write Governor Colfax and tell him his ideas on Social Security and Medicare are just plain wrong."

"They're more than wrong—they're mean-spirited."

"He's moving the country in the wrong direction. Franklin Delano Roosevelt is turning in his grave."

The commercial, dubbed "Ed and Helen" by the media, was estimated to have reached thirty-seven million viewers. It generated over a half million calls to the Colfax campaign. Almost no one questioned the motives of the group sponsoring the ad, the Coalition for a Prosperous New Millennium.

CHAPTER THIRTY-THREE

Colfax and Vandiver debated holding the news conference in Annapolis, Vandiver's hometown, but at the last minute decided on New York. The decision allowed the Colfax campaign to control the story and stay in the headlines between the Democratic and Republican conventions.

Television and newspaper reporters from around the country crammed into the main ballroom of the Waldorf Astoria. A few foreign journalists had begun following Colfax. The podium was jammed with microphones, and the crowd buzzed with excitement. The television ads that debuted over the last few days were well known by now, and most reporters speculated that Colfax was going to issue some sort of statement attacking the negative and misleading ads.

Just as the veteran reporters began to grow edgy, three minutes after the scheduled start time, Robert Colfax appeared alone from a side door. The room fell silent as he made his way to the podium. Sean McGowan silently scanned the crowd from Colfax's side.

"Good morning," began Colfax, looking out over the crowd. He knew they were intently studying his physical features to determine if the campaign—and the commercials—were taking any toll. "It is with great pleasure that I stand before you today to make three announcements."

The room remained quiet except for the cameras clicking.

"First and foremost, I would like to begin by announcing the selection of my running mate."

The reporters held their pens poised over their notebooks.

"It is my distinct pleasure—indeed, privilege—to have a person of such experience and integrity agree to join me as my running mate. This person has served in the halls of Congress, where she amassed an impressive record of passing thoughtful and effective legislation in a bipartisan manner. She has also served as a governor and demonstrated an uncommon willingness to set aside politics and do the right thing for the benefit of her state. And finally, she has served at the highest levels of our federal government, where she has distinguished herself as a global strategist and a compassionate advocate for America's foreign policy interests. It is with great pleasure that I announce the next vice president of the United States, former congresswoman, former governor and current Ambassador to the United Nations, Elizabeth Vandiver."

The room erupted with an explosion of strobe flashes as Vandiver entered from the side door.

As she took the podium by his side, Colfax prepared to speak again. The reporters were surprised Vandiver wasn't given the opportunity to speak.

"I also have the distinct honor of making a second announcement of major importance today. I would like to announce my selection for the secretary of Education."

A silence fell over the press corps. No reporter could recall a candidate naming in advance of his election a member of his cabinet.

"A former teacher, this man was selected as the Federal Teachers Union's elected official of the year in 1979 and again in 1991. In the last five years, having represented one of the poorest congressional districts in the country, he has become a relentless advocate for changing the way we fund our public schools. He is now an unabashed proponent of public school choice. It is with great pleasure that I give you Congressman Reginald Greene."

The recently defeated candidate for the Democratic presidential nomination sprang from the side door and made his way to the podium to join Colfax and Vandiver, wearing his large, Cheshire cat grin all the way. Greene savored the moment. It more than made up for the way Byrne and the Democratic machine treated him in Los Angeles.

By the time the news conference was almost over, every major network had broken into their regularly scheduled programming to share the announcements with the American public. Newspaper editors around the country were replacing stories about Byrne's growing momentum and the upcoming Republican National Convention with Colfax's surprise actions.

Almost lost entirely in the frenzy of the first two announcements was Colfax's third announcement. At the very end of the conference, Trent Hughes, a crusty old reporter from the *Birmingham Post Herald*, asked Colfax about his third announcement.

"I'm glad at least one of you actually pays attention to what I say," said Colfax, winking at the veteran reporter. "I do have a third announcement. I would also like to name my secretary of State."

The room was silent.

"Contrary to past custom and tradition, I actually intend to involve my vice president in my administration, and I will do that by utilizing her skills and talents as my secretary of State."

* *

Maria Taylor, a brash, opinionated congresswoman from South Chicago with strong labor ties, was a compromise vice presidential candidate after the labor unions balked at Byrne's first choice—Patricia Conklin, the senior senator from California and a vociferous advocate for free trade and an ardent supporter of open immigration.

Byrne and Taylor circled the country in the three days after the convention. Together, the pair had great success in recovering from the disastrous convention. Taylor, who was the opposite of Byrne in almost every way, would speak first and whip the crowds into frenzy by talking about those the prolonged economic expansion had left behind, the lingering social injustice that threatened to rip America apart, and the environmental degradation that corporate America was leaving for future generations. Byrne then followed up with a loosely defined set of policies that his administration would implement if he were elected president. The two worked well together and were beginning to gain in the polls until stories of Taylor's financial problems were revealed.

The *Chicago Tribune* was the first to report on the questionable $200,000 loan Taylor received from a banker who also lobbied her while she served on the House Committee on Banking.

* *

The August weather hung over the city of Philadelphia like a hot, wet blanket. The heat index, measuring both temperature and humidity, hovered around 111 degrees. It was worse inside the new arena hosting the Republican National Convention. The air conditioning system had been improperly installed.

The Republican Party had chosen Philadelphia for its 2000 convention because its leaders felt that to recapture the White House, they had to reconnect with the blue-collar and Catholic voters—the so-called Reagan Democrats—and Philadelphia was stocked with thousands of such voters. Furthermore, the city's motto of "brotherly love" was precisely the message the party knew it had to convey to the American public if it wanted to recapture the big prize in November.

Unlike the Democratic National Convention, where the lasting images of the event were the video of Greg Sajbel's beating, Martin Byrne's troubled victory and the labor unions display of raw political power, the Republicans were determined that their convention would be a model of orderly efficiency. If there was a negative criticism, Republican leaders speculated, it would come from the media, which would describe the three-day affair as a glitzy, highly orchestrated infomercial for the party. Jeremiah Laughlin was determined that that would not be the case.

* *

Stanley Cross' campaign manager viewed himself as a simple man, and he viewed the world in simple terms. He did not apologize for his views to anyone. He had great contempt for those who disagreed with him. But he held his greatest contempt for those he viewed as betrayers of the cause. In Laughlin's world, this meant Republicans who talked like conservatives early in the process, only to abandon those principles and "run to the middle" during the general election. Laughlin was convinced that these "wishy-washy" Republicans were the root of the party's problems. If America was to be cleansed of its ills, the Republican Party had to start first by purifying its own house. And in Laughlin's mind, that meant ridding the party of C. Elliott Prescott.

The strategy had played out beautifully so far in Laughlin's opinion. Stanley Cross had received enough delegates to demand a speaking role at the convention. Through intense negotiations, the Cross campaign had arranged for an eight o'clock time slot on Monday evening. The Prescott campaign and the Republican Party chair only agreed to the slot on the condition that Cross steer clear of all hot-button issues, namely abortion and homosexuality. So concerned was the Prescott camp that they required Cross to submit an advance copy of his speech and reserved the right to edit it. During negotiations, Laughlin did not vigorously protest the arrangement because he knew Cross never intended to keep it.

To Laughlin and Cross, the means justified the end: the moral fabric of America was being torn apart, and Stanley Cross was the only presidential candidate who could stop the damage before it became irreparable.

* *

The backyard of the governor's mansion was still set up from an official afternoon reception, so the Colfaxes decided to use the opportunity to eat outside on the patio. The brightly colored tents shielded them from the late afternoon sun. The turkey burgers, corn on the cob, salad, and iced tea were all laid out.

"Colleen, why don't you say grace?" asked Colfax, who had just returned from his news conference with Elizabeth Vandiver and Reginald Greene.

322

The ten-year-old thought about it for a moment and then began. "Dear Lord, thank you for the beautiful day and thank you for letting us have dinner as a family—finally. Amen."

"Amen."

"It seems like years since we all ate together," continued Colleen.

"'Have eaten,'" replied her mother, correcting her. "But you're right. What are the odds that your dad isn't campaigning or working, one of you isn't at a softball or soccer game, and I'm not at some board meeting? It's a small miracle."

No one responded. Everyone was loading up on food.

"You're right," said Colfax after a moment. "So how is everyone doing? Catherine?"

"Great."

"Care to elaborate?"

She just shrugged her shoulders.

"Ask her how Jeremy is," volunteered Colleen.

Catherine shot her little sister an icy stare. Both parents ignored Colleen's quiry.

"How about you, Colleen?"

"Super. Day camp is a blast."

"So what are you doing?"

"Swimming, biking, canoeing, softball. . . ."

"Anything educational?" asked Colfax.

"Oh, yeah. A lot of environmental stuff. How we can help clean the water, recycling—stuff like that."

"That's pretty important stuff."

"Yeah, it is, Dad," said Catherine, with an edge to her voice.

Colfax picked up on it. "Is something on your mind, Catherine?"

"Yes."

"Well, let's hear it."

"Why aren't you making the environment a bigger issue in the campaign?"

"Catherine," said Linda in a disapproving tone.

"It's okay. It's a good question. First though, let me ask you why I should."

"Because it's the right thing to do."

"Good answer. You'll be pleased to know that I'm going to Colorado next month, just after Labor Day, to outline my environment initiatives. Would you like to come?"

"Maybe. Depends on what you're going to announce."

Colfax was pleased with his oldest daughter's response.

"I'll go, Dad," interjected Colleen.

"Why don't Catherine and I do this one, Colleen? You and I will find our own special trip." His response seemed to satisfy his younger daughter.

"So, what are you going to say?" asked Catherine.

"My staff and I are still working on it, but I think you'll be pleased. I will be announcing an initiative to protect and preserve 100 million acres, including portions of the Everglades, the Rockies, the giant sequoias in the Sierra Nevada, and Alaska's coastal rainforest. I'm also going to announce the strictest air emission standards ever proposed. In short, I'm going to stop large corporations from plundering the environment at your generation's expense."

"Now that sounds more like it, Dad." Catherine added in mock seriousness, "On behalf of my generation, I say thank you."

"I graciously accept," responded Colfax, "but, as you said, it's the right thing to do. Even the Bible says so. Revelations 7:3: 'Hurt not the earth, neither the sea, nor the trees.'"

* *

Jeremiah Laughlin had been around presidential politics long enough to know that the Prescott team would take extra precautions beyond screening his candidate's speech in order to protect the illusion of unity at their convention. He knew they would attempt to control the teleprompter and the speakers just in case Cross began to deviate from the agreed-upon text.

Laughlin had never been fond of the media, but he was also never above using them when it suited his immediate political needs.

"How's it goin'?" said Laughlin in his thick southern drawl to veteran NBC political correspondent Jessica Williams.

"Fine," replied Williams, who openly despised Laughlin. The feeling was mutual.

"I've got an exclusive story for you. Are you interested?"

Williams looked suspiciously into Laughlin's narrow eyes, which had massive bags from too little sleep and too much caffeine and alcohol.

"That would depend on what it is and the conditions you're imposing," replied Williams, cautiously. She was always willing to set aside her personal feelings for an individual if he or she could help her advance her career. Williams was angling for a coveted spot on NBC's Sunday morning talk show, and if she could land an exclusive story, it might bolster her odds of achieving that goal.

"I'll answer the second part of your question first," said Laughlin. "I'll only make the story available if, after hearing what it is and you decide not to take it, you keep this conversation in the strictest confidence."

"You mean, not tell anyone else?"

"Do you have another definition of 'strictest confidence?'" said Laughlin with dripping sarcasm. *This is why I hate reporters,* he thought.

Williams ignored his remarks. "I can live with that. What's your story?"

Laughlin looked around to see if anyone could overhear his remarks before beginning. "Cross is going to speak tonight. As part of the agreement to allow him to speak during prime time, the Prescott camp has demanded to review the entire text of his speech. If they disagree with anything, they can pull it."

Williams had heard rumors of the agreement and was surprised to being receiving confirmation of it from such a high source. "You're kidding me? And Cross agreed to it?"

"He's not going to give the speech that he gave to Prescott's people," replied Laughlin. "Not only was the request unprincipled, it was undemocratic."

Laughlin's attempt at spinning the situation didn't work on Williams. She knew neither Laughlin nor Cross abided by principle. Still, she also knew a good story when she saw one.

"I agree," replied Williams, trying to figure out Laughlin's angle.

"The real story will come when Prescott's aides switch off the power on Stanley."

"You mean, cut off the speakers? I can't believe they'd be that stupid."

"I know they will. If anything goes wrong, they're going to claim it was caused by a heat-related power outage."

"It seems unbelievably risky."

"The stakes are pretty high. They're so prepared that they're even going to purposely knock out the power on an earlier speaker—Congressman Glynn, I think—just to make sure that if they have to pull the plug on Stanley, it doesn't look like an isolated event."

"I still can't believe they'd try something so stupid."

"Trust me, they will. But we have a staunch Cross supporter controlling the stage system, and he's willing to ignore the instructions of Prescott's people. If you catch the incident on video, it might top the one in L.A."

"And you want me and NBC there to cover the action?"

"Precisely. It could be enough to make you famous. I know that you dream of someday replacing Tom Brokaw. This could be your chance. This is your first step."

Williams knew Laughlin was right. She just hated the idea of owing such a coup to a man she despised. But after a second of thought, Williams asked for the details. Laughlin told her exactly where the stage booth was located.

* *

Laughlin stood next to his boss and felt a surge of adrenaline as a famous country-western singer belted out a rousing rendition of "God Bless America." As the singer hit the final few notes, Laughlin wished Cross good luck in his own unique way. "It's time to kick ass," he said. "Time to give it back to all those arrogant assholes that have criticized you and the true conservative movement for all these years. God bless you, Stanley Cross."

As Cross swaggered onto the stage, his diehard supporters cheered, wildly hoisting "Cross for President," "Cross = American Values" and "Cross 2000" signs and waving a variety of cheap plastic American flags that were—in spite of Cross' "America First" slogan—made in China.

While Cross waited for the cheering to die down, Laughlin made his way to the staging booth high above the convention floor in the rear of the arena. Once there, he saw that Jessica Williams and her cameraman were near the booth. He radioed his floor people and told them to halt the cheering.

Cross stood silently behind the podium. The longer he stood silent, the more silent the convention floor became and the more people's attention was directed at him. Finally, he spoke.

"The Republican Party is a grand party with a rich tradition," he began. "We were the first party to elect an African-American to Congress . . ."

The crowd applauded lightly.

"And we were the first party to elect a woman to Congress."

Again, the crowd applauded—this time with a little more enthusiasm. Prescott's people breathed a sigh of relief as he continued to read from the prepared script.

Then Cross added, "And we were the party of principle!"

Laughlin had told the Cross floor leaders that this phrase would trigger a "spontaneous" demonstration. On cue, all 658 Cross delegates responded with the energy of twice as many people.

Dan Miller, Prescott's campaign manager, noticed it immediately. "Oh fuck! He was suppose to say 'we *are* the party of principle.'" Miller instantly ordered the stage booth to cut his teleprompter and cut the speakers. "Shut him down!"

Two hundred feet above the convention floor, George Donovan, the stereo and lighting technician and an avid Cross supporter, ignored Miller's instructions.

326

Back down on the podium, Cross continued. "But no longer! We have become a party afraid of ideas—afraid of the truth. We are on the verge of becoming a party without principle. In fact, as I speak, party officials are trying to cut the power to these speakers."

Dan Miller was so busy shouting at the stage booth operator to cut off the speakers that he didn't hear Cross' remarks. He didn't know the world had been alerted to his efforts.

Back above the convention floor, Prescott operatives converged on the booth and struggled to physically remove George Donovan from his operator's position. It took them several seconds to figure out how to cut the power. While they did, Jessica Williams and her cameraman recorded the whole scene.

Cross used the few additional seconds to add, "They can silence me, but they can't silence the ideas of the silent majority!" And, as if on cue, the power was cut. Cross could not have orchestrated it any better.

Immediately after the power went off, NBC cut to Williams, who was providing the viewers with a detailed account of what was happening in the booth. Down on the convention floor, Cross delegates began to chant "Let him speak, let him speak." Quickly, the chant began to grow as even Prescott supporters, appalled at the tactics, added their voices to the chant.

Miller, recognizing his error and seeing that the scene was quickly growing out of control, ordered the speakers turned back on and Cross be allowed to resume his speech. Miller figured, incorrectly, that the damage was already done. He was wrong.

* *

Stanley Cross, who had run in 1996, had prepared for this speech his whole life. It was a speech for which he did not need notes. He had practiced it in his mind during the long drives across Iowa, on the plane trips to obscure southern towns, in the shower and even in his dreams. This was his moment to sell the conservative cause to the American public, and he did not let his supporters down. No stone was left unturned as he railed against the homosexual agenda, the perils of free trade, the evil nature of America's relationship with China and the rights of the unborn.

"If this party was true to its principles—as it was in Abraham Lincoln's day, when we were ready to pit the future of this great country on a question as profound as slavery and the threat it posed to freedom—then we must do the same over the question of abortion!" Cross paused, and his supporters roared their approval. "I hereby declare an Emancipation Proclamation for the unborn!"

For many of the pro-life activists on convention floor, it was an energizing moment. Stanley Cross had captured their hearts.

* *

Win Murdock was watching the convention proceedings on four different television screens in his plush office suite on the fifth floor of Holten's world headquarters. As soon as he saw Jessica Williams, he muted the other three stations and listened as she reported live on the attempt to silence Cross.

"I don't fucking believe this," yelled Murdock, turning toward his assistant, David Luther. "The Republicans are just as incompetent as the Democrats. I told Prescott not to let that redneck son of a bitch anywhere near the podium. Get Mance on the phone." In less than thirty seconds, Luther had Mance on the line.

"Are you watching the same fucking fiasco I am?" asked Murdoch, grabbing the phone from Luther.

"I am."

"The Republicans have just alienated half of the American population. The son of a bitch has practically declared a civil war against women. After this goddamn performance, I can't see any rational woman supporting Prescott—I don't care how moderate he attempts to portray himself. The Democrats are just going run Cross' speech over and over again until every person in this country associates his message of hate and intolerance with Prescott and the Republican Party."

"I agree, Win. It's not too late to switch our support to Byrne. We've run some ads against him, but the switch might actually work to our advantage. We can use it to demonstrate to the media that we are nonpartisan in our attacks."

Murdock pondered Mance's comments for a few seconds.

"Win? Win? Are you still there?"

"Yes. I just had an idea. Let me think for a minute." After a lengthy pause, he asked, "How many Electoral College votes are necessary to win the presidency?"

"Two hundred and seventy."

"That's what I thought. In the next hour, I want you and your team of lawyers to produce a state-by-state breakdown on the Electoral College and the latest polling information in every state."

"I think I see where you're going with this, Win."

"Good. Then by seven o'clock tomorrow morning, I expect to have on my desk a detailed analysis of how the coalition can expend its money to achieve maximum effect. I want to hit Colfax everywhere he is doing well, while simultaneously campaigning against Byrne and Prescott only in those areas where they are already doing poorly."

"The Prescott and Byrne camps won't be happy with writing off some key states."

"Fuck them. If they weren't so goddamn incompetent, they wouldn't be in this situation in the first place. I gave both of them every opportunity to try to win this thing on their own—and they have proven themselves incapable. I'm running this show now. You tell each campaign that I don't give a flying fuck which one of them wins, I only want to stop Colfax. And if that means that they have to write off a few states in the Electoral College, they can just kiss my ass." Murdock paused and slugged down a gulp of scotch before continuing, "And you tell them that if they choose to cross me and work against my plan, I will personally guarantee their defeat." Murdock signaled for Luther to refill his glass. "Do you understand, Jacob?"

"I do. I just have a few questions."

"Go ahead," replied Murdock, picking up a pair of sterling silver tongs and carefully placing an ice cube into his single-malt scotch.

"In our analysis, would you like us to figure a specific percentage of our revenues to be used against each of the candidates?"

Murdock contemplated the question before responding. "Yes. But the amount must be enough to seriously damage Colfax but not so great as to negate the illusion of the neutrality of the coalition in the eyes of the media."

"May I suggest that we start by directing fifty percent against Colfax and twenty-five percent against Byrne and Prescott. If necessary, we can later increase the amount against Colfax to something like seventy to fifteen to fifteen."

"I have a better idea. Let's dedicate twenty percent of our funds against each candidate on television ads. But the remaining forty percent will be used exclusively against Colfax—in the form of radio ads, push-polling, church money, et cetera. The media is too lazy to follow that shit."

"I like your thinking, Win," concluded Mance. "I think it'll work."

* *

Stanley Cross, with Jeremy Laughlin at his side, smiled as he entered the thirtieth floor suite. Laughlin spoke first, addressing Dan Miller, Prescott's campaign manager. "You're fucked," he said. "You have no room to maneuver."

"What's your deal?" responded Miller, biting his lower lip.

"Cross becomes Prescott's running mate. In return, we'll say that George Donovan acted alone." Laughlin sensed Miller's hesitation and pounced, "You've got one fucking minute to decide. If you don't, we're going to the press and spill the whole fucking thing. Your candidate will be forced to step aside in disgrace."

The following day, with Stanley Cross at his side, C. Elliott Prescott said he was acceding to the request of the delegates and making Cross his running mate.

At the follow-up news conference, Jessica Williams pressed Laughlin on whether the incident during Cross' speech played any role in the decision.

With a straight face, Laughlin said, "George Donovan acted alone."

CHAPTER THIRTY-FOUR

Jacob Mance didn't even make a token gesture to acknowledge either the Republican or the Democratic party chairs. Instead, he directed both men to chairs positioned across from him. He sat in a high-back leather chair, which stood a few inches higher than the other chairs. The arrangement was designed to give Earl Glenn and Paul Sutton the impression that they were being summoned to receive a lecture, which they were.

"Let me ask you," Mance began, "do either one of you feel comfortable that your candidate is going to win the election?"

Paul Sutton, a ten-year veteran of high-stakes presidential hardball, expertly recited his standard line, "Governor Prescott has the money, the message and the momentum—"

"Shut the fuck up," Mance barked. "I don't want to hear any of your verbal diarrhea."

Sutton sat motionless, his face red.

"Who the fuck do you think you're talking to? I'm not some goddamn schmuck who buys into your political bullshit. In fact, that's just the problem. No one is listening to your message, because it's so fucking pathetic!"

Earl Glenn cracked a slight smile.

"I wouldn't laugh, Glenn. You and your clowns are just as pathetic as the Republicans, maybe even worse. Your convention was a fiasco." Mance glowered at both men. "Colfax is running circles around both of you, and all you're doing is sitting here in Washington with your heads up your asses. Either that or you're trying to figure out where to place the blame when your candidate for president ends up in third fuckin' place." Mance repeated his last line. "Third fucking place!"

"If you called me over to rip me a new asshole, I've got better ways to spend my time," said Glenn, standing up as if to leave.

"Sit down! I called both of you over here to salvage you from your own pathetic performances. This is the deal. Shut up and listen."

Glenn sat, and Sutton shifted uncomfortably in his chair. Neither enjoyed being spoken to like a kindergartner, but both knew that if Jacob Mance said he could save them, he probably could.

"Glenn, you and the Democrats and Byrne are going to write off Texas, Pennsylvania, Ohio, Georgia, and Utah." Mance could see the Democratic chair about to protest. He held up a hand like a traffic cop. "Sutton, the Republicans and Prescott are going write off California, Michigan, and Illinois."

The two party chairs sat speechless.

"In return, the coalition is going to hammer Colfax relentlessly in the states where he is in first or second place in the polls. For the sake of appearances, we will be spending a few million dollars campaigning against your candidates in the states I just told you to write off."

"But," protested Sutton, "I can't do that . . . California is worth fifty-four Electoral College votes. That's suicide."

"Shut up," said Mance, glaring at Sutton. "If you had half a brain in your head, you'd notice that I have given the Republicans three states, while giving the Democrats five. The total number of Electoral College votes is exactly the same—ninety-four."

Glenn and Sutton looked at one another and then back at Mance.

"Assuming the coalition is effective at denying Colfax any Electoral College votes—although I think we can assume he'll win Minnesota's ten votes—that still leaves 340 for the two of you to compete over.

"The coalition is not attempting to determine the race between your two candidates. We simply want to stop Colfax."

Glenn and Sutton pondered the arrangement for a minute.

"You don't really have any choice, gentlemen. My employer is extremely unhappy with your performances so far this election year. We are offering you a wonderful deal. One of you will still win—which one will be your responsibility."

Glenn and Sutton looked at each other for a moment.

"Have you spoken with either of the candidates yet about this arrangement?" asked Glenn.

"No. That's your job. It is also your responsibility to keep my involvement in this matter a secret. If I find out that either of you has leaked any word of this to anyone, the full force of the coalition's resources will be directed solely at your candidate. Have I made myself clear?"

Sutton and Glenn nodded agreement.

Mance, with a simple tilt of his head, indicated that the conversation was over. As they were almost out the door, Mance called out, "And I expect to hear back from both you this evening by six o'clock. If I don't, you'll be odd man out."

* *

The commercial all but jumped out of the television and slapped the viewer in the face. It began with a loud, unruly crowd of tough-looking youths and minorities dousing an American flag with gasoline and lighting it on fire. The next sequence moved quickly to a scene shot during the Gay Pride parade in New York City. It showed a leather-clad man walking hand-in-hand with another man in a tight muscleman T-shirt and short shorts. The man in leather had his right hand on the other man's buttocks. The camera then swung left to show two lesbian women engaging in a deep kiss, while one of them held the hand of a young girl. The commercial then moved to a newspaper headline blaring: "Stock Market Plunges" and elderly old woman sitting alone on a park bench, silently weeping. The last scene was of a young black boy walking the halls of a dilapidated school. A voice then asked, "Is this your vision of America?" Then, the tape was rapidly rewound and restarted. Only this time, the deep voice said, "It is Robert Colfax's vision." Over the flag-burning the announcer said, "Robert Colfax does not support a common-sense Constitutional amendment to prohibit the burning of the American flag." As the commercial moved to the Gay Pride parade, the announcer intoned, "Governor of Minnesota, Robert Colfax signed a proclamation recognizing the special rights of homosexuals." The word "special" was emphasized as though it had a deep, insidious meaning. As the camera moved to the kissing lesbians and panned down to the little girl holding the hand of one of the women, the announcer informed the viewers that "Robert Colfax even supports allowing homosexuals to adopt children." As the frail old woman wearing a thin shawl wept over the stock market plunge, the voice said, "Robert Colfax favors privatizing Social Security and dismantling the Social Security safety net." Finally, as the young boy roamed the deserted school, the voice intoned that "Robert Colfax, despite the opposition of hundreds of thousands of teachers in every community in America, favors vouchers," stressing the word "vouchers" as though it was laden with ominous meaning. "Do we really want to take money from the poorest schools in America?"

The commercial concluded with a grainy black-and-white picture of Colfax, taken at an outdoor rally where his hair was swept by the wind. He had a serious, almost frowning look on his face, and his left arm lifted at an angle reminiscent of a Nazi salute. The tag line, read by the announcer, concluded, "Call Governor Colfax and share your vision of America with him." In tiny, almost unreadable print on the bottom of the screen was: "Paid for by the Coalition for a Prosperous New Millennium."

* *

Pete Sawyer just stared at the screen. He knew a commercial of this nature was inevitable. He thought that if he were in his opponent's shoes, he might run something similar. Still, the cold reality of the commercial stung as he rewound it and watched it over and over again. It did not get any easier to watch.

"Any idea how big of an ad buy the coalition has on this commercial?" Sawyer asked Wendy Little, the campaign press secretary.

"I just spoke with an old college friend at the Center for Communications and Media in Washington, D.C.—they do media buys—and she told me that over a million dollars has been allocated by the Coalition for a Prosperous New Millennium to run ads all the way through Labor Day." She added somewhat hopefully, "She couldn't say for certain if all the money was spent with the intention of running this specific commercial."

"Great," replied Sawyer with mock enthusiasm.

"For what it's worth," Little added, "my friend told me she and her friends—who have all seen the commercial—still intend to vote for Colfax. In fact, she said it made a few of her friends more likely to vote for Colfax." The antidote did not make Sawyer feel any better. "How do you think we should respond?" asked Little.

"I don't know. I mean, I don't want to respond to this trash because it allows them to set the agenda—but this one is going to hurt. What do you think?"

"I think we've got to sit down with the governor and get his opinion. The media is going to begin asking him about the commercial, and we need to develop a response."

"Let's go talk with him," said Sawyer.

* *

Colfax watched the commercial without emotion. When it was over, all he said was, "It's a good commercial."

"It's all bullshit, Governor. The whole piece is one big fucking lie."

"Calm down, Pete. It's politics."

"This isn't politics. It's pure, unadulterated sleaze. If we don't respond, this could kill you."

"I agree it could hurt—hell, it will hurt. But it's not as serious as you think."

"I don't know, Governor," added Little. "I agree with Pete. This is nasty, and we have to neutralize it immediately."

"No," said Colfax, with a clarity and certainty that surprised both of the young aides. "Have either of you ever read Sun Tzu's *The Art of War?*"

Both shook their head no.

"Well, you should. But that's not important now. I have my reasons for not responding. You have to trust me. But I do want you to know that we will respond—we will just do it at the time that is most opportune for us."

"Can you give us a hint of our strategy?" Sawyer asked, exasperation creeping into his voice.

"Peter," said Colfax in the tone of a teacher talking with a young student, "that commercial outlined one perception of where I stand on the issues. It was a decidedly negative view. It's my job—our job," Colfax corrected himself, "to use those same issues to paint a far different vision for this country. And I'm not only positive we can, I look forward to doing it. 'Where some choose to preach fear, I'll choose to preach hope. Where some choose to see only darkness, I choose to see light. Where others choose hatred, I choose peace.'"

* *

Anne Strong knew the Colfax campaign was going to kick into high gear following the Labor Day weekend and she would have little time to do anything in the next two months, so she jumped at the chance to return to Washington for the three-day holiday.

Since going on the campaign trail, Strong had been bothered by her inability to follow up on the connection between David Pollard's and Preston Briggs' deaths, and she was eager to do more digging. The reporter at the *Herald*, to whom she passed the lead, had done nothing with it.

Strong began by reviewing the short articles on Pollard's and Briggs' deaths. There had been only one follow-up story on Pollard's murder. It said the investigation had gone cold. Nothing else was reported on the suicide of J. Preston Briggs.

Strong also went back to Ellen Moriarty's web site and pulled up the old reports out of the archive. She searched under the phrase "Gibraltar conspiracy" and found Moriarty's first and only report on the subject. She read the story again, and this time made note of the source's codename, "the CyberCafe connection."

Strong returned to her *Washington Herald* database and, on a whim, searched under "CyberCafe." Thirteen articles were cited. Twelve were related to either technology trends or coffee. One reported that a young student, Troy Hall, died of a heroin overdose two hours after closing the CyberCafe. The story quoted the boy's mother as saying her son was not involved in drugs. The story was dated April 30—two days after David Pollard's murder and Preston Briggs' suicide.

Strong immediately called Tracy Hall, Troy's mother. "Hello, Mrs. Hall?"

"Yes?"

"My name is Anne Strong, and I'm a reporter for the *Washington Herald*. Do you have a minute to answer a few questions?"

"I'm busy," said Hall, ready to hang up the phone.

"Mrs. Hall, I don't believe your son died of an overdose."

The reporter had Hall's attention.

She continued, "I think your son's death was somehow related to his work at the CyberCafe." Without revealing any specifics, Strong suggested there may be a link to some other deaths. "What kind of a person was Troy?"

"He was a great boy," said Hall. "He was a year away from graduating from American University. He wanted to be a reporter, like you."

Strong asked a number of other questions, but they yielded no insight into why someone might want to kill Troy Hall.

"I'm so sorry for your loss, Mrs. Hall. If you remember anything—anything at all—that you think might be useful, don't hesitate to call me. I'll let you know what I find." Strong gave the woman a local number, but she heard nothing more before she had to return to the campaign trail.

* *

The commercials began airing Labor Day weekend, just as children all over America were preparing to return to school. Consumer research and the demographic segmentation of the television market made targeting young, affluent couples with kids incredibly easy. The National Sport Utility Vehicle Association joined the coalition because it wanted to oppose Colfax's proposal for stricter air emission standards on the highly popular but heavily polluting vehicles. But the manufacturers and dealers did not want to draw attention to themselves.

Jacob Mance was only too happy to accommodate the industry. He knew he could spin Colfax's proposal in such a way that Colfax himself would not even recognize it. Without mentioning the reason for the stricter standards, the coalition ad reasoned that the standards would inflate the price of a sports utility vehicle. And because sports utility vehicles were among the safest vehicles on the road, the commercial concluded that Colfax's idea was hostile to young families who wanted to protect their children because it made the cars more expensive. The commercial ended with a young mother holding an infant and saying: "Call Governor Colfax and tell him that he should be helping to protect our kids—not making it more expensive." Again, in small type, the ad revealed it was paid for and prepared by the Coalition for a Prosperous New Millennium.

CHAPTER THIRTY-FIVE

S tephanie Freeberg's seventh-floor office looked out over Connecticut Avenue. At 11:00 P.M., her light was the only one lit on the entire floor. She stared at her computer monitor and watched the three coalition ads in succession. First, she watched an ad directed against Byrne that described in great detail the devastating effect his support of the Global Warming Treaty would have on the oil industry; it ran in the Dallas and Houston areas. The commercial ended by asking the viewers to call Martin Byrne and urge him "to help keep energy affordable for all Americans."

Next, she reviewed an ad aimed at Prescott that ran in the San Francisco area. It featured the contorted black-and-white face of Stanley Cross and ended with a woman's voice asking voters how they could trust Prescott to stop hate crimes in America if he couldn't even stop his own vice presidential candidate. The tag line said: "Tell Elliott Prescott there is no room in the Republicans 'Big Tent' for small-minded people."

The last ad, of which there were multiple versions running in numerous smaller markets around the country, linked Robert Colfax's willingness to close military bases with a specific base in the particular market. The commercial took great artistic license in describing the catastrophe that would befall the community if the base were shut down. The ad encouraged voters to call Governor Colfax and demand that he "reconsider his position" on base closures.

Freeberg watched the commercials for over an hour, looking for some common thread. The coalition's willingness to run ads against all three candidates didn't make sense. It didn't fit her theory. There had to be a common link, she thought. She reviewed the old ads against Colfax and the more recent ads against Byrne and Prescott. For each commercial, she constructed a simple analysis outlining who it was meant to influence.

* *

Ira Bernstein was walking home to his Dupont Circle apartment after a late dinner when he noticed the lone light on the seventh floor. Knowing his protégé was working late, he decided to check in on her. Bernstein opted against using the elevator and instead walked up the seven flights to the office. Upon reaching the top, he was only slightly out of breath. Not bad for a man pushing sixty-five, he thought to himself. Freeberg, deep in thought, never heard him approach.

"Good evening," he said, leaning over her shoulder.

The young woman jerked up in her chair. "Jesus Christ," gasped Freeberg, "you scared the shit out of me."

"I'm sorry. I had no idea you were so captivated by the image of Stanley Cross," said Bernstein, referring to the anti-Prescott commercial that featured Cross' now infamous tirade at the Republican National Convention.

"I'm not. It's just that these commercials don't make sense. I understood the coalition ads against Colfax. I even understood the early ads against Greene and Graham. But now they're running commercials against Colfax, Byrne, and Prescott. I don't get it."

"Interesting," said Bernstein. "Is there any common theme? A theme that might shed some light on who—or whom—is behind the mysterious Coalition for a Prosperous New Millennium?"

"That's what I've been trying to figure out," replied Freeberg, finishing off the last of the lukewarm Diet Coke that had been on her desk since early afternoon.

"Let me see the commercials," said Bernstein, sitting down beside Freeberg. Together, the two watched the three ads in silence. "You're right," Bernstein replied after reviewing each commercial twice. "They don't seem to make sense. Where are the commercials playing?"

"The Colfax ads are scattered across the country, but they're clearly designed to harm him in every area where the military might possibly close a base. The Byrne ads are running in eastern Texas—primarily Houston and Dallas. And the Prescott commercials are running in the San Francisco area."

"Can you search the Internet for the latest poll numbers in each of the areas where the commercials are running?" asked Bernstein.

"Sure. I'll do a quick search of the major papers in each area. They're sure to have conducted a poll within the last few weeks." For the next twenty minutes, Freeberg searched the online databases of the San Francisco, Dallas, Houston, San Diego, Norfolk, Providence, and Indianapolis newspapers. As soon as she finished downloading the poll numbers from each city, Bernstein tallied them up on a flip chart.

When Freeberg and Bernstein were done, the common thread was apparent. "Whoever is behind the coalition is still pursuing an anti-Colfax strategy," said Bernstein, "and they're looking for cover. Just look at the numbers. Prescott is already behind in California, so he isn't really hurt by the negative ads in San Francisco. Byrne couldn't expect to win in Texas, given that he is already running third in the state, so the ads in Dallas and Houston are useless. They're preaching to the choir."

"But the Colfax ads," said Freeberg, "are hitting him in the states where it appears that he has the best chance of picking up some Electoral College votes."

"Precisely. He's only two percentage points behind Prescott in Virginia, he's ahead in Rhode Island, and it's a dead heat in Indiana."

"Why doesn't the coalition just come out and admit that they're against Colfax?" asked Freeberg.

"Probably because whoever is behind the group is afraid that it might actually help Colfax. My guess is that they're playing it safe with these other ads so that they can counter any accusations that they are simply a front group opposed to Colfax."

"So Murdock could still be the one behind this group?"

"Absolutely. In fact, after seeing this strategy I'm more convinced than ever that he's our man. The problem is that he has so effectively distanced himself from the coalition—and the coalition has so effectively positioned itself—that it will be impossible to prove that this is the plan or that Murdock is the one behind it."

"What if I provide this information to Anne Strong?" asked Freeberg.

"I'm not sure if the *Herald* will run with the story this close to the election."

"Maybe I could plant the story with Ellen Moriarty?"

"The Internet reporter?" said Bernstein, with open disdain.

"Yes. What do you have against her?"

"Everything, my dear. She represents everything that is wrong with the media today. She's a sensationalist, and her brand of media feeds speculation, rumor, innuendo, scandal, and conspiracy."

"But often the scandals are real, and sometimes there are conspiracies," replied Freeberg.

"Perhaps, but a great many of her reports tend to either leave out a lot of supporting information or she gets it wrong altogether. Her motto seems to be 'report first, confirm later.'"

"I don't think that's so terribly different from the traditional media," replied Freeberg.

"I just don't like it. But if the *Herald* doesn't pick up on your lead, I don't see what alternative we have. Why don't you try reaching Strong tonight?"

"That might be hard. I think she's travelling with the Colfax campaign."

* *

Anne Strong had been covering the Colfax campaign since early August. The stretch from Labor Day to Election Day had always been her favorite, and for the first time since 1980, when she covered the Carter-Reagan election for her junior high school newspaper, the race was in the final stretch and the outcome was still impossible to predict. The latest *Washington Post*/CNN poll had Prescott at thirty-seven percent, Byrne thirty-three and Colfax thirty percent. The question of whether Colfax would be included in the debates—despite Jacob Mance's dealing with this network contacts—was moot.

Although she would never publicly admit it, she was silently pulling for Colfax and was troubled by his slippage in the latest polls, which had skyrocketed in the wake of the disasterous Republican and Democratic conventions. Immediately after the conventions Colfax was ahead with thirty-six percent. In the last month, he had dropped six percentage points, and the hemorrhaging was giving no signs of slowing. In the last week alone, he had dropped two full points.

Pundits speculated that, like John Anderson in 1980, Colfax was suffering the plight of independent candidates: the nearer election day, the more likely voters were to turn away from third-party candidates either because independents ran low on money and couldn't respond to opponents' negative ads, or because the voters began to think that the candidate could not win and they didn't want to waste their vote.

Neither scenario jived with Strong's experience on the campaign trail with Colfax. Everywhere he went, he continued to enjoy strong and enthusiastic responses—even though Strong had begun to notice an increasing number of anti-Colfax placards on the fringe of his outdoor events. There was something about the protests that bothered her. The protesters seemed to lack conviction and passion. The protests seemed artificial—almost staged.

* *

Staff for the three campaigns had been jockeying for weeks over the details of the first presidential debate. What would the stage look like? Where would the candidates be situated? Who would be in the middle? Who would ask the questions? What would be the format of the questioning? Every trivial detail was reviewed, reconsidered and scrutinized in painstaking detail. It had reached a point where Pete Sawyer was ready to scrap the whole thing.

Eventually, the parties were able to agree that the first debate would be held in Boston and each candidate would open with a one-minute statement and finish with a two-minute closing. The order would be determined by a random drawing, conducted by a certified public accounting firm. In between the opening and closing statements, the candidates would be asked a series of questions, ranging from domestic policy to foreign policy, and each would get one minute to answer and thirty seconds to rebut. The date for the first debate was set for Sunday, October 3, 2000.

* *

"Do you understand me, Jacob?" screamed Murdock into the phone. "I don't care what the fuck they want. I want you to participate in both of their practice sessions."

Mance tried to get a word in, but Murdock continued his tirade.

"I want Byrne and Prescott working together to crush Colfax in this debate. If Byrne lands a right, I want Prescott to counter with a left—and vice versa. I also want you to supply those sons of bitches with enough ammunition to blow Colfax out of the water."

"I've got it covered, Win. I'm already acting as a behind-the-scenes advisor to both campaigns. I've been guaranteed that the man playing Colfax in both of their practice sessions is the same person."

"Who is he?" asked Murdock.

"He's our top opposition research guy. He's been researching Colfax and studying everything he has said or done for the last ten months. This guy knows Colfax flat. He's a very sharp lawyer—a Yale graduate."

Murdock wasn't impressed with either credential.

"I can guarantee you that their attacks will be perfectly coordinated."

"They had better fuckin' be. It's less than six weeks before the election and Colfax is still a legitimate contender."

"Five points," said Mance, "I can guarantee you Colfax will drop at least five points in the polls after we're finished with him in the debate."

"Your reputation—and your million-dollar retainer—is on the line, Jacob," said Murdock. "I trust you have been working with both staffs on the post-debate spin?"

Mance answered affirmatively.

"Good. I want us shaping the pre-debate expectations, then I want us commanding the flow of the debate, and finally I want us telling the American public what they thought they heard—just in case it differs from what we want them to think."

"I understand, Win. I've got high-level contacts inside the three networks and they're supplying talking points to each of the moderators. We will have a list of every potential question they could possibly ask. Prescott and Byrne will know exactly what questions are coming and in what order. They'll know what to say, how to say it and how to go after Colfax. As for the post-debate spin, we'll prepare remarks, based on Colfax's expected answers, to spin it exactly like we want."

Murdock poured himself two fingers of scotch as he listened to Mance. What he heard, in combination with the sweet smell of the scotch, made him feel better. "You're a true American patriot, Jacob Mance," said Murdock, with a laugh. "The citizens of this fine nation are in your debt."

∗ ∗

The timing of Freeberg's call could not have been better. Strong listened with great interest as Freeberg shared the information that she and Bernstein had found. "It all makes so much sense now," said Strong. "I can't believe I didn't see it myself."

"So, will you do a story?" asked Freeberg.

"I'll try, but I'll need more information. Can you help?"

"Anything," said Freeberg, enthusiastically.

"Can you get me precise information on how much the coalition has spent on ads against each candidate?"

"I don't know. I'll try. The coalition isn't required to reveal that information, but I can probably put together a fairly accurate account based on the number of ads they have run and the location of those ads."

"Great. Fax or e-mail me any information you put together. Once you do, I can confront Jacob Mance and asked him for his side of the story."

"He'll just deny it, don't you think?"

"I know he will . . . but if we've got the numbers to back us up, what can he do other than say 'No comment' or try to spin some ridiculous counterclaim. I think I might be able to squeeze him if we can prove the coalition is spending money on activities other than television."

"I've thought about that. Trying to determine the amount they're spending on consultants, pollsters, telemarketers, print ads and radio is much more difficult."

"I know, but I'm convinced they're doing it. In fact, I think it might be the coalition's low-profile activities that are hurting Colfax the most. I have been at every rally or speech he has had in the last six weeks, and I can sense a growing hostility on the part of those who oppose him. But I don't think it is a true grassroots opposition. It just feels weird—like it's being manufactured."

"I can get back to you with some preliminary numbers by tomorrow morning. Will that work for you?"

"The sooner the better. I'll still have to run the story by my editor."

"Will you have any problem?" asked Freeberg, wondering if she should leak the story simultaneously to Moriarty.

"I don't see why," said Strong.

Freeberg decided against contacting Moriarty for the time being.

* *

David Luther was pleased with himself for ordering the tap on Stephanie Freeberg's telephone. A minute after Strong and Freeberg hung up, he was on the phone with his boss, explaining the problem. Murdock listened intently. After Luther finished relaying the conversation between the two women, Murdock hung up the phone and called the senior political editor at the *Washington Herald*. The best place to kill a story was at the top, Murdock thought to himself. And the best time to do it was before it even became a story.

* *

Sean McGowan conferred with the lead agents for the Byrne and Prescott campaigns. Compared to what he had been working with for the past few months, the first presidential debate would be a piece of cake. A Secret Service advance team from Washington had conducted the preliminary security arrangements at Harvard the day before, and the director had assigned additional agents to help with many of the details that were typically left to local law enforcement officials. McGowan was so comfortable with the security that he took a rare afternoon break to confer with one of the Secret Service top profilers, Sharon Wilcox. He still was not comfortable that Bradford was the right man.

"I gave Wells my report on the profile of the subject about three months ago," said Wilcox, referring to the assistant secretary of Treasury. "It differs only slightly from the one that the FBI put together with the help of the CIA. But I have to agree with their assessment—I think Bradford is our man."

"How does your analysis differ?" asked McGowan.

"I think the suspect may have been a victim of sexual abuse. The FBI is less sure, and the CIA has ruled it out entirely."

"The CIA is always so damn sure of themselves. Why do you think the suspect was abused?"

"I said 'may have been.' I believe the suspect has a personal motive. I think the person feels Colfax somehow violated a special trust, and I think they have been violated before—either physically or mentally, or both. I say that because the shot at St. John's was so risky. There was something more than money or fame motivating the suspect."

"What's the second area of disagreement?' asked McGowan. He had a habit of getting right to the point.

"It's minor. The FBI is sure the assassin is a man. I think so, too, but I always leave the door open."

"Be open for anything," said McGowan, repeating a standard Secret Service motto.

"That's right."

"Why are you so sure?"

"Simple, really. The planned assassination was typical of a rural, white male with a penchant for hunting. It was a classic hunting trip—set the bait, hide, wait and shoot."

* *

The audience was predominately middle-class and white, but the debate sponsors made arrangements to ensure that minority groups were represented. They even made sure that the minorities were equally dispersed through the crowd so the national audience would see various segments of society represented. It didn't matter, however, because the audience was not allowed to ask any questions. Only four well-educated caucasians—three of whom were males—were selected to do the questioning. The questioners were all anchors or reporters from CNN, FOX, NBC and ABC. PBS anchor, James Kilgore, served as moderator.

"Welcome to Boston and the campus of Harvard University for the first of three presidential debates. I'm James Kilgore and I will be moderating this evening's debate." Kilgore, in his serious but unassuming manner, went to explain the format of the debate. As he did, the cameras, which were feeding the exact same shot to all the networks, panned across the three candidates. Governor Prescott was on the left. Colfax was in the middle and Byrne on the right. When he was done introducing the three candidates, Kilgore concluded by asking the audience to refrain from clapping or cheering.

Following the format, Vice President Byrne started the debate with a short speech. It was a speech that he had rehearsed endlessly over the last two weeks. Every line, every phrase and every word had been screened by numerous focus groups, and then modified by his handlers to elicit the most favorable response. Byrne's campaign advisors had even subjected a hundred randomly chosen citizens, all of whom were wired to a machine that tracked their physical responses, to the speech. Depending on where the needle went, the advisors made a note and further refined the sentence so that it yielded maximum emotional response.

The speech did not disappoint. From his opening comments about "the gap between the haves and the have-nots," to his concluding statement about "my three priorities, I call them the three E's of my administration: education, the economy and the environment," his remarks were well received.

Governor Prescott was next. He used his opening remarks to tell the people that he wanted "to restore the character and dignity of the office of the presidency, and bring honor, integrity, American values, and faith back to the highest levels of government." As with his Democratic opponent, every phrase had been tested in advance—including a remark acknowledging that he was "happy to be back at Harvard," his alma mater.

Colfax was the last to give his opening remarks. "Good evening," he began, flashing his easy and relaxed smile at the estimated eighty million viewers. He then paused a second. People not familiar with him thought he might be freezing under the pressure. "I couldn't help but notice that Governor Prescott, a Harvard man, is to my right and Vice President Byrne, a Yale man, is to my left . . . some would say the governor is to my far right and the vice president is to my far left."

The audience laughed loudly at the unexpected interjection of humor. And so it went throughout the debate. Prescott and Byrne never fully recovered, and Colfax, through his wit, was widely regarded as the winner.

CHAPTER THIRTY-SIX

B radley Schuman had been the editor for the *Washington Herald* since 1982. He had achieved his position in part because of a good word from Win Murdock to the owner of the paper.

In his eighteen years in the job, Schuman had never had a call from Murdock, although he saw him once in a while on the Washington social circuit. On those rare occasions, Murdock rarely talked business. So Schuman was surprised when he received a call from Murdock at his home in Alexandria, Virginia.

"Hello, Mr. Murdock."

"Good evening, Bradley. I'm sorry to bother you at home."

"No bother . . . what can I do for you?"

"I have a minor issue I'd like to take up with you."

"Yes?"

"This is a delicate matter, and I don't quite know where to begin," said Murdock, pausing. "It has come to my attention that a reporter of yours is writing a story about my potential involvement in the presidential race."

"I think you're mistaken, Mr. Murdock. I'm not aware of any such story. The only person who could order such a story would be me, and I've done nothing of the sort."

Murdock smiled. He had caught Schuman before Anne Strong could pitch him the story.

"Well, Bradley, I must say that makes me feel much better," said Murdock, telling the truth. He had been afraid the story might have been ordered from the top. "The only reason I ask is because a reporter—or least she said she was a reporter with the *Herald*—called and asked me about my involvement in an issue advocacy group."

"Can you remember the reporter's name?"

"Yes. Strong. Annette Strong, I believe," said Murdock.

"Anne Strong?"

"Maybe—yes. Do you have a reporter by that name?"

"I do, but I can't believe she would call you without first telling me. She's one of my best reporters."

"Like I said, Bradley, I don't have proof that she was who she said she was, but if it was your reporter, I would like to know the purpose of the story. It is getting too damn close to the election, and I don't want to be a factor in it."

"I don't follow you, Mr. Murdock."

"The reporter believes, incorrectly, that I'm somehow linked with a group that she says is opposed to Robert Colfax's candidacy."

"I see," said Schuman. He knew Anne Strong was not prone to pursuing bad leads.

"This is a rumor that seems to have some legs. It has been reported in various forms on the Internet. There is nothing I can do about that. I can't disprove a negative. Groups like the one Strong mentioned are not required by law to disclose their contributors."

"I see," mumbled Schuman again.

"But if the story were to be reported in a paper such as the *Herald*, it could have unforeseen consequences on the presidential race."

Schuman said nothing.

"Now, I have never made my political involvement a secret. It is a well-known fact that I support Republicans and Democrats alike. I'm proud of that, and if a story were to run along those lines, I'd gladly go on the record with my rationale for doing so. But I will not be dragged into the gutter about my alleged involvement in some group that I know nothing about."

"That's perfectly understandable, Mr. Murdock. I'll look into this immediately and get back to you. Is there a number where I can reach you?"

Murdock gave him the number of his direct line.

"If there is anything the *Herald* does not wish to do, it's influence the outcome of the campaign with incomplete, or worse, inaccurate reporting."

"I know you don't. That's why I called you directly, Bradley." Murdock added, "Holten's relationship with the *Herald* is very important, and I would hate to see anything tarnish our ability to keep working together."

Schuman paused for a second before responding. Was Murdock threatening him? He knew Holten did close to a million dollars worth of advertising with the paper every year. Was Murdock implying that if the story had merit and he went ahead with it, Murdock would stop doing business with the paper?

"No one values the relationship you and your company have with the paper more than I, Mr. Murdock," Schuman said diplomatically. "I'm sure if this is true, it is nothing more than a case of overly aggressive journalism," concluded Schuman, with more than a little bit of skepticism.

* *

The excitement was palpable on Colfax's campaign plane, named the *Bull Moose* in honor of Teddy Roosevelt's third-party challenge for the presidency in 1912. The first debate had given the Colfax campaign a tremendous boost. The candidate had just delivered a passionate speech about the need for young people to get out and vote in the 2000 election to a packed audience of college supporters, dubbed "Colfaxiacs" by the media, on the tarmac of the Charlotteville airport. Aides were confident that Colfax could win Virginia's thirteen electoral votes.

The whole scene had a surreal feel to it, thought Strong. People of all ages, races, and sexes stood illuminated by the flood lights of television cameras in the light drizzle, waving homemade signs in support of Colfax.

The *Bull Moose* was now enroute to Atlanta. Pete Sawyer believed that Colfax still had an outside chance to win Georgia. If nothing else, he figured that by campaigning in territory that was supposedly safe for Prescott, Colfax could force the cautious Republican candidate to "stay home" and shore up his base. The strategy worked. Prescott cancelled a trip to southern Illinois and instead made an appearance at the University of Georgia in Athens.

Anne Strong was having the time of her life. The camaraderie with the other reporters and the Colfax staffers was fueled by the knowledge that they all were witnessing a small piece of American history in the making. She couldn't believe that Prescott and Byrne, currently running first and second in the latest polls, were receiving the same kind of reception Colfax was getting. Strong could sense the momentum building.

The vibration of her pager ended her thoughts. It was her editor, Bradley Schuman. The typed messaged indicated that he wanted her to call as soon as possible. Strong thought he probably wanted a first-hand, live account from the campaign trail.

As soon as the *Bull Moose* landed at the Atlanta airport, Strong found a quiet area away from the throngs of people waiting to greet Colfax and placed a call to Schuman.

"Hi, Brad. It's Anne. I got your page. What's up?"

"How's it going?" asked the editor, still trying to figure out how to bring up Murdock with her.

"It's crazy—unbelievable, really. It's almost one in the morning, and there are probably a thousand people here at the Atlanta airport just trying to catch a glimpse of Colfax."

"Really?" said Schuman, genuinely surprised.

"Really. Colfax is even more amazing. We landed about ten minutes ago, and he's still out there shaking hands, exhorting his supporters to do even more in these last few weeks."

"How's he holding up?"

"The guy's a machine. I thought he'd catch some sleep on the plane, but instead he did three lengthy interviews."

"Which papers?" asked Schuman, almost by instinct. He always wanted to know what his competitors were doing.

"The *Chicago Tribune*, the *Boston Globe* and the *Seattle Post-Intelligencer*. Why?"

"Just wondering. My guess is that Colfax's press secretary is only granting interviews to reporters from newspapers in states that Colfax thinks he can win. What it tells me is that Colfax's people think he can win Illinois, Massachusetts, and Washington."

"I didn't think of that. You're probably right . . . I guess that's why you're the editor. Well, I'd love to sit and talk shop but, unlike Colfax, I can't perform on three or four hours of sleep. What did you want to talk about?"

Schuman got right to the point. "Are you considering writing an article about Win Murdock?"

Strong was stunned. "Ah—I was—I mean, yes. Yes, I was thinking about doing a piece on Murdock," replied Strong, regaining her composure. "But I haven't done a thing yet. How did you know? Did Bernstein from the Center of Ethical and Responsive Politics call you?"

"No. Win Murdock did."

"What! That's impossible. I haven't discussed this idea with anybody yet. You know I'd at least check with you before I started anything like that."

"I'm glad to hear it, Anne," said Schuman. He believed her.

"I just don't know how he could have found out. I mean—I haven't spoken with anyone about this . . ." said Strong, her voice trailing off. Now she knew for sure Freeberg was on to something.

"All I can say is that Win Murdock is a man with friends in a number of high places. If you said anything to anyone—either in person or over the phone, fax, or computer—he would have the ability to find out about it."

"You're kidding, right?"

"I wish I were. Anne, I'm not telling you not to pursue this story, but I'm cautioning you that the odds of getting enough background information to make the story publishable in the next two weeks is remote. And even if you do, I can't guarantee we'd run it. The implications on the outcome of the election might prove to be too great. Not to mention the threat of the lawsuit that I'm sure Win Murdock and his team of attorneys would file."

"I understand," said Strong, who could read between the lines. She understood that politics also invaded the newsroom on more occasions than she would like to admit. Murdock was pressuring Schuman. "It's just that I think that group, the Coalition for a Prosperous New Millennium, is working behind the scenes to harm Colfax, and I'm almost positive that Murdock is the person pulling the strings."

"Anne, even if he is, it's his constitutional right to spend his own money on issue advocacy. Furthermore, it is the law of the land that contributions to the coalition don't have to be made public."

"I know it's legal, but it still stinks. Don't the American people have a right to know if one individual—one individual who does billions of dollars worth of business with the United States government—is spending millions to influence the outcome of the election of the president? Don't you think the people have the right to know that?" demanded Strong.

Schuman remained silent. He didn't have a good answer.

"I mean, Jesus Christ, Brad, what this group is doing isn't about issues. It's about stopping Colfax. This coalition is making a mockery of our campaign finance system . . . a mockery of our democracy."

*   *

Stephanie Freeberg was surprised when Anne Strong called and asked if they could meet at the little Greek deli down the block from her office. "I didn't know you were back in town," said Freeberg, trying to start a conversation.

"I can't talk. I need to see you in five minutes," said Strong, cutting off Freeberg. She figured if someone had bugged Freeberg's phone, they wouldn't be able to get to the deli that quickly.

Freeberg left her office immediately and arrived at the deli a minute early. She wasn't even seated when a man with a thick Greek accent told her she had a telephone call. Freeberg started to question him, but he said, "The woman said it's an emergency." He directed her to a phone behind the deli counter.

"Stephanie, this is Anne. I'm not in D.C." Before Freeberg could even register a thought, Strong added, "And I think your phone is bugged."

"What?"

"Just listen. Is there anyone else in the deli with you?" Freeberg glanced around the small room. No one had arrived for lunch yet. It was not even 11:00 A.M.

"Just the two guys behind the counter."

"Did anyone follow you in?"

"No."

"Good. Look, I can't prove your phone is tapped, but my editor called me last night and asked if I was doing a story on Murdock. He said Murdock called him with a simple message—kill the story."

"You're kidding?"

"I wish I were. You and I were the only two to discuss the idea, and we did it over the phone."

"Oh, my God."

"Stephanie, I think you're onto something—you've got to be careful. Were you able to find any more information on the amount of money the coalition might be spending against Colfax?"

"Yes. Based on the radio figures alone—and I was only able to check a few key media markets in the states where Colfax is ahead in the polls—it appears that the coalition is spending about half of what it's spending on television."

"What about telemarketing or push polling?"

"I couldn't find much. But I was able to contact a friend who is a vice president for a political telemarketing firm. She confirmed they had been retained by the coalition to do an extensive phoning the last two weeks of the campaign. She said the coalition has earmarked six million dollars for the final three days alone."

"Six million?" exclaimed Strong. "These people aren't screwing around. Look, we don't have much time. I'm going to try to see if I can get someone else to run this story. Knowing Murdock, though, he's probably in bed with most of the editors across the country. I suggest that you try Moriarty."

"That's what I was thinking."

"Personally, I can't stand the bitch—but desperate times call for desperate measures.

* *

Freeberg spent the rest of the afternoon conducting research from Ira Bernstein's home computer. She read every edition of the *Moriarty Minute* for the last two months and was impressed with the caliber, content, and style of writing.

Freeberg hatched her plan after recalling her recent visit with her father. She recalled that he was an avid fan of the *Moriarty Minute*.

As Freeberg stood on the platform of the Orange line at Dupont Circle and waited for the next train to take her to Arlington, she looked around. Normally, she would have read a newspaper. Instead, she scanned the faces of everyone getting on and off at each stop. No one paid her any attention.

Strong's call had shaken her. Only four other people occupied the platform at 9:30 P.M., and they all seemed to be young, overworked attorneys. It took twelve minutes to reach her father's house, the house in which she had grown up with her two sisters. It seemed so small. She could hardly believe five people had once shared it.

Sam Matheny answered the door, and when he saw his middle daughter, a huge smile spread across his face. "Stephanie," he exclaimed, spreading out his arms and giving her a big hug. "To what do I owe this pleasant surprise?" He could see from her face that his daughter was troubled. "What's wrong?" he asked, escorting her into the house.

"I don't know, Dad," she said. "But I need your help."

Sam Matheny knew his daughter would only ask for help under the most serious of situations. She had always been the most independent of the three girls. It was this independent streak that had led her to join the Secret Service—and adopt her mother's maiden name, Freeberg.

"You've got it, Kitten," he said, motioning for her to sit on the couch in the living room.

Freeberg loved the smell of the house—it made her feel secure. She then noticed an Internet page was up on his computer monitor.

"Could I get you something to drink? A cup of tea?"

"How about a glass of wine? My nerves are a little frayed." She could tell by her father's reaction that he didn't have any wine. "A beer?"

"You got it. Two beers coming up. I can't let you drink alone," he said, winking at her. He quickly returned. "Now, what's the problem?"

"It's work. I think I have stumbled onto something big."

"Go on," said Matheny, twisting the caps off the beer bottles and handing one to his daughter.

"I think Win Murdock, the chairman of Holten, Inc.—"

"I know who he is," said her father, interrupting her.

"Well, I think he's trying to stop Robert Colfax from winning the presidency. I've got information proving it, and I think Murdock knows I have it. I tried to get it to the *Washington Herald*, but he blocked it. I also think he has my apartment bugged."

Sam Matheny sat and listened in silence. His worse fears were confirmed. The snippets of conversations he had been hearing over the last seven months were beginning to make sense.

"I remember you saying that you sometimes see Ellen Moriarty at the club on occasion."

"Maybe once a month."

"She's my only hope for getting this information to the public before the election. If you see her, could you pass it on to her?" Freeberg handed her father a thick packet of information.

"You're serious about this, aren't you, Kitten?"

She nodded. "I just don't know how to get her the information. Her phone is probably bugged, her computer can be hacked into, and she's probably being trailed."

"I suspect you're right," said Matheny, with a worried look. For the next half-hour, he told his daughter in great detail of the conversations that he had seen and overheard between Murdock and Jeffery Payne.

Freeberg was stunned.

"If what you've told me is true," said Matheny, "Murdock has taken this to a level that surpasses even Watergate. It also means that we're up against people who play for keeps."

Matheny then looked at his daughter and said, "We don't have to do this."

Stephanie smiled when she heard the word "we."

"Yes, I—I mean—*we* do."

* *

Baptista arrived at Manning's apartment late that night and informed the sniper his employer wanted another shot. What most surprised Manning was that Baptista said the shot would come from within the confines of the apartment.

CHAPTER THIRTY-SEVEN

Admiral Thomas Sewell, a decorated fighter pilot, former commander in chief of the Pacific Fleet during the Gulf War, and the first African-American to serve as chief of naval operations, had just finished a seven-mile run alone in the hills east of Oakland when he entered his workout room and flipped on CNN. As he cooled down on his stationary bike, the commercial came on. At first, he paid no attention. He became riveted as soon as he heard the Oakland Naval Yard mentioned.

"Governor Colfax supports the *Hammerschmidt Base Closure Report*," the announcer proclaimed, referring to Congressman Joseph Hammerschmidt's 1998 bipartisan report on military base closures. "If approved," the announcer continued somberly, "the city of Oakland will lose thousands of jobs." He emphasized the word "thousands."

Sewell shook his head. He knew the old naval base was long past its useful life and only survived because one of California's two senators relentlessly lobbied Congress for it over the objections of the Pentagon and the Navy. Sewell also knew the economy could easily absorb any workers who lost their jobs.

The announcer paused, and the picture of the shipyard faded away and was replaced by a photo of Robert Colfax. The announcer then continued by urging viewers to voice their displeasure with Governor Colfax directly. The ad didn't tell viewers how they might get in contact with the governor. That was not the purpose; the purpose was simply to leave the viewer with a negative impression of Colfax. On the bottom of the screen was a thin line of small print indicating that the ad was paid for and prepared by the Coalition for a Prosperous New Millennium. Similar versions of the ad were being run in every state with a military base listed for closure in the Hammerschmidt report.

"Bullshit," screamed Sewell, throwing his sweaty towel at the television. For the past few months, he had watched, with great interest, Colfax's quest for the presidency. At first, Sewell thought Colfax was crazy. But with each passing month, he had became more intrigued.

Sewell met Colfax as a fighter pilot onboard the USS Coral Sea when Colfax was temporarily serving as an intelligence officer on the aircraft carrier. Their paths later crossed when Colfax was secretary of the Navy and Sewell was CINCPAC. Never friends, each still admired the other—Sewell for Colfax's principled resignation in the wake of a presidential scandal, and Colfax for Sewell's stellar Gulf War performance.

The admiral continued to pedal on the stationary bike, the whole time thinking about the upcoming presidential race. Both Prescott and Byrne had asked if he would consider serving in either an official or unofficial capacity on their campaign committees. Sewell, a lifelong independent, declined the invitations, preferring instead to spend his time serving on the boards of various foundations and charitable organizations. In his free time, he picked up $50,000 per speaking engagement.

Ten minutes later, the same commercial came on. Sewell again swore at the television. *How much money does a man need?* he thought. In the past two years, he had made over four million dollars. He had a nice house in the Bay area and another in Steamboat Springs. His two kids had graduated from college, and he had a military pension worth close to $100,000 a year. His wife, Nancy, might even enjoy going back to Washington, D.C. They both had a lot of friends still living in the area. "That's it," he decided. Sewell recalled how General George Marshall came out of retirement to serve under President Harry Truman, and he felt he should do the same thing.

The admiral wiped the sweat from his brow and dialed 411. "Minnesota, please," he told the operator, "the Robert Colfax campaign headquarters." A minute later, Sewell was speaking with Doug Petit, a campaign volunteer at Colfax's Minneapolis campaign headquarters.

"Hello. This is Admiral Thomas Sewell. I'm trying to reach Governor Colfax's campaign manager."

"Admiral Sewell? Former chief of naval operations?" asked Petit, a retired Marine Corps officer who had decided to volunteer for Colfax after hearing him speak at his son's commencement address five months earlier.

"Yes. And with whom am I speaking?"

"Major Doug Petit. United States Marine Corps, retired."

"A pleasure speaking with you, Major. I'm trying to reach the candidate himself. Any idea how I might do that?"

"Let me put you on hold, sir. The campaign manager is in his office. I'll inform him of your call immediately." Petit sprinted into Sawyer's office. "Admiral Sewell is on the line," he said excitedly. "He wants to talk with the governor."

Sawyer stared in disbelief at Petit for a moment. "Are you sure?"

"Mr. Sawyer, I'm an ex-Marine officer. I know Admiral Sewell—and this is him."

Sawyer didn't know Petit—there were so many new volunteers at the campaign headquarters—but he could tell by his demeanor that Petit could be trusted.

"Well—fuckin' a," mumbled Sawyer. "Can you transfer the call?"

"I just started volunteering here yesterday. I haven't figured out the phone system. You'd better come and take it yourself."

The two sprinted past a pack of busy volunteers, a carton of lawn signs and stacks of campaign literature to Petit's desk.

"Hello," said Sawyer, almost out of breath, "this is Pete Sawyer, Governor Colfax's campaign manager."

"This is Admiral Thomas Sewell."

"How can I help you, Admiral?"

"I'd like to speak with the governor. Could you arrange a call between us?"

"Absolutely. I only need two things: your telephone number and the purpose of the call."

Sewell gave Sawyer his unlisted home number and then replied, "As to your second question, please tell the governor that the purpose of my call is to discuss my support of his candidacy."

Sawyer almost dropped the phone. He felt as though his prayers had been answered. The latest drop in the polls was giving him ulcers, and he needed some good news. Admiral Thomas Sewell's endorsement qualified as great news.

* *

Sean McGowan didn't endorse the plan but, having experienced past presidential campaigns, he knew that candidates wanted to increase their exposure as much as possible in the final weeks of the campaign. Robert Colfax was no exception. It was just that the idea of protecting him against 108,000 possible assailants breached the boundaries of common sense.

Robert Colfax saw it differently. The annual battle between the University of Michigan Wolverines and the University of Minnesota Golden Gophers had until recently been a cakewalk for the Wolverines, who had won twelve consecutive games dating back to 1987. Following a narrow loss in 1998 to Michigan, the Gophers substantially improved in 1999 and were picked by some in 2000 to return to the Rose Bowl for the first time since 1960. The Wolverines were determined to stop that dream, and the 108,000 partisan fans clogging the streets of Ann Arbor on Saturday, October 7, were demonstratively supportive of the same goal.

Three days earlier, a team of Secret Service advance agents had arrived in Ann Arbor and combed the stadium for possible dangers. They installed bulletproof glass in the executive suite where Colfax and the governor of Michigan would be sitting. They negated all possible lines of fire from the inside of the stadium to the suite. The Secret Service also identified the safest location for Colfax to greet people before the game.

In the hour before the start of the noon kickoff, Colfax greeted or was seen by over 35,000 fans as they entered the largest football stadium in the country. The response he received was overwhelmingly positive, especially from the students. A young man wearing a baseball hat backwards told Colfax, "You're the man!" A Ph.D. student from Nigeria, a recently naturalized citizen, informed Colfax that she was voting for him and was encouraging her fellow Nigerians—regardless of whether they could vote or not—to volunteer on his behalf. She also told the governor that she had a number of contacts at universities all across the country. Two nineteen-year-old sophomores wearing baggy gray University of Michigan sweatshirts were pleased to learn that he was pro-choice. Both vowed to vote for him.

"I don't just need your votes. I need the votes of everyone on your dormitory floor. Will you do that for me?" asked Colfax. They said they would. A campaign volunteer snapped Polaroids of Colfax and the women and handed each a photo.

*   *

Andrew Toby had no intention of shaking Robert Colfax's hand. The upcoming presidential election was the farthest thing from his mind. He had just started his freshman year at Ann Arbor, and college was everything that he had expected. The night before the game, he and two friends had persuaded an older brother of one of Toby's friends to buy a few cases of beer and some cheap Canadian whiskey. The beer was for Friday night. The whiskey was decanted into flasks for consuming during the game.

Before leaving for the stadium, Toby had tucked the flask securely inside his jeans where it was held in place by the elastic band of his boxers. He had forgotten it by the time he saw the crowd. Curious about who or what was causing the small commotion, Toby wandered closer. As he did, McGowan immediately noticed the slight bulge protruding from his pants. "Two o'clock," he whispered into his radio. "Young guy in the checkered blue and gray flannel shirt—wearing a Detroit Tigers cap."

Tom Daniels, a thirty-one-year-old Secret Service agent from the Detroit office, wore blue jeans and a navy blue wind breaker with a University of Michigan emblem as he stood on the outer right security perimeter. He picked up Toby immediately. "Got him," he radioed back to McGowan.

"Stop him if he moves for the concealed object or gets within fifty feet," said McGowan. Unaware of the surveillance and still in a fog from all the beer he consumed the night before, Toby continued directly toward Colfax. From McGowan's and Daniels' perspective it appeared that Colfax was the sole object of Toby's attention. The student continued straight at Colfax, and both Secret Service agents, whose eyes continued to alternate every half second across the throngs of people streaming into the stadium, kept coming back to Toby with increasing frequency. McGowan couldn't wait any longer. "Take him out."

So swift was Daniels that Toby never saw the Secret Service agent approach. Before Toby even knew what had hit him, his arms were pinned to his side and the whiskey flask was firmly in Daniels' possession.

Daniels quickly improvised. "Campus security," he said. "You weren't planning on taking this inside the stadium, were you?"

Toby was speechless. Daniels continued, "If you keep moving, we'll forget about this whole incident. If you don't, I'll arrest your scrawny little ass right now."

Toby shook off his hangover enough to say, "I'll keep moving." He was mad at losing his flask and its contents but figured that his buddies still had theirs. He never knew that he was only feet from Robert Colfax.

Daniels radioed back to McGowan, "Just a college kid trying to sneak in booze."

McGowan and Daniels both went back to scanning the multitudes of people walking by, looking for any quick movements. McGowan could not wait for the campaign to finish. He was verging on burnout but knew he could not let his guard down. His sixth sense told him the assassin was still out there.

* *

Colfax took the call from his campaign manager during halftime of the Michigan-Minnesota football game. The score was ten to seven in favor of the Wolverines.

"Are you sure it was Sewell?" asked Colfax.

"Positive," said Sawyer with an edge of excitement in his voice.

"And he said he was interested in supporting my candidacy?"

"Those were almost his exact words."

Douglas Headley, the governor of Michigan and Colfax's host for the football game, listened with rapt attention and tried to piece together the conversation he was overhearing. If he surmised correctly, it sounded like Admiral Sewell was going to throw his support to Colfax. If that were the case, Colfax's odds for winning the presidency had just improved dramatically. Ever a political animal, Headley, who had risen from the Grand Rapids City Council to the state legislature, to the attorney general's office and eventually to the governor's mansion, had always trusted his political instincts. He decided now was the time to act. Having been passed over as Prescott's vice presidential candidate, he figured he had nothing too lose.

"Give me his number," said Colfax, before listing off a number of other things he wanted his campaign manager to do.

"Bob?" said Headley, interrupting Colfax after he hung up, "I'd like to discuss coming on board your campaign."

Colfax turned and looked at Headley. He knew that the popular, three-term governor had overheard the conversation, but he was still impressed with Headley's ability to act fast. He was more impressed with Headley's willingness to take a risk. For all Headley knew, the conversation he overheard could have been manufactured.

"I know it's kind of late."

Always diplomatic, Colfax did not let on that the mention of Sewell might have persuaded Headley. "I'd be honored, Doug."

"The honor is all mine," replied Headley. "You know that I was hoping to be Prescott's VP. That didn't happen—that's life. I'm now in my third term. It's time for something new. I wish I would have had the courage to do what you did, but I'll settle for being a part of your administration. I really think you can make a difference."

Colfax was impressed with his candor. "You don't think Prescott can win?"

"Oh, I still think he can win. I just don't think I'll like what happens if he does. I don't think he can govern effectively. The special interests and the far right will pull all the strings."

"I think you're right. How soon would you be able to make your support for me public?" said Colfax, cutting to the chase.

"Immediately—whatever works best for you." Colfax thought about the man in front of him for a moment. Was he the ultimate opportunist, or did he invite him to the game to make this pitch? He knew Headley was widely respected in public policy circles as a leader in welfare reform and a thoughtful conservative. Colfax also knew he would be lucky to have his support, especially in Michigan with its eighteen Electoral College votes.

"Welcome aboard," said Colfax, extending his hand.

* *

The call went directly to Sewell's private line. It was 10:00 A.M. in California, and Sewell had showered and was watching the football game that Colfax was attending.

"Sewell," the admiral, answered.

"Thomas? Bob Colfax. How the hell are you?"

"Outstanding. And you?"

"You tell me," replied Colfax, getting directly to the purpose of the call—a trait that Sewell respected.

"I take it your aide told you why I called?"

"He did," said Colfax, placing one finger to his left ear to drown out the sound from the University of Michigan marching band.

"It's true. I was watching television this morning and saw those goddamn ads they're running against you."

"And which ads are those? There are so many I can hardly keep them straight."

"The one that claims you will render thousands of men, women, and children homeless because you favor the closing of that worthless piece of shit of a naval base they call the Oakland Naval Yard."

"Ah. *That* ad. It's just one of a hundred variations a group calling themselves the Coalition for a Prosperous New Millennium is running all across the country. Every area that has a military base listed in Hammerschmidt's report is being inundated."

"You're shittin' me. They've got to be spending millions against you."

"They are and there isn't a thing I can do about it. It's all legal."

"Well, there is something we can do about it," said Sewell. "I want to come out publicly in support of you—and I specifically want to help tell the American public that those bases have to be closed. Not one of those damn bases adds an iota to the national security of this country. They should—they must—be closed."

"I appreciate that, Thomas. Your support means a lot to me."

"You know, I was going to stay neutral in the presidential campaign, but that television ad pushed me over the edge. I might have had some respect for a group that was really opposed to the closing of the base . . . but for some nameless special interest group to blatantly appeal to people's raw emotions—it was more than I could handle. I might even have been able to live with it if they were willing to identify themselves—but they're not. They're cowards, pure and simple. I just couldn't sit on the sidelines any longer and watch the person I believe would make the best president be attacked and belittled by nameless cowards."

"Your support means the world to me, Thomas—and your timing couldn't have been better."

"You're welcome. I know you're busy, Bob. Keep up the good work. I'll speak with your aide, and we'll work out the details and the timing of my announcement."

"Thank you again, Thomas."

"No, thank you."

* *

Jacob Mance, after a berating telephone call from Murdock, dedicated four million dollars to a massive push-polling campaign. The target was likely Colfax voters. The questioner, who always presented him or herself as an independent pollster, asked a series of leading questions, each one was designed to make the recipient less likely to vote for the independent candidate.

"If you knew that Governor Colfax was opposed to the death penalty, would you be more or less likely to vote for him?"

"If you knew Governor Colfax opposed to a Constitutional amendment prohibiting the burning of the American flag, would you be more or less likely to vote for him?"

"If you knew Governor Colfax supported allowing more foreigners to come into the country, would you be more or less likely to vote for him?"

The questioner went on for seven more questions. The final question was, "Knowing what you know today, are you more or less likely to vote for Robert Colfax?" Jacob Mance's investment helped dissuade over one million once-likely Colfax voters from voting for the independent candidate.

* *

The second debate took place on the campus of Wake Forest University. What little bump Colfax had gained from the first debate had quickly given way under the massive push-polling campaign that had been directed against him at the request of Jacob Mance. Colfax drew the opening slot in the debate.

"Good evening," said Colfax, smiling warmly into the camera. "I am running for president because I believe the American people crave leadership. Leadership that is willing to take a position—take a stand—a stand borne not of politics or polls but of principle. If you are looking for the same thing, I ask you to vote for me on November 7th. You have my commitment that I will eliminate the national debt by instituting a one-time fifteen percent tax on the wealth of every American making over ten million dollars. I will work tirelessly to reform Social Security to allow you to invest a portion of your contributions in your own personal retirement account. I will preserve an additional 100 million acres of wildness for future generations. I will completely eliminate the insidious influence of special interest money. I will advocate for the toughest gun-control laws this country has ever seen. And I will work to give students and parents of the worst schools in this country the opportunity to choose a better future by selecting a better school. You may not agree with all these positions, but I believe they are consistent. They'll benefit the only special interest group I care about—our children."

* *

Later polling would show that the average voter liked Colfax instantly. And his plan to eliminate the national debt was supported by eighty percent of the voters. Furthermore, Prescott and Byrne's orchestrated attacks on Colfax, rather than working to beat him down, actually strengthened his standing among the public. One audience member interviewed after the debate said, "It looked like the vice president and Governor Prescott were beating up on Colfax. What I wanted to hear was how they intended to lead the country. Colfax was the only candidate who spoke to that."

Pundits also agreed that Colfax delivered a knockout punch to the vice president midway through the debate, when Byrne, in response to a question about what he would like his legacy to be, referred to the "three E's" of his administration: education, the economy and the environment. Colfax responded during his rebuttal by saying, "Martin, it's not the three E's that have me so concerned about your legacy, it's the other two E's that you never mention." Byrne fell right into Colfax's trap.

"And what might those other two be, Bob?" asked Byrne.

"Everything—else," said Colfax. The audience howled with laughter. "Seriously, Martin, you talk about education, the economy and the environment. But when you are talking to select groups of people, or when you are dialing for dollars with special interest groups, you're promising the moon. You talk about spending more money for health care, you pledge more money for workers displaced by trade, and you offer more money for farmers of this country. Even in your three E's, you talk about more money. More money for education, more money for the environment. What you never talk about is how—or who—is going to pay for these things. Martin, we have been down that path before, and I don't think the American people want to go there again. They understand that we can bolster our economy, improve our educational system and protect the environment by introducing competition and choice into the system. Our schools can be improved by letting the money follow the students, not by endlessly pouring more money at the teachers' unions." The dials in both the Republican and Democratic focus groups registered near "9" during Colfax's response.

* *

Win Murdock had no problem soliciting ten million dollars from a network of ten friends who he knew loathed Colfax's one-time plan to eliminate the national debt. Murdock promised his friends that the money would be dumped on Colfax in the final days of the campaign.

CHAPTER THIRTY-EIGHT

I t was a beautiful autumn day in Minneapolis, although the trees had passed their peak color two weeks earlier. The city was in the midst of a classic Indian summer. The temperature hovered around seventy and the day perfectly reflected the mood at Colfax campaign headquarters. There was a feeling of anticipation in the air.

The headquarters, which had only occupied the ground floor of the old brick warehouse four months earlier, now consumed three floors, and Pete Sawyer was in negotiations to sublet the remaining two for the final weeks of the campaign. On October 16, the warehouse hummed with an oddly efficient chaos—hundreds of individuals' actions blending together to achieve a common purpose, much like ants in a colony.

The first floor housed the core campaign activities. Colfax, Sawyer, and the press secretary occupied three small offices, and the remaining 3,000 square feet were devoted to telephones and computers to process the growing numbers of requests for volunteer information. E-mail inquirers received information immediately. Callers were transferred to the third floor, where they were referred to a Colfax volunteer coordinator in their area.

The second floor was reserved for media relations. Every town in America with a population over 35,000 was assigned a staff person to act as the liaison to the media in that community. Sawyer had directed that no inquiry go unanswered for longer than two hours. As a result, Colfax was receiving a disproportionate amount of media attention and editorial endorsements in the smaller markets. On October 16, the *Kenosha News* became the first paper to publicly endorse Robert Colfax for president.

A separate team, dubbed the e-truth squad, also worked on the second floor. Their purpose was to respond, via the Internet, to any and all negative ads directed against Colfax. No accusation was too small to go unchallenged, and no market was too small to avoid their electronic tentacles.

The third floor was dedicated to grassroots activity. Fifty-one staffers, one for each state and the District of Columbia, called the floor home for the last month of the campaign. On a single day, the local Dominos pizza franchise billed over $700 in pizzas to the staff and volunteers on the floor.

Pete Sawyer used the warehouse intercom system for the first and only time during the campaign. "Good afternoon, everyone," he said. His voice crackled over the entire warehouse. He then hit the microphone once more to ensure that it was working. It was. "Good afternoon," he repeated. "This is Pete Sawyer. I know everyone is extremely busy, but Governor Colfax has requested that I call a special meeting of the entire staff. He has a message that he would like to deliver personally. He has asked for everyone to convene on the main floor in twenty minutes. Thank you." After a pause, Sawyer added, "And, yes, food will be provided."

The stir the announcement created was immediate. Most staffers—paid or volunteer—had only seen Colfax once or twice, and he had personally addressed the staff once—and that was before most volunteers had started with the campaign.

Sawyer had ordered seven twelve-foot-long submarine sandwiches from a local sandwich shop and filled two coolers with soft drinks for the occasion. The staffers were still helping themselves when Colfax entered the campaign headquarters. They burst into applause as he made his way to the front of the room. Immediately, those still standing in line took a place on the floor where they could get the best view to see and hear the candidate.

"How's everybody doing?" Colfax asked.

The staff, not really anticipating the question, didn't respond.

Colfax laughed and repeated the question, "I asked: how's everybody doing?"

This time they responded with more enthusiasm.

"That's more like it. I know all of you have been busting your butts these past few weeks—months for many of you. And so have I," said Colfax, who had traveled over a 100,000 miles in the last three weeks alone and visited eighty-nine different cities in thirty-two states. "And I want you to know that I appreciate everything you have done for me—but I'm going to ask you to do even more over these next two weeks. We have an opportunity to make history—but to do it, we must work as a team."

Colfax looked out over the hundred-plus volunteers staring back at him—most were young faces, but there were older ones and a number of minorities. "I know most of you have either seen, heard or read the latest poll numbers, which show us dropping into third place. The pundits are now saying that the American people are beginning to question whether a vote for me is a wasted vote. Well, let me tell you a few things. First, my slide in the polls halts today! And second, the pundits are wrong. We're going to shock the hell out of them on Tuesday, November 7. Come Election Day, I'll be ahead in the only poll that matters—the one that takes place in the ballot booth!"

The volunteers went wild.

After the staff quieted down, Colfax continued. "The reason I say my numbers will halt is because tomorrow I'm going to make two major announcements that will surprise the political world." What little noise was still being made stopped completely. "First, Michigan Governor Doug Headley has agreed to publicly announce his support for my candidacy."

A chorus of hollers followed. After the cheering subsided, Colfax dropped the big news. "Second, former Chief of Naval Operations and Gulf War hero Admiral Thomas Sewell has agreed to serve in my cabinet when I'm elected."

The news took a second to register. When it did, the staff went berserk. Younger staffers were giving each other high-fives. Some of the older volunteers simply smiled. The momentum had finally switched.

"We will be making the announcements public in an hour," said Colfax. "A commercial featuring Admiral Sewell will begin airing tonight. I just wanted to have you hear the good news first. Folks, we're going to win. Now, lets get back to work," said Colfax with his crooked smile.

None of the staffers took any more soft drinks; the news had given them all the jolt they needed for the day—and possibly for the remainder of the campaign. Colfax could have told them he was working on endorsements from Jack Quinn, the maverick Republican candidate, and John Gordon, the thoughtful Democratic challenger, but he was afraid any leak might bring down immense pressure on those two from their own parties.

* *

The third and final debate was the most watched engagement in the history of presidential debates, surpassing the famous 1960 Kennedy-Nixon debates. The defining moment came over a question of heroes.

Laura Zoffer, the lone female panelist and a correspondent for CBS, asked each candidate to name a living hero. Governor Prescott, aware that the question was coming, used the opportunity to emphasize his position on character, honesty, integrity and values. He outlined characteristics that he felt defined a hero, but he never named one. When pressed, he responded, "Jesus Christ." Zoffer reminded him that Christ was not currently alive.

"Well, he's living in me and millions of other Christians," replied Prescott. His remarks struck many as inappropriate. Only among born-again Christians, a group already solidly in his camp, did his response go over well.

Martin Byrne went next and responded that his wife, Lucy, was his hero. "She has raised three beautiful children, donated generously of her time and talents in her community and made me a better person by demonstrating patience, kindness, and love throughout our thirty-three-year marriage."

Byrne's response fared better than Prescott's, but even among women—who were Byrne's intended audience—the sacchrine-like quality of the delivery and the content struck many as phony. One woman interviewed after the debate said, "You could tell he had that answer planted in his head. They weren't his words; they were some consultant's."

Colfax went last. "I think this country, contrary to the belief of many, has a multitude of heroes. I see heroes every day on the campaign trail. I've met with them and I've heard their stories," said Colfax, falling into his rapid campaign speaking style. "Tom Davis, a veteran cop from Baltimore, decided to get out of his squad car from which he simply chased criminals—after they committed a crime—and instead took up a walking beat so that he could interact with kids in the neighborhood and work to prevent crimes. Tom Davis is a hero.

"Dorothy Marbury, whom I met in Los Angeles, is another hero. Tired of gangs selling crack cocaine on her street corner—but not willing to pull down her shade—Dorothy decided to organize her neighbors to take back their streets for their children. Working together, they confronted the gangs and regained control of their neighborhoods. Dorothy Marbury is a hero.

"Everywhere I look, I see heroes. A hero is the parent who, after working two jobs in an effort to build a better future for their child, still finds the time to read to that child before bed."

A poll, conducted the morning after the debate, found that sixty-three percent of those watching felt that Colfax was the winner.

* *

"What choice do we have?" asked Jeffery Payne, with an air of resignation. "Colfax now has Sewell on board, and he kicked Prescott and Byrne's asses last night. He's on a roll. It's our only option."

"No," said Murdock with authority.

"But—" proclaimed Payne, who was so nervous he couldn't touch his salad.

"No buts. This thing is out of control, and the Vandiver card is the only card I have left. If I play it now, it'll be like pissing in the wind. It won't make a bit of difference. Colfax is too popular. A scandal involving a candidate for vice president doesn't cut it. The way things are going for Colfax, it'll probably increase his poll numbers."

"So we're sticking to the original plan?"

"That's right."

"It's too risky. I mean, Sewell is worth a few states. I'm not sure Colfax can be defeated."

"Neither am I, but he still has an uphill battle to reach 270 Electoral College votes," said Murdock.

"But if Colfax wins, his level of Secret Service protection will skyrocket. A second shot, especially after he has officially become president, will be next to impossible."

Murdock said nothing and took a sip of iced tea. Not wishing to stay any longer than necessary, Payne nodded his head in direction of the maître d', indicating that it was okay to serve the entrée.

As the maître d' approached, Murdock finally responded to Payne's comment about a second shot. "Not unless I know something the Secret Service doesn't."

* *

Baptista listened to Payne explain the plan. He asked a few questions but took no notes. Everything was committed to memory and would be reiterated to Manning flawlessly. Baptista's only other job was to supply the sniper with the equipment necessary to complete the job.

* *

Tracy Hall had been in a severe depression since her son's death. She had not even been able to bring herself to enter her son's room. Finally, on the six-month anniversary of his death, she mustered up enough courage to go in. A flood of memories rushed over her when she opened the door, and she almost turned around. She picked up a photo of her son in a Little League outfit and smiled. She then noticed the screen saver on her son's computer was still on—a school of colorful fish slowly swimming back and forth across the monitor. She clicked on the mouse and noticed that her son had hundreds of e-mails, mostly from friends who had forgotten to take his name off their mail lists. Hall scrolled through the messages, not bothering to open any. At the end of the list, she noticed the April 30 date instantly. The time was two hours before her son's estimated time of death. She took a deep breath before opening it.

Tracy Hall could not believe what she read. Her son had seen David Pollard the night he was murdered, which meant Troy had not died of an overdose. Her son had been murdered.

Hall frantically searched for Anne Strong's number. When the reporter didn't answer, Hall left a message. "Hi, this is Tracy Hall. We spoke about two months ago," said Hall, without taking a breath. "I have proof my son didn't OD. You were right. He was murdered. I have an e-mail that he sent to himself two hours before he died. He saw David Pollard."

* *

John Dalton had not been on the Chicago-St.Paul-Fargo run since May 16, the date of the attempt on Robert Colfax's life. As the train headed west out of St. Cloud, moving in the opposite direction it had the last time he made the trip, Dalton couldn't help but look around as he approached the area surrounding St. John's.

On May 16, he had no idea the university was even there. After the assassination attempt, he pulled out a map of central Minnesota and studied the location of the tracks relative to the campus. He still had the map.

The train was adjacent to the campus when he noticed County Road 53. It was then that it hit him. The last time he went by, a track foreman had ordered a "slow order" for this section of the track. He couldn't remember if he told this to the Secret Service agent who interviewed him. But he did remember that he had said it would have been difficult for someone to jump aboard the train. With a "slow order" in affect, that wasn't the case.

Dalton called the Secret Service office when he reached Fargo. It took only a minute for him to get through to Peter Tingley.

"Hello, Mr. Dalton," said Tingley, vaguely remembering the train engineer. "How may I help you?"

"It's about the assassination attempt. I have some important information that I think I failed to give you when we talked back in May."

"Go on."

"I remember telling you that someone couldn't have jumped on board. I was wrong. I think I slowed in the vicinity of St. John's—I just didn't know I was in the area of St. John's at the time. A 'slow order' was placed on a section of track just south of the campus."

"Just a minute, Mr. Dalton. Let me retrieve my notes." Tingley put the man on hold and pulled up his computerized notes of his interview and subsequent investigation.

"Are you sure, Mr. Dalton?"

"Positive."

"Why didn't you report this in May?"

"I don't know—maybe because I only slowed for a minute. Maybe because slow orders are so common. It could have been I didn't think I was anywhere near the university when I did it."

"We received the rail manifest for May 16. In fact, I'm looking at a copy right now, and there is no indication of any activity on the rail that day."

"Are you sure?" asked Dalton.

"Yes."

"I'm almost positive I slowed down because I remember thinking it odd because the order would have caused me to block the county road for a longer period of time than normal. At the time, I thought it had something to do with the recent acquisition of the railroad by Holten."

"Mr. Dalton, I'd like you to come back to Minneapolis for further questioning."

* *

David Luther heard immediately of the Secret Service's rekindled interest in the "slow order." Having learned his lesson from an earlier price-fixing investigation, Luther made sure all records—electronic or otherwise—were destroyed. Luther knew that he and John Dalton were the only two people who knew of the order. He also knew that it could never be confirmed if Dalton were no longer around.

The fifty-four-year-old train engineer's death received a tiny mention on page seventeen of the local section of the *Chicago Tribune* the day after it happened. Police had no leads or witnesses in the hit-and-run case.

* *

Anne Strong usually checked her answering machine religiously. But there was nothing usual about the final week of a presidential campaign. She did not retrieve her messages from October 30 until November 2. Strong listened to Hall's message in stunned silence, then punched in her number immediately.

"This is Anne Strong," she said.

"Thank God. I didn't know if you'd gotten my message. You're the only one I can trust. What do we do?"

Strong didn't know herself. She knew Bradley Schuman wouldn't let her run a story like this with only five days to go before the election.

"Do you still have the e-mail?"

"Yes?"

"Can you forward it to me, if I get you an address?"

"Sure."

"Better yet, give me your e-mail address. I'm going to send you a message. Once you get it, forward Troy's message to me." Hall gave Strong her dead son's e-mail address.

Twenty minutes later, Strong was sitting in a computer coffee shop in Minneapolis' Uptown area, sending out a short, innocuous message to Troy Hall.

Tracy Hall received the message instantly and forwarded the April 30 message to Strong. She noticed immediately that Troy had only sent a copy to himself and Ellen Moriarty. Strong reasoned it never reached her—probably for the same reason her story on Win Murdock had been stopped. Someone was monitoring their activities.

It took Strong only minutes to locate Stephanie Freeberg at her father's house. Freeberg and Sam Matheny read the message together. Both looked at the other. The April 30 e-mail linked everything together. Now they just had to get the story to Ellen Moriarty.

CHAPTER THIRTY-NINE

Ellen Moriarty finished her last sip of decaffeinated coffee and silently cursed that she had spent over $100 on lunch and hadn't even seen anyone remotely resembling a person of power. Her next report was looking pretty bleak. She was about ready to leave when she noticed the maître d' coming toward her.

"Ms. Moriarty?" Matheny asked.

"Yes."

"I have a package for you. It was just delivered by special courier," he lied. He had been waiting three weeks to personally deliver it.

"Who is it from?" asked Moriarty.

"I don't know."

"Did you sign for it?"

"No. It was delivered by a young man," lied Matheny again.

Before Moriarty could even say anything, Matheny, familiar with the ways of Washington and knowledgeable enough to know that suspicious packages weren't necessarily welcomed, offered to discard the package. His ploy worked. Moriarty laughed off the risk.

"Would you prefer that I open it?" he asked. The thought that it might contain an explosive hadn't even occurred to Moriarty. His offer did make her pause for a moment.

"No thank you, Sam, that won't be necessary."

Matheny was surprised she knew his name.

"No need for you to fall victim if some Unibomber-like character is really gunning for me," replied Moriarty, with a small laugh.

"That's very kind of you, Ms. Moriarty, but I do feel as though I bear some responsibility. I should have asked for some verification from the deliverer."

"Nonsense. I'll open it. You could, however, have my waiter bring over some more coffee. I take it black. It looks as though the package contains a goodly amount of reading information."

"Coming right up, Ms. Moriarty."

Matheny's job was done. The waiter removed Moriarty's old cup and saucer and replaced them with a fresh set. Two cups later, Moriarty, buzzing more from the contents of the package than the coffee, set the papers down and said, "Holy shit." She then smiled. The $100 lunch had more than paid for itself. If what the information in the package said was true, Moriarty not only had her next report, she had enough information to last her to election day—and well beyond.

* *

Peter Tingley was unable to debrief Sean McGowan on his conversation with John Dalton until McGowan returned from the campaign trail. McGowan's initial reaction was just what Tingley had expected.

"How the fuck did we miss this? How the fuck did Dalton just forget something like this?"

"I don't know, Sean. He claims the train only slowed for a minute, it was nothing unusual. Plus, I didn't specifically ask the question."

"Pete—how could you?"

"It slipped. He had been interviewed the day before—and it was my tenth interview of the day."

"Jesus Christ." McGowan took a deep breath and tried to regain his composure. "But there is no confirmation of the slow order?" asked McGowan.

"None."

"So, it's the engineer's word against that of officials at Holten?"

"I guess . . . but we'll never know. Dalton was killed in a hit-and-run case last night."

"What? That's too much of a coincidence," said McGowan. "Something's not right. I talked with Wells last night about Holten, but he told me that the FBI remains convinced Bradford is their man. And maybe he is. But I've looked at his background, and the guy was not very bright—his high school grades and his military evaluations reeked of mediocrity. There is no way he could have pulled this off alone. I mean, where does a guy like Bradford get custom-made depleted uranium bullets? He had to have help."

"He's evaded the FBI search for over five months. He can't be that stupid," said Tingley. He saw McGowan's face change immediately. "What?"

"Unless Bradford isn't even our guy. I remember Wells saying earlier that there were three other people still under investigation. I want you to get photos of all three and search the video archive of Colfax's appearances since February and look for possible matches. Whoever shot at Colfax probably did some advance surveillance. We didn't find Bradford anywhere. Let's see if one of these other three appear. Give this your highest priority. If that son of a bitch is still out there, I want to know it. Let me know what you find."

* *

Ellen Moriarty posted the *Moriarty Minute* at precisely 03:42:27 on November 3. David Luther read the report at 3:47 A.M. By 3:59, a team of sophisticated computer hackers, hired by Jacob Mance, had disabled the web site and inserted a photo of Ellen Moriarty's head superimposed upon the body of a woman dressed in provocative leather dominatrix outfit. The hacker job was meant to look like it was a prank pulled by a college-aged computer geek.

The one factor beyond the coalition's control was the few copies that had been downloaded from the Moriarty web site in the twelve minutes between when the report was posted and the site was disabled. Of the handful of people who accessed the report, only one downloaded an electronic version of it.

* *

It was 2:00 A.M. and Josh Parker couldn't sleep, so he folded up his Murphy bed, showered and left his cramped efficiency apartment for the campaign headquarters. The building was only three blocks away. On his way in, he stopped at a convenience store and grabbed his usual breakfast of a massive cup of Mountain Dew and box of chocolate donuts.

With only four days to go before the election, someone was always at the headquarters, so the door was open. Parker headed straight for his computer. He scanned the latest news from CNN, the *Political Insider*, the *Washington Herald*, the *Washington Post* and the *New York Times*. Next, he reviewed ESPN's site and silently bemoaned all the interviews from New York Yankees players following their third-straight World Series championship two weeks earlier. He thought that if he ever had a minute alone with Colfax, after he became president, he would ask him to review baseball's antitrust exemption—it was ruining baseball, Parker thought. Lastly, he opened the *Moriarty Minute*. The time was 2:51 A.M. On the East Coast, it was an hour later.

* *

The headline blared out from the screen of the *Moriarty Minute* web site: GIBRALTAR CONSPIRACY UNVEILED. "This newsletter originally reported about the Gibraltar Conspiracy on March 8 of this year. It has not been reported on since because members of the Coalition for a Prosperous New Millennium have hacked my site and stolen information that unveils their plot. I will now—thanks to sources that cannot be identified for reasons that will soon become obvious—tell the story."

In great detail, Moriarty described David Pollard, the role he played in trying to identify the members of the coalition, and the details surrounding his unsolved murder on April 28. She explained J. Preston Briggs' relationship with Pollard, the work he done for the law firm of Lawrence, Mance & Scott, the connection between the law firm and the coalition, and the details surrounding his April 29 suicide. Next, Moriarty sketched her brief encounter with Troy Hall and her request to the young man. She included a copy of his April 30 e-mail. Moriarty outlined the puzzling circumstances surrounding his alleged overdose.

The story, Moriarty admitted to her readers, still did not explain the reason the coalition had been formed. That, she wrote, was filled in by the details of the Coalition for a Prosperous New Millennium's anti-Colfax Electoral College strategy, which she took almost verbatim from the notes Stephanie Freeberg had provided in the packet that Sam Matheny had delivered to her the previous day.

The man behind the coalition, Moriarty reported, was Win Murdock. For the safety of her source, she wrote, she could not provide any more details. Moriarty simply concluded by saying, "Win Murdock is not acting alone. The Gibraltar Conspiracy reaches to the highest levels within government."

* *

"Holy shit," said Parker, printing a version of the report. Before he rushed into Sawyer's office, he downloaded a copy of the report.

"Have you seen this?" said Parker, bursting into Sawyer's office frantically waving a copy to the *Moriarty Minute* at him.

"Slow down, Josh," said Sawyer, who had fallen a sleep in a corner chair and was still groggy. "I don't even know what you've got. What is it?"

Parker had no idea that the information in his hands was less than ten minutes old. "It's a copy of the *Moriarty Minute* and she is reporting that the 'Gibraltar Conspiracy' is real!"

It took Sawyer a moment to remember the specifics of Moriarty's earlier account of the conspiracy. He recalled it had something to do with Win Murdock and the

Coalition for a Prosperous New Millennium. At the time, it had made sense, but he hadn't seen proof of it in the past few months and had completely forgotten about it.

"Let me see," said Sawyer as Parker handed him the report and watched his face while the campaign manager read it. "Sweet Jesus! When did this come out?" Sawyer asked.

Parker asked for the report back. "It says it was sent at 3:42 A.M. Eastern Standard Time. So that means it's not even fifteen minutes old."

"Fantastic. Any of the major networks reporting it?"

"Not yet. I just read the most recent electronic updates from CNN, the *Herald*, and the *Times*. It's probably too fresh. Moriarty has scooped the majors again."

"Stay right here. I'm going to check with a few editors and find out what is going on," said Sawyer, rifling through his Rolodex looking for CNN's number.

"I can help you put all your contacts on a computer Rolodex, so you can instantly call up whatever number or person you want," replied Parker, watching Sawyer flip through scores of business cards. Sawyer didn't respond. Finally, he found the number he was looking for and dialed it.

"Morrie Vitale, please," said Sawyer to the receptionist at CNN. "Tell him Pete Sawyer, Robert Colfax's campaign manager, is on the phone."

The receptionist informed Sawyer that Mr. Vitale was not expected to arrive for another two hours. Sawyer suddenly remembered it was only 4:00 A.M. on the East Coast.

"Could I speak with the most senior news director available?"

The receptionist replied that that would be Joan Rummel and forwarded the call.

"Rummel," answered the twenty-six-year news veteran.

"Hello, this Pete Sawyer—"

Before he could even finish speaking, Rummel asked if he was Colfax's campaign manager.

"One and the same," replied Sawyer, happy to know that she knew who he was.

"What can I do for you?"

"Are you aware of the story that was reported in the *Moriarty Minute* this morning?"

"No," replied Rummel. "But you're the second person to call in the last five minutes about it. I tried to have a staff assistant pull up the story, but she said the web site had been hacked."

"What?"

"Apparently there's a picture of Moriarty superimposed on the body of a woman dressed in leather with a collar in one hand and a whip in the other," said Rummel, laughing.

"What about the story?" asked Sawyer, growing frustrated.

"What story?"

"The Gibraltar Conspiracy!"

"The what? I haven't seen anything. All I know is that some hotshot lawyer just called and said that if we ran with any portion of the story, we would be sued—and in his words, sued 'big time.' I told him I didn't know what the hell he was talking about. That seemed to satisfy him."

"Do you know who the lawyer was?"

"Someone from Lawrence—"

"Lawrence, Mance & Scott?" said Sawyer.

"Yeah, that sounds right."

"So you're telling me that Lawrence, Mance & Scott is threatening to sue you for a story you didn't even see?"

"Basically. Although, like I said, I'm having an assistant try to locate a copy of the report."

"Doesn't it make you a little suspicious?" asked Sawyer. "First, hackers take down the site and then you receive a threat not to run a story that doesn't even exist?"

"A little. But I can't get too spun up about something I haven't even seen. But you're right—it is a little suspicious. What's in the report?"

"I'll e-mail and fax you a copy," said Sawyer, looking at Parker. "The gist of the story is that Win Murdock, through an organization called the Coalition for a Prosperous New Millennium, is pursuing a strategy that will deny Robert Colfax an Electoral College majority. There's a lot more—but I know what I just told you is true."

"Does she provide any details? Any names? Sources?"

"Plenty of details, but nothing on the sources," said Sawyer, knowing what Rummel would say next.

"Until we get some verifiable sources, I can't do shit. Even if the lawyers weren't breathing down my back, I wouldn't run with the story."

"Look," said Sawyer, "I appreciate the position you're in. Once you read the story, you'll see why the sources have to remain anonymous. I just ask that you keep after this story. It's got merit."

"But you're Colfax's campaign manager. You get paid to think it has merit, especially if it benefits your candidate."

"Look, just keep after the story. Please."

"That's what we get paid to do," said Rummel.

After he hung up, Sawyer looked at Parker. "The big boys are fucking with us. They've threatened to sue anyone who airs the story. I'm sure they're already working to discredit the story. We have only one option."

Parker looked at him and smiled. "Consider it done. I'll have it out to our supporters in less than a hour and on our web site in two. By eight o'clock, it'll be in the hands of all our media contacts."

"Thank God for the Internet."

CHAPTER FORTY

The final ninety-six hours of the campaign were run on pure adrenaline. Every state and every single Electoral College vote was crucial. The Coalition for a Prosperous New Millennium had allocated three million dollars for television ads on Saturday and Sunday, five million dollars for Monday and up to five million dollars for Tuesday, if necessary. The money was strategically targeted to keep the likely Colfax voters at home and get Prescott and Byrne voters out to the polls. The campaign tactics were as varied as the people they were trying to influence. Pro-life voters received literature through their churches and were inundated with last-minute phone calls reminding them of Colfax's willingness "to trample on the rights of the unborn." Union members were warned that Colfax's free-trade policies were "jeopardizing your job, your future, and your family's way of life."

Television and cable ads were running around the clock. A person could hardly turn on the television or radio without seeing or hearing an anti-Colfax ad. It didn't matter what the person was watching or whether they were listening to country, rock and roll, or talk radio. The coalition understood the demographics and how best to attack Colfax.

Individual members of the coalition were busy exerting their influence where appropriate. The Committee to Protect Social Security distributed over thirty million pieces of literature to elderly Americans telling them Colfax's plan to partially privatize Social Security was "an attempt by Wall Street bankers to make the rich, richer and the poor, poorer." Teachers' unions inundated their members with telephone calls urging them to "Tell Robert Colfax to protect public education." The callers reminded members that Colfax's support for vouchers "was the first step to dismantling the American public school system."

The American Legal and Judicial Society, the largest association of trial attorneys, was more sophisticated than some of the other groups and quietly went about informing its members of Colfax's support for tort reform. Most members didn't need to be told what Colfax's plan to cap excessive nonpunitive damages meant—they knew it would take money out of their pockets.

* *

Sean McGowan returned to his apartment overlooking Lake Calhoun in Minneapolis' Uptown area. It was a treat to be in his bed so close to the end of a presidential campaign—even if it was only for five hours. Sawyer had notified McGowan that Colfax intended to campaign nonstop the last seventy-two hours of the campaign, and McGowan knew he needed every second of sleep he could get. Before he laid his head down, however, he had two calls to make. The first was to the director of the Secret Service, whom he called at home.

"This is Agent McGowan. Sorry to call you at home, sir."

"We still don't have anything," said Max Walters.

"That's not the purpose of my call. Gibraltar has decided to campaign nonstop for the next three days. I need some assistance. The crowds are getting larger everywhere we go. My team is on the verge of exhaustion. I need support."

"What's his itinerary through election eve?"

"We're in Boston tomorrow A.M. We then fly to D.C. for a rally on the Mall. Afterwards, we go to Atlanta and then Miami. We fly overnight to San Antonio, stop quickly in Phoenix before working our way up the California coast all day Sunday, hitting L.A., San Jose, and Sacramento. Next, it's off to Portland and Seattle. In each city, we're making brief appearances. We arrive in Denver for a midnight rally. Monday starts with an early-morning rally in Chicago, then Milwaukee, Detroit and Cleveland—all before 1400. Then it's off to Louisville, St. Louis, Wichita, Dallas, and finally, early Tuesday morning, he wraps things up in New Orleans before heading to Minnesota to vote."

"How many cities?" asked Walters, incredulous.

"Twenty-one."

"Get me a copy of the itinerary. I'll make sure you have the support you need. It'll be tough, though. The other candidates—and their running mates—are making the same last-minute mad scramble." Walters let out a sigh. "Any chance Gibraltar will commit to limiting all the stops to the tarmac? That'll make crowd control easier."

"He's already agreed to it—he's a little sensitized to the issue since St. John's. He did ask that an exception be granted in New Orleans. He wants to speak at a park on the Mississippi River at dawn on Tuesday."

"You'll have all the support you need, Agent McGowan," said Walters.

McGowan almost didn't make the second call, but he saw that he had one remaining message. He wanted to sleep so bad that it physically pained him not to lay his head on the pillow. Instead, he pushed the play button.

"Hi, Sean, this Stephanie. Please call me immediately. I've got to talk you. Soon," she pleaded in her message. "Don't call me at home. I'm staying with a friend from work right now." She then listed the number to Ira Bernstein's home. McGowan knew from her voice that something was wrong.

Ira Bernstein answered the phone on the second ring.

"Hi. Is Stephanie there?"

"Is this Sean?" asked Bernstein, in a protective manner.

"It is."

"One minute."

McGowan heard Bernstein talk to Stephanie. She answered almost instantly.

"Hi, Sean," she uttered in a flat, emotionless tone.

"Are you okay?"

"Oh Sean, you won't believe this."

"What is it?"

Freeberg hesitated for a moment.

"What is it?" repeated McGowan.

"I've got more information linking Win Murdock to the Colfax assassination attempt."

"What?"

"Just listen, Sean. Have you read the story in the *Moriarty Minute?*"

"I'm aware of it," said McGowan, who had been given a copy by Sawyer. "It's just speculation—another wild Internet conspiracy theory." The truth was, he hadn't stopped thinking of the possibility since the coincidence of the Holten train being in the vicinity of St. John's.

"I'm the one who gave her the story. I tried to run it in the *Herald*, but someone bugged my phone and got to the editor and killed the story before it got anywhere."

McGowan listened in stunned silence.

"I also think the CIA is involved."

McGowan started to protest.

Freeberg persisted. "You remember my Dad?"

"Yes."

"Well, he's the maître d' at the Congressional Country Club. He has seen Murdock and the deputy director of the CIA meet on a number of occasions, including the days before and after the St. John's assassination attempt. And he saw them meet again briefly yesterday. And when he delivered their food, he overheard Murdock say, 'Unless I know something the Secret Service doesn't.'"

"So? That doesn't mean anything."

"It does in the context of Payne's question."

"Did your father hear the question?"

"No—but he saw it."

"What? What the hell are you talking about?"

"Remember my sister Lisa?"

"Yeah—she's the one at Gallaudet," replied McGowan, referring the university for the deaf in Washington.

"That's right. Well, my Dad taught himself how to read lips so he could help teach Lisa the skill. He's been doing it for more than twenty years. Anyway, he couldn't make out Payne's entire question, but he is positive that he saw Payne say something to the effect of a second shot being impossible after Colfax becomes president."

"Tell me again what Murdock said."

"He said: 'Unless I know something the Secret Service doesn't.'"

Freeberg also shared with McGowan the earlier conversations her father had overheard. The first statement, "Your man should only attempt a shot if it is a sure thing," gave McGowan a little hope. The second, about the assassin returning "to St. Paul as soon as things cool down," sent chills down his spine.

Immediately after hanging up, McGowan called Tingley and told him to concentrate his video search on Gerald Weber, Buford Hansen, and Derek Bosseli—in that order. McGowan did not get any sleep that evening.

* *

Carmen Jimenez received Josh Parker's e-mail describing Win Murdock's attempt to defeat Colfax, along with the copy of the *Moriarty Minute*, and went into high gear. First, he translated the *Moriarty Minute* and Parker's analysis of it into Spanish. Next, he forwarded copies to his database of 230,000 Colfax supporters. He asked everyone on the list to print as many copies of the report as they could afford and distribute them. Many of the recipients, receiving the report early on Saturday, posted copies in their churches in time for Sunday services. A number of priests made the story the topic of their sermon. By Monday, the "Gibraltar Conspiracy" was well known among Latinos all across the country. Most couldn't wait to cast their ballot for Robert Colfax.

* *

On university campuses all across the country, the same thing was happening with Parker's e-mail. From the University of Alabama to the University of Alaska, more than 1,700 institutions of higher learning received his e-mail. Copies of the *Moriarty Minute* were downloaded, printed and slid under thousands of dormitory doors in the middle of the night. Copies were posted in large lecture halls and stapled to telephone polls from upstate New York to southern California. By Sunday night, Internet chat rooms were buzzing with support for Colfax. Students, tired of politics as usual, were responding to Colfax's message. And, as with the Latino community, the fact that a group of very powerful special interests wanted to stop Colfax made them even more eager to cast their ballot for the independent candidate for president.

* *

Jacob Mance and David Luther convened a hastily called meeting of the coalition. The marching orders they delivered were clear and succinct: use any and all means to discredit the Gibraltar Conspiracy.

"I want all of us to stay on message," said Mance, looking over the room. "The report does not name a source. I want each and every one of you to work that angle to the hilt—this story is wild-eyed fabrication of some goddamn conspiracy buff. If asked why you're bothering to respond, tell the truth: it would irresponsible not to. We are three days away from the presidential election. People are taking this hair-brained conspiracy fantasy seriously. It'd be a travesty if the election were effected by this piece of garbage." Mance paused. "Feel free to openly mock the part about Mr. Murdock working with the CIA to thwart Colfax. That is as ridiculous as it sounds."

Mance knew otherwise, and others in the room had their suspicions, but none let on. Most had known David Pollard. More important, they knew what had become of him.

The group was successful beyond Mance's expectations. No major media outlet gave any credence to the Gibraltar Conspiracy.

* *

Peter Sawyer watched the commercials and smiled. The campaign's efforts of trailing Byrne and Prescott and recording their speeches paid off. Sawyer wanted to make Colfax's two main challengers pay, and he wanted to make them pay in the biggest state of all—California.

The commercial was a simple compare-and-contrast piece. Unlike the ads running against Colfax, Colfax did not distort his opponents' positions. He used their own words. The first clip showed Colfax outlining his strong stance on gun control. The commercial then cut to Elliott Prescott speaking before a convention of gun enthusiasts in South Carolina: "My idea of gun control is plugging six straight shots in a three-inch grouping." The all-white, all-male crowd roared approvingly at Prescott's remarks.

The next scene cut to Martin Byrne speaking in a filled auditorium before the country's third-largest trade union. "As the next president, I understand your position and you have my commitment that I will always favor your jobs over the environment." His words were contrasted with Colfax's speech in Colorado, where he promised to preserve 100 million acres for future generations. The tag line read: "Robert Colfax. Strong on gun control. Strong on the environment. Just like California."

* *

The second floor of the Colfax headquarters was a flurry of activity. Since the *Kenosha News* endorsement, a spate of endorsements by small newspapers had trickled in. The numbers peaked on Sunday with 243 newspapers—all with circulations of less than 25,000—endorsing Colfax. The strategy of courting the small newspapers was paying off.

* *

The commercial was elegant in its simplicity. It began with the two former candidates looking directly into the camera.

"Hi, I'm Jack Quinn," said Quinn.

"And I'm John Gordon," said Gordon. "We had both hoped at one time or another that you would be voting for us next Tuesday."

"Unfortunately for us," said Quinn, with a smile, "that's not going to happen."

"Too bad, really," quipped Gordon. "We would have been good."

"Real good," replied Quinn.

"Luckily, for us—and for you—there is still one candidate in this race who can make a positive difference for this country," said Gordon.

"And that candidate is Robert Colfax."

"Now, neither of us agrees with every position of his—"

"But we do believe he is the most qualified to lead this country," said Quinn.

"We also agree that he is the only candidate who is committed to ending politics as usual—"

"And putting an end to the corrupting influence of big money and special interest groups."

"This Tuesday, I hope you will join the two of us in voting for Robert Colfax."

"He's the right man for the job," said Quinn, as the commercial cut to a photo of Colfax and his web site.

The commercial ran in thirty-nine states and was later estimated to have given Colfax the edge in Quinn's home state of California and Gordon's home state of Florida, for a total of seventy-nine Electoral College votes.

* *

The knock on the door was not unexpected. Manning had spent the last two days in the apartment waiting for Baptista to show up. When he did, he carried a thin, long case. Inside was a single-bolt McMillan M86.

"The plan is on," said Baptista, walking toward the window at the rear of the apartment. Outside, the cold fall weather had dispersed the last leaves. The line of sight to the golf course was perfectly clear.

"I won't miss this time," said Manning.

"I know you won't," replied Baptista. "We expect that Colfax will arrive sometime between 0530 and 0600. It'll still be dark out, so you'll need this," said Baptista, handing Manning an infrared scope. "You'll probably first pick him up as he comes over the green on the seventeenth hole. He'll then turn to his right—your left—and run down the length of the fairway to the eighteenth green. You'll have approximately thirty seconds to determine his pace and then about twenty seconds to fire the shot."

Manning went to the window and looked out. The sight selection was perfect. The golf course was visible from the apartment window, but the window was difficult to see from the golf course. In the predawn darkness, it would be almost impossible to see.

"Do you need anything else?" asked Baptista.

"Although it didn't work at St. John's, I could use some assistance gauging the wind," said Manning. "With no leaves on the trees, it'll be difficult to determine the speed and direction."

"It's already done. A pin will be in the green. Look for yourself," said Baptista, directing Manning toward the window and handing the assassin a pair of binoculars. Manning spotted the small flag, situated in the middle of the eighteenth green. It was limp.

"That'll work."

CHAPTER FORTY-ONE

Win Murdock poured over reams of polling data from around the country. Every state had been surveyed, and the results were enough to make Murdock feel like vomiting. Prescott held a statistically insignificant lead over Colfax, but that was fast slipping away. Colfax had the momentum. Byrne trailed both men by three percentage points.

"Mother fuck," said Murdock under his breath. "He might actually do it. If these numbers hold, he'll win 273 electoral votes."

"How much money do we have left?" he asked, turning to his aide, Luther.

"It's all been spent."

"How much has been allocated to Arizona, Washington, Illinois, and Indiana?"

Luther referred to a spreadsheet. "A million each, with the exception of Indiana, which only has $500,000."

"We need more. Colfax has a slim lead in each of those states. How much more media can we buy in those state's top markets?"

"I'll have to check."

"Then check. Get me an answer. No, hold it," said Murdock. "Just buy whatever's available. What isn't available—see if they'll make it available. I'm willing to spend whatever's necessary. Use our connections at the networks to get more time."

"I'll also see which of our candidates for Congress have remaining time slots," said Luther.

Murdock smiled at the suggestion. "Excellent idea. I know I've contributed to Senate candidates in Washington and Indiana. In fact," Murdock laughed, "I've supported all four candidates. Take all of their goddamn media time. If any of their campaigns complain, tell them to call me directly."

By noon on Tuesday, an astute observer of the Seattle, Phoenix, Chicago, or Indianapolis television markets would have noticed that all references to local races had vanished and Robert Colfax had become the sole target of the last-minute negative ads—ads that bore no resemblance to the truth.

* *

Sean McGowan had grown accustomed to the runs. He enjoyed Colfax's fast pace and even admitted to himself that he was probably in better shape because of the candidate's daily dedication to his running habit. What the Secret Service agent did not like was Colfax's fondness for sometimes turning his five-mile runs into seven or even ten miles.

"How are you feeling this morning?" Colfax asked his lead protector.

"I feel great, sir."

"So do I—I'm going to add an extra two miles on this morning. The rally on the Mall doesn't begin until noon."

"Sir," replied McGowan, who was dripping with sweat from the unusually warm November morning in the nation's capitol. "I can't recommend that. The path up ahead has not been secured."

"That's bullshit. How well is this part of the run secured?" Colfax asked.

McGowan had to admit the candidate had a point. The Secret Service was still stretched so thin that an elaborate search could not be conducted along the entire course, which was always randomly selected. "Sir, the course has been cleared by an advance team."

"That's what you said last week when we were in Natchez. We ran five extra miles there, and nothing happened."

"Yes, sir, but—"

"Look, Agent McGowan, I've said this before: If someone really wants to kill me and they are somehow lucky enough to guess that I'd be running along this particular isolated course, there is little you or anyone can do about it."

"Sir—"

"Look, I know you're worried about what happened at St. John's. So am I. But I'm not going to let some nameless son of a bitch keep me from doing one of the few things I really enjoy."

Colfax safely completed his seven-mile run, and McGowan and his team of agents breathed a sigh of relief. There were only three days left in the campaign.

* *

"How much money do we have left, Pete?" asked Colfax on flight from Miami to San Antonio.

"Less than three million dollars. We're getting our ass kicked by the coalition. A consultant friend of mine estimates that they spent five million dollars in television ads against you last night alone. To make matters worse, they're likely saving their big guns for today and Monday."

"You're probably right. It's time to fight back—time to turn their strength into a weakness," said Colfax. "Do we still have time blocked off with the major networks for commercials?"

"We do. Do you want to do something other than run the ad with you and Admiral Sewell?"

"I think we've ridden that horse as far as it's going to go," said Colfax, referring to the ad that featured Sewell praising Colfax's character and experience. "I know the Coalition ads are hurting. It's time that I take them head on."

"Thank God," said Sawyer, who had been privately advocating a more direct approach. "I was wondering when we were going to go on the offensive."

"In the words of General Israel Putnam, I had to wait until I could see the whites of their eyes. I wasn't able to do that until I read the *Moriarty Minute* and saw the commercials they were running against me. The enemy is the community of Washington-based special interest groups and lobbyists. They don't care whether Byrne or Prescott wins—because they know that neither will rock the boat and disrupt their privileged lifestyles. They know they're not reformers. They are, however, scared of me. They know I won't play by their rules. They're paralyzed by the fear of real change."

Colfax then turned his head and stared out the airplane window. He had a far away look. It was a look very similar to the one he had when he was concentrating on the finish line of the state cross-country championship thirty-four years earlier. He could see the finish line in sight, and nothing was going to stop him from coming across the line first. "I want to talk directly to the American people."

* *

It was unseasonably hot all across the South on the morning of Sunday, November 5. The temperature inside the unairconditioned church hovered above ninety degrees. The official temperature in Charleston was eighty-five, and it wasn't even noon.

Pastor Phillip George stood six feet, six inches tall and possessed a shock of black hair that made him look a full two inches taller. When he finished reading the gospel from his podium high above the congregation, he said nothing for a full minute. He appeared deep in thought. Nobody seemed inconvenienced by his unnatural delay. In fact, the congregation's anticipation grew with each second the pastor remained silent.

Finally, in his booming baritone voice, George thundered, "The choice is clear." The word "clear" reverberated over the 500 people sitting in the wooden pews. "The choice is clear," he thundered again. "As citizens of God, we have a responsibility—nay, a duty—to help this country return to the path our Founding Fathers originally intended us to walk." Again, there was a lengthy pause. George wanted his congregation to contemplate what that path might be. "It was never the intention of our Founding Fathers for us to live in a country void of any reference to the Almighty. They did not intend for us to turn a blind eye on the plight of the unborn. They did not intend for homosexuals to be given special rights and held up as models of normality." George paused again, this time to take a cloth hanky from the sleeve of his robe to wipe the sweat from his brow. "And yet that is the path two of the men running for president will take us—if elected president. Your responsibility," he said to his congregation, "is clear. Vote for Elliott Prescott."

George rambled for another fifteen minutes outlining the vices of Colfax and Byrne, and praising the many virtues of C. Elliott Prescott. George sincerely believed it was his duty to share his political views with his congregation. The fact that he had been paid $1,000 by the coalition to spice up his remarks only reinforced in his mind that he was doing the work of the Lord.

* *

All across the country in black parishes and neighborhoods, ministers had been offered a similar deal to make use of their pulpits to promote the vice president. A few accepted the bribe, figuring that the outcome of the election would make no difference to their members. Most, however, refused. For many, it was the ethical thing to do. For others, it was political. Many knew that Reginald Greene and Admiral Sewell would play large roles in Colfax's administration—and they wouldn't just be tokens.

* *

Robert Colfax sat on a tall bar stool. Behind him was a simple gray wall. In the front, a single camera. Two lights stood to each side of the camera so no shadows fell on him. A director stood in front of Colfax and said, "Take one, Colfax commercial, 11-4-2000." He moved off screen, and Colfax came into focus.

"Good evening. I'm Robert Colfax and, as you probably know by now, I'm running for president. For the past three months and with increasing frequency these past few days, you have seen me and my ideas portrayed through the eyes of my opponents.

I have been called an enemy of public education, a foe of Social Security, a slasher of Medicare, and an opponent of unions. You have seen ideas of mine taken to ridiculous extremes in an effort to frighten and scare you—and it has probably worked.

"But what you have not seen is the people who are behind those ads. You have not seen them because they do not wish to be seen. And unfortunately, our campaign finance system allows them to remain unseen.

"The truth is, our campaign finance system has been taken over by special interest groups and lobbyists. They are using money to their advantage—and to your disadvantage. The special interest groups don't want me to become president because I will not do their bidding for them. I don't take their money, and I will not grant them special access to my office," said Colfax, pausing. "And that scares the hell out of them." He paused again. "Instead, I'm running for president to represent you. Every ad directed against me has been targeted at a specific narrow segment of the population—be it teachers, seniors, union members, people who live in a district with a military base—you have all seen the ads. What you have not seen is an ad that talks—I mean, *speaks* to you as an American—not as an African-American or Mexican-American or farmer or teacher or senior citizen.

"That is what I want to do tonight. I do not wish to refute the claims of my opponents. Rather, I want to call you—and this country—to a higher purpose, a more noble purpose. It's time we rise above the petty, partisan, special interest politics that seek to separate us.

"I want to unite us, and I intend to do that by telling you about the only special interest group that motivates me. It a special interest group that all Americans—regardless of race, color, and creed—will recognize. It is a very special interest group—one that has no high-powered lobbyists to do its bidding. This group is our children.

"As president, every action I take, every bill I sign, everything I do will be done with one purpose in mind: to make this country better for our children. Look at where I stand on all the issues, and the one constant you will see is that I have sought to provide maximum opportunity for our children—to give them a chance to go to the school of their choice, or invest their own money as they see fit, or leave the environment in better condition, or free them from the crushing burden of our national debt.

"By looking out only for ourselves, we will perish. By uniting on behalf of our children, we will prosper. I'm Robert Colfax and I need your vote this Tuesday. Thank you and God bless you."

"Cut. That was great. Do you want to take another cut? Work out that rough spot?" said the director, referring to where Colfax had stumbled over the word "talk."

"No," replied Colfax. "That's what I wanted to say. I don't want to run it by any focus group. I want the American people to hear what's in my heart. I also want them to see that I'm not perfect. Warts and all."

The commercial, cut on a short stay over in Los Angeles, included the clip of the director starting the filming and the last part asking Colfax if he wanted to "take another cut," along with the candidate's response. Unlike Prescott and Byrne's commercials, which had gone "positive" in the remaining days of the campaign—and showed the candidates in warm, glowing terms—the Colfax commercial actually caught the viewers' attention.

The commercials began airing Sunday night, and the response was overwhelmingly positive. The unrehearsed flavor of the commercial came across as sincere, and the last section, which Colfax ordered to be kept in the commercial, was a stroke of genius. The viewers did want to hear what the candidate felt in his heart.

The three million dollars didn't buy a lot of air time, but the commercial was also on Colfax's web site. It was later estimated that more than two and one-half million undecided voters had either heard of the ad or accessed it before entering the voting booth.

* *

Sean McGowan opened the door of the *Bull Moose* and immediately scanned the name above the airport hanger. He had been catching a quick catnap when the plane landed and had no idea where he was. The sign told him he was in Sacramento. It was his ninth city in the last twenty hours, and he still had twelve more stops to go before the 2000 presidential campaign came to an end. It could not come too soon, thought McGowan, who was on the verge of complete exhaustion.

Colfax did not suffer from the same fatigue. He bounded down the stair dolly to the awaiting podium. From the hastily constructed stage, Colfax looked out over the considerable crowd that had gathered on the tarmac. Intermixed with the regular Colfax signs were a healthy number of "*Viva Colfax*" and "*Ganamos con Colfax*" signs.

Pete Sawyer smiled. His strategy of courting the Latino vote was paying off. The campaign manager knew that Latinos represented the swing vote in the seven largest states—representing 210 Electoral College votes. It was why he had insisted that Miami, San Antonio, Phoenix, Los Angeles, San Jose, Sacramento, and Chicago all be included in the final three-day blitz across the country. Carmen Jimenez, through his Internet alerts, ensured boisterous crowds awaited Colfax at every stop.

"*El sue—o Americano es para tu,*" said Colfax, to the delight of the crowd, "the American dream is for all of us—"

* *

The final onslaught of commercials was the television equivalent of the Allied Forces bombing of Dresden in World War II. No section of the country, however remote, was left unscathed. The goal: suppress voter turnout for Robert Colfax. The first commercials began running during the daytime soap operas. Targeted at the predominately female population, the coalition ads focused on diminishing Colfax's appeal to lower-income women by highlighting his willingness, as governor, to cut welfare programs for single parents. The ads did not tell the full story. They did not say that Colfax provided training for welfare recipients so that they could find work or that he pushed thorough legislation allocating extra money for health and child care for working parents. The commercial ended with the line, "What's next on the cutting block, Governor Colfax? Head Start programs? School lunch programs? Call Governor Colfax and tell him to protect our children."

"That's bullshit," said Deb Lindmeier, a fulltime nurse and a single mother who had pulled herself off welfare, returned to school and worked the night shift so she could spend afternoons with her children. After watching the commercial, Lindmeier decided to vote for the first time in her life. She planned to cast her ballot for Robert Colfax, and she urged all of her co-workers to do the same.

* *

By five o'clock, the coalition had changed tactics and was targeting the elderly, upper-middle-class voter during the national evening news. Colfax's proposal to make well-off elderly Americans pay more by means-testing Medicare was being touted "as the first step to the complete deconstruction of Medicare. Tell Robert Colfax to leave Medicare alone—thirty-seven million Americans count on it."

Paul Cotter, a sixty-seven-year-old retired physician, one of the well-off Americans who would pay more under Colfax's proposal, turned to his wife, "That's the problem with this country. Right there," he said, raising his voice and pointing at the screen. "Colfax is the only candidate with the balls to ask us greedy geezers to pay a little bit more for our Medicare insurance. It's still a great deal. I think his proposal would mean that we would pay about twenty dollars more a month. Two hundred and forty measly dollars a year. His proposal doesn't take a dime from those who are less well off. Yet to hear this coalition for the . . . whatever, tell it, Colfax is just a cold-hearted SOB who's going throw all of us into the street. What a crock! I think he's the only one that gives a rat's ass about our grandchildren's future."

His wife nodded silently in agreement. "I'm going to vote for him," declared Cotter, a lifelong Republican, as though it were an earth-shaking event.

His wife, a closet Democrat, smiled and said that she had come to the same conclusion three months earlier. It was the first time since they both voted for John F. Kennedy that they didn't cancel out each other's presidential vote. That night they called their five children and persuaded them to vote for Colfax.

* *

By prime time, the coalition ads were as varied as the shows during which they ran. In most cases, the intellectual caliber of the anti-Colfax commercial was only one step above that of the show. The majority of commercials, all of which fit a very tight script, were almost universally ignored by viewers. As soon as most people recognized it was a political commercial, they checked out either physically—to get a drink or go to the bathroom—or mentally. The one commercial that did capture their attention was the one-minute black-and-white commercial that Colfax ran.

* *

Kenny Starrett lived in a high-rise apartment in Chicago's Lincoln Park. He worked as a floor trader on the Chicago Board of Trade. For the past few days, he had heard a lot of his buddies talking about Colfax's proposal to allow younger people to invest some of their Social Security withholding in the stock market. Starrett liked the idea. He got pissed every time he saw how much money Uncle Sam was withholding from his paycheck for Social Security. "I'm never going to see that money," he always thought.

Starrett was watching the Monday night football game between the Oakland Raiders and the Green Bay Packers when Colfax's commercial came on. The ad immediately caught his attention. As the commercial faded, he caught the web address of the Colfax campaign. The game was a blowout, so he brought up Colfax's web site on his TV. He clicked on the section outlining Colfax's Social Security proposal and printed 250 copies. Between midnight and 2:00 A.M., Starrett slipped the flyer under the door of every apartment in the building. The young professionals in the building liked what they read the next morning.

Chapter Forty-Two

Fifteen minutes past midnight on Tuesday, November 7, 2000, the first exit poll was complete. The citizens of Hart's Location, New Hampshire, always the first in the country to vote, began telling the paid station pollsters their choices. A true sampling of the fifty-seven voters would have revealed twenty-one voted for Colfax, nineteen for Prescott, and seventeen for Byrne. The coalition, afraid that the exit poll would reflect positively on Colfax's prospects for victory—and thus be reported on the morning news in time to influence millions of voters who had been led to believe his chances to win were slim, bribed two pollsters to file false reports.

Jacob Mance watched with delight as he sipped his freshly squeezed orange juice and listened to the handsome, well-known morning anchor regurgitate the coalition's fictitious numbers: "In the nation's first exit poll, it appears as though Governor Prescott has a razor-thin lead over Vice President Byrne, with Governor Colfax finishing a respectable but distant third. I caution our viewers that this is just a sample from one small town, in one small state, and is by no means scientific." His cute sidekick stepped in effortlessly and added, "So what you're saying, Brad, is that our viewers should still get out and vote." The weatherman chimed in and said he was going to vote immediately after the show. The two anchors ignored him and moved on to a live report from Miami, where the vice president was just touching down at the airport for a final pep rally.

Mance polished off his juice and said, "Perfect." He hoped Colfax's ficticious third-place showing would dampen turnout and fuel the "wasted vote" syndrome.

* *

Lee Manning was awake before the sun rose but had no intention of being the first in line to vote. In fact, no one other than Baptista knew the sniper was in St. Paul. Instead, Manning drove four hours one way to sight the rifle that would likely fire a single shot in the next day's early morning darkness.

On the afternoon before, Manning had measured the distance to every visible landmark on the golf course. From the perch of the third-floor of the apartment building, Manning knew that the pin on the eighteenth green was precisely 364 yards away. The large oak tree where Colfax would come into view was 291 yards away.

The night scope tested fine, and Manning used a glasscutter to cut three sides of the window. The remaining side would be cut the next day.

* *

The warm, humid New Orleans air enveloped the 6,000 Colfax supporters in the predawn hours as they waited for their candidate to arrive. Due to Internet postings showing Colfax's estimated arrival time, many arrived only minutes before the candidate. Others arrived hours earlier to get a good seat. Everyone in attendance was thoroughly searched, run through a magnetometer and required to stay within a specially constructed holding area that the Secret Service had erected. No handheld posters and banners were allowed. The Secret Service was concerned that they might be used to conceal a weapon and hamper the ability of the agents to catch a gunman's movements.

The *Bull Moose* touched down just as the sun was rising. The sky was a beautiful mixture of dark and light blue, intermixed with a soft orange. Colfax savored the impending sunrise and the crowd for a moment before climbing down the stairs of the plane, just after his wife. Sean McGowan followed right behind him.

At the base of the stairs, McGowan was informed through his radio that the sector to the left of the candidate was the most secure. It was also the closest to the waiting limousine. McGowan subtly directed the candidate toward that section of the crowd. He knew Colfax, who hadn't slept more than two hours in the last three days, needed contact with his supporters to keep going. He also knew that the candidate was going to mingle with the crowd one way or another. It was his job to limit the danger Colfax put himself in. "Governor, right this way," said McGowan softly, directing Colfax to his left.

The crowd lunged forward as Colfax approached the barriers. For a minute, McGowan was reminded of the situation in Ghana a year before and felt a surge of panic course through his body. Luckily, the crowd was only about twenty people deep, and the pressure on those pressed up against the steel barriers was nothing more than an uncomfortable inconvenience. It was an inconvenience soon forgotten as Colfax reached out and touched their hands.

Colfax made his way down the barrier, shaking every hand within reach.

Sensing that Colfax was not going to voluntarily quit, McGowan diplomatically reminded the candidate that he had another speech scheduled to start in twenty minutes. Because the Secret Service had sealed off roads and a portion of the interstate, McGowan did not wish to delay the morning commuters of New Orleans any more than necessary.

Colfax arrived at St. Bernard State Park, near the mouth of the Mississippi, at precisely 6:43 A.M. Tuesday, November 7, 2000—Election Day. The setting was perfect. Behind the podium, the massive Mississippi River slowly flowed toward the Gulf of Mexico and bright orange sunrays appeared temporarily frozen against the light blue sky.

"Today," said Colfax, turning slightly with an open hand toward the sunrise, "is a new day in America."

The large crowd of supporters erupted. The scene was being covered live by over fifty United States and foreign television stations and would be replayed throughout the day—although Jacob Mance, through his connections with executives at the national networks, had seen to it that it would not be aired on any of the national networks. He had personally reminded the network executives of the money they stood to lose if Colfax were elected and fulfilled his promise to end the billion-dollar digital broadcast spectrum giveaway. It was enough to convince the executives not to provide Colfax any more coverage than absolutely necessary.

"Almost 400 days ago, at the headwaters of the Mighty Mississippi, I began this campaign. Since that time, my family and I have traveled this country far and wide, meeting and visiting with Americans of all different walks of life. But I have always come back to the Mississippi. I visited the towns and cities of the Mississippi—the backbone of this great country—from my hometown of Minneapolis to Davenport and Cape Girardeau to St. Louis and Natchez and finally here," said Colfax, "New Orleans." The crowd went wild. Colfax continued on for a few minutes before concluding. "And just as the waters of the Mississippi nurture the fertile land to the east and west and allow its people to live and grow prosperously, throughout this campaign I sought to find the fertile ground between the extremes of the two major parties that will allow this country to prosper."

The crowd again erupted.

"And I will continue to do that as president. Thank you, New Orleans, God bless you, and God bless America!"

* *

By the time the candidate and his entourage returned to the airport, the crowd had swelled to over 10,000 people. Colfax gave an impromptu speech at the pep rally before boarding the plane. It was 7:00 A.M. Central Standard Time. The polling booths had been opened for an hour on the East Coast. By 7:15, the first reports of high voter turnout were being broadcast. Experts had been predicting only a slightly larger voter turnout than in 1996. Many speculated that the massive amount of negative campaigning that had filled the airways would cause a large segment of the population to stay home. They were wrong.

* *

Agent McGowan breathed a sigh of relief as he secured the airplane door behind Colfax. Ever since the failed attempt at St. John's, fears of a copycat assassin had consumed his days. Each airport visit and every campaign stop had required every ounce of mental and physical energy he possessed. If the campaign went on much longer, McGowan thought, he might suffer a breakdown.

McGowan glanced around the plane and wondered how the campaign staff and the reporters on the plane still had so much energy. A Tom Petty song played over the intercom system—"No, I won't back down—I'll stand my ground." Two veteran reporters savored an early-morning Bloody Mary. The candidate retreated to a private room in the back of the plane with his wife.

"How are you?" asked Pete Sawyer, looking equally exhausted.

"Relieved," said McGowan in a soft tone. "Please tell me the candidate isn't directing the pilot of plane to make one last campaign stop or that he wants to go for an unscheduled run."

Sawyer laughed. "No. But that's not a bad idea. We'll be flying over Iowa in an hour. We can make a stop there for old time's sake," said Sawyer. "You missed all the fun we had in Iowa in January and February of this year."

"I've worked plenty of campaigns in Iowa, believe me," replied McGowan, honestly. "I'll try to catch you in 2004."

"If we don't win today, I don't think there'll be a 2004."

"I don't know what the papers or the polls have been saying," said McGowan, "but I've worked a lot of campaigns—I've even covered the president—and, to be honest, I've never seen crowds like Governor Colfax has been getting."

"That's nice to hear you say."

"I spoke with my counterparts at the debate last week. We compared notes. Your candidate has been generating crowds two to three times the other candidates'."

"You'd never know that from the network reports," said Sawyer, pushing his weary body out of the seat next to McGowan, "Well, I've got to make sure our get-out-the-vote operation is hitting on all cylinders. I can't rest until the polls in Hawaii and Alaska close—I gotta make sure our people vote." Pausing, he turned to McGowan and asked, "Have you voted?"

"Absentee ballot. Two weeks ago."

"Can I chalk one up for Colfax?" asked Sawyer, hopefully.

"Secret," replied McGowan, with a wink. "Secret Service policy." Deep inside though, he wanted to tell Sawyer that it was the first time he had ever voted for the candidate he was assigned to protect.

* *

Greg Sajbel read the text of his e-mail message one last time. "Only one candidate had the courage to immediately and unequivocally come to my defense after the hate crime perpetrated against me—and, in a sense, the entire gay and lesbian community—in Los Angeles this past summer. That man is Robert Colfax. I believe he has earned our respect. I urge you to cast your vote for him." A single keystroke sent the message to over 325,000 people who had registered at his makeshift web site in the three months since he was attacked. Later polling would show Colfax received a stunning sixty-two percent of the gay and lesbian vote.

* *

"Dear Colleagues," the e-mail began. "The first presidential election of the new millennium is upon us. One candidate stands head and shoulders above the others in promoting individual freedom, the power of the free market and the free exchange of ideas and commerce. That candidate is Robert Colfax." The one-page message outlined Colfax's positions on Internet taxation, increasing the number of visas for high-skilled foreign workers, and free trade. It concluded with a reminder that regardless of how they intended to vote, they had a responsibility to vote. The message from the head of Trident Software, a man who had never before voted in an election, awaited each employee of the multibillion-dollar Austin, Texas, company as they powered up their computers on November 7.

By mid-morning, the message had been forwarded and reforwarded to hundreds of thousands of people. By mid-afternoon, the Internet chat rooms were buzzing with speculation that Colfax was ahead. Informal Internet polling showed him receiving forty-three percent of the vote. Among voters under the age of forty, Colfax was receiving fifty-one percent.

The combination of young voters, coupled with Carmen Jimenez's efforts and the support of Texas Congressman, Reginald Greene, helped Colfax collect Texas' thirty-two Electoral College votes.

* *

Diane Kilgore had spent the six months since Colfax's speech in Cape Girardeau mastering the Internet. Kilgore had active chapters in forty-eight of the fifty states, and she was linked to each one electronically. In turn, many state chapters had local branches. The result was that her network of tax reform advocates voted for Colfax in overwhelming numbers.

* *

Patty Nelson stood just inside the polling station in State College, just north of the campus of Penn State, and stared in disbelief. The seventy-six-year-old election judge had worked every election since 1952 and was sure she had never seen lines form this early in the morning. She knew for certain that she had never seen lines at any time wrap around the corner of the block. As a stalwart believer in democracy, Nelson was tickled-pink that college kids were finally voting, but the memorandum from both the Republican and Democratic parties was explicit: "Every voter must be screened to ensure that they are registered voters." Nelson was reminded that every voter must present proof of residency, and they must have registered at least thirty days in advance of the election. No exceptions.

The memoranda, signed by Earl Glenn and Paul Sutton, had been sent to every state chair at the bequest of Jacob Mance. The purpose: limit the number of new voters. Coalition polling revealed that among people voting for the first time, Colfax was their overwhelming favorite—winning by a margin of more than two-to-one. Mance knew that if Colfax were to be denied victory, the coalition had to severely limit the number of first-time voters. Only three states in the country had same-day voter registration, which worked strongly in the coalition's favor. Unless the students had planned thirty days—and in some states, sixty days—in advance to vote, Mance knew they could be denied the opportunity to cast their ballot.

What Mance had not planned for was Josh Parker. Shortly before Labor Day, Parker came to the same conclusion. He knew all of his hard work organizing colleges and universities would mean nothing unless the students met the voting requirements in their state. Parker individually researched every state and disseminated, via e-mail, specific instructions to every person on his listserve. He also assigned each campus a coordinator responsible for following through on the instructions. To a person, the coordinators fulfilled their duties admirably.

Ellen Johnson, Penn State's coordinator, was particularly diligent. Of the thirteen hundred new voters that passed through Patty Nelson's station, less than a hundred were turned away because they failed to meet the registration requirements. Colfax carried College Station and the surrounding area by nine hundred votes.

Colfax did not carry Elliott Prescott's home state of Pennsylvania, but because the college-aged vote, he did pick up Massachusetts. The state was organized by Mardi Arbeit and Julie Romero, the two women Colfax had met in New Hampshire in February. They had taken a semester off to volunteer for his campaign. The college vote also proved decisive in victories in Iowa and Delaware—allowing Colfax to just edge out his competitors there.

* *

Peter Tingley had not slept in the last seventy-two hours. The Secret Service's Visual Intelligence Branch, due to the high number of requests in the final days of the campaign, could not give his request high priority, which meant he had to search the immense database himself. The search included every public event Colfax had attended since receiving Secret Service protection. There was over 300 hours of videotape. He searched according to the preference that McGowan had requested. The sensitive nature of the equipment also yielded a number of "false-positives"— hits that the equipment thought were matches but were not. The time was 6:00 P.M., November 7.

McGowan's internal clock was completely screwed up. Twenty-one cities and countless time zone changes in three days had left the agent utterly exhausted. Still, the dream always woke him with terrifying realness. Only this time, it was different. It wasn't his little brother lying on the bottom of the shallow lake. It was Robert Colfax.

Drenched in a cold sweat, McGowan lay awake doing what he always did after the dream. He tortured himself with "what ifs" about his brother's accident. But this dream wasn't about his brother, he kept telling himself. It was about Colfax. And Colfax was still unharmed. *What if*, he thought, turning the phrase into a question rather than a statement of regret. *What if . . .* Then it hit him. Be open for anything. *What if . . .*

Instantly, he was on the phone with Tingley.

"Pete, this is Sean. Have you found anything yet?"

"Nothing."

McGowan paused before continuing. "What if the suspect isn't a man?"

"What?"

"Think about it for a minute. This is what we know—or what we think we know. The suspect weighs between 120 and 145 pounds, is right handed and probably comes from a military background. We also think he or she has been sexually abused and may have felt Colfax had violated a special trust. We also think the person has the characteristics of a rural, white, male upbringing. *The characteristics of . . .*"

"Shit!"

"Listen. I remember Wells once telling me that the FBI crossed off two potential suspects just because they were women. One, I think, was pregnant. Find out the names of both of them but begin your search with the one who wasn't pregnant. Do it quickly!"

CHAPTER FORTY-THREE

T he polls are now closed—except for Hawaii and Alaska," said Sawyer as he entered Colfax's private study. He was surprised to see that Colfax was reading a book instead of monitoring the election results.

"Is it going to be a long night?" the candidate asked as he looked up from his book, a biography of Otto von Bismarck.

"I'm afraid so. Exit polls show us slipping in Illinois and Washington and hemorrhaging in Indiana and Arizona." His comments elicited no response from the candidate. "The networks are projecting Michigan for Prescott. I guess Governor Headley wasn't much help," he added.

"I thought something like this might happen," replied Colfax.

"According to our coordinators, the barrage of TV ads against you in the final hours was unbelievable. In Arizona, the coalition resurrected the old ad showing shadowy figures streaming across the border, saying 'and they keep coming.' It looks like it was effective," said Sawyer, with an air of resignation. The final ninety-six hours had physically and mentally exhausted the young campaign manager. He couldn't understand how Colfax stayed so calm and relaxed.

"That's the ad twisting my refusal to build a 2,000 mile security fence across the entire southern border into a de facto support for illegal aliens?" asked Colfax.

"That's the one. They ran even worse ones in Indiana. Do you want to hear about those?" asked Sawyer.

"Would I even recognize myself?" asked Colfax.

"No. In Washington, in the more socially liberal areas of the state like Seattle, the coalition ran ads questioning your commitment to a woman's right to choose and asked viewers to call 'conservative Bob Colfax.' They then turned around and ran ads in the more conservative areas of the state highlighting your pro-choice position and urged people to call 'liberal Bob Colfax.' What's really ironic is that in both commercials they cited your refusal to use the abortion issue as a litmus test for your Supreme Court justices as proof that you could not be trusted." Sawyer turned and looked out the window of the study. Down below he saw a Secret Service agent and wondered if the agent would even be around the next day. "Doesn't it piss you off?" he asked, turning back to Colfax.

"That's politics, Pete. We knew what we were getting into."

"I know, but did you ever think it would sink to this level? I mean, the ads that they run bear almost no relationship to you and your positions. If we were in any other business, we could sue for libel."

"I'll admit that it has been difficult to watch at times, but what's really hard is knowing that Catherine and Colleen have to see me portrayed in this light."

"Have you ever questioned your decision to limit the amount of your own money you would spend on the campaign?"

Colfax looked at his campaign manager with a sense of detachment. "Never," he replied. "The 8.5 million dollars that we raised through the Internet was phenomenal. Matched with my own money, that gave me more than seventeen million dollars to articulate my vision. That was sufficient." He then added, "The solution is not to join my opponents in the cesspool that has come to represent modern-day politics. The only way to truly reform the way things are done is to demonstrate that a candidate can win on his own terms."

"That's great," said Sawyer, with an edge to his voice, "but if you lose because you were unwilling to engage them at their level, aren't you conceding the game to the very people you despise?"

"Perhaps," said Colfax softly, "but I chose—and will always choose—to place my faith in the people. They're smart enough to figure it out for themselves. They know my opponents have outspent me ten to one."

* *

Lee Manning finished cleaning the rifle for the second time and gently placed a large piece of cotton cloth over it. The sniper then reweighed three Federal Match .308 bullets to ensure that they would perform precisely as required. Next, Manning turned on the TV. Every station had live election coverage. The first station was saying the race "was too close to call." Manning changed channels and heard the another anchor say, "The race is shaping up to be the closest since John Kennedy defeated Richard Nixon in 1960."

The assassin changed channels again. Another reporter was talking about the Electoral College. Manning listened to a college professor say that "Few people understand that they are not actually voting for their candidate but rather for a slate of people who will, in turn, elect their candidate in the third week of December." The civics lesson was lost on Manning. Baptista had been quite specific in his instructions. If Colfax showed up on the golf course, he would be the president-elect and had to be assassinated. If Colfax didn't show, it meant he had lost the election, and Manning could quietly go into retirement.

Manning turned off the television and set two alarms, one for 3:00 A.M. and another for 3:10 A.M. Sleep didn't come easy. The sniper spent two hours mentally visualizing the shot before finally slipping into a light, unsatisfying sleep.

* *

The drive from the governor's mansion to the new arena, home of Minnesota's professional hockey team, The Wild, took less than five minutes. The steel-plated limousine was escorted into the bowels of the complex, and Colfax was shepherded up to a holding room overlooking the Mississippi River. The buzz outside the room was palpable. Missouri and Wisconsin had just been declared for Colfax. News anchors from every major network were reporting that Robert Colfax was just thirty-three Electoral College votes shy of a majority and appeared ready to make an announcement. Many speculated that Colfax was going to give a victory speech since it now appeared mathematically improbable that either Byrne or Prescott could reach the 270 votes necessary to become the next president of the United States.

Five minutes later, after the Secret Service had confirmed the room safe, the door opened and Colfax emerged into a throng of supporters. Camera lights from every direction were pointed at him. The room was so packed, the candidate was barely able to reach out and shake the hands of his supporters.

It took Colfax and his family three minutes to cover the short distance from the door to the podium. Enthusiastic supporters held signs and mocked-up versions of newspaper headlines declaring "Colfax Wins!" Others shouted "Mr. President." Colfax himself just smiled, pausing only to recognize those friends who had been with him throughout his political career.

The crowd erupted as he reached the stage and appeared above them for the first time. The celebrants began to chant, "Mr. President, Mr. President." Colfax held up his hands in an effort to quiet the crowd, but they continued for a full minute. Colfax acknowledged friends and supporters in the crowd with waves and smiles as he waited for the noise to die down. "Please," Colfax finally said into the microphone, "please."

The crowd quickly quieted down.

"Thank you. Thank you from the bottom of my heart. I appreciate the title many of you have already bestowed upon me," said Colfax, referring to the chant. "Unfortunately, it is an honor that I have not yet earned."

The crowd began to respond, but Colfax again signaled for quiet.

"I am told," he continued, "that it is going to be a long night."

Just as he said that, a small cheer erupted from the back of the room where banks of television monitors were tuned into various networks. Most were covering Colfax's speech live but one, CNN, was reporting that South Dakota with its three Electoral College votes was being projected for Colfax.

Sawyer, the only other person on the podium with Colfax besides his family, whispered the news into the candidate's ear.

"The night just got a little shorter," said Colfax, correcting his earlier statement. He shared the news of South Dakota with the crowd and the decibel level shot through the ceiling. Colfax then publicly thanked a number of key supporters, including Josh Parker, Carmen Jimenez, and Greg Sajbel, and concluded by saying, "I hope the next time you see me, I'll be able to accept the title."

The crowd took his cue and started the "Mr. President" chant. Colfax grabbed his wife's hand and together with Catherine and Colleen, they left the stage. Four Secret Service agents formed a shield around the family and began to work their way back through the crowd.

* *

Win Murdock flipped through the same networks that Manning had earlier viewed. Unlike Manning, Murdock understood the conversation about the Electoral College. By midnight, Murdock was halfway through his bottle of scotch. He would have been farther along, but after every glass he took a sip of Pepto-Bismol. The alcohol soothed his nerves, but the Pepto-Bismol settled his stomach.

Murdock knew his business and his power were jeopardized by a Colfax presidency. He understood that Holten wouldn't be able to make a profit without federal subsides. The ethanol subsidies alone added 750 million dollars annually to Holten's bottom line. Without that funding stream, the company was not competitive. Murdock had always known that the only way for his company—and himself—to survive was to redirect a portion of the money he received from the federal government back into supporting the same people who gave him the money in the first place, Congress.

Murdock loved the simplicity of it all. He was bribing the citizen's representatives with the citizen's own money. Only in America, he thought, could you spend a few million dollars to support politicians who in return would lavish you with billions of dollars in subsidies, tax breaks and other sweetheart deals. Although he was not the only person to play the game—every other lobbyist and special interest group had also figured it out—he was by far the system's biggest winner.

Murdock also understood that to keep the "inside the Beltway" game going, he had to keep open the channel through which the money flowed. The only person capable of closing the channel was a president who wasn't afraid to wield his considerable clout to reform the system. Colfax was such a man. Murdock also knew Colfax would not be bashful about using the presidential veto pen on his pet projects. Murdock had no choice but to go ahead and use Lee Manning.

✳ ✳

Tuesday turned into Wednesday and the nation still didn't know which man had been selected to become the forty-third president of the United States. Sean McGowan had been positioned outside Colfax's study since he returned from the arena, and his shift was almost up when the candidate emerged. "I see you're still here," said Colfax, cracking a smile at the exhausted Secret Service agent.

"Yes, sir."

"Then I assume that I'm still in the running for the presidency."

"No one's told me that you're not, sir," said McGowan, lightheartedly.

"Are my daughters in bed?" asked Colfax, knowing that from where McGowan stood watch, he had a direct line of vision to the girl's bedrooms.

"Yes, sir. Neither has left her room since we returned."

Colfax walked down the hall and entered Catherine's room. He heard the television from outside. "How's it going?" he asked, peeking his head around the door.

"You're so close, Dad, you're only twenty-two Electoral College votes away. How can you be so calm?" she asked.

Colfax noticed his oldest daughter had chewed her nails down as far as she could, a habit he thought she had broken years before.

"Faith," he responded. "We've run a good race, Catherine. It's now in God's hands," he said, resting his hand softly on her shoulder. He bent down and gently kissed her cheek. "Try to get some sleep," he said, moving toward the door. He knew she would stay awake until a winner had been declared.

He then walked into Colleen's room, which adjoined Catherine's. The light was out, and his youngest daughter was fast asleep. Colfax smiled. Colleen had always possessed a strength of character that allowed her to remain peaceful when others around her could not. He liked to think that this characteristic came from his side of the family, but he knew his wife deserved equal credit. Colfax stood over Colleen for a minute and just stared at her blissful sleep. Finally, he bent over and made a sign of the cross on her head. "May angels always watch over you," he whispered.

She stirred but did not wake.

Colfax then walked back toward his study and approached his lead Secret Service agent. "Agent McGowan, regardless of what happens, I would like to thank you for your service. I owe my life to you. I'll never forget what you did at St. John's." Colfax extended his hand.

"The pleasure's been all mine, sir," said McGowan, shaking Colfax's hand. "I'd do it all over again."

"Get some sleep," said Colfax. "You look as bad as me."

* *

Peter Tingley worked straight through the night. McGowan's periodic calls didn't help matters. The tape of the Easter Day service was not put in until 3:20 A.M. This time, however, the evidence was indisputable. The video clearly captured the former police sergeant fumbling the Catholic ritual of taking the host, and as the sniper turned back down the aisle, the camera captured Lee Manning's thin face and narrow brown eyes.

"Mother fuck!" Tingley was on the phone to McGowan at once.

"Are you positive it's her?" asked McGowan excitedly.

"Absolutely. It's Manning."

"That means she is probably still here in St. Paul."

"Possibly."

"All right. I want you to search the records of new service from the utility companies—concentrate your search around St. Thomas. I also want to know the names and addresses of everyone who rented an apartment after October 1999."

"You got it, boss."

* *

Manning arose at precisely 2:59 A.M.—a minute before the first alarm was scheduled to go off. Without turning on a light, Manning walked to the bathroom and cut the final side of the window out of the pane. Using a suction cup, the sniper lifted the glass away. The cold November air rushed through the opening. Nothing now stood between the end of the barrel of the McMillan M86 and the golf course. Methodically, Manning attached the scope and cleaned the barrel again to ensure that absolutely nothing, not even a speck of dust, lay between the bullet and the barrel. The assassin was ready.

With time to spare, the sniper, careful not to leave any fingerprints, turned on the battery-operated radio and waited patiently. At 4:46 A.M., the news that Manning had been waiting to hear was finally reported: Illinois and its twenty-two Electoral College votes were projected for Robert T. Colfax, the next president of the United States of America.

*　*

Less than three miles away, Colleen Colfax, having awoken from her sleep, heard the same news Lee Manning had just heard. CBS was projecting Robert Colfax the winner with a plurality of forty-one percent of the vote. The caveat the announcer placed on Colfax's victory went unnoticed by the ten-year-old girl.

"Daddy, Daddy!" she screamed, running down the hall toward her father's room. Agent Parish, on duty outside the room, had just been informed of the projection over his radio and smiled as the young girl approached. He opened the door for her.

"You won, Daddy! You won!" she said excitedly, hugging her father.

Colfax lifted his daughter off the ground and returned the hug. Setting her in the middle of the bed, he reached over her and hugged his wife. Catherine, who had heard Colleen yelling, was only seconds behind. She too jumped into the bed, and Colfax embraced his whole family. From the doorway, Agent Parish observed the scene. Pete Sawyer, who had not slept the whole night, also watched, as did Sean McGowan, who had been napping in a spare room at the end of the hall. The family huddled together for almost a full minute.

Sawyer approached the bed cautiously. Colfax stood up and shook Sawyer's hand and pulled him into a hug saying, "We did it, Pete."

Sawyer was about to remind him that it wasn't exactly official—he understood the caveat the announcer had placed on Colfax's victory—but decided that now was not the time to burden the candidate's family with the realities of the Electoral College or the imperfect science of network projections. The small group talked and celebrated for another half-hour.

"Call a staff meeting for 7:00 A.M.," said Colfax to his campaign manager. The time was 5:20 A.M. "But right now, I need to go for a run. I need to clear my head and get my thoughts in order." Looking at his daughters, Colfax said, "Go try to get some sleep. It's going to be a long day."

After everyone left, Colfax turned to his wife, "Are you ready for the next four years?"

She didn't really know, so she just embraced her husband and said a silent prayer.

Colfax quickly put on his running suit and laced up his shoes. Agent Parish, having heard Colfax say he wanted to go running, ordered an advance team to secure a secret route that had been determined a week in advance.

"The Secret Service is ready, Mr. President-elect. You'll notice that you'll have an additional three agents this morning," said Parish. Colfax said nothing. As the pair walked down the hall, Colleen came out of her room and ran to her father. Bending down on one knee to greet her, Colfax embraced her in a fatherly hug.

"I love you, Dad. I'm so proud of you."

"Thank you, Colleen. I love you, too," said Colfax, pleasantly surprised at the sudden outburst of affection from his youngest daughter.

"God bless you," she gently whispered. She then made the sign of the cross on his forehead, just as he had done to her so many times when he tucked her into bed. "May angels always watch over you now that you're president, Daddy."

A tear came to his eye, but Colleen could not see it because he had pulled her close for another hug.

CHAPTER FORTY-FOUR

Luke Parish had directed four agents to secure a four-mile corridor along the eastern side of the Mississippi River as soon as he heard Colfax wanted to go running. It was a route that had not been used by the president-elect before, and it could only have been anticipated by a would-be assassin through random luck.

Colfax and the Secret Service agents ran silently for the first three and a half miles down the east side of the river to the Franklin Avenue Bridge and then back up the Minneapolis side to the Marshall Avenue Bridge. Colfax used the time to gather his thoughts. The next few days were going to be chaotic. He needed more time.

"Agent Parish, I'd like to extend the run."

"Sir, I can't recommend—"

"Agent Parish," replied Colfax sternly, "I need to extend the run." Colfax did not mention the sentimental reason he wanted to extend the run.

"Sir—"

"There is a golf course just up Marshall Avenue. I know it's open. You can radio the advance team and have them secure the route."

Parish was aware of Colfax's habit of extending runs. "Yes, sir," he said, immediately radioing the change to the advance team along the Mississippi and directing them to the Town and Country golf course. Sean McGowan received the same message back at the governor's mansion.

* *

"The Town and Country golf course?" said McGowan to himself. He thought about the name for a second. It sounded familiar, but he didn't know why. A comprehensive Secret Service review would later determine that McGowan's lapse in not linking the nickname of "Tommie Loop" to the Town and Country golf course was caused by severe sleep deprivation. "Why the change in plans?"

410

"Gibraltar simply demanded it. He's giving us the opportunity to secure the course, however. The advance team is already on the scene." The latter remark gave McGowan some comfort.

"Did you advise him against it?" asked McGowan.

"Of course, I did," said Parish, "but you know how he is when he makes up his mind."

* *

Agent Brix greeted Colfax at the entrance to the country club. "Congratulations, Governor—I mean, Mr. President-elect." The time was 6:24 A.M.

"Thank you, Agent Brix."

Parish took up his position on Colfax's right, and Brix took a similar position on his left. In front and back of Colfax were two new Secret Service agents, Agents Stan Wiley and Al Jackson, who had been dispatched overnight from Washington. Forming a diamond shape around Colfax, the group continued running.

No one could see that one block away, a window was missing a single pane of glass. In the predawn darkness, the house itself was barely visible.

Colfax, still operating on pure adrenaline, set the pace. For the first mile, he ran a seven-minute pace. Lee Manning first saw the contingent come up the fairway of the seventeenth hole. The time was 6:31 A.M. Colfax was not visible—only the lead Secret Service agent. Colfax was still over half a mile away.

* *

It took Peter Tingley exactly three hours to locate the information. The officials from Northern States Power and US West were extremely cooperative. The time was 6:28 A.M.

"This is it," he said, slamming his fist down. He was instantly on the radio to McGowan.

"A Lee Murphy moved into the third floor apartment at 433 Carroll Avenue this past January. There is no record of the person at the university, and the apartment doesn't have an active phone line."

"Go," screamed McGowan. "I'm on my way."

* *

Manning had assumed Colfax was running at a slower pace. The president-elect reached the turning point almost a minute quicker than Manning imagined he would. It was now 6:34. Colfax was still well covered by Secret Service agents.

Agent Brix's position on Colfax's left side blocked Manning from a clear shot for nearly a minute. But as they continued to run, an angle opened up on Colfax, allowing for an unobstructed shot.

As the angle was materializing, Colfax, reliving his championship "kick," picked up the pace even more. He easily moved into a sub six-mile minute pace. The increase in speed temporarily threw off Manning's timing. Colfax pulled even with the lead Secret Service agent and again unwittingly obstructed Manning's shot.

* *

McGowan did not recognize his mistake until it was too late. He did not know that Lee Manning's apartment had a line of sight to the Town and Country until he reached the address. It was at that moment that he remembered the term "Tommie Loop" actually referred to the Town and Country golf course. "The area is not secure," screamed McGowan into his radio. "Repeat, the area is not secure!"

* *

The lead Secret Service agent, Al Jackson, the one on point and the one with whom Colfax had just pulled even, slowed when the radio call came in. Colfax oblivious to the news, blew past the stationary agent. At the same instant, Parish, from his position behind Colfax, spotted the flag in the pin on the eighteenth green and knew it was too much of a coincidence. He remembered the flag at the St. John's cemetery and knew there was no rational reason for a pin still to be in a hole in a Minnesota golf course in November. Colfax was now ten yards away from him and increasing the distance.

Parish yelled for him to stop, but Colfax was in another world. He was reliving his championship kick. Parish sprinted after the candidate.

Three hundred yards away, Manning was too focused on Colfax to notice that the lead agent had stopped. Manning also failed to notice the other agent gaining on Colfax from the rear. The sniper's rifle barrel easily kept pace with Colfax's head.

Parish used the precious time to close the distance between him and Colfax to five yards. "Stop," he screamed again.

Colfax ran even faster, still oblivious to the commotion.

As Manning let out one last breath and waited for the perfect moment, Parish gained another three yards. Colfax, just as he did on that cool fall day in 1966, dug a little deeper and increased his pace yet again. Manning squeezed the trigger.

412

The first bullet flew a fraction of an inch behind Colfax's head and just in front of Parish. The Secret Service agent heard the distinctive whistle sound and dived for an accelerating Colfax.

Agent Brix screamed "Shot!" into her radio.

Parish, arms stretched out, wrapped his arms around Colfax's knees and tackled him to the ground. The pair hit the frozen November grass and lay in a heap. Parish scrambled to cover Colfax.

Manning coolly lined up a second shot. This one found its mark and would have killed Colfax instantly had Parish not placed himself in the bullet's path. The Federal Match .308 hammered into Parish's back, just above his shoulder blade.

Parish, writhing in pain, continued to cover Colfax. As he did, Manning calmly took aim again and pumped the third and final bullet into the crumbled mass of bodies on the ground. The bullet smashed squarely into Parish's chin. The Secret Service agent was dead.

Agents Wiley and Jackson, having caught up with Colfax and Parish, offered additional protection and returned fire in the general direction of the three shots. Agent Brix did the same. "The shots are coming from the east," she screamed.

* *

McGowan raced for the side stairwell. As he reached the base, he heard Manning's second shot discharge. It was followed quickly by a third. McGowan had not even reached the second floor.

* *

Manning assessed the damage through the infrared scope. Either Colfax or the Secret Service agent was still moving. The assassin ignored the shots being fired at the apartment; they were wildly off the mark. Manning expertly jacked out the spent cartridge and inserted the next round.

Just then, the sniper heard the front door of the apartment break open. Manning didn't care. If Colfax was still the one moving, the job had to be finished. Colfax was going to die for his arrogance, Manning thought. She would prove to him that she could have done the job in the Persian Gulf. The sniper locked the bullet tightly in the chamber and pulled the trigger taut.

McGowan, knowing precisely which room Manning occupied—it was the only one facing the golf course—fired desperately through the wall. Manning jerked up ever so slightly. The fourth bullet sailed harmlessly over Colfax. The sniper turned and faced the door.

413

McGowan crashed into the room, dropped to one knee and fired. The sniper fired at the same time. In a fraction of a second, the two bullets viciously moved into opposite directions. The sniper's shot hit first, violently crashing into McGowan's Kevlar vest and throwing him around.

McGowan's shot effortlessly sliced through Lee Manning's forehead. She was dead instantly.

CHAPTER FORTY-FIVE

It took the media less than twelve hours to put together the first profiles of Lee Manning. The *Washington Herald* reported that Lee Manning had been born R.E. Leigh Manning. Her father had chosen the name to honor the famous Confederate general. Her mother had agreed on the condition that the feminine spelling, "Leigh," be used. In 1986, Manning officially changed her first name to Lee in an effort to fool the application committee at the Citadel. It worked—until she showed up on campus. A few psychologists, hired by the media to report on the assassin, speculated that the incident might have fueled her hatred of men. The media was not yet reporting that her father had sexually abused her.

In 1987, after being denied an opportunity to attend the Citadel, and wanting to get away from her father, Manning enlisted in the U.S. Marine Corps and was accepted into an experimental program for female snipers. She quickly qualified as a master sniper. In 1990, she was deployed to the Persian Gulf. But as a result of a policy decision made by the secretary of the Navy, Robert Colfax, to not allow women to engage in combat, she spent her time working in a mess hall. Most media psychologists agreed this was the most plausible motive for her attempted assassination.

In the days following the second assassination attempt, even more information on Manning came to light. A number of theories abounded. One psychologist speculated that the rape of her best friend was a contributing factor. Others speculated the racist views that she adopted from her father were the reason she wanted to kill Colfax. These theorists reasoned that a Colfax victory would have allowed at least two African-Americans, Reginald Greene and Admiral Thomas Sewell, to receive prominent positions in his administration.

* *

Sean McGowan had not been able to move. The doctors had told him that it would hurt to breathe for a few months, but he should be able to return to limited protective duty about the time Robert Colfax was inaugurated.

The problem was that Colfax's inauguration was not assured. Contrary to the national network projections, Illinois and its twenty-two Electoral College votes did not go for Colfax. A surge of last-minute voters, late reporting precincts and absentee ballots were cited as reasons the state switched to Martin Byrne. Arizona, Indiana, and Washington also were taken away from Colfax. As a result, Colfax had fifty-three fewer Electoral College votes than originally reported. He now only had 224, well short of the 270 needed. Martin Byrne was second with 167 and Elliott Prescott was a close third with 149. For the first time since 1876, when Samuel Tilden defeated James Buchanan by 264,000 votes, it was possible that the person with the most popular votes would not become president. It also meant that the House of Representatives—and not the American people—would decide who would be president.

Although Colfax had received a plurality of the vote with forty-one percent, he had no legislative allies in the House of Representatives. His election by the Electoral College, scheduled for Monday, December 18, was not guaranteed. This was not something the general public understood. Win Murdock, however, did.

With the outcry in the media over the unfairness of the Electoral College system and the accusations hurled at the major networks for erroneously declaring Colfax the winner, the fact that the Coalition for a Prosperous New Millennium had spent over four million dollars in negative advertising in the four states where the vote switched went unnoticed. Jacob Mance, using his connections, saw to it.

Only the *Moriarty Minute* gave the story any credence. But Jacob Mance also saw to it that the *Moriarty Minute* itself was the subject of massive negative public relations campaign. The story was promptly discredited and summarily dismissed by the mainstream media.

* *

Stephanie Freeberg had taken a temporary leave of absence from her job at the Center of Ethical and Responsive Politics. Ira Bernstein encouraged her to do so. It was important for her to be with McGowan as he recovered, he said.

Although it was mid-November, there was still no snow on the ground in Minnesota, which allowed Freeberg to push McGowan, who still had trouble walking because of his broken ribs, around Lake Calhoun in his wheelchair.

"I can't believe this Electoral College crap," said Freeberg, starting the conversation. "Colfax won. He came in first. He should be president."

"I agree, Steph, but that's not how the system works."

"Well, that's how it should work. I just get this weird feeling that the powers that be are conspiring against Colfax. The Republicans and the Democrats would each rather have their traditional opponent in the Oval Office than Colfax. At least with each other, they know their opponent. Colfax will shake up the system. I think they're petrified of him."

"You're right," said McGowan, who had been using his convalescence to read up on the intricacies of Electoral College. "I think the vote will be decided in the House. Those guys are too weak to go against the wishes of the public."

"I don't know. The people don't control the House—special interests do. I bet they pass it up to the Senate and let them decide the issue," said Freeberg, "because most of the senators aren't up for election for four or six years, they're a little freer to go against the public's will."

"Do you think they'd really have the gall to select either Prescott or Byrne as president over Colfax?"

"I'm sure they do."

"You know what really concerns me?" asked McGowan, looking around. They were the only ones walking around the lake on the cold fall day. "'The Gibraltar Conspiracy.' Although your father got the sex wrong on Manning, I still think he overheard something relevant. I just don't buy the theory that the media is reporting. Manning could not have set up Bradford. It doesn't fit—too many pieces don't add up."

"Such as?" asked Freeberg. She could tell McGowan was debating whether to share something with her. "You can tell me, Sean."

"I know I can. It's just if I tell you, I may be putting you in danger."

"As long as we're together, I'll be okay."

"I am going to accept the job as Colfax's head of detail—assuming he's our next president."

Freeberg smiled. It was McGowan's way of telling her that he would be with her. "So, tell me."

"I've been searching around, going over old Secret Service reports. Too many points argue against Manning setting up Bradford. First, the papers found in Bradford's trailer . . . one piece had the word 'bullshit' scribbled on it. It was meant to be Bradford's. Our analysts have determined it was neither his, nor Manning's, writing."

"Meaning there was a third person."

"At least a third. Second, there is the mysterious missing 'slow order.' Holten claims that their train never slowed down. The engineer says it did. And now he's dead. Three, I spoke with a lot of people up at St. John's, and everything points in a different direction from Manning. Brother Linus recalls a man calling and asking about Father Otto's funeral. The person said he was a former student. But he was interested in the tolling of the bells—it was the tolling that masked the shot. Krebsbach, the cook, recalls seeing a man running with Otto shortly before his death, but we've never been able to find the man. Also, Father Bechtold saw a man planting a flag in the cemetery—it was an American flag."

"So?"

"So, the American flag was left at the foot of a German monk who died in 1868."

"And you think the flag was used to help Manning gauge the wind from her hide."

"Yes. But the clincher is this: we've gone over the voice recordings that came into our office after the first assassination attempt. There's a male voice telling us someone threw a rifle over the train bridge into the river. I believe it was the voice of a person involved in the conspiracy. Voice analysts said that the voice was stressed—meaning that whoever it was, was trying to cover up their real voice."

"Why isn't this getting out?"

"Why are some of the Kennedy assassination records still sealed?" asked McGowan, rhetorically. "Why, in both the Kennedy investigation and this case, was the Secret Service taken off the case, and the investigation handed over to the FBI?"

"I don't know."

"Neither do I."

"Let's go to Moriarty," said Freeberg. "It's our only option."

"You're right. Whoever wanted to kill Colfax is still out there."

* *

On Monday, December 18, 2000, the Electoral College, for the first time in 124 years, failed to reach a majority of 270 votes. The decision of electing the next president, as required by the Constitution, was passed to the United States House of Representatives.

* *

Jeffery Payne entered the private dining room from a secluded entrance in the rear of the club. It was the first time he had met with Murdock since the failed assassination seven weeks earlier.

Murdock did not get up to greet him. "You didn't tell me the assassin was a bitch."

418

"I didn't know," replied Payne. "Like I said months ago, the less I know, the less trouble I can get into. My contact handled all matters with Manning."

"Well, it doesn't matter now," said Murdock. "We still have a chance to keep Colfax out of the White House."

"Is this your Vandiver plan?"

"Yes."

"Can you share it with me now?"

Murdock looked around. The room was empty, except for themselves. "I secretly caught her on videotape a year ago having an affair with a high-ranking foreign military officer."

"Are you serious?"

Murdock smiled. "I intend to leak the tape to the media just before the House of Representatives votes on the election. The ensuing uproar will effectively kill Colfax's chances—no one will vote to have a compromised vice president a heartbeat away from the Oval Office."

Payne laughed. "Jesus, Win, why didn't you use this ace earlier. It could have saved us all a lot of time."

"I was hoping that Vandiver would become president after we killed Colfax. Then I planned on using it to leverage Vandiver for some really big concession."

A half an hour after both men left the club, Sam Matheny cleared the plates and collected the miniature recorder from the centerpiece. He delivered it straight to Ellen Moriarty, who delivered it to the Secret Service—but not before writing her story.

∗ ∗

Win Murdock and Jeffery Payne were quietly arrested early the next morning by the director of the Secret Service, Max Walters.

EPILOGUE

On Friday, December 29, 2000, eleven days after the Electoral College deadlocked, the United States House of Representatives was called into an extraordinary session for the sole purpose of selecting the next president of the United States.

Fresh on the heels of the startling news of Win Murdock and Jeffery Payne's involvement in the Colfax assassination attempts, every representative was deluged with thousands of calls, letters, and e-mails demanding that Colfax be elected president. Most citizens, including scores of Prescott and Byrne supporters, argued it was only fair—Colfax had won by over three million votes.

By a vote of 435 to zero, Robert Thomas Colfax was elected the forty-third president of the United States.

* *

A light snow began falling on the nation's capital just after midnight, January 20, 2001. By morning, the white blanket of snow seemed to be a visible sign of the new era that the citizens of the country hoped the first-ever independent president, Robert Colfax, would usher in.

A sea of people crammed the Washington Mall to witness the inauguration of Robert Colfax. He stood across from the chief justice and, with his wife and daughters by his side, placed his left hand on the bible that Father Otto Wilhoit had given him.

"—I, Robert Thomas Colfax, do solemnly swear—"

* *

Sean McGowan, from his position at the base of the platform, swept the Mall with his eyes looking for any sudden movement. He did not see the unimposing, middle-aged man with gray hair watching the drama unfold from the anonymity of the crowd, but he had a feeling someone was still out there.